Speechless

# Speechless

## yvonne collins
## & sandy rideout

RED
DRESS
INK
TM

First edition February 2004

SPEECHLESS

A Red Dress Ink novel

ISBN 0-373-25049-5

Visit Red Dress Ink at www.reddressink.com

**Printed in U.S.A.**

Thanks to our families for their interest in our projects, right down to the smallest detail.

Thanks also to our friends for their support—and for sharing their stories of workplace divas and bullies.

A special thanks to Kathryn Lye for her role in bringing Libby to life.

Last but not least, we are grateful to Dave for rescues great and small. Whether it's resuscitating a laptop after an unfortunate collision with a cup of tea, researching obscure facts or indulging a craving for sushi, Dave always delivers. What's more, he knows when to keep the champagne on ice and when to grab the schnauzer and run for cover. We appreciate his patience and encouragement.

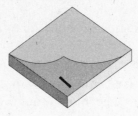

I'm in the ladies' room when my big moment arrives. It's no coincidence. The event: Emma's wedding. My mission: to avoid the ceremonial tossing of the bridal bouquet. I almost pull it off, too. As a bridesmaid (my seventh tour of duty), I've had access to the script, which states that the toss is to occur at 11:45 p.m. precisely. At 11:35, I skulk off to the last stall of the hotel's fancy washroom, sit down on the toilet's lid and haul my feet up onto the seat. It won't take long for the search party to give up. In the meantime, I can lean against the cool marble bathroom wall and rest my eyes.

"Found her! She's asleep!" Emma's six-year-old niece yells. She's peering under the stall door, a wide grin on her annoying little face.

"I was *not* asleep," I say, opening the door to find two bridesmaids in buttercup yellow dresses identical to mine glaring at me. "I've got a migraine."

"You don't get migraines," Lola says, grabbing my arm with one hand and hitching up her special Maid-of-Honor chiffon cape with the other. "Cut the crap and let's get this show on the road. The sooner it's over, the sooner we're back at the bar."

As they escort me to the dance floor, the delighted flower girl skips ahead, shouting, "I found Libby! She was asleep on the toilet!"

I should have known better than to attempt escape with Lola in charge. She's cranky because yellow makes her look sallow and worse, Emma made her promise not to smoke tonight. The honor of being chosen maid of honor is hardly compensation enough. In fact, no one is more oblivious to this sort of honor than Lola and no one is less willing to be on her best behavior. That's why I expected the Maid-of-Honor nod myself, but Emma probably wanted to leave me free to enjoy my own brand of nuptial notoriety.

For five minutes at every wedding, I am a bigger star than the bride. My role is to catch the bridal bouquet. It isn't staged, it just happens. No matter how poorly the bride throws, nor how eager my competitors are, the bouquet is always mine. All I have to do is show up. I stand among the single women, hands at my sides and it flies straight at my face. At the last moment, I inevitably raise my hands in self-defence. Like I could afford twelve nose jobs on a government salary!

Twelve bridal bouquets. Now, there's a claim to fame. At six foot two (six-five in yellow satin bridesmaid pumps), I suppose I'm an easy mark. I prefer to blame my unlikely talent on my height than accept that Fate is playing a cruel joke on me. After all, everyone knows that the girl who catches the bridal bouquet will be next to marry—it's a tradition. Yet, somehow, I remain single despite my twelve trophies.

When I caught my first bouquet at age eight, I was thrilled. When I caught my third at age twenty, I was cautiously hopeful. When I caught my eighth at twenty-eight, I was mortified. And when I caught my tenth at thirty, well, I asked my friends to stop inviting me to their weddings.

They didn't, obviously. These days I get invites from people I barely know, just so that they can see me in action. I've become a party trick.

Being a little superstitious, I held on to the bouquets long after I gave up all belief in the tradition. Lola found them hanging in my closet last year. "This is *seriously* weird," she said, as if she'd stumbled upon Bluebeard's wives. "I'll destroy them to spare you from ridicule." As if anyone who's caught that many bridal bouquets is a stranger to ridicule! Still, I was relieved when she took responsibility for dumping them. Given my history with men, I can't afford to be sending that kind of message out to the universe.

When I agreed to be her bridesmaid, Emma promised to show some restraint. "Don't worry, I won't get all bridey," she said moments before launching herself into a vortex of white lace and tulle. After that, it was Fairy-tale Wedding by the book. Pathetic optimist that I am, I even believed her when she told me she'd keep the bouquet toss simple. "Just the basics," she said.

Many have been less considerate. They embraced the variation on the tradition where the woman who catches the bouquet has to dance with the man who catches the garter because they're destined to marry each other. People love seeing the look on my face as the garter-catcher—usually a single-for-good-reason guy in a bad suit—comes to claim his dance. It makes for great wedding video footage. Take the following scene from Emma's, running unedited at nine minutes:

*Emma, resplendent in $2000 worth of strapless, beaded taffeta, is beaming from the podium as she prepares for the bouquet toss. The camera cuts to the crowd of single women, where my big, bushy head looms above the crowd. There's a sullen expression on my face. Lola stands guard over me, a drink in one hand, a partially hidden smoke in the other. Two eager young women flank me. They're sizing me up and, judging by their smirks, they don't* *consider me much of a threat. Lola pretends to burn one of them in the butt with her cigarette and we both make faces behind them. We have forgotten the camera.*

*Emma winds up for the pitch and the video slips into slow motion. The bouquet shoots out over the crowd. The camera captures my expression as I assess the bouquet's trajectory. Closer…closer… The two youngsters jockey for position, elbowing me. I step backward to avoid them. Arms outstretched, they hurl themselves into the air. You can see the hope on my face: this time I am finally going to miss it! But no, the teens careen into each other. One stumbles off her platforms and into Lola, who "accidentally" spills red wine on the teen's tight white dress (never wear white to a wedding). The bouquet travels like a missile over their perfectly coiffed heads, my hands go up and…yes! It's a direct hit, ladies and gentlemen. Turning, I hold the bouquet high and curtsy for the crowd. The teens check out my butt and sneer, confirming my suspicion that there is no good angle in a yellow stretch-poly frock.*

*I offer the photographer a big, fake smile before stepping to the sidelines to make way for the single men. The D.J. cues the stripper music and Bob, the groom, removes the garter from Emma's leg and snaps it into the air. There's a flash of blue as it streaks across the dance floor, the camera panning to follow its path. Over the heads of the single men it goes, until its flight is suddenly arrested…by my forehead. It snaps my head back with its force, then drops into the bridal bouquet I'm still holding. Heads are swiveling. No one knows where the garter landed. The videographer speaks up: "Libby caught it!"*

*Stunned, I pluck it from the bouquet and hold it aloft. The single guys turn as one and race toward me. There's a brief struggle as they grab my arms, my waist, my legs and hoist me into the air. I stop resisting when I realize that the more I thrash, the less coverage my dress provides. The D.J. plays the Village People's "Macho Man" and the guys pump me up and down to the beat. As the song ends, they deposit me—quite gently, really, when you consider the trays of tequila slammers they've consumed— before the bride and groom. I surrender the garter with a dizzy flourish. Bob snaps the garter again; this time a tall guy grabs it casually out of the air. Emma grins in my general direction before whispering something in the D.J.'s ear. He steps to the mike: "Would Libby McIssac please step forward again? Tim Kennedy will now place the garter on Libby's leg and the two will share a special dance."*

*I look stricken, but Tim is smiling as he walks toward me and bows. He leads me to a chair in the center of the dance floor. I lift my own bridesmaid gown and place my foot on the chair. Tim slips the garter over my foot and slides it up my leg. The video does not capture the snag in my thirty-dollar stockings.*

*"Let's give Libby and Tim a hand, everyone," the D.J. shouts. "We'll see them united in wedded bliss sometime soon!" (I hate this guy.)*

*The camera follows us briefly as we start dancing, then finally cuts back to the bride.*

"Well, Libby," Tim says, "are you always this popular at weddings?"

"I'm afraid so. I can't help competing with the bride for attention," I say. I'm starting to breathe again, but I can't meet his eyes.

"*Very* bad form." He's smiling and although I'm staring over his shoulder, I can't help but notice it's a nice smile.

"Not as bad as beating a bride senseless with her own bouquet. She deserves it for this dress alone!"

"Oh no, it's very becoming," he says, laughing. When I roll my eyes, he adds, "I've seen worse."

My blood pressure must be entering normal range, because it's starting to register that Tim is quite handsome. He has that dark-haired, blue-eyed combination I can never resist. Eventually I summon the nerve to look right at him, and miracle of miracles, I'm staring into his forehead. Without these stupid yellow pumps, he's got an inch on me. Maybe Fate isn't heartless after all.

"Let me get you a drink—and some ice for that welt on your forehead," Tim offers as the song ends.

He pulls a chair out for me before heading to the bar. He probably feels sorry for me, but hell, I can live with that. Besides, I need a few minutes to recover before joining the bridal party again. My left foot has begun to tingle; the damned garter is cutting off the circulation. I remove it with more uncharitable thoughts about Emma. I'm mad enough to march over there and swing her around by her veil. Instead, I take a few cleansing breaths and smile over at Tim in the bar line. He smiles back. That's when it occurs to me that Bouquet 13 could be my lucky one. It's a cut above any other I've landed, the rosebuds being a deep red and fully two inches long. At least Emma had the decency not to get a substandard minibouquet for tossing, as brides used to, before my fame grew and I started making demands. Now I tell them straight out, if you're going to put me through this, I expect the real thing.

My nose is buried in the bouquet when Tim returns carrying two highballs of bourbon and a bag of ice. I drop the flowers on the table, take the ice and hold it to my forehead.

"Technically, this belongs to you," I say, offering the garter to him.

"Don't you want to keep it as a memento? The bouquet won't last forever, you know."

"I won't have any trouble remembering this evening. Emma will torment me with the video for decades to come."

"What are friends for?"

The adrenaline is draining away faster than I can replace it with bourbon. Tim takes the ice pack back and wraps it in a linen napkin. I hadn't even noticed the water dripping down my arm and onto my five-hundred-dollar yellow dress. Spinning the garter on my finger and smiling as coyly as a girl with a bespattered décolletage can, I ask, "Your first?"

"Yeah. Every guy dreams of this." Uh-oh. He's funny too.

"All those years in Little League culminate in this one perfect moment."

"I imagine you train constantly yourself."

"Not at all, I'm a natural."

"Care to share your stats?"

"A lady never reveals her age nor her bouquet quota," I demur.

"So what do you do between bridesmaid gigs?"

It's come to this so soon! I hate talking about my job. Tim is the cutest guy I've met in a year and I can't bear to tell him I'm a government hack. It will suck the life out of the conversation and I'm having such fun. Maybe I can deflect his question with idle banter?

"I'm writing a book," I say.

"Really? What's the story?"

"Well, it's a combination of memoir and how-to, based on my extensive experience as a bridesmaid."

"I'll put it on my Christmas list," he says, smiling.

"You'll laugh, you'll cry... And how about you?"

"Yeah, I'm writing a book too, isn't everyone? It's about my career as a dog trainer."

I can tell he's kidding, but I'm not sure if he knows that I am, too. "Breed of choice?"

"Jack Russells—the toughest breed on the planet. The first chapter is about my technique for establishing I'm the alpha dog."

"How do you do that?"

"I can't just *give* away my secrets. You'll have to wait for the book."

"Does it have a title?"

"*The Man Who Listens to Terriers.* Don't laugh. Dog training is serious business in my family." He's leaning toward me now and, judging by the flickering candles in the table's centerpiece, he's releasing dangerous gusts of pheromones. "In fact, my father and I have broken off our relationship over it."

"Really? Tell me about it. I promise I'll still buy the book."

"Well, okay," he says, taking my hand and gazing into my eyes. "Two years ago, his best friend bought an Afghan hound and my dad fell in love—with the dog, that is. He gave up terriers to train Afghans exclusively."

"Ah, the blond bombshell of the dog world…" Our faces are inches apart and I am grinning like a fool.

"Careful, Libby," a woman's voice cuts through the fog of love chemicals "—you can see right down your dress." Lola has appeared from nowhere to ruin my good time. But she's right: if Tim chose to look (and I certainly hope he did), he could see my navel. I clap my hand to my chest and glare at Lola. Tim smiles innocently and shrugs.

The dreaded disc jockey steps up to the mike: "Time for the last dance, everyone. Emma and Bob want Tim and Libby—we see you hiding in the corner, you two!—to join them on the dance floor."

"Hold on a sec, Libby," says Tim, reaching for a cocktail napkin. The ice pack has trickled water into my eye and he gently wipes mascara away. It drains the clever banter from my mouth.

"Mop up the drool while you're at it," suggests Lola.

*"Lola!"*

"Forget it, it's our big moment," Tim says, leading me to the dance floor. Soon I am swaying in Tim's arms, coasting effortlessly across the floor on a sea of pheromones. He quickly breaks the spell by asking, "So, how much truth is there in this garter tradition?"

"Given my experience with bouquets, I think you need to reach a critical mass before the tradition kicks in. At a single garter, you're probably pretty safe."

"That'll be a relief for my girlfriend. She's just accepted a job in Vancouver and it will be hard enough to keep our relationship going long-distance without planning a wedding, too."

I've just wilted faster than a nosegay on a hot day, but somehow I manage a brave smile. "Try hanging the garter from your rearview mirror. It might work its magic long-distance."

Mercifully, Tim and I are soon swept up by the crowd of guests swarming the dance floor to hug Emma and Bob. Emma asks me to help her change into her going-away outfit and the night ends in a blur of duty and booze.

I'm at home and in bed when I remember the wedding cake. "You're hopeless," I tell myself, but I get up and dig the piece of cake out of my purse and slip it under my pillow. Maybe I'll dream of Tim. Maybe his girlfriend will dump him for some west-coast hippie in a VW van covered in flower decals. He deserves it. And as for Lola, I'm never speaking to her again.

2

It's almost noon when I roll over to behold the bouquet on my dresser. Drooping already. So much for superior quality. The squashed wedding cake falls to the floor as I get out of bed, reminding me of a hazy dream about John Lennon. Figures, twenty years in the grave. I'd never last a round with Yoko, anyway.

I shuffle to my tiny kitchen and put the kettle on. While the water heats up, I gulp chocolate milk out of the carton and rub my forehead where the garter struck me. The only thing I'd like more than a cup of strong coffee right now is to call Lola to discuss the wedding, but of course, I can't, having written her off. Better to call Roxanne, although she missed the wedding and therefore won't be fully able to share my lament over Tim. I'll call her later, I decide, when the sour taste in my mouth has disappeared. I eat a blueberry Pop-Tart to speed the process along—my standard hangover therapy.

Cornelius, my gray tabby, is weaving around my feet. I lean over to pick him up, careful to lift with my legs. He's so stout that Lola once asked, "Is that a cat or a coffee table?" Corny's wondrous purr isn't enough to prevent the Curse of the Bouquets from washing over me. It happens every time. Sometimes

I can't shake the blues for weeks after a wedding, and that's without the cute guy in the picture. How could I fall for that dog-whisperer schtick? Thirteen bouquets and I am still the biggest sucker in the world. But this time will be different. I am done with guys, I mean it. I will not waste a single second moping. In fact, I will prove it by going out and raking the backyard as if nothing happened. I'll plant some flowers. Better yet, I'll start a medicinal herb garden. I'm already reaching for my jacket when I remember I don't own a rake. Besides, I'm just a tenant; there's a reason I don't do yard work.

I go to the office instead. I may be a boring civil servant, but I take pride in being a hardworking one. There's a pile under my office door because I was off work Friday to prepare for the wedding. I sort through it, wishing I hadn't told Tim I'm writing a memoir. I doubt he took me seriously, but still, I shouldn't even pretend my life is that interesting. I'm not a *real* writer, I'm a "communications" person, which means I write briefing notes, fact sheets and news releases about education policy. I have 45 e-mails for one day's absence, though, so I must be important. Clicking through them, one catches my eye: a job ad for a speechwriter to the Minister of Culture. Hmmm… Not qualified. Keep clicking, government hack, then go write that fact sheet on private-school funding.

Half an hour later, I retrieve the job ad in my electronic wastebasket and open it again. A speechwriter? Now, that could be fun. It's a political job and I'm a bureaucrat, but it's Culture—how tough could it be? Nah! The impact from the garter has addled my brain. I have no interest in politics and I've only written five speeches, two of which were never delivered. Better to hold out for my dream career. I'm bound to intuit what that is any year now, especially at the rate I'm reading those woo-woo discover-yourself books. Nothing wrong with being a late bloomer.

In the end, I collect some writing samples and submit them with my résumé. Today, for some reason, I am able to tune out the inner shrew whose mission is to ensure that my reach never exceeds my grasp. After all, no one needs to know I applied.

By the time I get home, I have eight bouquet-related voice-mail messages. Good news travels fast. The first is merely a long, loud guffaw, which sounds suspiciously like my brother Brian. Emma's mother must have called my mother, who sent out a family bulletin. Message two confirms it: my mother telling me, in her most soothing voice, that she's heard about the bouquet and there's nothing to worry about, even though it is "Unlucky thirteen." (So she *is* counting!) The third and fourth are hang-ups; I know it's Lola because there's a distinctive pack-a-day wheeze. The fifth is Roxanne: she's heard from Lola, she says, voice oozing sympathy. I am not to take it seriously, although it *is* hugely fluky and she can understand how I'd be freaked out—it's just a tradition. Number six: Rox, again, asking if I want her to come over; she's made chocolate chip cookies and we could debrief on the wedding. Number seven is Lola hanging up after a prolonged whistling sigh. Probably smoked an extra pack today. Rox again for number eight: "Libby, do not—I repeat *do not*—do anything desperate with that bouquet. I'm on my way over to pick it up. I'll make a big batch of potpourri out of it for Lola. Her place always reeks of smoke."

Lola snorts when I tell her I'm scheduled for an interview at the Ministry of Culture. Although she's an underchallenged copy editor at *Toronto Lives* magazine, she's always giving me a hard time about my restlessness, or, as she calls it, "repressed ambition."

"Why would you want a job like that?" she says. "You'll get your fifteen minutes of fame when I convince the magazine to profile you and your bouquet collection."

I should have stuck with my plan to write her off, but as usual, she got around me. And also as usual, she relents and helps me prepare for the interview. Her sleuthing at the magazine turns up an in-depth article on Clarice Cleary, Minister of Culture. It won't be published until next month, but if I take a vow of silence, she'll get me a copy. This article, with its current research and interviews, gives me an edge, but it still takes me a whole weekend to write my "take-home" speech assignment.

The interview goes far better than I expect. The Minister is called away unexpectedly and advises the human resources rep to proceed without her. Laurie O'Brien, the office manager and events planner, attends in the Minister's place.

"This is *very* good," Laurie pronounces after reading my sample speech, "but how do you know about our plans to increase funding for after-school arts programs? We haven't announced this publicly."

"A reporter never reveals her sources," I say, smiling. (Not if she wants to keep her friends, she doesn't.)

In any case, they're convinced I have my finger on the pulse of government: three weeks and a police check later, the job is mine.

Visions of oak paneling dance in my head as I walk toward Queen's Park, the pink sandstone fortress that houses Ontario's Legislative Assembly. It's my first day and I'm more nervous than I ought to be, considering I've had a shiatsu treatment and two intensive yoga sessions over the weekend. Maybe I should have gone the chemical route instead. Still, I'm optimistic. It's an elegant building and there probably isn't a bad office in the place. I just hope it's quiet, because I expect I'll be in seclusion writing speeches most of the time once I'm up to speed. During the interview, Laurie warned that I'd need to attend dozens of events in the first few weeks to get a sense of the business and how Mrs. Cleary likes to work. Cool. Free food and entertainment. Culture-loving guys, maybe. What could be wrong with that?

I don't notice the dead rat until I'm standing on its tail. I'm practically on the doorstep of the Pink Palace, so I stifle my scream and step away from the rat. *"This is not a bad omen,"* I tell myself. *"There are no bad omens."* No, this job is going to be great. Straightening up, I brush cat fur from my black jacket and skirt (you can't even tell they're from the Gap), fluff my hair, and stride through the imposing front door with renewed confidence.

"Welcome to the Minister's Office," says Margo Thompson, the Minister's executive assistant, looking me over from shoulder to foot. "You're *very* tall."

At barely five feet, Margo clearly isn't thrilled about my having the height advantage, but at least she isn't going to be one of those people who looks up at me and says, "I've always wanted to be tall. You're so lucky." No woman who has been addressed from behind as "sir" is likely to feel lucky about being tall. It's not as if I'm tall in a supermodel, waiflike sort of way. Rather, I'm tall in a big-boned, size-twelve-feet sort of way. But there is a notable advantage to looming above the crowd: you can tell a lot about people by checking out their roots.

Margo's do-it-yourself henna is a month past its "best before" date and the wide stripe of gray running down the center of her head worries me. No one who invites comparison to a skunk is likely to become an inspiring boss. I try to keep an open mind, but it's hard, because Margo refuses to meet my eyes. She leads me to a sleek boardroom, settles into a chair at one end of the gleaming mahogany table and motions me toward the chair at the other end. I'm sure I look smaller from a distance, but she still can't meet my eyes. Instead, she examines the ends of her long, ruddy hair while delivering a half-hour monologue on the importance of protocol in the Minister's Office. My questions on program priorities and upcoming events are dismissed with a wave.

"Make no mistake," she says, "Mrs. Cleary cares a great deal about appearances. She has to."

"Of course," I say, conscious that my hair is swelling. There must be a storm front moving in. "When can I meet her?"

"She's away today at an off-site meeting—a policy seminar—and is attending a gallery opening tonight. You'll probably get some face time with her tomorrow."

Face time. Oh my. Margo hands me a binder of speeches and advises me to review them carefully to study the Minister's style. Laurie will show me to my office, she says, eyes fastened on my left shoulder. Laurie's roots are in excellent condition and as she also appears to have a sense of humor, I am optimistic.

"I'm so happy you accepted the job," Laurie says, "I think we're going to get along great."

"Me too," I reply, encouraged, "but Margo doesn't seem happy I'm here."

"She's only been here a few weeks herself and is still getting her bearings. I think she wanted to choose her own speech-writer, but Mrs. Cleary wouldn't wait."

"What's the Minister like?" I ask.

"Wouldn't want to ruin the surprise. Far better to experience her firsthand."

"Okay, then what's the off-site meeting about?"

Laurie sizes me up for a moment before saying, "It's a pretty heavy agenda: hair; nails; exfoliating; massage."

"Don't spas fall under the Ministry of Recreation?"

"There's more overlap than you might imagine," Laurie says, stopping beside a cubicle along the inside wall. I must look aghast, because she smiles and asks, "You were expecting oak paneling?"

"Uh, yeah, actually." I run a finger over the bristling beige carpet on the walls and across the wood-look desk.

Laurie is sympathetic. "Don't despair. I've been working on Margo to give you more space, but in the meantime, I'm afraid this is it." She leaves me with my binder of speeches and I do the first thing that comes to mind—call Roxanne. Thank God she doesn't leave for her movie location until later in the week.

As camera assistant to the city's busiest cinematographer, Rox is often away from home for months at a time.

"Rox," I whisper, "they've put me in a cage."

"You're exaggerating."

"I never exaggerate. It's a cubicle, for Christ's sake. There's no window and it's in a high-traffic area. I'm an artist! How the hell am I supposed to create in this environment?"

"Maybe it's temporary. Besides, it's the work that counts and this is a *great* opportunity, Lib. What's the Minister like?"

"Haven't met her. She's either at a policy seminar or a spa. Margo, the Minister's handler, has already lied to me. If I were still speaking to Elliot, he'd tell me he gets very bad vibes about her."

"What do you mean, if you were 'still speaking' to Elliot? He's a psychic, not your boyfriend. What could you be feuding about?"

"Last week I made the mistake of asking him if this dry spell in my love life is ever going to end. He had the nerve to say he sees me sitting on a rock in the desert wearing a sign that reads, *I'm available. Fuck off.*"

"Oooh, that's a little harsh."

"Rox, you don't think he's right, do you?"

"Not really, Lib, but ever since things didn't work out for you and Bruce two years ago you've been a little…*cautious*… with men."

"No kidding. That's what happens when your boyfriend of two years suddenly admits he never loved you. And what about that guy I met at Emma's wedding? I let him charm the garter right off me before he mentioned his girlfriend. Men are scum, Rox. You'd better hang on to Gavin."

"You can have him if you think he's such a catch, but remember, Daisy comes with the package."

Daisy is Gavin's dog and Rox always feels like "the other woman" in the relationship. They met five months ago while bidding on the same antique armoire at an auction. He got the armoire, but she got the guy when he invited her over to see how great it looked in the century home he's renovating in St. Thomas. Gavin has an unfortunate habit of expressing his feelings through Daisy, whose supposed prejudice against downtown living is wearing out the tires on Rox's new Jeep.

"Being away for three months on the shoot will tell you a lot about your future with Gavin. Are you packed and ready to go?"

"I sent the camera gear off this morning, but I haven't started on my clothes yet. The weather changes hourly on the Isle of Man, which means I need to take everything in my closet yet leave room for treasures. Want me to look for something special for you?"

"Yeah, a nice Manx guy."

"Forget it. I'm keeping the nice Manx guys for me. How about a nice linen—"

My gasp cuts her off midsentence. Two round hazel eyes have appeared above the cubicle, looking above me, around me: Margo. She mumbles something into the beige wall.

"Sorry, I've gotta go." I'm chagrined to be caught in a personal call on my first day. "Yes, Margo?" I say, smiling brightly as I put the phone down.

"The Minister's seminar is starting later than expected so she can see you briefly."

I trail after her, a battle cruiser following a tug, into the Minister's corner office. Ah, so here's the oak paneling I crave. The desk, massive and oak again, would bring a tear to my eye with its beauty if the Minister didn't look so funny behind it. Like Margo, she is tiny. When she comes around the desk to shake my hand, her height only allows her to reach my armpit, which is probably as disconcerting for her as it is for me. Obviously I've been hired for contrast.

"I'm Clarice Cleary," she announces regally, gesturing to a leather club chair in front of the desk. "Please call me *Minister.*"

She's wearing the most beautiful suit I've ever seen, with two Cs on the buttons—Coco Chanel or a Clarice Cleary original?

"Libby has been reviewing your portfolio of speeches, Minister," Margo offers.

"Yes, lovely, Margo." Looking me directly in the eye, she asks, "So tell me, Lily, what can you do for me?"

I am too intimidated to correct her. I can live with "Lily." Besides, I'm busy berating myself for not reviewing the lines I prepared for the interview. Finally, after a long pause, I say I've noticed inconsistencies in the tone and style of her speeches, due to the fact that she's been using several freelance speechwriters. I can ensure she develops "one strong voice." I'm rather pleased with this observation, but she looks unimpressed, so I add that I want to see her speeches reflect her obvious love for the arts—a love that I, incidentally, share. (No need to mention that I'm more Bon Jovi than Beethoven. I'm a quick study.) The Minister and Margo sit watching me in silence, so I ramble for a bit about how excited I am to have this excellent opportunity.

Pushing her chair back, the Minister opens her top drawer. It's filled to the brim with beauty aids. I continue to speak while she flips up the lid of a gold compact and dusts her face with powder. She selects a tube of lipstick from a tray of at least two dozen and applies it, blots and checks her teeth. When she pulls out a mirror and starts back-combing her short chestnut bob, I finally rumble to a stop, overcome by the realization that I am so boring people forget I'm in the room even while I am speaking.

The Minister eventually looks over her mirror at me and says, "I must make a call if you don't mind.... Thank you, Lily."

Thus dismissed, I retreat to my cubicle. I've always known that my downtown polish is only skin deep. It's no surprise that the Minister saw right through me to the shack in the suburbs where I started out.

I'm still studying the sample speeches Margo gave me because I don't have much else to do. I can barely concentrate anyway, knowing that there's a baited rattrap under my desk. It's well out of pedicure range, but if that baby ever snaps, I will too.

Laurie says the rodents have been running amok since the building's refurbishment project kicked off three months ago. The construction has rousted them from their usual lairs and despite the best efforts of a pest-control company, every employee in the building must have a rattrap in his or her office. According to the running tally on the staff-room chalkboard, five rats have already met their end in the trap lines. Laurie has the Rat Guy on speed dial. No matter how bad my job may become, his is definitely worse.

I check my trap every morning, less worried about finding a dead rat than about finding a *half*-dead one. Elliot once awoke to a strange noise in the night and found a bloody, mangled rat dragging a trap across the hardwood floor of his hip downtown loft. It was as big as a dachshund, he claims, and its heartrending squeals drove him to seize the only weapon at hand—a plunger—and put it out of his misery. I keep a sturdy umbrella in my cubicle for just such an occasion. A speechwriter must be prepared for anything.

To date, Margo has assigned only stupid, make-work tasks. I suspect it's part of her plan to beat the "attitude" out of me before it surfaces. She already senses it's there, because I can't even feign enthusiasm for my list of chores. Mind you, I've done worse in my time than pick up dry cleaning and book appointments. It's just that I'm anxious to start writing speeches—surprisingly so, given that all this came about so recently. The Ministry of Education would only give me an eight-month leave, so I don't have long to get something out of this job. When I hesitantly raise the issue with Margo, she says, "Oh, I can't see your writing speeches for *months,* Libby," she says. "There's so much you need to learn first."

She tells me to dust the collection of "art" given to the Minister by students in her travels around Ontario. A learning opportunity, to be sure. My attitude must be showing, because Margo lifts her thin upper lip and bares a row of tiny, perfect teeth.

"We don't stand on ceremony around here, Libby," she says. "Even the Minister pitches in."

I doubt the Minister has ever turned her hand to dusting this papier-mâché beaver family, or the clay moose for that matter. Whenever I see her, she's checking her makeup or patting her stomach to make sure it's still flat. Not that I dare talk back to Margo. I may be twice her size, but she scares the hell out of me. Her smile is eerily reminiscent of the doll in the Chucky movies, especially now that she has a fresh, carroty henna. I'm relieved when I hear that my field training is to commence. At least it gets me out of my cubicle.

I've been trapped for three hours in a car with two women who refuse to acknowledge I exist. It's not as if they could miss me: I'm in the front seat with Bill, the Minister's driver, while they cosy up in the rear. A retired army officer and a widower, Bill has a heart of gold under his gruff exterior, which I notice he is careful to conceal from Margo and the Minister. In fact, they both seem a little intimidated by him, lucky man. Today he's taking us to Sarnia to launch a new YMCA after-school arts program, which the Ministry is funding.

Under cover of a sneeze, I ease the window down half an inch and crane upward for a breath of fresh air. The Minister's habit of liberally spritzing herself with perfume is wreaking havoc on my allergies.

"Margo, close that window," the Minister snaps. "My hair is blowing around and there will be photographers."

"Libby, close that window!" Margo snaps in turn, but I already have my finger on the button.

The Minister goes back to reviewing her speech, occasionally breaking the silence with the squeak of a yellow highlighter as she colors over certain words for emphasis. I sneak a glance over my shoulder. Margo bulges her round eyes at me and I look away quickly, but not before seeing that most of the top page is yellow.

The Minister emerges from the car, switching on a high-beam smile. The YMCA staff, volunteers and kids cheer. Margo and I walk ahead to open the door and as the Minister passes us, she thrusts her purse into my hands without even turning her head. Margo and I then fall into step behind her and proceed in this way through the halls to the auditorium. We stand by the stage as she reads her speech, then fall behind again as she reaches the bottom of the stairs and begins to work the crowd.

I've become a lady-in-waiting.

Later, when I break from the procession briefly to speak to a student about his painting, I hear the Minister say to Margo, "Where is *the girl* with my handbag?"

I slouch behind an easel, determined not to spring forward

to press the Gucci into her hands, but Margo tracks me down. "The Minister is in the staff washroom and needs her purse to freshen up," she says before rushing off to deal with a reporter. I locate the washroom myself and knock tentatively.

"Who is it?" comes the Minister's muffled voice.

"It's Libby, Minister."

"Who?"

"Libby. Your speechwriter." Silence. "With your purse, Minister."

She cracks open the door, sticks out her hand and pulls the bag in without so much as a thank-you.

Yet the crowd loves her and she seems sincerely proud of the program. She even volunteers to stay for a silkscreen demonstration by the Grade Ones, despite Margo's pressure to leave. As we finally head to the car, one of the kids runs up to the Minister and hugs her around the waist. I suspect Margo of deliberately arranging a cute photo op for the local papers, but realize it's impromptu when I see the handprint in blue paint on Mrs. Cleary's butt.

I see no reason to break the silence between us with the bad news.

I hate flying—especially in planes with motors no bigger than a blow-dryer's—but I will not give the evil duo the satisfaction of seeing how nervous I am as we embark on a couple of meet-and-greets in small-town Ontario.

Minister Cleary sweeps onto the plane in an elegant wrap and takes her seat. Since Margo is offering flight advice to the pilot, I clamber aboard and sit next to the Minister. Eventually Margo gets on, takes the seat opposite, and glares at me: she must normally ride shotgun. In revenge, perhaps, she says, "Why don't you let Libby read your speech aloud, Minister, so that you can see how it sounds?"

The Minister turns to me as if she's never laid eyes on me. "Yes, certainly. Did you write this one, Lily?"

Before I can reply, Margo jumps in. "Oh no, Minister, one of the freelancers wrote it. Libby needs to study you in action for a while before writing speeches herself."

"Yes, of course," agrees the Minister, losing interest immediately and turning to stare out the window.

Once we're in the air, I reluctantly pull out the speech. "Minister...?"

"Yes, yes, go ahead," she says, without turning.

I read a couple of paragraphs, my voice quavering. Damn it! They'll think I'm afraid of them when I'm just afraid of being airborne in this tin can with wings. I force myself to read on, but the Minister suddenly reaches over and grabs the speech out of my hand, seemingly appalled by my dreadful delivery. She reads it aloud herself to illustrate how it *should* be done, emphasizing all the wrong words. When she finishes, Margo applauds and exclaims,

"Well, done, Minister! That was *excellent!*"

"Excellent," I echo weakly, nursing my paper cuts.

The Minister pulls out her highlighter and begins coloring over her favorite words.

Another day, another small town, another terrifying plane ride. I spend the flight comparing my expectations about this job with the reality. So far, I've only been right about the free food. Mind you, I am acquiring something I never expected from this job: a regal bearing. Putting in the time walking behind the Minister and carrying the royal handbag is paying off. When I return to my home Ministry, my special talent will propel me up the ranks. "Who cares if she never wrote a single speech," the Education Minister will say, "anyone with that polish *must* be good!"

Roxanne keeps telling me to calm down, it's early days yet, but I feel as though I've stumbled onto one of her film sets: the Minister is the star who is perpetually in hair and makeup. Today I sneeze seven times during her prelanding touch-up and she has the nerve to look at me with distaste. I'm tempted to wipe my nose on my sleeve. She'd notice. While she may not acknowledge I exist, I've caught her casting covert glances at my clothes, my shoes, my teeth, my nails and she doesn't look impressed.

I have a single moment of pleasure today. As we hurry from the plane to the waiting car, a damp breeze wipes all life from both the Minister's and Margo's hair. Mine expands at the same pace theirs droops. I see them checking it out and exchanging disgusted looks. The Minister actually rolls her eyes. Once in the car, with my back to the ladies, I give it a good fluffing. Take that, you limp-locked hags.

I try not to look too excited by the brownies on the refreshment table, but there are so few rewards in this job, so far. I set the purse on a chair and reach for a plate.

*"Libby!"* I withdraw my hand guiltily. Margo is wedging a sandwich into her mouth and has several more on her plate. "Do not—I repeat—DO NOT leave the Minister's purse unattended even for a moment." At least, I think that's what she says, her mouth being full. It's definitely a rebuke.

The good news is I discover I can hold a briefcase, two purses and a notepad and still get a brownie into my mouth. Someday those two will realize how much talent I pack into this pear-shaped body.

I'm on the subway en route to my first glamour event, wearing Roxanne's lucky dress—as in "get lucky." She insists I borrow it while she's away because she won't have much use for it on the Isle of Man.

The dress is sexy despite offering enough coverage to be appropriate at a quasi-work function. The secret is in the flow of the fabric, although there's less flow now than there was when I tried it on last month. Blame it on the brownies. In fact, the dress is pulling slightly across the thighs, but I wear it anyway, because I only have one other formal dress and I vowed never to wear it again after getting dumped in it after a wedding a year ago (tenth bouquet). Until Margo coughs up a clothing allowance, there will be no new frocks. I hate dressing up anyway and I'm not very good at it, judging by the fact that I snagged two pairs of fifteen-dollar stockings and put on my tights in the end. The dress is floor-length on Rox, mid-shin on me, but it still hangs several inches below the coat I've borrowed from Lola. This wouldn't bother me so much if I had a ride to the event, but no, it's public transit for me, while the Minister and Margo ride in the car sent by the sponsors of the event. No room for Libby now that she's put on a few, I suppose.

I arrive at eight sharp, by order of Margo; she and the Minister are late. I explain I am on the Minister's staff and make small talk with the organizers while I wait. They chat me up, imagining I have some influence. At last the Minister arrives, brushing by me without acknowledgment. Wait, she's coming back my way, and…yes, she passes the handbag. Margo beckons and I heel like a well-trained poodle. We follow in the Minister's wake, a few discreet paces behind. I am at leisure to look around, however, and another dream implodes: no handsome eligibles in this crowd. Just as well. They'd hardly be impressed with my role as lady-in-waiting.

I'm speaking to a woman I know from the gym when the crowd parts for Margo.

"Libby. Please go to the washroom."

"Actually, I just went, Margo, but thanks." My friend looks at Margo as if she's nuts.

Margo is not amused. "The Minister needs you."

Meaning she needs her handbag. I excuse myself and locate the Minister by checking for her size fives under the bathroom stalls. I knock on the door. No response.

"Your purse, Minister."

She sticks her hand out under the stall and I slip the DKNY

clutch into her waving fingers. When she emerges, I lean against the counter pretending not to watch as she reapplies a full range of cosmetics and sprays perfume around her head in a cloud. The other women in the washroom are also watching, as she goes through the ritual. I try to look serious and powerful, as if I might be a police officer overseeing my VIP. Then the Minister hands over her purse and back into the crowd we go. She signals that I am to stick with her by snapping her fingers quietly at her side, yet she does not introduce me once as she works the room. When she takes the stage to speak, I pause by the stairs with the royal bag. Despite her lackluster delivery of a mediocre speech, the host gushes and presents the Minister with an enormous bouquet, which she subsequently shoves into my arms.

Suddenly I realize that all my years of training at weddings haven't been wasted. I'm just getting paid for my efforts now. Next time I'll wear the peach satin bridesmaid dress and see how that grabs the Minister.

I am disappointed about Rox's (get) lucky dress and when the procession passes a pay phone, I call her to tell her so.

"Your lucky dress *isn't*."

"I've never known it to fail."

"That's when *you're* wearing it. I'm cursed, remember? Toronto's eligible men don't seem to attend charity events."

"Wait a second, Lib, are you on the pill?"

"I went off it last year to see if my ovaries work. You never know, I could still need them."

"Didn't I tell you that the dress only works when taken *in combination with the pill?* Taking the pill sends a message to the universe that you're available."

"Yeah, yeah." But it's true that Rox has never really had a dry spell.

"Don't 'yeah' me. Get your prescription filled, my friend. Take it and they will come."

"All right, I will. So when's your flight?"

"Seven a.m. I've already said goodbye to Gavin and—"

"Libby, I've been looking for you everywhere!" Margo strikes again. "The Minister needs her handbag."

"She just freshened!"

"There are photographers everywhere. You're here to work, remember."

"Listen, Rox—"

"Never mind, go. And don't talk back to Margo!"

I emerge from the ladies' room in the Minister's wake, reeking of her perfume and in some discomfort because I couldn't use the toilet myself. There was nowhere I could safely put the Minister's purse and the flowers—plural now, since two additional bouquets have arrived. The Minister, holding me by the wrist to ensure I don't disappear, approaches a tall, attractive man and trills, "Why, Tim, how nice to see you!"

"Minister Cleary, the pleasure is all mine!"

I am about to gag when I realize it's Tim Kennedy, the garter-catcher from Emma's wedding. He recognizes me immediately and says, "Well, hi there! How's the forehead?"

The Minister looks momentarily displeased, then slaps on a wide smile for a passing photographer. The smile disappears as quickly as the photographer, and the Minister turns her attention back to Tim. "Oh, so you already know..." she struggles for my name "...Lily?"

"Uh, yes," Tim says, confused. "We met recently at a wedding."

"Isn't that lovely. So tell me, Tim, how is your work going?"

The Minister releases my wrist and steps directly in front of me. This would be a more effective blocking strategy if she were a foot-and-a-half taller, but I take the hint and escape into the crowd.

"Oh, Lily! Lily!" It's Tim calling me in a singsong voice.

"Shut up."

"Now, Lily, is that any way to greet an old friend?"

"You're not funny, old friend."

"You're just grouchy because you've caught yourself another bouquet."

"Make that three."

He's grinning and I can't help smiling myself. "So, what's the deal?" he says. "I asked Clarice whether you are working with her and she said, 'I believe so.'"

"Well, it's only been a month, she'll figure it out."

"I thought you were writing a book?"

"Uh—yeah." So he did take me seriously. Well, now is not the time to enlighten him. "That's right, but I couldn't turn down this excellent opportunity to—"

"—carry the Minister's flowers."

"*And* her purse. The job isn't as easy as it looks."

"Knowing Clarice, it wouldn't be."

"Actually, I'm supposed to be writing sp—"

"Libby!"

"Oh, hi, Margo. This is Tim Kennedy."

"We've met. So sorry to interrupt, Tim, but the Minister needs Libby urgently."

I sigh, excuse myself and head to the washroom.

Margo actually offers me cab fare home, but only because she wants me to stop at a retirement home and donate the three bouquets. It's almost 1:00 a.m. and I suspect the seniors won't welcome my arrival. Besides, now I really need to pee. So, in my first act of outright defiance, I flout Margo's orders and take all three bouquets home with me. She's got me so spooked, however, that I examine them for tracking devices. If she asks where I left them, I'll tell her I couldn't read the sign on the senior's home in the dark.

I load the flowers into juice pitchers and I distribute them around my tiny apartment. The funereal quality suits my mood.

★ ★ ★

I already have a "sneak" voice mail from Rox when I get up. She was at the airport before dawn and was the first to see the photo of the Minister and me on the front page of the *Toronto Star*.

"My dress looks *great* on you," she says, "but lose the flowers, okay? You've got enough trouble with wedding bouquets."

On my way to work, I stop at my local café to find Jeff, the owner, has pasted the photo above his espresso machine. The Minister is smiling broadly and looks stunning in her beautiful blue gown. I am standing beside her, arms full of flowers and handbags. Thank God one of the bouquets strategically blocks the tightest part of the dress. But wait—there's a man's face in profile in the upper right corner of the photo. It's Tim and he's smirking. At least it looks like a smirk to me.

I field calls from fans all day. Emma gets through first: "What was Tim doing there?"

"You tell me."

"Well, he's a music teacher at the Toronto School for the Performing Arts, but he's also involved in all kinds of youth causes. This must have been one of his things."

"Well, he's annoying and I hope I've seen the last of him. Is he still with his girlfriend?"

"Yeah, and last I heard she got some hotshot job with the Vancouver school board. She's a child psychologist."

"Not that I care."

"Of course not."

"It's just that I looked like a fool carrying those flowers and the Minister's purse."

"He probably thought the designer purse was yours."

That I doubt, but I feel cheered just the same.

In the realm of romance, I peaked at age nineteen. That's when Scott, the perfect boyfriend, moved to Halifax to attend Dalhousie University. We'd been together for two years, nine months, five days and seven hours. Scott was a ringer for Jason Priestley from *Beverly Hills 90210*. He was also very kind. His pals teased him about my height constantly, and he never let on it bothered him. I only figured it out when I overheard him claiming he was five-nine, when he was really five-six. As a gesture of support, I began claiming that I was five-eleven, although I hit six-two in Grade 10. Despite this agreeable fiction, however, Scott had to stand on the bottom stair of my parents' front porch to kiss me good-night.

We vowed to stay together while half a country apart. He called every Sunday without fail, but at Christmas he went to Hawaii with his parents and on reading week he went to Fort Lauderdale with his pals. I didn't realize I'd been dumped until he passed through Toronto en route to the west coast for a summer of tree planting. Roxanne and I bumped into him at a local bar, where he was hovering over his new girlfriend, Kelly, who like her *90210* counterpart, was blond, beautiful and petite.

While Rox distracted Kelly, I asked Scott, "Did it occur to you to mention we broke up?"

"Lib, we haven't seen each other in almost a year (eight months, 18 days). I thought you *knew.*"

So the bastard wasn't perfect. Kelly, poor thing, didn't survive the summer, having been supplanted by the even smaller Marta, a Granola Girl who stunk of patchouli oil and didn't shave her legs. After that came a succession of girlfriends that diminished in size to the point where the guests at his wedding needed a microscope to find the bride.

Elliot says I "lost courage" after Scott, but I think I was damned brave to go out with the number of men I dated during my twenties. Finally, I met Bruce and it seemed as though I may have found it—*it* being, in Elliot's view, Scott all over again, but without the good looks. Not that Elliot is really in any position to criticize: his longest relationship lasted six months. Coincidentally, it, too, was with someone who strongly resembled Jason Priestley. Or so he tells me.

When I arrive at the Manhole, Elliot's favorite bar, he's holding court at his usual table, which happens to afford an excellent view of both the bar and the door to the men's room. A waiter is sitting across from him. At first it looks like they're holding hands, but then I realize Elliot is reading the guy's palm. Not that I'd have been surprised: Elliot's charm is legendary and he's particularly dashing this evening.

"The positive energy is rolling off you in waves!" Elliot greets me with a delighted squeal, sending the waiter scurrying off to get me a beer. "And you look *hot,* too," he adds, leaning over to kiss my cheek. "Scorching! Too bad it's totally wasted in my domain."

"Not at all," I say, smiling. "I've been hit on here before."

"That's nothing to brag about, doll," he says, but he's laughing, because he enjoys it more than anyone when I'm mistaken for a drag queen.

"Buy me a martini?" Elliot asks. It's his way of telling me he's picking up psychic signals about me and is willing to share them—for a price.

"Do I want to know?" Elliot is not the type of psychic to spare one bad news.

"I'd say so, Flower Girl, but enter at your own risk."

Elliot's presence in my life is entirely Lola's fault. I would never have consulted a psychic myself, but she took to him during a fact-checking phone call five years ago. They clicked over their mutual interest in great food, exotic smokes, and getting laid (not by each other, clearly). Elliot has ranked first in *Toronto Lives* "best of" edition as *the* psychic to see for the past four years—the one "most likely to make you feel great about yourself."

At first I paid fifty dollars a session and cringed over his carnival-barker–style delivery. Now he gives me the ten-dollar "family" rate if I meet him at a boy bar and buy him a drink. I've grown to find his performances hilarious. Although he never makes me feel great about myself, he's frequently dead-on with his predictions. For example, Elliot said that Bruce and I wouldn't last two years; we survived only twenty months. Mind you, anyone who saw Bruce and me together might have predicted that. My brother, for example, said, "Pay me five bucks and I'll predict your future with 'Bwuce.'"

"Tell me all about the Minister, first," Elliot says. "Has she mentioned me yet?"

His crush on Clarice Cleary predates my employment. She's all about appearances and he respects that. Besides, Elliot is an artist as well as a psychic and has been the grateful recipient of several Ministry arts grants.

"She hasn't even acknowledged *I* exist yet, but I do have some news." He leans forward with unexpected focus, given the constant parade of handsome men past our table. "She's been shopping—two Armani suits and an Ungaro ball gown this week alone."

"Jewelry?" Elliot is practically drooling.

"Not this time, but last week she picked up a stunning tennis bracelet and two new Kate Spade handbags."

"And you didn't call me?"

"I wasn't speaking to you."

"Oh right, you were still in a snit. Look, it's not my fault if the universe sends me messages you don't like. I am merely a medium."

"Yeah, but would it kill you to keep your mouth shut if you know I won't like the message?"

"It would." Elliot is smiling over my left shoulder and I don't have to be a psychic myself to sense that fresh prey looms on the horizon. "Oh my, the man of tonight's dreams," he says, already out of his chair and gliding toward the men's room.

I have a moment of worry that he'll be too distracted to give me the good news he's coaxed out of the cosmos about me, but he's back presently, with a beautiful, bashful youth in tow.

"Libby, this is Zachary," he says, "never *Zack*." It takes another hour and a second martini before I can get him to focus on the reading. "Okay, Libby, if we must talk about you, fine. I intuited something remarkable about you today, which intensified as you walked through the door. Something different from anything I've picked up in months…years, even. In fact, since I've known you. Zachary, you would not believe Libby's luck with men." Zachary smiles in silent sympathy.

"Elliot, get to the point."

"Don't interrupt the energy flow." Which means he wants to put on a show for Zack. "It's been a long time since Libby's had sex, if you must know, Zachary."

"*Must* he know, Elliot?"

"He must." Elliot's hand is now resting on Zack's forearm. "How else will he appreciate the significance of this news? Because, Libby, honey—(pause for dramatic effect) *you are going to get laid*."

I'm silent for a moment, then, *"Really?"*

"Don't sound so surprised. It has happened before—just not in recent memory." Zack is giggling and gazing admiringly at Elliot. "But what's truly amazing, is that it's going to happen more than once. And with different people."

I'm staring in stunned disbelief.

"I absolutely feel this in my bones," Elliot continues, voice rising. "You will have several opportunities in the coming months, some of them quite *unorthodox*. And for a change, I actually see you taking them."

"Can you sense anything about the men?"

"Who said anything about *men?*" Elliot says, laughing, but then his brow furrows. "I also sense conflict, and on many fronts."

"What else is new?" I shrug, undaunted. This news was worth a dozen martinis.

Zachary excuses himself and I taunt Elliot about his penchant for youth. "You're a cougar," I tell him.

"And you're jealous," he responds.

"I don't know how you do it," I sigh. "You were gone less than five minutes and returned with Zachary clinging to your arm. What am I doing wrong?"

"I told you, it's the sign. Take it off."

"Don't start with me."

"Okay, leave the 'I'm available,' and strike a line through the 'Fuck off.'"

"And we've been getting along so well…"

"Actually, you need to get along home."

*"Fine,"* I say, becoming huffy in an instant.

"I just want to woo Zachary. You know I'd do the same for you."

He would, too, but it's never been necessary. I slip my coat over my raised hackles, reach for my purse and grudgingly kiss

Elliot goodbye. On the way home, I stop at the drugstore and fill my prescription for the pill. Best be prepared for all that sex.

I hear my admirer long before I see him. That's because he is singing—and quite loudly—in the dreary halls of the Pink Palace. Not the worst item in the catalog of male flaws, but it's unusual, even by government standards. Every day for two weeks, he's warbled up the long hall to my cubicle, stopped abruptly, then started again ten feet past me. Since male birds sing to attract a mate, I put two and two together.

No doubt sensing I'd prefer to remain anonymous, Margo hastens to introduce me to my songbird, Joe Connolly, an analyst with the Ministry's policy branch. After a few days of dropping by with policy papers and arias, he gets the nerve to leave me a note inviting me for a drink. Elliot's predictions in mind, I pick up the phone. Joe might be a weird opera lover, but he's the only canary chirping by my cubicle; I can't afford to send him down the coal mine just yet.

We meet at a pub up the street and I am pleased to find, on closer inspection, that Joe is actually cute in a nerdy sort of way. Unfortunately, it becomes clear with the first pint that we have very little in common. The man loves a debate, and the more heated, the better. I, on the other hand, loathe debating because I exhaust the full extent of my knowledge on any issue within five minutes. Besides, I have a tendency to cry during a heated discussion, which rather undermines me in an argument, even of the recreational variety. When his efforts to engage me on political issues fall flat, he takes another tack.

"So, how do you feel about marriage?"

I inhale a lungful of beer but this doesn't deter Joe from interrogating me about my wifely qualities. By the time the second pint arrives, I tell him I'm uncomfortable, so he switches to the abstract, as in, "Is a good marriage possible in these difficult times?"

There isn't a third pint.

★ ★ ★

I can tell from the expression on Margo's smug, slappable face that she has something on me and mentally scroll through my sins.

"I saw you with Joe Connolly last night," she blurts.

Who knew she ever left the building? No matter when I shut down at night, she's still at her desk, and she beats me in every morning. I've assumed she just hangs herself up in the corner like a bat and catches an hour's sleep at dawn.

"And?"

"And it's inappropriate to date colleagues."

"*Dating* isn't the word, Margo."

"Well, you were talking about marriage when I walked by, so you can see how I got that impression."

"We're not dating."

"Maybe he thinks so. He came by this morning singing."

"He's always singing."

"It was something from Andrea Bocelli's *Romanza* and he was carrying a rose."

"A rose? (gulp) It was probably for the Minister."

"Not likely (witheringly). He left with it when he saw me."

"Look, Margo, there's no rule saying I can't have a drink with a colleague after work."

"No, but in this office, we're governed by special considerations. You're not in the bureaucracy anymore, Elizabeth. We must avoid the perception of *preference* among the staff. I am sure that Father Connolly understands the nature of your position, but—"

"Father Connolly?"

"He didn't mention the seminary?" I am speechless. "Well, he may not be a full-fledged priest," she qualifies, "but he left the seminary just last month. You can see why it would be awkward for us if you got involved. There would be *talk,* and the Minister can't afford talk. Protocol is everything in our business."

She smiles and her perfect teeth look like fangs. Then, as I stand to leave, I notice that Margo appears to have doubled in size: I am diminished. Nonetheless, when my minstrel later appears (without the rose, which probably died in Margo's presence), I propose dinner. I'm determined to see him again simply to defy Margo. Besides, I'm intrigued by the seminary thing.

At a restaurant far out of reach of the Minister's Office, I try to bring the discussion around to the priesthood, but he evades my clumsy efforts. I can't come right out and ask; it just seems so personal. Too bad I'm not more like Margo, who has no trouble shoving her nose in where it doesn't belong. For example, when I walk into the office the next morning, she casually throws out, "And how was your dinner with Father Connolly last night?"

Unbelievable. She must be consulting with Elliot, too. "Oh, lovely, thanks."

*"Good!"* she replies. Full-fang smile.

Around noon, I hear strains of "Con Te Partiro" in the hall and quail. What's the point, when I don't feel any sparks? This must be another of my romantic dead ends. But somehow, when Joe invites me to meet him at his new condo before catching a movie, I find myself agreeing. In the end, it's the sight of his single bed that emboldens me. It says so much about his hopes for a wild new life outside the monastery walls.

"What's this I hear about the priesthood?" I ask, standing before a crucifix on the otherwise bare walls.

Joe explains he left the seminary following a "year of grave doubt." The door is always open for his return, he says, and he's not sure what the future holds. I'm quite sure of what it holds for us as a couple, so when he walks me to the subway and leans up to kiss me, I present my cheek. Surely he will get the message?

I arrive at the office to find a voice mail from Joe asking me out again. He's humming as he hangs up. There is nothing for it but to call Elliot.

"A *priest?* Are you crazy?!" Elliot squawks.

"Look, you told me there were guys on the horizon. I'm trying to be available."

"I said *un*orthodox, if you'll recall. Put that sign back on right now, Libby and get back to your rock until I tell you otherwise."

He's no Jason Priestley, Joe, but he's very sweet. I suppose that's why I find myself picking him up one sunny Saturday morning en route to the parade. The "Pride" parade, to be exact. As in "Gay Pride." It's a major event in Toronto, and I look forward to it for months. Elliot always holds a raucous Pride Day party that starts after the parade and lasts through the next day.

Joe is as anxious as any Pride Parade virgin. The nudity, blaring music, water guns and S & M gear are quite shocking and the only way to get past it is to set free one's inner prude. A shirtless woman in jeans and work boots throws her arm around my shoulder and plants a kiss on my neck, not being able to reach my cheek. Joe lurches away in horror, but I just laugh.

Elliot and Zachary soon cruise into view on the float sponsored by the Manhole. Zack is wearing nothing but a skimpy Speedo bathing suit and when he spots me on the sidelines, he leaps off the float, races over and drags Joe and me to the float. Elliot stops dancing to "YMCA" long enough to pull me onto the moving stage, and hands me a water gun to fire out into the crowd. Meanwhile, Zack, Speedo askew, is doing his best to hoist Joe onto the float but Joe is flailing and resisting.

"Come on up, Joe!" I yell. "The view's amazing!"

Elliot blasts me full in the face with his water Uzi and I'm laughing so hard I almost choke. By the time I can see clearly again, Zack is back on the float, leaving Joe flat on his back in the street. A tall man in fish-nets, a leather miniskirt and red platform sandals is trying to help him to his feet before the next float rolls over him. I catch a last glimpse of Joe as his companion leads him—and his inner prude—into the crowd.

I hope he realizes it isn't me.

5

My cousin Amy's wedding triggered the bouquet curse. I was eight years old and thrilled to play the role of "junior bridesmaid." The dress was powder blue and I daydreamed for months about walking up the aisle in it, carrying a beautiful bouquet of daisies and pink roses. By the time the big day arrived, however, I had grown and the dress pinched terribly under the arms. Amy handed me a bouquet of polyester flowers in powder blue and white, and I burst into tears. "It doesn't even *look* real," I wailed, to my mother's shame. "But it matches your dress perfectly and you'll be able to keep this bouquet *forever,*" Amy said.

The universe has been making it up to me ever since.

My mother made me keep the fake bouquet so as not to hurt Amy's feelings. It sat on my shelf for years until I eased it past Mom and into the basement. I urged her to sell it in the annual family garage sale, but she was convinced that Amy—who had relocated to Winnipeg in the late '70s—would catch her in the act. My mother is the nicest woman in the world. Although this is admirable, for me it's a lot like driving with the emergency brake on all the time: I've got my foot on the gas, but something keeps slowing me down.

I tried to weasel out of attending the bridal shower my mother is hosting for Amy's daughter. I barely know Corinne, who recently left Winnipeg to attend the University of Toronto. Hell, I barely know Amy, she's been gone so long. But I do know Amy's mother, my father's eldest sister, Mavis. She brings out the worst in me. Even my mother acknowledges Mavis is "difficult" but that doesn't mean she'll let me off the hook for the shower. While she doesn't insist, she refuses to say I *don't* have to come and she knows full well I'll be driven by my own guilt to show up. That's how the nicest woman in the world manages me. It's called Emergency Brake Psychology.

I arrive at the family homestead—a standard gray-brick bungalow in Scarborough—an hour early, ostensibly to help my mother prepare, but really to stake out my turf before Mavis takes over the house. Mom doesn't need my help. She's been throwing the same shower about twice a year for decades and she's got it down to an art. The cardboard wishing well is ready and waiting to be filled with gifts for Corinne, the child bride. Pink-and-white crepe-paper bells and streamers hang over the easy chair that serves as the bride's throne. Otherwise, the basement looks as much like the set of *Wayne's World* as ever. Mike Myers grew up a few blocks from here and our parents obviously had the same taste. Mom, however, refuses to redecorate even now. Whenever I complain that my brother Brian's old Def Leppard posters still adorn the walls, she reminds me that the posters are all she has left of him—as if he's dead, rather than thriving on the west coast. And when I suggest that the rust shag has seen its day, she says that it's in perfect condition. Ditto the swag lamp.

But there it is, *home.*

No need to open the refrigerator to know what's on offer for the luncheon. If it's a shower, there must be pinwheel sandwiches—peanut butter spirals with a banana in the middle, and pink-tinted cream cheese surrounding a gherkin. The cranberry-lemonade punch (alcohol free) is already in the bowl. The daisies and pink roses adorning the cake remind me to suggest to Corinne that she simply hand me her bouquet at the wedding. Why risk putting out my eye when we all know where it's going to end up? Not that I'm bitter. Well, I am bitter that there's no booze in the punch, but I found my way to my parents' bar at age fourteen and I can do it again today.

Fortunately, there's plenty of vodka, because Mavis is definitely on her game.

"Libby!" she exclaims as my mother leads her down the stairs. "What a surprise to see you. Who's carrying Minister Cleary's flowers today? Yes, we saw your picture in the paper, dear. Corinne thought you looked a little heavy, but the camera really must add ten pounds, because you look fine now. Mind you, the light in this basement has never been good, has it, Marjorie?"

My mother turns on the swag lamp and gives me a pained smile that says, "I don't like this any better than you do, but look how well I am bearing up." I kiss Mavis's cheek, excuse myself, and add a little more vodka to my punch.

"Libby, darling, could you get some tape and a paper plate for the bow hat?" Mavis trills. "I wouldn't like to guess how many bow hats you've made in your day. Still hoping to wear one yourself?"

"No immediate plans, Aunt Mavis, but never say die." I get the paper plate, stalling in the kitchen long enough to hear Mavis telling my mother, "I can't imagine how you feel with Libby still alone. Amy was only seventeen when she married Earl, but I was so relieved. And now Corinne engaged early, too… We *have* been blessed."

Amy, visiting from Winnipeg, hugs me as she comes in with Corinne. I've forgiven her for the fake flowers. It was the '70s, after all.

"I don't know what the boys are thinking, Libby," Mavis says. "Amy had been married almost twenty years at your age."

"I was at the wedding."

"That's right, you caught the bouquet, didn't you?"

"It almost knocked me over. I was only eight."

"But you were always very tall for your age, weren't you?"

"Yes, and I just read that some people continue to grow even after they die, Aunt Mavis."

"Marjorie, your daughter is having sport with me."

"Get your aunt some punch, Libby."

I make the bow hat, as I always do. Corinne's bridesmaids are too busy giggling in the corner and cooing over the gifts. It is quite a haul: a full set of china, dozens of plush towels, bottles of wine and champagne, crystal vases, a stackable washer-dryer for their new condo (gift voucher only in the wishing well) and a certificate for a day at a spa.

Once the gifts are open and on display, my mother enlists my help to circle the room with trays of sandwiches and exchange pleasantries with various aunts, cousins and family friends. That's when I discover I've become an object of considerably more interest now that I'm working for a "personality." I'm not surprised that everyone has an opinion on Minister Cleary and I manage to say the right things. She's lovely in person, yes. No, I don't think she's had any "work" done. Yes, she really is a size zero. And yes, she's every bit as nice as she seems. *Classy* is indeed the word. It takes a swig of spiked punch to coax this last comment out of me.

I am, however, surprised to find that people suddenly expect me to discuss politics. It's not as though I didn't hear opinions during my tenure at the Ministry of Education, but everyone recognized I was just a bureaucrat and left me in peace. Now that I've gone over to the dark side, people want to engage me in spirited debate. I guess I'd better get used to taking a stand if I'm going to write political speeches.

But not today. Today I can watch from the sidelines as the

debate heats up, with the shower guests, led by Mavis, jumping between culture and education. Most of the women in the room are mothers or grandmothers and they're concerned about rumblings of government cuts to music programs.

"My great-granddaughter, Madeline, has a marvelous voice but her school has canceled its choir," Mavis says. "How do you explain *that,* Libby?"

"Teachers aren't leading extracurricular activities this year, Aunt Mavis. They're 'working to rule' because they've been forced to teach an extra class each day."

"And what is your Minister doing about it? Can you talk to her? Maddy's school *must* have a choir." Mavis's ruddy face has flushed and her sparse gray curls are bobbing as she angrily swivels to make sure the rest of the guests support her.

"Minister Cleary is launching several programs that give kids access to the arts, but school choirs are out of her jurisdiction, I'm afraid. That's a Ministry of Education issue."

"But it's a choir and music is culture. This is outrageous! Maddy is born to sing!"

Mavis is almost shouting now and the room has fallen silent. I look around to see my mother hovering anxiously near the door. Amy looks embarrassed and Corinne is pouting on her throne. Mom hurries over to press more pinwheels on Mavis.

"Now, Mavis, have another sandwich."

"No, Marjorie, I have had enough. And I have had quite enough of what this government is doing with my tax dollars. Why, I—"

"Aunt Mavis?" I say, bravely. "Could I speak to you alone? I need your advice."

"Well, of course, Libby," Mavis, says, mollified. "I'm always glad to help."

We adjourn to a corner. Mom watches us, grateful, but suspicious.

"I'm having boy trouble, Aunt Mavis, and I can't talk to my mother about it."

"Small wonder. Marjorie never did understand men the way I do. It's a miracle she and your father have stayed married." Actually, Uncle Harold only survives Mavis because he has virtually moved into their garage with his huge model train set. "So, what's the trouble then?" Mavis, having recovered her appetite, takes a bite of cake.

"I've met this really nice man at work."

*"Really."* Aunt Mavis stops chewing and rests her plate in her paisley-covered lap.

"Yes, he's very bright and talented. He sings, you know—opera."

"Opera! Well, you know, little Maddy is quite a singer. It's such a shame she hasn't been able to develop her talent through a choir—"

"That's what reminded me to ask your advice about Joe. He's such a fine man, but there's a slight problem."

"What is it?" she asks, taking another mouthful of cake.

"Well, he's Catholic, and—"

"Catholic! That won't do at all, Libby. He'll want a large family and you are already thirty-seven."

"Thirty-three, actually. I still have a few good eggs left—I've gone on the pill to conserve them. Anyway, the problem is not that Joe is Catholic, but that he's just left the seminary and is still torn about becoming a priest."

"A priest! My goodness, are you crazy?" Mavis inhales the last of her cake.

"Aunt Mavis, be careful! Here, drink my punch." I smile as my aunt swallows the better part of a glass of spiked punch, then I quickly offer to get her some more.

Mom intercepts me at the bar. I expect she is going to blast me for baiting Mavis, but instead she holds out her own punch for a shot of vodka. She comes closer to grinning than she has since running over my father's new experimental jazz CD with the vacuum cleaner. I clink my glass against hers and whisper, "I'm going back over the wall. Wish me luck."

Mavis has briefed the crowd by the time I return and I feel I've earned more respect, simply by becoming a temptress luring a man from the arms of God. Amy raises her eyebrows and smiles at me.

"How's the speechwriting working out?" she asks.

"Well, they're easing me in, but I think I'm going to like it when I get going."

"Amy is an excellent writer," Mavis announces.

"Mother, I am not."

"You are a gifted writer, Amy. If you had just finished high school before marrying Earl, I expect you'd be writing for the premier by now. Don't roll your eyes at me. This is a talent you and Libby both got from my mother, who had beautiful penmanship."

I escape up the stairs to the kitchen and start washing up. Mavis's voice floats up after me. "Libby is doing very well for herself. We are all very proud of her. I always advised her to pursue a career in political writing. I just wish Amy had had the opportunities Libby has had to develop her skills. But then, Amy devoted herself to raising her children and family does come first. Corinne is just like her."

An hour later, I collect my father from his hiding place in the backyard and tell him to boot Mavis out. As her baby brother, he's the only one who can handle her. He's pressing the door closed behind her when she says, "Libby, give up on the priest. It will never work."

"I think you're right, Aunt Mavis. I'll take your advice."

"What priest?" Dad asks, curious.

"Never mind, dear," Mom says. "Shower talk."

It's a relief to be alone with my parents. We sit down with the last of the punch and as I tell them about the past few weeks, I realize how stressful it's been. I haven't wanted to worry them, because they were so enthusiastic about the new job. But now I spill the story of Margo, the cubicle, the joe-jobs and the damned handbag. Soon they're on their feet, taking action. Mom hurries to the kitchen and gathers the ingredients for brownies. Dad steps outside to start the barbecue so that he can grill me a burger. I've told him I'm a vegetarian countless times over the years. He always smiles vaguely and pretends I am speaking an incomprehensible language. Even my mother prefers to think of this as a bad phase. She indulged me for a year by creating a succession of unusual bean dishes, but today she's thawing beef patties in the microwave. I've decided this isn't a battle worth fighting and become a vegetarian by convenience.

"First pick goes to the speechwriter-who-doesn't," Dad says, holding out the plate of burgers. "Choose carefully." It's an old family joke. Years ago, Dad used to get tipsy while waiting for the charcoal to heat up and sometimes he'd drop a patty into the fire, or worse, into the dirt beside the barbecue. He'd put a safe burger on mom's plate, then let my brother and me take our chances with the rest, laughing heartily if one of us got a mouthful of grit.

"I'd still like to know about the priest," Dad says. The man knows when he's on to something.

"Reg, don't pry."

Mom never pries—wouldn't be nice. Besides, I don't think she's all that interested in my love life. She has never put any pressure on me to marry. At least, I don't think she has. Sometimes I wonder if it's so subtle I can't see it, yet it's slowly driving me insane. Why else would I be so worried about being single? Overtly, at least, she's always had very moderate expectations of me in all things. "Just do your best is all I ask."

Dad is more forthcoming about his ambitions. Each year on my birthday he allows himself a joke about adding something— maybe a few head of cattle—to my dowry, just to see if he can't stir up some interest.

Tonight, however, Dad only jokes about the Minister and Margo. And Mom gets out the Baileys Irish Cream to serve with the brownies, as if it's a special occasion. When I climb into my beat-up Cavalier and drive home, I am stuffed, but somehow feel ten pounds lighter.

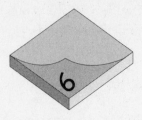

Laurie is pacing up and down, wringing her hands. The Minister is hosting a dinner for a Spanish ambassador tonight and as in-house events manager, it's Laurie's job to ensure that the elaborate dinner is perfect. Mrs. Cleary has decreed that each table will feature a centerpiece of magenta tulips, her favorite flower. The buds are to be three-quarters open when the guests arrive—no more, no less. About really important matters, the Minister is always quite precise. The florist, however, is more freewheeling, having delivered twenty gilded pots of pale pink, tightly-closed tulip buds.

"Those flowers are all wrong," Margo announces, inspecting the pots Laurie has arranged on the boardroom table.

"Tell me about it," Laurie says. "The Minister's going to flip and there's no time to get more. The event starts in an hour."

"The success of an evening is in the details, Laurie," Margo intones.

Laurie turns on her. "What would you have me do?"

"Actually, I've got an idea," she says, turning to me. "All these need is a little heat to bloom. Since Laurie is busy, Libby, why don't you fetch the Minister's blow-dryer and heat up the flowers?" I feel my eyes rolling skyward of their own accord. Noting this, Margo adds, "I hope you'll be more agreeable during our trip."

"What trip?"

"The road show to the eastern townships to promote Kreative Kids."

It's the first I've heard of any road show for Kreative Kids, the new arts program sponsored by both the Ministries of Education and Culture. With the teachers' unrest in Toronto, the Premier's Office has obviously decided our Ministry should do the promotion. The teachers are already on record as saying that the government's funding cuts killed school arts programs three years ago.

"How long is the trip?"

"Maybe ten days. You'll need to get someone to take care of your cat."

How does she know I have a cat? Is she having my house watched? Worse, do I just look like someone who'd have cats?

"Will I be writing speeches?"

"Of course not. A tour is no time to begin writing. Besides, I'll need you to support me with the logistics and coordinate the freelance writers."

In other words, I'll be a makeshift event planner, and planning isn't my strong suit. My sour look must have reappeared, because Margo smiles and waves me away. "Go get the blow-dryer. I'll give you a hand moving the tulips to your office."

"You mean my cubicle."

"Whatever. You'll have to take care of them there, because the Minister is meeting some of the guests in the boardroom before dinner."

At least she hasn't asked me to spray-paint them magenta, I think, directing hot air at the first pot. The blooms quickly overheat to the point of collapse; my efforts to revive them at the water cooler are unsuccessful. The second pot works beautifully, however, and I am at work on the third when a man's voice shouts "hello" over the screaming blow-dryer. Startled, I drop the dryer and knock the pot to the floor. Tim Kennedy is standing behind me.

"So, Clarice has found another way to use your skill with flowers," he says, with a delighted grin.

"I'd take the time to laugh if I didn't have a deadline to meet," I reply sarcastically, stooping to collect the flowers and stuff them back in the pot. "The least you could is help."

"And get my hands dirty before dinner? I don't think so." But he kneels to collect the blow-dryer from under my desk. "My God, what's *that?*"

"A rattrap."

He's silent for a moment. "What did you say your job is?"

"I didn't." I'm disgruntled enough to be rude.

"Oh, come on, Libby, lighten up."

"Fine," I say, sighing as I start on a new pot. "What brings you to my humble cubicle this evening?"

"I'm meeting with Clarice before dinner. I manage the Ontario Youth Orchestra, which your Ministry generously supports. Now, tell me what you do here."

"I'm the Minister's speechwriter and flower wrangler. My mission today is to ensure that these tulips are precisely three-quarters open by the time you pick up your salad fork."

"Did you write tonight's speech?"

"No, but I *coordinated* it."

"What does that mean?"

"It means I collected it from the freelancer and blew up the point size so that the Minister can read it without her glasses."

Tim snorts. "Here, let me give this a try." He takes the blow-dryer from my hand.

"Careful, now. Three-quarters, no more, no less."

"So, how's the book coming along?"

Still with the book. Ah well, it's way too late to explain now. "Fine, I guess. It's hard to make a lot of progress while working full-time…."

I'm lying with newfound ease because Tim has flipped the dryer to high and can't hear me anyway. He is leaning in for a closer look at the tulips when Margo's head suddenly pops over the side of the cubicle. Tim fumbles the dryer, knocking the pot to the floor again. He drops to one knee to pick up the battered buds.

"Don't, Tim, Libby will get them," Margo says. "The Minister is waiting for you."

He grabs his briefcase and squeezes my arm. "Sorry, Libby."

Margo tows him away, looking back over her shoulder at me, one Vulcan eyebrow raised. The rattrap is probably big enough to take her down if I can find the right bait.

I'm taking matters into my own hands. If Margo won't assign me a speech, I'll create my own opportunity. With this in mind, I review the Minister's calendar to find an event for which no speech is required. I plan to craft brief but compelling remarks and ask her to review them. At best, she'll decide to deliver the speech; at worst, she'll offer advice on improving. It's a desperate move, I suppose, but at least she'll see me as eager.

The most promising event is the upcoming visit to a junior school where the Minister is to judge a poetry contest. Recalling that the Spanish ambassador who visited yesterday is a well-known poet in his country, I decide to propose that Mrs. Cleary tell the kids about his visit, read a poem and comment on how poetry can transcend borders and unite us as human beings. Wonderful sentiment! How could she fail to recognize my genius?

Laurie sneaks the Spanish ambassador's books out of the Minister's office for me and I select a poem that seems appropriate for children. By midafternoon, I have a draft, but I'm stumped about my next move. If I give the speech to Margo, she'll refuse to share it with the Minister, but how can I slip it directly to the Minister when Margo never leaves her side? Then it hits me: I'm joining the dynamic duo at the unveiling of a portrait of a former Premier in the Queen's Park lobby this afternoon. It's a short event, but chances are good that the Minister will need to freshen up. When I escort her handbag to the washroom, I'll seize my opening.

Sure enough, the velvet curtain is barely drawn when the Minister turns and snaps her fingers at me. I follow her down the corridor to the public washroom and take my position beside her stall, heart pounding.

"Minister?"

"What?" (Ever gracious, my lady.)

"You're judging a poetry-writing contest at Earl Gray Public School on Friday and I thought it might be a nice opportunity to mention the poetry of the Spanish ambassador who visited yesterday." Silence. Voice shaking, I continue. "I drafted a few lines of introduction—about how the arts draw people together—and selected a poem that the children can understand. Would you like to review my draft?"

"I suppose so," she says, and flushes the toilet.

"Shall I slip it into your handbag?" I shout over the running water.

Taking the lack of response as permission, I click open her purse and tuck the speech between her glasses and the massive cosmetic bag. The Minister swings open the stall door and snatches her purse from me with a disgusted look. She continues to cast hostile glances at me while touching up her makeup, before finally saying,

"I'll look at your speech because it's my job to spread the word about culture, Lily, but please don't corner me in the washroom again. This is private time."

My delight over my coup outweighs my embarrassment at the reprimand. Later, however, I overhear Mrs. Cleary talking to Margo when I'm passing her office.

"Her remarks were quite good for a first attempt, Margo, but the poem is utter drivel. It makes no sense at all. Maybe it lost something in the translation? I'm so glad I didn't read any of his poetry before we honored him at dinner. I couldn't have kept a straight face...."

Disappointed, I take comfort from the fact she saw some promise in my remarks. Margo soon arrives to admonish me: "Nice try, Libby."

"What do you mean?" (innocently)

"All material for the Minister must be vetted by me so that I can ensure everything has the proper tone and content. Your draft, incidentally, did not."

"Really? It must have lost something in the translation," I say. Margo flushes blotchy puce. "Don't do it again."

I've just logged on to my computer to send Roxanne an e-mail when Margo pops her head around my partition to tell me the good news. I'll be rooming with her on the trip. My shrill protests do nothing to dissuade her.

"Elizabeth, this job is all about optics. We can't be seen to squander taxpayers' dollars. The Minister will have her own room, of course, and the rest of us will double up."

I manage to extract from her that the "away team" is comprised of only the Minister, Margo, Laurie, Bill and me. Obviously Bill and Laurie aren't doubling up.

To: Roxnrhead@interlog.ca
From: Mclib@hotmail.ca
Subject: My sad life

Rox,

Glad to hear you've arrived safely in Douglas, although the constant rain sounds depressing. If it's any consolation, the micro-climate here at Queen's Park is equally miserable. Remember that trip we're taking? Margo is making me share a room with her. Since no one else is doubling up, I have several theories about her motivation: a) she has a crush on me;

b) she's worried I'll be off writing speeches and slipping them into
   the Minister's handbag;
c) she suspects Laurie and I will plan a mutiny if we spend our
   nights together; or
d) two of the above.

I have every reason to think that Margo hates me as much as I
do her, so it's likely choice (d).

Well, she's a brave woman. I will have nine opportunities to
smother her while she sleeps. Try to make it home in time for the
trial, will you?
Libby

I've been freakishly hungry since I started this job. My stomach always seems to be growling, despite the fact that my waistband is constantly cutting off my circulation. The day of the
pre—road show speech-planning meeting, the internal grumbling escalates to a howl. Although I've dealt with the freelance
speechwriters for weeks, it's the first time I've met them in person. I've already developed a burning resentment of them, simply because they get to write while I "coordinate." One of the
writers is forgettable—or would be if only she'd stop talking
about communing with her "muse" (she needs a new muse—
her writing isn't that good). The other, Christine, is considered
the "intellectual," which is reason enough to hate her. She also
has a frightening wiglike growth on her head. I promptly christen Christine "Wiggy."

Mrs. Cleary is surprisingly engaged in the meeting and
Wiggy and Forgettable are vying for her favor. I'm pleased to
note that Forgettable is frequently on the receiving end of the
blank Ministerial stare—I presumed such moments were my
exclusive domain. Mind you, I am totally excluded from the
discussion and sit in silence until my stomach speaks on my
behalf, gradually increasing in volume until Margo turns to me
and says, "Libby, can you keep it down?"

After the meeting, I realize that what I am experiencing is
not hunger, but low-grade indigestion brought on by common

jealousy. I never used to be a competitive person, but frustrated ambition has possessed me like a demon, which explains why I've been eating for two.

Fortunately, I have a little project underway that will simultaneously improve my profile while improving the Minister's speaking style. I've attended enough events by now to know the latter also needs work. The problem is two-pronged. First, the Minister only occasionally reviews her speeches prior to delivering them. Second, she won't wear her glasses. Instead, she demands that her remarks be formatted not in the standard speech font of 14 points, but in a 40-point font that wouldn't be out of place on a street sign. At this size, very few paragraphs fit on a page; even a brief greeting can run to twenty pages, while a keynote address rivals the phonebook in bulk. This does not faze the Minister. She simply heaves her portfolio onto the lectern and stumbles through the speech as fast as her long nails allow, grabbing a breath wherever there's an opportunity.

"This is ridiculous," I whisper to Margo one day during a lengthy page-flipper in a high-school auditorium. "She *has* to wear her glasses. Her delivery is so disjointed people are tuning out."

"You're exaggerating."

"A teacher in the second row is *snoring.*"

"You'll need a lot more experience under your belt before taking this on," she advises.

So I launch Project Diminishing Font. One day, I reduce the font to 38 points, with no discernible impact on the Minister's delivery. Then I try 36, after which I ease it down half a point at a time until I have the Minister reading a 28-point font with apparent comfort. Even this has made a big difference to the amount of text I can cram onto the page. Obviously, she never needed 40 points in the first place.

The Minister slips a streamlined folder onto the lectern and starts into her speech. We're at a conference for teachers of children with disabilities sponsored by the Hearing Society and the National Institute for the Blind and she's tearing through the first page quite smoothly, considering she didn't read it in advance (as evidenced by the lack of yellow highlighting). By the second page, where the text is denser, she starts laboring. By the fifth, she is getting some of the words wrong and by the eighth, she keeps pausing to guess. After leaning in so close to the lectern that all we can see is the top of her head, she finally lifts the speech and holds it inches from her face, muttering into the page. Meanwhile, a teacher standing behind her struggles to simultaneously translate her remarks into sign language.

Perhaps my decision to dip to a 26-point font was a little ambitious.

At the end of the event, I scurry to the car and sink as low in the front seat as possible.

"Ask her," the Minister says to Margo in the back seat, in an eerily calm voice.

"What happened to today's speech, Libby?" Margo's voice is calm too.

"What do you mean?"

"I mean, what size is the font?"

"I'm not sure," I hedge.

"Give us your best guess."

"Well, it's pretty big. Maybe 32 points."

"Did you reduce it deliberately?"

Recognizing that evasion is futile, I confess. "Actually, I did. I couldn't understand why it's usually so large. It's difficult to deliver a speech smoothly with so little text on a page. And besides…"

"Yes?" Margo asks.

"Well, flipping that many pages is very hard on a manicure."

"Libby, when you're ready to think for yourself, we'll let you know. Let's return to a 40-point font, shall we?"

Much later, the Minister says, "Margo, you don't suppose anyone thought I was mocking the people from the Institute for the Blind?"

"Of course not, Minister. You could barely tell there was a problem."

Margo, who is sitting behind me, hoofs the back of my seat.

I'm about to become a glorified roadie. During the Ministerial tour through the eastern townships, I'll be part of the "advance" team that sets up the show. This could actually be fun, since Bill and Laurie comprise the rest of the advance, but with Margo, nothing comes easily. Bill and Laurie will drive ahead in a Ministry "limo" (a government-issue sedan), while the Minister flies from place to place in the tiny government plane. I really want to travel by car, but Margo apparently considers me "plane-worthy." I'm certain this has less to do with wanting me on the plane than with *not* wanting me to have a good time in the car. It's her "divide and conquer" philosophy.

This means Bill will often have to leave an event site, pick me up from the closest airstrip, and rush back to ensure all is ready for the arrival of the Minister. Meanwhile, Mrs. Cleary and Margo will stall for time in a separate car with a local driver so that they can make a grand entrance. It's a pain in the ass for all concerned, but Margo has somehow convinced the Minister that it's a sound strategy. It's Margo's special gift: she can dress up any stupid idea in flawed logic and present it as viable to the Minister. Since the Minister does not appear to be a fool, I assume she has her reasons for accepting Margo's decisions.

We three roadies have prescribed tasks. Laurie will schmooze the event organizers and keep the kids calm. They're always wound up at these events, even though they don't have a clue who the Minister is. Bill and I are to make sure the auditorium is set up properly, and the sound system is working. My special job is to ensure that the podium is appropriately situated to display the Minister to good effect. Specifically, it must be low enough so that she's visible and properly positioned to allow the lights to gleam off her burnished locks.

My biggest challenge is that we require lecterns that accommodate an 8.5 x 14-inch folder, the standard being 8.5 x 11 inches. The Minister has decided, as a result of Project Diminishing Font, I presume, that her speeches will be printed on legal-size paper to get more 40-point text on each page. Besides, this way she'll barely need to lower her head to read. Looking down is unflattering around the chin line and even having a prominent cosmetic surgeon as a husband cannot completely erase the effects of time.

Not that I'm totally insensitive on this score. My many years of rebound dieting foretell of early wattle. Maybe the Minister will grow to like me and give me a voucher for some cosmetic work in her husband's luxurious clinic. I plan to age gracefully, but if the nip-and-tuck were a gift, well, it would be rude not to accept it.

To: Mclib@hotmail.ca
From: Roxnrhead@interlog.ca
Subject: Roughing it on the Isle

Hi Libby,

Bridget Wilkinson refused to come out of her trailer and shoot her scenes today. It all started when the local caterers assumed her request for turkey bacon was a joke. You don't laugh at Bridget! The executive producer stormed over but despite all the yelling, Bridget never appeared on set. I know how much you love the Diva Report, so I hope you'll still be able to access your e-mails during your trip.
Rox

P.S. I haven't missed Gavin at all, which doesn't bode well. I suspect I've seen the last of him and his mangy mutt.

I try reverse psychology on Margo with good results. Fearing she will forbid me to bring the laptop on our journey, thereby cutting off my electronic lifeline to Roxanne, I blithely announce my intention of leaving the computer behind.

"You must bring it," she declares.

"Why?" If she weren't staring at my shoulder, she'd surely detect the desperation behind the bravado. Rox e-mails often when she's on location and I've been relying on the celebrity gossip more than ever lately to distract me from my woes.

"Because it will be useful, that's why."

"But I'll have to carry it around and it's heavy. It's not like I need it to write speeches."

"You'll need it to revise the freelancers' speeches."

"Well, okay, but I have back trouble, you know."

"You can get Bill to help you carry it, but I've made my decision."

To: Roxnrhead@interlog.ca
From: Mclib@hotmail.ca
Subject: Victory

Rox,

If they fire Bridget Wilkinson, tell your director I'm ready for my close-up. My superb performance this afternoon convinced Margo that it was her idea to bring a laptop along on our trip. I even managed to look annoyed and resentful when she put her foot down. It wasn't much of a stretch, since it's becoming second nature anyway.

Can't say I'm surprised about Gavin. Country boys were never your type.

Lib

With the trip less than two days away, my worries about rooming with Margo haven't diminished, particularly as her food issues become more obvious. We're constantly being offered refreshments at events and on several occasions, I've caught her slipping food into her bag for later, presumably because she never goes home. Or maybe she lived through the Irish potato famine in a former life.

Today I catch her removing a plastic cup covered with a napkin secured by an elastic band from her briefcase (i.e., there was planning involved). In the cup are a dozen large shrimp in cocktail sauce. I recognize them from the buffet table at an event we visited hours earlier.

"Margo! You're not going to *eat* those are you?" I say. "It's salmonella waiting to happen!"

"Never mind!" she retorts, slipping them back into her briefcase and stalking out of her own office.

No wonder we have a rat problem. And no wonder her clothes are often a mess, with stains and her shirttail hanging out. The Minister frequently whispers, "Margo, your blouse…"

Still, as much as it pains me to admit it, Margo is actually quite attractive. What's more, for all her compulsive eating and hoarding, she barely tips the scale at a hundred pounds. Maybe she could get me a similar pact with the devil. I imagine she has some pull.

"Are you drunk, Libby?" my mother asks when I call to tell her we're shipping out at dawn.

"No, why would you say that?" I counter, scooping the ice cubes out of my glass so that their clinking won't give me away.

"You seem a little withdrawn, that's all. And you're slurring."

"I am not slurring."

"You'd drink a lot less if you had Mrs. Bingham living next door, monitoring your recycle bin as she does mine."

"I don't drink enough to interest the Mrs. Binghams of the world. Worry about my chocolate consumption if you must worry."

"You've been miserable since you started this job."

"I'm fine," I slur soothingly. "How's Desdemona doing?"

"Desdemona? The Binghams' poodle? Good Lord, she died in the '70s!"

"Yeah, but they had her stuffed and standing by the fireplace last time I was there."

"That was a decade ago. I'm sure they've thrown it out by now."

"*Her.* Desi was a girl. Maybe they sold her at their garage sale last year."

"I think I'd have noticed *that.* I'd have bought her for your father."

"He could keep her beside his recliner."

"Don't suppose your diversionary tactics are working, by the way. They may work on your aunt Mavis, but they're wasted on me."

"Not if I'm sober, they aren't."

"So you *are* drinking!"

"Mother, you'd be into the bourbon too, if you were facing the week I am."

"Never bourbon," she says. "I'm sure it won't be as bad as you fear. And when you get back, I'll make some Nanaimo bars you can take into the office to sweeten Margo up."

They'll be just the thing to tempt her into the rattrap.

The Royal Tour is off to a majestic start. Witness this day in the life of the average political speechwriter.

7:00 a.m.: Libby arises immediately upon alarm, only to have tiny, fleet-footed Margo stampede by into shared washroom and slam door. Boots up computer instead and checks hopefully for e-mails from Rox.

7:30 a.m.: Showers while Margo throws personal effects into suitcase and races off to all-you-can-eat buffet at motel restaurant.

8:10 a.m.: Rushes into motel restaurant only to hear Margo announce there's no time to eat—plane awaits.

9:00-10:00 a.m.: Another terrifying flight in the provincial crap can with wings.

11:15 a.m.: Arrival at public school. Royal entourage attends lengthy theatrical production of Harry Potter adventures, tours art and music rooms, and listens to choir recital (songs from *Lion King*). Lib smiles until gums dry out.

1:30 p.m.: Lunch in school cafeteria. Mix and mingle.

Highlight: Student, age 7, asks Minister, *"Do you work in a church?"* Minister looks annoyed.

Lowlight: Student, age 7, asks Libby, *"Are you pregnant?"*

Result of Lowlight: Baggy sweater destroyed by sundown.

2:30 p.m.: Departure for school number two. As rare treat, Lib rides with Laurie (Margo evidently has top secret biz to discuss with Minister). School itinerary virtually same as before, except theatrical production is scene from *Free Willy*. Boy in black-and-white costume flops around the stage as Willy. Choir's tunes are from *The Little Mermaid*.

Highlight: Student, age 5, remarks to Minister, *"You smell."*

Result of Highlight: Minister grabs handbag and applies even more expensive cologne in staff washroom.

Lowlight: Whale child cited previously rediscovers arms and legs, snatches Ministerial handbag from chair beside Libby, and runs off with it. Lib pursues. Ruckus is sufficient to provoke Minister to whisper savagely, *"Lily, I would appreciate your attention during my remarks. You need to set an example for the students."* Libby glares menacingly at purse-snatcher at snack time, noting nonetheless that Margo stashes two butter tarts in briefcase.

4:00 p.m.: Departure to Town Hall for glad-handing of boring local politicians. MPP, age 70, holds Lib's hand too gladly and too long. Margo, generally so quick to interrupt, is nowhere to be seen.

6:00 p.m.: Arrival at Lakeside Inn, located not by a lake but a major highway. Margo promptly disappears. Lib skulks to Laurie's room to make plans for dinner.

6:20 p.m.: Margo arrives at Laurie's door, shifty-eyed with paranoia. Could Lib and Laurie be plotting mutiny? Lib blurts out that she is simply borrowing curling iron from Laurie, who promptly produces one. Returns to room to add fake ringlets to hair under Margo's watchful eye.

6:30 p.m.: Margo decides that the Minister needs contact lens solution and sends Lib to town to buy it. Lib picks up submarine sandwich en route, dazzling "sandwich technicians" with curls.

9:00 p.m.: E-mail to Rox, bitching and whining.

10:30 p.m.: To bed, too exhausted to read.

11:00 p.m.: Margo crashes into room, turns on all lights. Consumes butter tarts with snuffling noises. Prepares for bed as loudly as possible.

12:00 a.m.: Lib lies awake listening to Margo snore.

Another day, another town, another school visit. It's 7:00 p.m., and we've just checked into the Downtown Motor Lodge, which (surprise) is a twenty-five-minute drive from downtown anywhere. I feel at home immediately, because the rust, orange and brown decor is reminiscent of my parents' basement. Having gained a small head start on Margo, I switch on the swag lamp and throw my things on the bed closest to the washroom. I'm stretched proprietarily across it when Margo crashes into the room and I smile innocently in response to her glare. There was a candy machine in the lobby; maybe I'll curl up with a bag of pretzels and watch mindless sitcoms on TV. That's about all I feel up to tonight. I hide the remote while Margo unloads her beauty aids in the washroom, then start digging through my wallet for change.

"So, Libby." Damn. It speaks. "I've made some revisions to tomorrow's speeches. I want you to input the changes and have them printed."

I look at my watch pointedly before responding. "And where do you propose I do that, Margo? It's almost 7:30 and we aren't in the heart of a thriving metropolis."

"It isn't my job to help you figure out how to do yours. I'm sure you'll find a way. I'll be in Mrs. Cleary's room if anyone needs me."

I throw my shoe at the door as she closes it behind her. Okay, I wait a few beats first so she can't hear the thud, but the act of defiance still makes me feel better. I input her changes, which, in my humble opinion as speechwriter/lady-in-waiting/flunky, were completely unnecessary, and head over to the motel office, computer disk in hand. My faint hope that someone there can help with the printing flickers when I find Dwayne, the night manager, hunched over the front desk crafting a *Gents* sign with a wood-burning kit. But he surprises me.

"Sure, we have a printer, honey. Come on in."

At this rate, I may even be able to catch the second half of *Will and Grace.* My heart sinks when I see the primitive piece of junk they call a printer. I explain politely that my disk is not compatible with their printer and Dwayne directs me to a place in town that can do the job. I collect the keys to the government "limo" from Bill, who's ensconced in his room with a detective novel and a large pizza. He offers to come along for the ride, but fraternizing with Laurie is what set Margo off in the first place, so I decline.

During the drive, I imagine all the ways I could tell Margo to shove it. If the copy shop is closed when I arrive, I'll head right back to the motel and compose a snotty resignation letter, I decide. Oh, right, no way to print it. Fortunately, the shop is open and I am soon on the road again, having surmounted another of Margo's obstacles. Hard not to feel good about that! I perk up even more when the Golden Arches appear on the horizon—I *do* deserve a break today. And how nice to discover a new talent on my drive back to the motel… Like my father before me, I am able to eat a Big Mac with one hand and steer with the other. Since I'm starting to feel quite good about myself, I chant my affirmations between bites: "I am an accomplished speechwriter. I embrace my challenges with grace. I accept all the blessings the universe offers me."

Then I wipe my mouth on my sleeve and burp. What the hell?

The extra duties Margo assigns me are obviously part of her scheme to isolate me and break my spirit. She wants me out, of that much I am sure, and if she sees me as a threat she must sense my potential. Well, bring it on, baby. I am not going anywhere because *I embrace my challenges with grace.*

Full of renewed enthusiasm, I burst into our room, only to

find it empty. Well, if these speech revisions are so damned important, I'll deliver them personally into the Minister's hands. Maybe I'll even convince her to rehearse them for a change.

When I knock at the Minister's door, Margo's dulcet tones ring out.

"Who is it?"

Ignoring the fact that it's Margo, I carol out, "It's me, Minister. I brought your revised speeches for tomorrow!"

"Is that you, Lily? For heaven's sake, Margo, get up and get the door."

"No problem, I've got it," I call, pushing the door open and freezing at the sight of Margo on her hands and knees in front of the Minister.

"Well, come in, Lily," says the Minister. "Don't be shy."

Flustered, Margo scrambles to her feet, dropping a bottle of black-cherry red nail polish in a cloud of cotton balls. I've interrupted a pedicure. The Minister, quite oblivious to Margo's dismay, leans back in her chair, smoothing the feather trim of her diaphanous lounge outfit.

"Be careful," she says as Margo stumbles over a pair of feathered mules. "Do you realize how much those shoes cost? Lily, what was wrong with the speeches?"

"Margo made a few changes and sent me into town to—"

"Some minor but critical edits, Minister," Margo interrupts smoothly. "Libby was good enough to see they were made."

"Thank you, Lily. I hope you got dinner?" Mrs. Cleary masterfully hoists a California roll to her mouth with chopsticks.

My jaw drops even further. Is she warming up to me? Or just warming up to the open bottle of wine on the table? And where the hell did they get that fine spread of sushi in this backwoods town?

"I did, yes, thanks."

"Well, we have enough to spare if you'd like to—"

"Libby can't stay. She has work back in our room," Margo says, pushing me out the door.

"This little piggy stills needs polish, Margo," the Minister says as the door closes behind me.

Speeches still in hand, I head back to our room, retrieve the remote from under the mattress and flick on the television. Only one channel is clear enough to watch and at the moment it's running *Dukes of Hazzard*. I turn down the volume and call my answering machine. It would be nice to hear the voices of family and friends just now.

"You have no new messages."

And the sun sets on another fine day.

Everything looks better in the morning—or so says my mother, the incurable optimist, who has never met Margo. Still, it is going a little better today. First, I was victorious in the shower wars, thanks to my proximity to the bathroom. I raced in the moment I heard her stirring, and then deliberately took twice as long as usual to style my hair. By the time Margo got her turn, Laurie was knocking on our door to warn us about checkout in ten minutes. Margo chose to spend the ten minutes shovelling scrambled eggs into her mouth and has therefore been running around without makeup, her wet hair drying in pleasing strings. We're on the plane before she gets a chance to pull her cosmetic bag out of her briefcase.

Mrs. Cleary, who has been idly flipping through a decorating magazine during the flight instead of reading her speech, wrinkles her perfect little nose and exclaims, "Good Lord, what is that *smell?*"

At first, all I smell is her own cloying perfume, but then I detect an acrid odor. The Minister's gaze is fixed on Margo, who is shrinking behind a green Clinique hand mirror, as she applies her eye makeup.

"Margo? Answer me, please."

"I have no idea, Minister," my roomie replies, looking guilty as she casually snaps the lid of her briefcase closed with her elbow.

"Open it," the Minister commands.

"My briefcase? Why? There's nothing in it but notes."

"Let me see for myself," says the Minister, more bemused than harsh.

"Why don't I ask the pilot? It smells like chemicals."

"Margo, *open your briefcase.*"

Margo clicks it open reluctantly to reveal a few date squares from Monday's school visit, half a tuna sandwich of relatively recent origin and an ancient orange, molded almost beyond recognition.

"Eeeew!" the Minister and I exclaim in unison. "Get rid of that immediately," the Minister adds.

Sheepish, yet defiant, Margo stashes her treasures in the plastic bag I hand her. The Minister turns to me and rolls her eyes dramatically and we both laugh. We are actually having "a moment." I laugh even harder when I notice that Margo has only applied her makeup to one eye and is looking like a "before and after" picture. Unfortunately, the Minister notices too.

"Fix your makeup, Margo, we'll be landing soon."

I must look too happy, because she turns to me and says, "As for you, Lily, your eyebrows are unruly. Margo has her waxing kit with her and I recommend letting her help you with them."

Margo pauses in the middle of her application of mascara to raise one penciled-in eyebrow at me over the edge of her mirror. How will I sleep tonight?

Today was the lightest day of the tour circuit and we move into Fort Everest's Have-a-Nap Hotel by 4:30 p.m. I have rest and relaxation on my agenda, but thankfully, Margo is here to rescue me from that.

"What we really need, Libby, is a *scrapbook* of our trip and this would be a great project for you, since you're so creative. I want you to get started tonight, while it's all fresh in your mind."

And there you have it, folks, the spirit-busting task of the day. I knew she'd punish me somehow for my beautiful moment with the Minister, but this is an inspired move. I lack the "craft" gene and Margo knows it. Time to put my foot down, I decide. Skill with scissors and glue is not required of a speechwriter. I practice the words in my head: "Margo, I've worked some long days lately and I really need to take it easy tonight." But when I open my mouth, waffle-talk trickles out.

"Well, Margo, I'm not sure if I'm the right person for a job like that. I wouldn't know where to begin."

Where's my father's legacy now? This is the man who once asked his boss, *"Would you like me to shove a broom up my ass and sweep as I go?"* Wait, he got fired from that job. Which explains why I soon find myself wandering the aisles of a local dollar store, filling my basket with art supplies from Margo's list.

Back at the Have-a-Nap, I begin pasting photos, speeches and programs into the scrapbook. Running my glue stick across the pages is actually quite soothing and I don't even mind when Margo pops her head in the door to let me know that she and the Minister are heading into town to see a late movie. Eventually, I become so relaxed that I'm forced to call it a night lest Margo return to find me glued to the table by my own bushy eyebrows.

I am sound asleep when Margo comes into the room. In fact, I'm having an amazing dream about Tim in which we're having dinner together at Lavish, the trendy new restaurant I can't afford in my waking life.

*Tim looks gorgeous; I look thin (dreams take off ten pounds). He's entranced by my conversation, and no wonder: every word that falls from my lips is a perfect gem. When the waiter brings the dessert menu, Tim orders chocolate mousse and tries to tempt me with it. He's describing how he's wanted to rip my clothes off since the night we met. Soon we tumble into a cab, where we grope each other like sex-starved teenagers. Buttons and bras are springing open seemingly of their own accord. Suddenly a cell phone rings—one of those annoying musical rings, like the William Tell overture. Tim lets go of me to lunge for his phone and my head hits the backrest with a thud. Confused, I hear Margo's voice squawking away in the distance. I can't make out what she's saying at first, but her voice gets louder and clearer and I hear my name.*

"Libby! Libby, wake up!

The lights are on and my eyes are open but I'm groggy enough to wonder what Margo is doing in the back of our cab. Then she reaches out to shake my shoulder and I remember where I am. Squeezing my eyes shut, I struggle to hang on to the feeling of Tim's lips on the back of my neck, of his hands in my hair and—

"What are you grinning at?" Margo asks.

"Grinning? I'm not grinning, I'm *grimacing* because you're standing over me in the middle of the night for no apparent reason."

"The Minister is upset! We're leaving!"

"Leaving?" I glance at the clock on the bedside table. "For God's sake, Margo, it's 2:30 in the morning. What's going on?"

If it were anyone other than Margo, I'd be on my feet already, certain that tragedy had struck. Because it is Margo, I can only guess that the Minister has broken a nail and I am about to be dispatched for an emergency repair kit.

"Never mind, just get Bill to find us another motel right away." Maybe it's resentment over being torn from my dream, but I find the nerve to stare back at her without flinching. I will wait for an explanation. "All right," she yields, "if you *must* know, the Minister found something in her bed and refuses to stay here."

"What? A cockroach?"

Silence. I hold my ground. I will stage a bed-in until I get a response.

"It was a condom—a *used* condom." I throw back the covers and pull on my jeans, all thoughts of sex extinguished. "When you've taken care of the arrangements, come and get me," Margo says, rushing out.

Bill finds us new digs and pulls the car around. Laurie emerges from her room and stands, dazed, beside the car.

"You and the Minister can leave now," I tell Margo when she opens the Minister's door. "Bill will come back for Laurie and me later."

The Minister sweeps out in a gorgeous yellow silk kimono, matching head scarf and dark sunglasses. Somehow I manage not to laugh as she clatters toward the car in those feathered mules and slides into the back seat. While she's pulling her leg in, there's a flash, as if someone has taken a picture. We all spin to see a man running around the corner of the motel. Bill slams the car door and races to the driver's side, while Margo hurls herself into the passenger seat. "Libby," she calls out the window as they squeal off, "go after him! Get the film! Then grab our things."

I look at Laurie questioningly and she shakes her head; we've sacrificed enough for our province. Instead, we return to our rooms to pack. Handling Margo's belongings is plenty heroic for me, since it means disposing of the garlic bread she lifted at dinner. By the time Bill returns, we're ready to roll and the three of us laugh ourselves sick all the way to the new fleabag motel.

"Remember the last time we had a crisis on the road?" Bill asks Laurie. "Cleary canceled the rest of the trip. Maybe we'll get lucky again."

Bill invites Laurie and me to his room, where he produces a bottle of premium bourbon. Turns out these two can play as hard as they work. In fact, by the time I finally weave my way back to my room and fall into bed, the sky is beginning to brighten.

I feel as though I've only been asleep for minutes when I awaken, sensing an evil presence. I struggle to open my puffy eyes, only to see someone standing by my bed, silhouetted by the light streaming through the window. She's staring at me intently. Waiting. I swallow a scream and croak, "What are you doing?"

"Waiting for you to wake up."

"If you're thinking about waxing my eyebrows, forget it."

"This is no time for your jokes. We have a crisis."

"I haven't recovered from the last one yet."

Margo is still wearing her suit from yesterday and it's looking decidedly worse for wear. Craning to see the clock, I realize that I have only been asleep for an hour. I also realize that I'm still tipsy. Keeping my face averted to prevent premium bourbon vapors from enveloping her, I raise both eyebrows in a question. She holds up a newspaper, forcing me to lift my pounding head for a closer look. It's the *Fort Everest Chronicle-Times,* and there on the front page is Minister Cleary, just as she appeared during last night's exodus. It is just a black-and-white, so regrettably, the impact of the yellow silk robe is lost. The photographer caught her with mouth agape, one bare leg and a feathered mule dangling out the car door.

"Good thing you did that pedicure," I say.

"I'm surprised you see any humor in this situation."

"Sorry. Read me the headline." I ease my head back onto the pillow.

"Minister Storms Out of Have-a-Nap At Midnight—Motel Staff Mystified."

Margo tosses the paper at me and sits on her bed, which hasn't been slept in. The story quotes motel staff speculating on the Minister's hasty departure: *"Her husband is very rich, you know. Maybe our beds aren't good enough for her."*

"The Minister refuses to do today's events."

"That's just going to make things worse."

She ignores me and continues: "The Minister wants to know how the reporter found out about it. She thought you might know."

"How would I know?" When she doesn't reply, I sit up so that I am eye-to-bloodshot-eye with her. "I hope you're not implying I called the local paper and leaked this in the five minutes before Bill found us another motel."

"Not at all, Libby, but we do want you to drive over to the Have-a-Nap and apologize for the Minister's abrupt departure. See what you can find out."

"Just let it go. The more we react, the more coverage we'll get."

"The Minister wants action, so get out of bed and get going." She hands me the car keys and walks out.

The definition of "speechwriter" just gets broader every day. I consider telling her I'm too drunk to drive, but she'd only run to Bill, then Laurie, and discover they're worse off than I am. Instead, I swallow headache pills and head for the car. I can't believe they think I alerted a paper I didn't know existed to the newsflash that the Minister would be appearing out-of-doors without makeup for the first time in her life.

At the Have-a-Nap, I chat up the clerk and apologize for our hasty exit. There's a stack of newspapers on the counter and the unflattering photo is already on display in a cheap plastic frame by the cash register. Gesturing toward it casually, I say, "I can't imagine how the paper knew we'd be leaving just then."

"The editor was leaving Millie's Roadhouse next door as your driver pulled around," the clerk offers. "Between you and me, he's *thrilled,* because there's so little real news around here. Apparently they've picked up the story in Toronto, too." I must look shocked because she adds quickly, "The Minister's not upset about all this, is she?"

"Not at all! She has a great sense of humor," I lie. "I'll let her know that the folks back home will see her in the news."

I knock at the Minister's door and when Margo opens it, I can see the Minister lying on the bed, forearm over her eyes, overcome by the drama of it all. The table is strewn with hair-brushes, makeup and nail polish. Clearly, Margo has been trying to soothe some shattered nerves.

"You'd better step outside," I tell Margo. She is so shaken by my news that I actually have to restrain her from heading to our room to write a huffy rebuttal to the local paper—and all three Toronto papers, just in case. "Don't. You'll inflame the situation. Leave it alone, and it'll die out."

"And where did you get your degree in Political Science, the University of *Kentucky?*" I guess she's onto the bourbon.

She's blocking entry to the Minister's room, but realizing I can turn my personal hygiene issue to my advantage, I lean in nice and close and let the fumes wash over her: "I may not have the degree, Margo, but I know something about public relations."

My breath has the desired effect and Margo backs away, allowing me to slip past her. "Minister?"

"Who's there?" comes her weak reply.

"It's me… Libby. I have something I need to tell you."

Margo attempts a body slam in the doorway and we stumble into the room together.

"Stop it, you two, my head is killing me. What is it, Lily?"

"I think you should do this morning's event."

"I am not leaving this room."

"The children have been preparing for weeks. They'll be so disappointed."

"Can't you see I'm ill?"

"Surely you could stand for an hour, Minister… Remember, children don't read the newspaper."

She lifts her head to glare at me. My imagination must have been working overtime when I thought she was warming up to me.

"I'll send regrets saying that you're unwell, Minister," Margo says.

"If we don't generate a fresh story, the paper might do a follow-up piece about last night's hasty retreat and what they make up will be worse than the reality." Sensing that I'm getting through to her, I continue. "You could put on your new Dolce & Gabbana suit—it's stunning—and say something funny and self-deprecating to the teachers and parents before your speech. How about I write up a funny line or two to defuse the situation? What do you say? The show must go on, Minister."

"All right, I'll do it," she mutters.

Margo is livid, especially later, when I am proven right. The Minister rises to the occasion, striding onto the school stage looking like a million bucks.

"Hello, everyone," she begins, "I do hope I'm looking a little better in person than I did on the front page of your paper this morning?"

When everyone laughs, she relaxes and delivers the rest of the speech with ease. Afterward, people surge over to offer support; no one mentions the motel incident. My rare moment of satisfaction is enhanced by the fact that Margo isn't speaking to me. Later, as we drive to the airport, Margo breaks the news to the Minister about the Toronto paper picking up the photograph. I expect tempers to flare, but much to my surprise, Mrs. Cleary takes it all in stride.

"Well, Margo, we'll just face this the same way we did today. I managed to maintain public affection quite effectively."

I won't hear any praise from them, but I know I earned my pay today. And I did it all with a hangover. I am good.

9

By some miracle I manage to fall asleep during the forty-minute flight to Ottawa. Maybe Margo slipped a sedative into my Diet Coke, but it's a welcome reprieve. All good things must come to an end, however, and by the time we pull up to our motel on the outskirts of the city, Margo has clued in to the fact that ostracizing me isn't having the desired effect and resorts to her old tactics.

"While you were asleep, the Minister mentioned how much she's looking forward to seeing your scrapbook."

And I look forward to showing it to her—almost as much as I look forward to sharing a room with Margo. The Minister continues to maintain that her staff cannot squeeze the public purse (though some may be forced to carry it). Rest assured fellow citizens, your tax dollars are not being wasted on me.

Overnight, Mrs. Cleary works herself into a lather about the main event of the road trip—a reception for outstanding youth achievers to be held at Rideau Hall, the Governor General's residence. Although it doesn't start until 11:00 a.m., she rings our room at 5:30 to summon Margo, who crashes around long enough to make sure I'm awake. Finally she leaves with *the suitcase*—the one she keeps locked all the time. I used to think it contained a voodoo doll with big hair just like mine, but when I interrupted the pedicure the other night, I discovered that it's really a portable spa filled with high-end beauty products. I think she swallows the key each night.

Despite the early awakening, I'm in great spirits when I slide into the vinyl booth of the motel coffee shop across from the Minister and my bunk buddy. My mood fizzles before the coffee arrives. The Minister, dry toast untouched before her, is holding forth about the importance of reaching the impressionable youth of this country.

"Here's our opportunity to *make a difference,*" she says, looking expectantly at both of us. Margo is impassively working her way through a large stack of flapjacks, eggs, bacon and hash browns while I study my coffee. "We're role models for these kids," the Minister continues, voice rising, "and we must use our influence to set them on the right course *while there is still time.*" She bangs a fist on the arborite table for emphasis, spilling tea into her saucer.

I can't tell from Margo's expression if this is an old rant or a new idea hot off the presses. All I know is that the Minister has spoken to hundreds of kids in the past month alone without any apparent desire to influence them for the good. It's not till I'm halfway through my waffle that I realize that she's not worrying about making an impression on young minds, she's worrying about making an impression on Juliette Moreau, the Governor General. The latter is a lawyer, a generous patron of the arts and a style maven to boot. It seems that the Minister is intimidated.

I try to distract her during the drive by suggesting she rehearse the speech Wiggy prepared weeks ago. "You know, Minister, I have your speech right here in my bag. Would you like to review it?" I turn around in my seat to find her plucking at invisible lint on her dress.

"Can't you see the Minister has more important things on her mind right now, Libby? Honestly, you have no sense of timing."

The Minister stares out her window as if our exchange hasn't registered and by the time we reach Rideau Hall, I've become a little nervous myself. It doesn't help when I see the banner strung across the entranceway: "The Governor General Welcomes Minister Cleary and the Ontario Youth Orchestra." Fabulous, another opportunity to embarrass myself in front of Tim. On the other hand, I'm wearing a fetching outfit and I'm having a rare good hair day. He could do worse. Maybe this will be the day I turn things around and prove I've got it together. Some affirmations will put me in the right frame of mind: *I will not be a fool. I will not be a fool. I will not—* Wait a minute, affirmations are supposed to be positive. *I am a skilled and confident woman. I am poised and centered. I am sexy and articulate....*

"Libby, stop daydreaming and get the Minister's door."

Scrambling out of the car, I fling open the back door for Her Nervousness. A cloud of powder blue sweeps by and I trot along in her perfumed wake. In the lobby, I scan the crowd for a glimpse of Tim. Fortunately, he stands a little taller than the rest of humanity, so he's not too hard to locate. Of course, the same applies to me, and when he sees me a second later, he smiles and raises his arm to wave. My heart does a little leap. More affirmations.... *I am poised and confident.... I am skilled and centered....*

The Governor General is introducing Mrs. Cleary. I should be paying attention, but I've just realized that my arm is still in the air, waving at Tim. How long has it been up there? I'm yanking it down when—WHACK!—a bulky Michael Kors shoulder bag hits me square in the chest so hard I stagger backward.

Mrs. Cleary is at the podium now and beginning to speak. I'm trying to focus on what she's saying but my eyes slide toward Tim to see if he noticed the handbag debacle. Judging from his grin, he saw it all right. I turn back to the stage, muttering aloud, "I am poised and confident. I will not be a fool...."

"Ssshhh," Margo hisses.

Slow, deep breaths....Keep eyes averted....Recovery of dignity is still possible.

The Minister is several minutes into her speech before I can fully concentrate. She's waxing on about the glacial landforms in the eastern townships. Have I missed a connection to culture? Maybe this is part of her new effort to inspire today's youth. Oh, there it is—she's claiming the landscape inspires our artists. That's original.

"As I traverse the highways and byways of this great province, I am astounded by the beauty of the landscape. Yesterday we passed through Prince Edward County and never in my life have I beheld such a spectacular penis...."

She stops cold, turns the page, freezes. Laughter ripples across the room. Even the teachers are grinning. The Minister, poor thing, is totally nonplussed, nervously shuffling pages of the speech, wondering how to back out of this corner. It seems like hours before she finally speaks.

"That would be *peninsula*. 'Never in my life have I beheld such a spectacular *peninsula*.' Of course, I've never beheld a— But never mind. Excuse me."

The laughter turns to hysteria and the kids start high-fiving each other with delight. This is an event they will remember for a long, long time. Suddenly, the room erupts with a chant: "Pee-nis, pee-nis, PEE-NIS." The teachers are working furiously to calm them and just as they're making headway, a shrill voice rings out over the crowd:

"SHUT UP! JUST SHUT UP!"

The audience falls silent. I turn to see Margo standing on a chair, chest heaving in rage. The kids are still laughing, but uncertainly now. The teachers and the Governor General look grim. Finally, the Minister begins speaking again and stumbles through the rest of the speech. At the end, she hurries off the stage, grabs her bag from my arms and makes a beeline to the ladies' room. I collect the speech from the lectern and scan it anxiously, knowing I could end up wearing this. To my horror, I discover that it *is* partly my fault. When I formatted the text of Wiggy's speech two weeks ago into the 40-point font, I split a word between two pages: penin-sula. She read the first half as *penis*. Shit, shit, shit. She'll be in dire need of a scapegoat right now and I expect I'll be the one baaa-ing.

I'm barely through the bathroom door when the refined, elegant little woman turns on me.

"What were you *thinking,* Lily?" she says, tapping a polished finger against her own frontal lobe. "Did you even read the speech? You've humiliated me and I can assure you, speechwriters have lost their jobs for less!"

She's practically screaming and the reverberation propels a teacher out the door. Yanking her perfume out of her purse, Mrs. Clearly squirts it savagely into the air and steps through it. Then she fiercely dusts her face with powder as I stand by, trying to look contrite. I consider mentioning that this wouldn't have happened if she'd wear her glasses, but chicken out. At the moment, she's quite capable of drowning me in a toilet bowl. Finally, she clicks her purse shut and shoves it at me with a parting blow: "Maybe if you weren't so busy *flirting,* you could concentrate on what we pay you to do."

Ouch. She's gone before my burning face confirms my guilt. Smiling at Tim didn't cause this screw-up, but I'm ashamed that she knows I was thinking about boys on company time. Besides, I should have paid more attention to the formatting.

When I emerge a few minutes later, the Minister is chatting with Tim and his expression when he sees me confirms I've been named the villain of the piece. Maybe he even overheard her tirade. Now she's clinging to his arm for support, so I slink by to join Laurie and Bill in the audience. The Minister doesn't have the pleasure of Tim's company for long, however, because the Governor General soon introduces his orchestra.

Now that my opportunity to impress him has vaporized, I shift my focus to counting the ways he's all wrong for me, anyway. He's a teacher, for example. Teachers get no respect and they're grossly underpaid. What's more, they're expected to be role models and their wives probably have to be role models, too. I have enough trouble getting myself through the day without trying to inspire anyone else. Tim is obviously not my prince. My prince is a wealthy man, a man who hangs out with high flyers. A man who is comfortable in Armani. A man who…knows better than to wear athletic socks with a suit. Tim, it appears, does not. His arms are raised to summon the woodwinds when I see the telltale flash of white.

My eyes happen to be in the sock region because they've drifted down from his butt. It's a pretty great butt and it's too bad I'll miss out on it, but happily, I'll also miss out on a lifetime of wardrobe monitoring. The man is in the presence of royalty, or at least a vice regal. Socks matter. As if orchestra conductors don't have enough strikes against them already! Look at him waving that silly baton around. And what's with the jutting of his rib cage in the general direction of the horns? The grimace at a squawking bassoon? The blissful radiance over a perfect chord? It's too much—and it cancels out the great butt, which is a shame, because they aren't that common.

Having confirmed that no romantic interest remains, I spend the rest of the event hoping to talk to him. I may find him repellant, but I don't want him thinking *I'm* a complete waste of skin. I won't get a chance to enlighten him today, however, because my lips are firmly attached to the Minister's derriere. Margo has disappeared and my guilty conscience is driving me to support her through this disaster. In the endless receiving line, I observe the Minister when she meets the Governor General's husband. A notorious ladies' man, he not only compliments her on her lovely suit, he also takes the liberty of looking down her blouse. Pulling her out of line, I whisper, "When you reach Mrs. Moreau, make a joke right away about using *that word*. Say you've been on the road too long without *your* husband or something. Then mention that Margo is undergoing a personal crisis. And maybe you should do up your blouse."

I push the Minister back in line before she can protest. I watch her lean over to whisper something to the Governor General, who giggles, then looks sympathetic—right on cue. No time to thank Lily, though. The minute she's through the line, the Minister starts toward the door.

Margo is waiting in the car and it looks as though she's been crying. I'd feel sorry for her if I didn't know she's already devising a way to add her share of blame to mine.

There's a wonderful moment when I awaken, where I actually believe yesterday was just a bad dream. Margo, perched on her bed opposite, is quick to assure me otherwise. She's already dressed and between bites of a donut, she sets the tone for the day.

"Well, it's good to see...that *some* people can relax...when things are falling apart around them.... If you aren't too busy lounging around...you might want to get packed.... Our plane leaves in an hour."

With that, she stuffs the remaining chunk of cruller into her mouth and walks out. I don't need this crap. Maybe I should just make a break for it at the airport and grab a flight back to Toronto. I could be sipping espresso on College Street by 10:00 a.m. Tempting as this is, my departure would only bring joy to Margo's pathetic life and that's not in the cards. So I pack my bags and I head out to the car to wait for the ladies. Twenty minutes later, Bill and I are still waiting. He goes into the motel to roust them out and when they finally appear, we're thirty minutes behind schedule. He drops us at the airport, but a glitch brings it to forty-five, and by the time we land in Clarington, it's a full hour. Everyone is on edge.

"Where's Laurie with the car?" I ask Margo as we step off the plane.

"I asked her to rent a car and get to the school very early

this morning," Margo replies. "We can't afford to have anything go wrong today."

Bill, traveling behind us in the official government "limo," won't arrive until the event is almost over.

"Are we taking a cab to the school?" I ask suspiciously.

"Oh no, the Minister would never allow that on an official visit. I've reserved a rental car. You'll drive, of course."

Of course. A chauffeur. Why didn't I think of that? Oh right, because I'm directionally challenged, a source of great shame to my father. Margo sends me over to the rental desk while she and the Minister repair to the washroom. The clerk escorts me to a compact with standard transmission. I haven't driven a five-speed since high school, I tell him. We can't take this car.

"But there's nothing else available," he says. "It would take hours to bring one in from Ottawa. Miss Margo assured me on the phone that this would be fine."

Then Miss Margo had better grab her neck brace, because she's in for a bumpy ride.

Soon I'm behind the wheel of the tiny vehicle, praying that gear-shifting is stored in my memory alongside bike-riding. I take a moment to examine the map but I can't even locate the airport. All those lines and colors… Who wouldn't be confused?

"Exactly how late are we, Margo?" the Minister asks pointedly in the back seat.

"An hour and fifteen minutes by my watch. Are you planning to set off today, Libby?"

When I put the map on the passenger seat, there are damp handprints on either side. I can't remember the name of the school and I'm unwilling to ask. It just isn't fair that I'm expected to— Wait a second. *Fair…* Fairview Public School. That's it! Libby, you're a genius. I reach for the map again, but a huffy sigh from a back-seat diva dissuades me. How big can the town be anyway? I'll just drive around until I see it.

I depress the clutch, rev up the gas and by some miracle, get the car into gear on the first try. My luck continues as we approach the first intersection and the light remains green. I head right on through and ease the car into second. It *is* like riding a bike. But the next light is red and I forget what to do. Clutch? Brake? Clutch-and-brake? I hit the brake only, lurch to a stop and stall the car.

"Good Lord, what happened?" the Minister sputters.

"Bubble in the gas tank," I say.

I stall again pulling out from the light and a guy in a Jeep lays on the horn behind me. I make the first right to escape him, stall a third time and look up to behold Fairview P.S. My father is wrong about me: I *am* a natural navigator! Shifting into first, I crawl forward so that I don't have to gear up, then cut the engine in the school parking lot just as Margo's cell phone rings. After saying hello, she passes the phone to me.

"Libby, where the hell are you?" It's Laurie, and she sounds stressed.

"We've had some car trouble, but don't worry, we're in front of the school now."

"I don't think so."

"What do you mean? We're right outside."

"Yeah? Well I'm standing at the front doors of Fairmount Public School with about forty bored kids and six frustrated teachers and I don't see you."

"Fair*mount?*" I feel queasy.

"What's going on, Libby?" asks Margo.

Then the Minister finds her voice again, but apparently forgets I can hear it.

"Margo, please tell me she hasn't fouled up *again*. I cannot endure such incompetence."

Does she think an invisible glass partition is standard issue in a Ford?

"I'm so sorry, Minister," I say. "It seems I have the wrong school. But we're only a few blocks away and I'll get you there quickly, I promise."

I tell Laurie we're on our way, turn the car around and gun

it out of the gravel parking lot. This might have been impressive had I not stalled the car as we hit the road, flinging Margo into the Minister's lap. All of a sudden I feel a little better.

"Margo, stop this at once!" the Minister says. "I'm getting whiplash! And you're crushing my skirt."

"The gas quality is simply appalling out here," I offer. "I'm afraid it makes for a rough ride, ladies. Hold on now!"

Laurie is standing in the middle of a rowdy throng of students as we bunny hop up to the front door. Margo springs from the car and opens the Minister's door with a grand flourish. Mrs. Cleary emerges in her commanding turquoise Yves Saint Laurent suit but the kids don't even notice her. What they notice is that Margo is pulling bags of chocolate bars out of her briefcase. They surge over to the car and while the Minister fights her way into the school, Margo tries to generate a little goodwill.

Laurie leads us to the auditorium, where the teachers encourage the children to take their seats. Finally, there's enough of a lull for the principal to introduce her esteemed guest. The Minister strides quickly to the microphone, looking a little nervous, and no wonder after yesterday's cock-up. She senses that the kids are not going to settle for long. That's the only explanation for the way she speeds through her speech, ruthlessly chopping paragraphs as she goes.

"She's not making any sense," Laurie whispers to me.

"I know, but the kids aren't listening anyway."

"Good point. And I've been thinking, why don't I drive your car to the airport and you can take the automatic?"

I practically throw the keys at her. "Laurie, I love you. I can't afford another screw-up. The Minister basically called me incompetent earlier."

"Her bark is much worse than her bite," she assures me, handing me her car keys in return. "And remember, this is the civil service. They can't fire you for getting lost."

I'm starting to relax, knowing that the easy part is coming. Mrs. Cleary will tour the classrooms, fuss over the kids and win their hearts with her charm. But today, the trouble is just beginning. As we walk down the corridor to the classrooms, the kids—blood sugar soaring from Margo's chocolate bars—rush ahead to prepare their presentations, screaming and yelling and pushing each other out of the way. When we arrive at the art room, several eight-year-olds are arguing about who will get to demonstrate a particular painting technique for the Minister. Their teacher tries to defuse the tension by calling, "Kids, kids, it's time to make our rainbow for the Minister."

But ever-patient Margo takes matters into her own hands. "Just STOP IT, all of you," she shouts. "The Minister doesn't have time to listen to your bickering." It's like the woman has lost control of her mouth. Who makes the same gaffe two days in a row?

Disaster strikes and it seems to happen in slow motion. Margo has startled a big kid, causing him to step backward, lose his balance and sit down hard on one end of a folding table holding art supplies. The other end of the table shoots up, launching several open paint cans across the room. From my vantage point just inside the door, I see the paint rain down on the students. One kid bathed in green returns fire at the big kid with an open can of bright blue paint and—score!—Margo takes it in the face.

Other students join the fray and paint is soon flying in all directions. I scuttle backward through the door, but the Minister and Margo are caught in the cross fire and pretty soon the YSL suit looks like an original Jackson Pollock. Margo's glasses are covered in paint and she rubs a fat blue streak right across her cheek. It's a scene out of *Lord of the Flies.*

Bill suddenly arrives on the scene, charging by me to restrain the two ringleaders. Laurie leads a bewildered Mrs. Cleary out of the room while Margo stumbles blindly behind. Knowing that seeing me standing there unscathed will infuriate them more, I slip behind the door as they pass.

I give them a few minutes to clear the school, then follow them to the front doors. There's a chance I can avoid them until we get to the airport, by which point they may have cooled off. I'll wait until they're in the car with Bill and when they pull out, I'll jump into Laurie's car and trail them.

When I get to the door, however, I see that Bill has already pulled into the street. Seconds later, the Ford reverses quickly out of the parking spot, and it's sent gunning after Bill. Wow, Laurie really knows how to handle a stick shift! But wait, it doesn't look like Laurie behind the wheel. It looks more like... the Minister! She expertly maneuvers the car out of the lot, accelerates smoothly through several gears and passes Bill in moments. I catch a fleeting glimpse of Margo alone in the back seat. Laurie's car is sitting empty in the lot, so she must have gone with Bill. I can't imagine why the Minister is driving (who knew she was even capable?), but there's no way I can catch them now. I might as well help the teachers clean up, then call Laurie for directions later.

Back at the classroom, it occurs to me that there's no need for anyone to know I escaped the melee unscathed. All I need is a daub of paint here and there and no one will be any the wiser. The teachers are herding the kids out of the classroom, so I step in, reach into a can of becoming pink and spread a little on my cheek.

"Why are you putting paint on your face, lady?"

Whirling around, I see an adorable little girl, maybe six years old. Across the room, two teachers are starting to clean up, but they seem oblivious to us. Why not try my charm? It's useless with men, but occasionally effective with kids. Switching on a best-pal smile, I crouch down in front of her.

"What's your name, cutie?"

"Ashley. What's yours?"

"Libby," I answer. It's working! She's taking to me.

"Why are you putting paint on your face, Libby?"

Never hesitate to lie to a child when one's credibility is at stake, I always say. "No, no, sweetie. I'm not putting paint *on* my face. I'm cleaning it *off*."

"But you ran into the hall when the fight started, I saw you."

"I did not *run*." She's staring at me with round, questioning eyes, so I add, sighing, "Well, I may have hurried."

"Why?"

"It's complicated, Ashley."

"Why?"

"When you're older—and have a horrible job—you'll understand."

Laughter erupts across the room and I find that the two teachers have overheard this exchange.

"Ashley, we're out of paper towels," one says. "Please run and get us some." To me, she says, "Hi, Libby, I'm Jan and this is Maureen. Don't feel bad about escaping. Wish we could have done the same."

Grinning sheepishly, I offer to help them clean up. Jan and Maureen are such good company, I don't even care that I am legitimately getting covered in paint from my efforts. At least I'll be able to face the troops now.

Half an hour later, I collect Mrs. Cleary's purse, which she's left behind, and walk to the front doors of the school. The spot where Laurie's car had been is now empty. But it can't be gone, I tell Maureen and Jan, I have the car keys. I pull Margo's cell phone out of my bag and call Laurie. Her phone is turned off, as is Bill's. I'm stuck. My eyes water up and Jan puts a comforting arm around me, assuring me they'll notice I'm MIA soon enough. I'm more worried about what will happen when I do unite with Margo and the Minister again. What if the Minister fires me?

Half a dozen calls later, Laurie answers. She's at a local medical clinic with two students who got paint in their eyes during the fight. We piece together that she was in the school nurse's office when I went to the door the first time. Later, she drove off—using her spare keys—when I went back to the classroom. Surprisingly, the Minister offered to drive the Ford so that Laurie would have room in the larger car for the kids, a teacher and two parents.

"I'm really sorry, Lib," Laurie says. "I just assumed you'd hook up with Bill."

And Bill, who arrives moments later looking for me, just assumed I was staying to help Laurie. Margo and the Minister, Bill admits, didn't notice my absence until they arrived at the airport and the Minister reached for her Gucci. Margo then called Bill, who was speeding along the highway to our next event by that point, and sent him back for me.

The ladies are drowning their sorrows in a good bottle of wine in the airport's tiny lounge when Bill drops me off. They've washed, although Margo's complexion remains slightly blue (oxygen deprivation, one can only hope). The Minister is wearing a clean suit and her hair is freshly coiffed, but she's without makeup. I've evidently been carrying the entire cosmetic collection. No wonder my arm aches.

"None of this would have happened if Libby hadn't made us late," Margo is saying as I approach the table.

"I agree and I'm telling you, there is absolutely nothing wrong with that car. It handled perfectly for me. I have no idea what she was on about."

"It was like she was having spasms."

"Maybe she has a disorder. She's certainly oddly attached to my purse. Have you noticed how I always have to hunt her down for it?"

"Ladies," I say, pleasantly. They don't even have the decency to be embarrassed. "Sorry I'm late. I thought it would be good public relations to stay and help with the mess."

"Well, next time you decide to stay behind, Lily, perhaps you'll let us know. Don't assume that Bill is at leisure to chauffeur you around."

With that, she snatches the Gucci and disappears into the

washroom, the Smurf close on her heels. I take my chances in the men's room for a hasty wash-up. When I return, I see that there's plenty of Beaujolais in the bottle and I don't hesitate to pour myself a glass. The makeover will probably continue until the plane is ready and there's no sense in wasting good grape.

10

It's the end of another long day, but a day that has been curiously short on disasters. Three separate events went off without a hitch. We arrived on time, the Minister performed well, and the audiences were receptive. What's more, the local press somehow missed the story of the great paint fight. I could almost relax if Margo and the Minister weren't behaving so oddly around me. Neither one has said anything abusive for two full days. Not that they've been friendly, mind you, but they have been more or less polite and professional. It's disquieting.

The Tranquility Lodge, our abode for the night, is just another motel sprawled alongside a busy stretch of highway. To reach the driveway, we have to detour around a construction site where workers are blasting through limestone to expand the highway. Signs in the motel lobby warn that the pool and recreation areas may be evacuated occasionally prior to detonation.

Ignoring the warning signs that an explosion is about to occur in my own room, I enter unarmed.

"Libby," Margo says without ceremony, "you just aren't measuring up."

Here we go. I sit down on the edge of the bed and prepare

for the worst. Margo is already red in the face and she's pacing back and forth over the worn gray carpet.

"The Minister is concerned about your lack of attention to detail and we're both extremely disappointed by your poor judgment. You've really let us down."

*My* judgment is poor? Which one of us shouted at children during two recent visits? But I remain silent because I have no experience in this sort of confrontation. I've always been considered a strong performer.

"I talk to you until I'm blue in the face, but your work doesn't improve."

"Could you give me some concrete examples of how my performance is unacceptable?" I ask, wishing my voice weren't so hoarse.

This request appears to take Margo aback, because she hesitates. "Well, the formatting mistake in the speech was clearly a major blunder on your part. Then, you made us terribly late the next day when you got lost. Your driving is deplorable. And you have made little progress on the Minister's scrapbook."

"I see. Is there more?"

"Actually, yes," she says, warming to the task. "Our biggest concern is your *attitude.* You are sullen and resistant to the most basic requests, Libby. This is a tight team and our effectiveness depends on each member playing his or her part. I'm afraid you just don't fit in." It's as though I'm back in school, the girl on the outside, the one who isn't allowed into the cool group. "I assume you have *some* strengths, but I have yet to discover what they are. What really surprises me is how your references can be so good. HR spoke to four people at length and no one had a bad word to say about you."

BOOM! A blast from the road makes the windows rattle and shakes my tongue loose.

"My references were good because I was applying for a job as *speechwriter.* I doubt anyone commented on my abilities as a scrapbook engineer, baggage handler, private investigator or chauffeur. I'm disappointed too, Margo. Never once in the interview process did anyone mention that writing would be the last on my list of duties."

"You see, this is the attitude I was talking about."

"Well, I take my work seriously. I can live up to my good references if you'll let me do what I was hired for."

"If things don't improve, Libby, we'll need to talk again."

I dig through my bag for my shampoo and head for the bathroom. Fifteen minutes later, I'm still under the shower, feeling defeated. I manage not to cry, though. It's not as if she can *really* fire me. In government, it's only possible to get rid of people if they've died at their desk. Even then, the absence of life signs must be thoroughly documented. However, Margo *could* end my contract and send me back to my home position with two weeks' notice and the shame of it would kill me. Not that I'm deluding myself: I do have an attitude problem. I resent being assigned tasks for which I have no aptitude and I feel I'm being set up for failure. If only they'd give me an opportunity to put pen to paper, I know I could turn things around.

By the time I step out of the bathroom, Margo has left. I dress quickly and when there's no answer in Laurie's room or Bill's, I decide to go for a walk. Some fresh air would do me good. Maybe I can find an ice-cream shop and drown my sorrows. Half a mile down the road, I discover a bar and a drink seems more appropriate for the occasion than ice cream. The place looks a bit run-down, but it's got to be better than my own room at the moment. Once inside, I find it's actually quite a nice little pub. I head for the bar, pull up a stool and take a moment to appreciate the young man stacking cases of beer behind the counter. Watching the way his muscles move against his white T-shirt is helping me forget my worries. He looks around and shoots me a flirty smile.

"Hey, there! See anything you like?"

Busted! Well, maybe not. He's gesturing to the array of bottles behind him but the playful look on his face suggests he knows what I'm thinking.

"Yeah, does he know how to make a good Cosmopolitan?"

Did I just say that out loud? Margo's inability to hold her tongue must be contagious. It's like I've stepped onto the set of *Sex and the City.*

"Everything he makes is pretty good," he says, smiling suggestively, "but you'll have to talk me through the Cosmopolitan."

"I think I can handle that."

Did I just giggle? I'm almost old enough to be his mother, for God's sake. He's probably still living at home. And what could he see in me, a wizened government hack who's almost been fired? Still, I flirt my way through the list of ingredients and when he slides the drink across the bar, he also offers me his hand.

"I'm Danny."

"Libby."

"Where are you from, Libby?" he asks, still holding my hand.

"How do you know I'm not from around here?"

"Your hair isn't big enough."

He's funny and gallant too, because if the ladies in this area have bigger hair than mine, they'd never fit through the door. Ageism is an unacceptable form of discrimination, I decide, and by the time I've talked him through a Mudslide, I'm over the whole May-December issue. The bar is filling up, but Danny keeps coming back to chat to me between filling orders. I continue to flirt outrageously and all my inhibitions vanish by the time I lean across the bar and whisper the secret behind a good Slippery Nipple into his tanned, perfect ear. He returns with my concoction and studies me for a moment.

"How old are you?" he asks (as they must).

"Twenty-eight," I lie (as we must).

The light must be kind in here, because he isn't laughing. He tells me he's twenty-four, which is good, because I draw the line at a decade.

"What's on your mind tonight, Libby? You can tell me. A bartender is the closest thing you'll find to a shrink in this area."

I find myself telling him about my job, about Margo and the Minister, about feeling undervalued.

"They're bullies," he says. "You're a bright, talented woman and you should stand up to them. What have you got to lose?"

Several of the guys from the road crew have joined me at the bar. Danny knows them all by name and introduces me. I'm having a fabulous time and, one Manhattan later, find myself recounting a few stories about the evil duo. I get up and demonstrate the ceremonial passing of the handbag. When I describe the great "penis" moment the guys are howling as if I'm the funniest gal in the room. Actually, I'm the *only* gal in the room (it must be true about the big hair), and I like it. The guys introduce me to the rest of the house as "Purse Carrier to the Stars" and pretty soon, everyone has come over to shake my hand or buy me a drink.

By the time Danny announces last call, there are half a dozen beers lined up in front of me along the bar. I offer them to the guys, because I've switched to water in a belated attempt to sober up. We move to a booth, and Danny, who's sitting beside me, puts his hand on my knee. Oh my. I may be hazy, but *that* I can feel. The minute our chaperones drink up and leave, Danny and I are all over each other.

"I'll drive you home," he says, kissing my neck. He locks up the bar and we climb into his truck. On the grounds of Tranquility Lodge, he cuts the engine. "I could come in, if you like."

"Oh, I'd like," I say, amazed at the way my bra has magically come undone, "but I'm afraid my roommate wouldn't."

"Roommate? On a business trip?" He looks at me doubtfully, wondering if I am trying to get rid of him.

"Hey, I told you this Ministry is cheap. Besides," I add, allowing my hand to slide up his thigh, "my room isn't nearly as spacious or as comfortable as this truck."

The boy knows how to take a hint. In less than a minute, my seat has been adjusted to the fully reclined position. Danny produces a condom from the glove compartment with an ease that would worry me, were I in my right mind. As it is, I can only consider it auspicious.

Later, as Danny wipes the condensation from the windows,

I wonder what has happened to my brain. Taking a youth—however experienced—for a test-drive in a pickup truck just isn't me. And what about getting plastered alone in a bar and spilling company secrets? I've been inappropriate in every possible way. If I get away with this indiscretion, I'm luckier than I've been feeling lately.

"Are you all right?" Danny's voice silences the self-recrimination.

"Yeah, I'm all right."

He massages my shoulders and I can feel myself relaxing again. The seat is surprisingly comfortable for two.

"No regrets, I hope?" His hand is beginning the slide south and I send one of my own on a reconnaissance mission. The appeal of a younger man is immediately obvious.

By the time I climb out of the truck, I'm feeling better about our little fling. Hell, everyone needs to blow off steam once in a while and with Margo and the Minister conspiring against me, I've been ready to explode. This was therapy.

"I'll call you," he says (as they must).

"That would be nice," I say (as we must).

And with one last kiss, he leaves. I realize before I'm in the motel door that I never gave him my phone number. Well, tonight wasn't going to be the start of anything and we both knew it.

Margo is snoring in deep, wheezy gusts as I creep into our room. How nice that worry about my whereabouts didn't keep her awake! I undress quickly in the dark and get into bed. If I had the strength, I'd grab my spare pillow and put an end to that racket. Instead, I lie grinning and thinking about Danny until I drift into a deep, satisfied sleep.

A bright light is piercing my aching eyelids and my head feels heavier than a sack of wet cement. Bang…bang…bang…KA-BOOM!!! For a second the racket seems to be coming from inside my head. Then I feel bits of plaster raining down on my face and remember the road crew blasting in front of the motel. My synapses are beginning to connect. I drank way too much last night. Fancy drinks with funny names—one had a brain-like blob of Baileys in it, dripping with grenadine "blood." My stomach doesn't feel so good. I had a good time, though, that much I remember. There were lots of men around and…a truck. A red pickup truck and— *Oh my God!*

My eyelids snap open and I'm momentarily blinded by the sunlight streaming in the window. More plaster sprinkles from the ceiling and into my eyes and I squint at the shadow above me. As it comes into focus, I realize it isn't plaster hitting my face at all, but bits of scone. Margo is standing over me, chewing.

"What are you doing?" I ask.

She crams the remaining chunk into her mouth and chews. "Iztimtogetuph."

"Excuse me?" I close my eyes briefly while she chews the wad enough to answer.

"I said—*urp!*—it's time to get up."

"Why? This is a down day for us. There's nothing scheduled."

In fact, we were originally scheduled to fly home today but with all the mishaps we've had on this tour, Margo recommended we pick up a couple extra engagements to recoup from the bad press.

"We may not have anything booked, Libby, but there's still plenty of work to be done. We don't pay you to lie around in bed all day."

Sounds as if I'm still on the payroll, although that could change quickly if they find out where else I've been lying around. I must have a death wish. What if another local newspaper editor was at the pub last night? A quick firing would be the best I could hope for if the story gets out that the Minister's Handmaid mocked her in a public setting, then had it off with a boy toy in a pickup truck. Panic is creeping through me, but at least it's overpowering the worst of the hangover. I ease myself out of bed and walk carefully around Margo and into the bathroom. As I close the door, she calls, "You could finish that scrapbook today. The Minister is impatient to see it."

Again with the scrapbook! I sense she knows I'm in considerable pain and wants to turn the knife but I don't have the strength to protest. I'll finish the damn scrapbook but first, I need extra-strength Tylenol.

After a long, healing shower I head to the newspaper rack in the Tranquility Inn's lobby. Finding it empty, I set off across the parking lot to the nearest convenience store. Halfway across the lot, I freeze at the sight of the road crew. They've noticed me too and have stopped working to wave—just as Margo and Mrs. Cleary emerge from the front door. They'll be upon us in moments. Forget about the newspapers: it all ends here, in the parking lot of a tired old roadside lodge.

"Good morning, Minister!" I call out in an overly cheery

voice, hoping I might deter the guys from shouting anything embarrassing.

"Hello, Lily." Her tone is icy, but at least she's speaking to me. "Margo tells me you had a little trouble getting up this morning. Not coming down with something, I hope?"

I've got too much on my mind to worry about Margo. When I look over my shoulder, however, I find that the guys are all hard at work, seemingly oblivious to our presence. Did I imagine that they recognized me? Then one allows himself a wink in my direction and I realize my secrets are safe with them.

Mouthing "thanks" to the guys, I hurry across the street and into Nick's Convenience, where I half expect the kid behind the counter to announce, "So *you're* the older woman who seduced Danny!" I grab a newspaper from the stand and the tension drains from my body when I find no mention of last night's debauchery. So far, the town has been silent on my bad behavior. With the immediate disaster averted, I cruise the aisles to find my hangover cure: Pop-Tarts and chocolate milk.

The room is empty when I return. I jack up the volume on MuchMusic, spread my collectibles on the bed and dive in. The work is surprisingly therapeutic and I'm in no hurry to finish. Soon though, the scrapbook is complete—and it looks damn good, if I do say so myself. I'll never admit it to Margo, but this morning was a nice reprieve. Besides, it's not as if I could risk wandering around town. I have no major regrets about last night's close encounter of the meaningless kind, but if I run into Danny, I'll probably say something stupid and ruin the memory. No, the only discussion I want to have about it is with my friends. And with that in mind, I call my voice mail at home to see if any of them miss me.

BEEP—"Hi, dear, it's Mom. Haven't heard from you in a while. Hope everything went well on your business trip. I have my doubts, since we saw that picture of Mrs. Cleary in the Toronto papers. It was a lovely robe, though. Give us a call when you get a chance. It's your father's birthday next Sunday, and we should take him out for a nice dinner." As she hangs up, I hear my father in the background, "Tell her to bring the priest along—I've got something to confess." He's not the only one!

BEEP—"Hey, government hack, it's Lola! How goes life on the road? You're not missing much here. All's quiet on the social front, although Emma and Bob are hosting a cocktail party Saturday night. You'd better be there. Don't leave me at the mercy of couples comparing mortgage rates. By the way, anything coming through on the guy front? Elliot is convinced you're *getting some*."

BEEP—"Flower Girl, it's me! Something is going on, I can feel it! Last night I had a dream that you were hitchhiking along a dreary little stretch of country road and some guy in a pickup stopped for you. Listen, be careful. I'm not saying don't do him—I certainly would—just take all necessary precautions. But enough about you, it's my quarter. I can't *wait* to tell you about this new guy I met. Zachary is history. He's just too young for me. Well, the new guy is even younger, but you know what I mean, he's more mature. He has that whole Jason Priestley thing going on—but don't get any ideas, because—" BEEP!

BEEP—"Christ, who makes the rules with this technology?! I'd like to meet the gay man who can keep a message to three minutes! Anyway, as I was saying, on my first date, I tried this great new restaurant called Storm. Let's go when you get back so you can tell me how my predictions are panning out. If I'm as right as I sense I am, you're buying! But I'll see you at Emma and Bob's party first. Love ya!"

BEEP—"Hi, Libby, it's Emma. Bob and I are having a cocktail party Saturday night. You have to come because we're showing the wedding video and you, my friend, are a star! Wait till you see it. God, I laughed so hard I need Botox. Mind you, I noticed that Lola was *smoking* and it didn't look like you were trying to stop her. We'll discuss it at the party. Starts at eight. Don't worry about your look, there won't be any single men. Tim can't make it, either. But it will be fun, honestly! See you Saturday."

I hang up and try Lola's work number.

"Lola Romano."

"Hey, it's Lib."

"Hi, there! You home?"

"Nah—Margo's prolonging the agony. We're not home until Saturday morning."

"You're coming to Emma's party, right?"

"Are you kidding? Wouldn't miss the wedding video! Fair warning, though, she's on to you about the smokes."

"Shit! I'm in for it. But can I help it if I'm a pathetic addict? So, how about Elliot's prediction?"

"Actually, last night I had a fight with Margo and went to this pub down the highway, where I got pretty wasted and seduced the 24-year-old bartender."

"Congratulations, you're officially a cougar!"

"Great."

"Nothing to be ashamed of—it just means you're mature enough to be able to enjoy sex for sex's sake without getting all caught up in the relationship bullshit."

"Really? So why don't I feel mature? I kinda used the guy. I've been so down lately, Lola. It's not working out with this job. Margo bullies me and now the Minister thinks I'm totally incompetent."

"You're way too hard on yourself, Lib. From what you've told me about Margo, she isn't very bright, and she's obviously threatened. You know you can outsmart her."

Occasionally Lola surprises me. "Do you think I can take her?"

"We couldn't be friends if you weren't a fighter. You're *sneaky,* too—and I mean that in a good way!"

"I'll take it as a compliment. And I shouldn't feel guilty about jumping a guy in his pickup?" Oops.

"A *pickup truck?* You slag!" Lola squeals.

But her laughter is infectious and I find myself giggling too. By the time I hang up, I'm feeling much better. I have family and friends who care about me and even think I'm an intelligent, competent (if sneaky) woman. What's more, I can still attract young bootie. Well, fuck it, if I'm a cougar, I might as well show some teeth. I'll deliver this scrapbook to the Minister's room and throw in a piece of my mind as a bonus. Time to show the hags that Libby McIssac has a spine.

Quietly chanting affirmations, I march toward the Minister's room: "I am a cougar. It is a good thing to be a cougar. Cougars are strong and invincible. Cougars leap upon bullies and savage them...."

Margo is chattering away inside the room when I reach the door and I'm conscious of uncougarlike terror. When no one answers my knock, I call and the chattering finally stops.

"It's Libby, Margo. I'm delivering the scrapbook."

I hear the Minister say, "What scrapbook?" and Margo replies in so low a tone that I can't make it out. Finally the door swings open. I look over Margo's head to see the Minister, hair in Velcro rollers, lounging on the bed. She's flipping through a glossy brochure and sipping a glass of wine. There's a tug on my hand as Margo pulls the scrapbook from me. She tosses it casually on the coffee table.

"Well, thanks, Libby. You can go, we're in the middle of something right now."

Yeah, an expensive bottle of Chardonnay. I'm about to launch into my *Give Libby a Chance* speech when a wistful sigh escapes the Minister's collagen-plumped lips and she tosses the brochure on top of my scrapbook. It's promotional material for the Ottawa School for the Arts. We're flying back there tomorrow for one of Margo's bonus engagements.

"Kids today have so many advantages," the Minister says. "Look at what this school offers!"

Given what I know of Mrs. Cleary's privileged background, I'm puzzled. "Didn't you go to a private school, Minister?"

"Well, yes, Lily, I did. But it wasn't like *this* school. They offer harp lessons. I always wanted to play the harp, but my school couldn't afford one so I had to learn the bassoon instead. Playing the harp would give me such comfort now. The bassoon is not a soothing instrument." Another heavy sigh as she recalls her deprived childhood.

Margo is quick to sympathize (read: kiss some ass): "The problem with kids today, Minister, is that they don't know how lucky they are. They have it too easy. And worse, they have *no respect* for their elders."

"I have to agree with you. In my day, students would never display the boorish behavior we have witnessed on this trip. I can't say I've ever regretted pressuring Julian to get a vasectomy."

A voice surprisingly like mine says, "The problem isn't the kids, Minister—it's your approach." And it must be mine, because they're both staring at me. The voice speaks again. "You take these things too seriously. Far better to laugh it off."

Margo recovers enough to say, "You are in no position to tell the Minister what she needs to do. I said I'd let you know when you're ready to think for yourself."

But I'm in no mood to be squelched: "You've been coming across as *humorless,* Minister. Look what happened when you joked about the bathrobe photo. People loved it. Why don't you set up a couple of visits to women's groups the Ministry funds and talk about being a woman in politics? You can describe how it feels to have people focus on your appearance instead of on the real issues. We might get a couple of great stories to finish up our road show."

The Minister is staring into her Chardonnay and Margo's face has taken on the hue of her freshly hennaed hair. I decide to flee before she finds her tongue.

Bill is having a late lunch when I enter the motel restaurant.

"Well, Bill, it's been nice knowing you."

"What's Margo done now?"

"Actually, this time it was me and my big fat gob. I practically gave the Minister a lecture."

"They can't fire you for sharing your ideas, Libby. Remember, you're a government employee. Relax…and try the tuna melt."

Bill's cell phone rings as my sandwich arrives. After a short, agitated discussion, he hangs up, saying, "Sorry, I've got to go."

"What's up?"

"Margo wants me to set up a meet-and-greet for tomorrow at the Ottawa YWCA and something similar for Friday. I'll be on the phone for the rest of the bloody day."

I manage to be sympathetic but grin to myself when he leaves. I got through to the Minister! She's actually taking Lily's advice. There's further evidence of my success when I return to our room to find Margo on the phone with Wiggy, asking her to draft remarks for the next two events.

"Tell her they have to be casual," I say.

"Quiet," Margo snaps.

"It should sound off-the-cuff," I continue. "And they have to be *funny!*"

These should be mine to write, but one must not ask for too much at once. I just hope the event goes well. My future may depend on it.

I know I'm stressed when a passing plate of homemade brownies piled high with icing has no effect on me. It's 3:00 p.m. and I've been a nervous wreck since Wiggy's remarks arrived on the motel fax machine this morning. They were serviceable, but by no means sparkling, and I need this event to sparkle. I took the liberty of writing my own ideas and comments in the margins before giving copies to the Minister and Margo. And a minute ago, as she made her way to the front of the room, I slipped the photo taken during our hasty departure from the Have-a-Nap into the Minister's hand.

"Use it!" I said. "They'll love it." (I hope.)

Now the Minister is at the mike and I'm so nervous my palms

are sweating. The Minister's bag slips from my grasp and I bend down to pick it up.

"This is your great idea," Margo hisses at me. "You could have the decency to pretend you're interested."

If only she knew. Never in my short time at the Ministry have I been so interested in what the Minister has to say. I take a moment to scan the room and see there are only about thirty women in attendance, but I suppose that isn't so bad considering it's short notice. And thankfully, a couple of reporters came out. From the stage, I hear:

"I have moments in this business, ladies, when I wonder why I bother."

The Minister is holding up the photograph and smiling ruefully at the audience. Everyone laughs and the Minister, encouraged, launches into her speech. She delivers it beautifully and I experience a small thrill every time she uses one of my suggestions. When the speech is over now, everyone applauds enthusiastically. The reporters fire insightful questions at the Minister and she fires back some terrific responses.

All in all, the event is a roaring success, and now that I can relax, I make a beeline for the brownies. I'm polishing off my third when Laurie approaches. "It's a hit, Libby. Congratulations."

I thank her and smile proudly. All I need is a little acknowledgment from my leaders and here they come now. They can't possibly ignore the fact that this, the best event of our whole trip, was *my* great idea. I prepare to accept their praise graciously. The Minister reaches me first.

"Get the door, Lily."

Margo "accidentally" shoves me as she sweeps past.

They love me.


At the motel, I hurry to our room and test out both beds before flinging my bags onto the more desirable one. Then, without bothering to change or unpack, I head for the door. Laurie and Bill are taking me out for a celebratory dinner tonight; I need to escape before Margo arrives. As I reach for the knob, it jiggles and there's a yelp from the other side. Then the door swings open and Margo steps into the room, struggling more than usual under the weight of the beauty supply suitcase. Her hair stands on end with static electricity and she yelps again as she receives a shock from the metal doorknob. I watch in silence, sensing my dinner plans are going up in smoke. The only sound is the scrape of her cases as she drags them along the shabby carpet toward the empty bed, too tired to care if it's the better one. With an air of defeat, she leans back against the metal desk then jumps away again when she gets another shock—this time in the backside.

Poor Margo has had a tough day. Libby's ratings have climbed a notch or two out of the muck and that makes Margo miserable. I accept that I'll be paying for this, but I don't want her to collect tonight, so I ease toward the door. I almost have it closed behind me when she speaks.

"I hope you're not going anywhere, Libby." She's struggling to free her skirt, which is clinging to her panty hose.

"Just getting a breath of fresh air," I say. Then I remember my recent spine transplant: I'm supposed to be standing up for myself. "Actually, I'm having dinner with Bill and Laurie."

"Cancel. The Minister's speech at the National Gallery tomorrow is very important—not like one of those YWCA toss-offs. I need you to go over it with a fine-tooth comb and check all the facts." She's already digging the papers out of her briefcase.

"Christine wrote the speech and she's a stickler for detail," I protest. This isn't a lie: Wiggy's a regular Dick Tracy when it comes to accuracy and Margo knows it. "Anyway, I've worked almost every night of the trip and tonight I need a break."

"Look, if you want to be a member of this team—and it seems that you do—you'll have to accept that the job comes first. When do you ever see the Minister and me relaxing?"

She's plucking a bottle of wine and a video out of her bag

while she speaks, and as she walks out the door she hands me the speech file. At least I have the comfort of seeing her get zapped one last time by the door handle. I flop down on the bed and consider my options: I could dig out the laptop and do as Margo asks, or I could just blow it off and go out for dinner. Wiggy isn't careless and damn it, I deserve a nice dinner. Why should I be their slave? Enough already, I am going out.

I call Laurie and cancel. Old habits die hard. I hit a home run at the Y today, but you're only as good as your last success. So, I collect quarters from my purse and hit the junk food machine down the hall. Then I call Wiggy to request a list of her sources. She's insulted, but she gives it to me, and I start going over every word of the speech, checking and rechecking the facts. By the time I crawl into bed at midnight, I'm practically an expert on the acquisition and funding of modern Canadian art.

During the night, my sleep is disrupted by the weird dreams one might expect after a dinner of potato chips alone. In one, I'm locked in a gallery of modern sculptures, each a rendering of a small woman with scarlet hair. A huge rat crawls out of the mouth of one statue and scurries toward me. I almost surface to consciousness at this point, and am dimly aware that the noise is actually coming from inside the motel room. Margo must be back. There's rustling, then a beep, but I'm too tired to open my eyes and find out what she's doing. Next thing I know, it's 6:00 a.m. and Margo is snoring so loudly, I decide to get up and take advantage of the extended shower time.

Collecting the speech file, I head over to the motel restaurant to review it over a nice long breakfast. Before my coffee arrives, however, I discover the folder is empty. The speech must have slipped out when I picked it up. I'm not overly worried until I creep back into our room and start looking around to no avail. Finally, I flick on the light, thereby waking the slumbering dwarf.

"What's going on?" asks Dopey.

"The speech for the National Gallery. I can't find it." I'm trying to keep the panic out of my voice as I get down on all fours and check under the desk and then under the bed.

"What do you mean, you can't find it?"

"I mean, it's not here—it's missing!" That definitely came out an octave higher than I wanted it to.

"You lost the Minister's speech? How could you be so careless?"

"I didn't *lose* it, Margo. I couldn't have. I worked on it all night and I put it back in the file before I went to bed. Are you sure you didn't take it when you came in?"

"Quite sure." With a dramatic sigh, she slips out of bed and begins to dress. "Well, I suppose we'd better find the Minister and tell her what you've done."

"Not just yet. I have it on disk and can track down a print shop while you're at breakfast."

She dashes out of the room, eager to deliver the news—although I suspect she'll hold off till I'm present, so as to enjoy the show.

My suspicion that she's behind the speech's disappearance intensifies when I scan my disks and discover the electronic version of the speech has also disappeared. Which explains the mysterious "beep" in the night. She must have deleted the speech and flushed the hard copy down the toilet. Even my call to Christine is futile, as no one answers.

Out of options, I head over to the restaurant, where the Minister is enjoying a cup of tea and picking at a slice of dry toast. Margo is already feasting on a fry-up. I explain that the speech has disappeared.

"Well, what's your solution?" the Minister asks irritably. She won't be improvising.

"We still have over an hour before the event. I can draft something for you," I say. "I reviewed that speech for hours and am familiar with the content."

"No!" protests Margo. "I'll call Christine and get her to fax it."

"Tried that," I said. "No answer."

"Margo, what on earth did we hire Lily for, if not to write speeches? If she can't do it, we may as well discover it now."

If Margo did steal the speech to sabotage me, this was obviously not the outcome she had in mind. I sit down at another table and write the speech by hand, in huge block letters on legal paper. An hour later, I hand it to the Minister, who's still picking at the same piece of toast. Then I go out to wait in the car.

"Fix this up, Lily," the Minister says thrusting the pages of the speech over the seat as she climbs in.

She has reversed two lines, which means I have to rewrite a whole page during the bumpy drive to the Gallery. Otherwise, she has not changed a single word. I can feel Margo's glare boring through the back of my skull, suggesting that the Minister ignored her feedback on my first speech. Or maybe she's just pissed about the two excellent reviews of yesterday's YWCA event.

The Minister delivers the speech with ease and the response is positive. And as we drive to the final event of the trip, Mrs. Cleary again overwhelms me with praise: "You can see how reordering that passage made it much stronger, Lily. But you will learn as you go and I will do my best to advise you."

Yes, I have much to learn from her.

Bill, Laurie and I have escaped to one of Ottawa's finer restaurants and I feel pretty good as I tuck into my shrimp linguine. Despite many hellish hours over the past ten days, the trip is ending on a positive note. The Minister's final speaking engagement was another success, with almost eighty women in the audience. Then, I slipped out of the motel before Margo could conjure something up to occupy my evening. She herself was called upon for beauty duty.

"Okay, so tell me," I say as Bill tops up my wineglass, "why doesn't Margo find it demeaning to act like the Minister's personal hair and makeup artist?"

Bill and Laurie exchange quick glances. "Because she *is* her personal hair and make-up artist," Bill says. "Always has been."

"Margo used to own Beauty 911, which offered the full range of beauty treatments to people in their homes and offices," Laurie explains. "Mrs. Cleary has been a client for years and she was so impressed with Margo's business acumen that she convinced her to come on board as her executive assistant just before you arrived. I doubt Margo realized she'd be doing double duty as lady's maid."

"So few consider combining those important roles," I say, shaking my head.

"The lines are always blurred around here, as you've learned. You're her first staff speechwriter though, so she's still figuring out how to use you."

"Her *first* staff speechwriter?" Something else I didn't know.

"We've only used freelancers so far. The Minister didn't see the need, fancying herself quite the wordsmith and all."

"I've noticed that," I say, "and it's obvious that Margo doesn't want me around. So why was I hired?"

"The Premier insisted on it after Mrs. Cleary made too many changes to an important speech and ended up insulting the Minister of Education."

"Why didn't she just compliment his *spectacular penis?* I plan to make it my standard approach."

"Works for me!" Bill says, raising his glass. "Here's to Libby!"

I smile and touch my glass to his. "And here's to going home!"

## 12

The sun is already slipping below the Toronto skyline when the cab pulls up in front of my apartment. Our flight was delayed six hours; I have a scant hour to beautify myself for Emma and Bob's cocktail party—nowhere near enough, given the wear and tear of this trip. But first things first: I must collect my angel from Mrs. Murdock upstairs. She always minds Cornelius when I'm away and each time he comes back fatter and meaner. No matter how much I plead, she slips him extra treats and as a result, he adores her. Tonight he wails and hisses all the way down to my apartment. It warms my heart to see how he's missed me. Still, as roommates go, Corny on his worst day is a vast improvement over Margo.

My little hovel has never looked so good as it does to my travel-weary eyes tonight. Some might call it run-down, cramped and poorly decorated, but I see a cozy haven. I hope the same rose-colored glasses will transform my wardrobe, because last time I looked it consisted mainly of rags—certainly nothing *In Style* magazine would sanction as appropriate cocktail attire. I don't own dressy suits or shapely little frocks.

After a quick shower, I start pulling things out and trying them on, but the spirit of Goldilocks has possessed me: this outfit's too hot, this one's too cold, nothing is just right for cocktails at a suburban bungalow. I'm about to give up in despair when I recall Emma's voice mail advising me not to worry about my appearance—that no single men would be there to notice. She's given me permission to choose comfort over style: I slip on a favorite pair of flowing silk pants and a tank top, both black.

By this time, my hair is well on the way to becoming an afro of Mod Squad proportions and wrestling it into a "come-hither" tousle exhausts me to the point where I can only try three different jewelry combinations. Time to stop fussing, or I'll be late.

Cornelius has been watching the fashion show impassively from his perch by the door. He's planning to make a break for Mrs. Murdock's as I leave. Just to offend him, I give him a big hug—and I take another five minutes to scrape the cat fur off my suburban cocktail attire. Finally, unavoidably, I am on the road.

I've offered to pick Lola up en route to Emma's because I hate walking into parties alone. Actually, I hate walking into parties period, unless I've had a couple of shooters beforehand. Either way, I tend to make a poor first impression. Lola, on the other hand enjoys parties and is waiting on the porch for me. The minute I see her red sheath I understand what proper cocktail party attire is, and how far short of the mark I've fallen. The dress complements her generous curves as well as her ebony eyes and hair. No one will give me a second glance.

"Do you mind if I lie down in the back seat so that I don't wrinkle my dress?" Lola asks.

"I'm a lousy chauffeur, so get in the front and buckle up, glamour-puss."

"You were never harsh before you started this job."

"Oh, I was, but I internalized it. I'm finally learning to share."

"In that case, I won't ask how you like the bouquet I bought for Emma. I'm hoping she'll be so besotted with it that she'll forgive me for the cigarettes. I could get two cartons for what I paid the florist."

Lola is in nicotine withdrawal by the time we reach Emma's new house, which isn't far from my parents'.

"I've gotta have a quick one before we go in," Lola says as we're walking up the front stairs. "Emma won't let me smoke inside."

She hands me the huge bouquet so that she can light up. Suddenly, an automatic sensor light flashes on, freezing us in its beam like raccoons caught rifling a garbage can. The door opens, framing not Emma, but Tim Kennedy, and he's wearing a tuxedo. Clearly, someone is even more confused about cocktail party attire than I am.

"Libby! Is the bouquet becoming your signature style?"

"Tim, what a pleasure to see you. Where's the rest of your wedding party?"

"Battle positions, everyone," Lola says, smoke streaming from her scarlet lips. Why can't I be that cool? And why do I have to get shrill and defensive every time that man shows up? He's obviously just teasing me.

"Come in and play nice," he says.

I hand him the flowers as I pass: "Take a walk in my shoes, pal. If you're any good, you can give me a hand at the next Ministry event."

"Is it a peace offering?"

"It's flowers, already, you can't get nicer than that."

Emma takes my coat and I follow her into the bedroom, glaring at her.

"Look, he told me he wasn't coming," she explains, shrugging. "He's got a fund-raiser downtown in an hour—hence the tux. It was awfully sweet of him to drive all the way out here. He even brought us a bottle of champagne."

"I wouldn't have worn *pajamas* if I'd known he'd be here, Emma. I'm at a psychological disadvantage with this drawstring waistband."

"It sounded like you were holding your own," Emma says, patting my back reassuringly.

She leads me to the kitchen, where Bob pours me a bourbon. I barely have time to taste it, however, before he's cueing up the wedding video and herding us to the couch. Tim suggests he and I sit on the floor so that we won't block anyone's view.

"Okay, but I don't think the etiquette books would approve of your sitting on the floor in a tux," I say. The moment we sit down, Bob's beagle, Barney, gambols over and covers both of us with slobber and dog hair. "For God's sake, Tim, show him your Alpha Dog moves."

"They only work on Jack Russells," he says, unsuccessfully fending Barney off.

We sit waiting for the show to start while Bob shuts the dog away. I smile at Tim in what I intend to be a warm, friendly way, but he sees through it.

"You'd rather get down on your knees and kiss Clarice's pricey pumps than sit through this video, wouldn't you?" he asks.

"You already know me so well," I reply.

The video is painfully long, a fact to which Emma and Bob seem happily oblivious. Everyone laughs heartily at the bouquet toss and even I have to concede it's the video highlight. Bob replays the scene twice and is about to hit Rewind again, when Tim speaks up: "Let's keep going, Bob, I want to see the whole thing before I go."

"Thanks," I whisper to Tim. "I owe you."

"Then let up about the tux," he replies.

"Fair enough," I say, laughing.

The laughter sticks in my throat during the garter scene, however. To my mind, there's an expression of pathetic longing on my face during my dance with Tim. Fortunately, Lola is not sufficiently drunk to point it out. When I look over my shoulder at her, she simply pretends to get pinged in the forehead with a garter.

The torment over at last, I clamber to my feet and hasten to the kitchen for another drink. Why did I offer to drive? Now I'll have to eat a huge amount and stay till the wee hours to burn off the booze. Tim reaches the counter at the same time as I do, and pours me a couple of fingers of Maker's Mark. With anyone else, I'd consider remembering my favorite drink as a sign of interest. As it is, I can only assume he's socially gifted. No wonder the Minister loves him.

"Are you ready to go back out there?" he asks.

"In a minute. I need to gather my strength. You know what they're talking about, don't you?"

"The wedding?"

"No, fool, flooring."

*"Flooring?"*

"That's right. And tiles. Grout, contractors, housekeepers, strollers, nannies and preschool."

"How about life insurance?"

"That comes later in the evening, along with retirement savings plans and wills."

"I think you're wrong, as least as far as the guys are concerned." We peer out into the living room via the pass-through. The women and men have already divided into different sections of the room, with the common ground being the dining table, where Emma has arranged canapés. "They're talking about sports, cars, sports again—and maybe stock portfolios. At least, those are *my* topics of choice at parties."

"And you're in here with me, where your knowledge is totally wasted."

"No, if I met *you* at the canapé table, I'd immediately refer to 'conversation starters for girls,' which includes books, pets, tulips and, my personal favorite, bad bosses."

"Don't get me started."

He seems to be releasing the very same pheromones I fell prey to at the wedding. I get this light-headed feeling when he's around that I certainly never noticed earlier this week with Danny. Mind you, I was too drunk for such subtleties. Now, with only the slightest buzz clouding my judgment, I could swear the man is flirting with me. And he's off-limits.

"Shall we?" I ask, gesturing toward the living room.

"Do we have to?"

I sense that he'd like to linger and chat, but it's a little dangerous for my tastes. I've done the "other woman" thing and it's not a role I enjoy. No, we'd be far better off sparring with a table of hors d'oeuvres between us.

Before I have a chance to take the moral high road, Lola and Elliot burst into the kitchen.

"Libby, Elliot is *dying* to hear all about Danny and the pickup truck," Lola says. The evil glint in her eye tells me she's deliberately interrupting.

"Yes, tell Elliot all about it, Flower Girl," he says.

Tim looks curiously from Elliot to me and, panicking, I do the only thing that occurs to me: walk away with a brusque "Excuse me." Elliot grabs at my arm as I stalk by. "Later, Elliot."

Well, that was certainly cool. No danger of my making Tim's "other woman" list after all. I search out Emma and find her in the middle of a discussion on backyard water features. She hurries toward me when she sees my woeful expression.

"What's wrong?"

"Oh, it's just the Tim thing."

"What, was he mean to you?"

"No, he was nice—too nice."

"Maybe not," she says, smiling coyly. "Tim told Bob earlier that the girlfriend is history."

"Really?" My heart picks up the pace. "Then it's a shame I was just rude to him. Well, I guess I don't want to be his transitional girl anyway. That never lasts."

"Oh yeah? I'm a transitional girl and look how that turned out."

"That's right! Everything but the white picket fence."

"It's coming," she says. "Listen, Tim would be lucky to get you, Libby, but try to be nice, okay?"

Before I can thank her, Lola and Elliot swoop down on us.

"I'm *so* sorry, doll. Obviously my radar is impeded by this," Elliot says, waving a rather large martini.

"I expect better from a psychic—especially one who's predicted romance."

"I predicted *sex*. And I believe I also mentioned conflict."

"Look, the guy is taken anyway," Lola interrupts.

"Apparently not," I reply, Emma having left to welcome another guest.

"Then your rude exit probably didn't help your cause," Lola says, brightening. She now considers Tim fair game.

Given the power of a red dress, I realize I'd better initiate damage control measures immediately. I excuse myself and head into the kitchen again, where I find Bob alone, filling a cooler with ice.

"He's gone, Flower Girl."

"Who's gone? And don't call me that!"

"Why not? Elliot always does."

"Elliot is gay, so he gets away with murder. When you start waxing your chest like he does, you can use his nicknames."

"Snap at me if you like, but Tim's still gone," Bob says. He's blushing at the very thought of waxing, though, which gives me some satisfaction.

"I am not looking for Tim, I am simply getting a refill. Anyway," I say, contrite, "thanks for stocking my favorite drink. I know that was your doing."

"You're welcome," he says, hugging me. "Look, Tim's a good guy—and he asked about you tonight. That's all I'm saying. Like a wise straight man, I'm staying out of it."

He pours just a touch of Maker's into my glass and reminds me that I'm driving. Emma found herself a good one.

By the time I leave the kitchen, Elliot is nowhere to be seen and Lola is now deep in conversation with Michael, Bob's buddy from the squash club. She looks enthralled by his conversation and keeps fluffing her hair. Now she's touching his arm. What's the deal? She's met this guy a half a dozen times and has never shown the slightest interest in him. In fact, I'm sure he's the one she dismissed as a techie nerd. Emma's sister catches me staring at them and says, "Could she be any more obvious?"

"What do you mean?"

"Lola is way out of Michael's league and she knows it, but I just mentioned the runaway success of his dot.com company, and suddenly she's all over him."

I end up trapped on the couch between Emma's sister and another woman, and look up to see Lola sneaking out the back door with Michael. Gee, thanks, pal. Here I am, caught in the conversational cross fire.

"With interest rates declining, Stephen and I have decided to refinance and invest in a minivan."

"Yeah, Dylan and I did that when we were expecting our first, too. Have you chosen a car seat for your precious cargo?"

My eyes are glazing over but I can still focus enough to see Elliot ushering Emma back into the room. They've been on the grand tour.

"Emma, you must tear down this ghastly wallpaper. It's so 1999." Then he spots me and senses a rescue is in order. "Libby darling! Get your sweet ass off that sofa and tell me all about the road trip."

Saved! And not a moment too soon—my glass is empty and I'm sucking on the ice cubes for residual bourbon. I excuse myself and join him at the table. He's examining one of the dips suspiciously.

"What's that in the salsa?" Elliot lives in fear of "double dippers."

"It's a speck of hummus. I'm sure it's fine." He backs away from the table. "Safer to stick to the veggies, Elliot."

"I don't know… Bob might have cut them up. I doubt he washes his hands properly. Did you see antibacterial soap by the sink?"

I make a show of stirring the salsa with a carrot stick before popping it into my mouth. "Mmmm, germs!"

Disgusted, he tries to divert me by asking about Danny. "Was he hot?"

"He certainly was."

"Nice ass?"

"Very. But enough about *my* sex life. Tell me all about your new victim."

"Ah, Günter…the most beautiful man I've ever seen." Elliot's usually sharp voice softens noticeably.

"Where did you meet him?"

"At a benefit concert. He's the lead singer in a glam revival band." Elliot gets a dreamy look and absentmindedly dunks a bagel chip into the "contaminated" salsa. Wow, this is serious. "You have to come see him perform. You're going to love him."

At the end of the evening, I head outside to retrieve Lola from the porch. She's still with Michael and if they're discussing the vagaries of the high-tech world, it clearly has them spellbound. But even Lola's interest in Michael hasn't prevented her from lighting up; she's holding the cigarette at her side and the smoke is curling up around them. Although I know I shouldn't sink to her level, I can't resist: "So… Are you two discussing the perils of secondhand smoke inhalation?"

"Libby," Lola says in a pleasantly cold voice, "have you met Michael?"

"Many times! You seem like a nice man, Michael, don't you care about your lungs?"

"No comment," he says.

"Lola, I need to get going."

"Already? Michael and I are just getting to know each other."

"It's after midnight and I've had a long week. But if you'd rather make your own way…"

"No, no, I'm coming." The prospect of being stranded in

suburbia obviously isn't appealing; she's not *that* fond of Mr. Dot.com. "Why don't you go warm up the pickup—er, the car? I'll join you in a minute."

Lola's smile verges on a snarl, but I am unafraid. She has no idea how the Minister and Margo are toughening me up.

## 13

There's nothing in the world I enjoy more than an early-morning run. Actually, that's a lie; what I enjoy is *claiming* I enjoy it. If I liked running that much, it wouldn't take three coffees and half a row of Oreos to get me on the road. The fact that I'm setting out this morning despite my post–road-trip fatigue is a statement less about my desire for fitness, than about my desire for Tim Kennedy. I'm launching the McIssac Renovation Project.

Twenty minutes into a plod around my neighborhood, I see someone resembling Tim cross to my side of the street half a block ahead. I'm gaining on him when an old lady with a cane hobbles into my path. I dodge around her, sidestep her poodle and run full tilt into a parking meter. Hearing my squawk as I collapse to one knee, the guy turns: it's not Tim. Complaining that I scared her half to death, the old lady helps me up. I've bruised my pride and God knows what else, and for what? I promptly lean against a storefront and remove my shoe to retrieve the five-dollar bill I keep under my insole for emergencies. Then I limp into Dooney's and order a mochaccino— skipping the whipped cream since I'm officially on a run.

Later, after laundry duty, I call my folks to invite them out for a fancy dinner at Storm, the hot new restaurant Elliot recommended.

"Hi, Dad, I'm home."

"Nice to hear from you, dear, I'll get your mother." Never one for long-winded telephone conversations, my dad.

"Libby! How are you, honey? How did the trip go?"

"It ended up all right, but I hate this job, Mom."

"Well, it's still early days, dear," she says, and there's trepidation in her voice. Once, when I was fifteen, I quit a part-time job after two horrible weeks and ever since, she worries that when the going gets tough, Libby gets going.

"Oh, don't worry, I'm not going to quit—yet—but I don't think I'm going to get enough out of this job to make putting up with Margo and Mrs. Cleary worthwhile. They really are bitches." I don't like to swear in front of the nicest woman in the world, but sometimes it's necessary to go to extremes to make an impression.

"Now, Elizabeth, it's not right to speak of our Minister of Culture that way."

"Mother, I say it with all due respect. And Margo is even worse." The whining has officially started.

"Margo must be a very unhappy woman. Keep in mind that one can never fully comprehend what may be happening in someone else's life, dear." This is going nowhere. Mom is pretty stubborn about seeing the bright side.

"So," I say, switching tactics, "I went to Bob and Emma's last night."

"That's nice. How are they?"

"They made us sit through an hour-long wedding video, that's how they are."

"Well, isn't it wonderful that they're so happy together?"

"Would *you* want to sit through their wedding video?"

"I'm sure Emma looked lovely. She's a beautiful girl."

"Arg!"

"Don't worry, dear, your turn will come."

Cutting my losses, I extend the invitation for next weekend's dinner. Then I turn to the cold comfort of e-mail, listing my complaints in a very therapeutic note to Roxanne, who is apparently enjoying the Isle of Man about as much as I enjoy life in the Minister's office.

Mrs. Cleary is still steaming over the mishaps of the road trip despite a positive finish and amazingly, she is blaming Margo for them. She's even addressing Margo in the dismissive tone of voice usually reserved for lesser beings like me. Mind you, I think Margo's relegation to the doghouse is really due to the Minister's breakout. Laurie heard that Margo introduced a new exfoliater late in the trip. Whatever the cause, the Minister's alabaster skin is a mess.

Perhaps by way of punishing Margo, the Minister summons me to her office alone to discuss upcoming speeches. Laurie is standing beside the Minister's desk, speaking on the phone when I arrive. The Minister, meanwhile, is leaning into her magnified makeup mirror, carefully concealing blemishes. Neither one of them notices my arrival.

"You wanted to see me, Minister?"

Laurie turns and shoots me a smile but the Minister doesn't raise her eyes from the mirror.

"Yes, Lily. My schedule is very tight right now and I don't think I'll have time to write my own speeches for the junior school talks next week." Since I've never known the Minister to attempt her own speeches, this is no surprise.

"Good news, Minister," Laurie interjects as she hangs up the phone. "I was able to book you for facials every morning except Friday, when you're already scheduled for a trim."

The Minister shoots Laurie the evil eye and, given the mirror's magnification factor, the view from where I'm standing is quite threatening. "You can go now," she advises Laurie coldly.

"Anyway, Lily, I think you can handle drafting these three speeches and I'll use your material as a jumping-off point."

"You want me to write *three* speeches?"

"You are the speechwriter, aren't you?"

"Yes, but…"

"You can't hide under Margo's coattails forever." She turns her attention back to her concealer and thus dismissed, I back out of her office.

Laurie is lurking in the hall and walks me to my cubbyhole.

"What just happened?" I ask, stunned.

"You just got a break."

"But why now?"

"Well, you got her some good press on the last two days of our tour, which puts you on the radar. But she's also pissed at Margo and knows this will annoy her."

Whatever her reasons, I'm thrilled and I waste no time starting the research.

Next morning, I'm again called to the Minister's office. This time, Margo is there as well. She's been keeping a low profile since her slide from grace began, whereas I'm already feeling pretty cocky about my new relationship with the boss. Now that the Minister has acknowledged me as her speechwriter, I expect it won't be long before she invites me to lunch at her club.

The Minister is in midrant when I walk in, rehashing the events of the trip.

"My favorite suit was absolutely ruined, Margo. This *cannot* happen again."

"It was a beautiful suit," I offer, causing Margo to frown at me. She is probably sensing I'm the Minister's new favorite.

"Ruined," she repeats, shaking her head. Then, still looking at Margo, she adds, "And my handbag was *never* available when I needed it."

What can I say? It's hard to get good help these days. By the time the meeting is over, my dreams of quiche at the club have fizzled, but it's obvious Margo won't be dining there anytime soon either.

"Just a minute, Libby," Margo's voice is so close behind me I jump. How does she move so fast with those scrawny little legs? "We need to talk about what's on your plate right now."

I list off my many tasks, citing each and every minor make-work item she's assigned me, then finally, when I can avoid it no longer, I mutter that the Minister has given me three speeches to write.

"*Three!* With all the other work you have to do, you won't be able to write three. You'll have to reassign two of them to the freelancers."

"I can manage three."

"Libby, let me make myself clear: you are to write speeches only when all your other duties are under control. Judging by the condition of our reference shelf, that doesn't seem to be the case. I want that shelf reorganized this week."

I retreat to my cubicle to assign two speeches to Wiggy, but I vow to boycott all of the useless tasks Margo has in store for me. Instead, I spend the day working on the one school speech I've retained and by late afternoon, it's finished. I think it's pretty good—and kid-proof, too. The only problem is that I'm now left with nothing of value to do and it's too early to leave. Leaning out from my desk, I peer around the partition and down the hall at the reference shelf. It would only take half an hour to clean it up, but I'm a speechwriter, damn it—the Minister said so. I can find something more important to occupy my time.

I'm rooting around in my snack drawer when the phone rings: it's the Minister calling from her office again. Heaven forbid she take the trouble of walking down the hall to see me in person. Just as well, because Margo took away my "guest chair" recently when she discovered Laurie sitting in it.

"Lily, it's Minister Cleary. How much progress have you made with the speeches I assigned you?"

"I've finished one, but Margo directed me to reassign the other two to Christine."

"Why, may I ask?"

"She'd like me to focus on my other priorities."

"And what might those be?" There's a little menace to her tone, but it's less intimidating over the phone.

I rhyme off a dozen useless tasks, finishing with tidying up the reference shelf.

"The reference shelf?"

"Yes. It's in disarray. Margo says it's my number one priority for the week."

"Really? Well, I expect to see drafts of all three speeches on my desk by noon on Friday, and I expect *you* to write them. Consider *that* your priority."

"But I've already called Christine."

"Call her back," she says and hangs up.

I assure the dial tone that I'll get right on it.

I'm sipping my morning mochaccino—extra foam, no whip, out of respect for the Libby Reno project—when it occurs to me that I'm actually enjoying myself. My cubicle is cluttered with piles of paper and books from the Legislative Library and I'm well into the research for the speeches I reclaimed from Wiggy.

"What are you working on?"

Startled, I dunk my nose in mocha foam. How does she materialize out of nowhere like that? I wonder if she casts a reflection?

Wiping milk and chocolate shavings off my nose, I offer a smile. "Good morning, Margo. I'm working on the speeches for the junior school talks."

"Speeches? As in *plural?* I told you to reassign two of them."

"You did, and I did. But then the Minister called to find out how I was progressing. When I told her that I'd reassigned them, she told me to take them back."

"I see. Well, then, while you're at it, you can write a fourth. I just accepted a last-minute invitation for the Minister to speak at the Spirit of Youth Awards on Friday. In fact, the organizers have lost their venue and asked that we hold it here."

"But it's already Wednesday and the Minister wants the three I have by Friday! Besides, don't you think the Youth Awards is too major an event for me to tackle so soon?"

"Not at all, Libby. I have full confidence in you. In fact, it's the perfect opportunity for you to show your skills—there will be several dignitaries in attendance. I look forward to seeing your draft tomorrow."

And with that, she disappears. Vindictive cow. I'm just about to stick my tongue out after her when her head reappears around the side of my partition.

"By the way, I just checked the reference shelf and it's still a mess. You will take care of it, won't you?"

Half an hour later, I pass her office at the right moment to hear her saying, "The Minister would be *delighted* to present your awards next week, and what's more, we'd like to invite you to hold the ceremony here at our offices."

She accepted a last-minute invitation on the Minister's behalf simply to torment me. And the woman doesn't miss a detail: since we're holding the event here, there will be constant commotion around my cubicle while I'm courting the muse.

It's 10:00 p.m. and I'm still slaving over my keyboard. I've been working hard on the Youth Awards speech and I finally have a solid draft. If I can polish it up by noon tomorrow, I'll still have a day and a half to write the other two school speeches. I pack up my things and am heading toward the elevator when I hear the Minister's voice drifting out of Margo's office. Why would she still be here at this hour? As I get closer, however, I realize she's on the speakerphone with Margo, who must think the building is empty.

"How could you confirm my attendance without asking me first?" the Minister screams. "What were you thinking? I have personal plans that day and worse, my husband's friends will be at those awards and, *thanks to you,* my face is still a mess. And furthermore, Lily isn't ready to write this speech. Tell her to give it to Christine, or be prepared to rewrite it yourself if it's a disaster."

So Margo really did set this up just to sabotage me—and mission accomplished, because thanks to the Minister's parting comment, I instantly lose all confidence in myself.

My phone rings an hour before the Spirit of Youth Awards Ceremony.

"Lily, I've revised today's speech myself," the Minister shouts over the sound of a blow-dryer. "I don't have time to explain where you went wrong now, so listen closely as I deliver it and try to learn."

I listen very closely indeed when she delivers the speech at the ceremony, having memorized every word, but I find that Mrs. Cleary has merely replaced half a dozen of my words with her own. Obviously, I did fine and maybe she'll even come over and tell me so. However, the only person I see heading my way is Margo and she's carrying a tray of hors d'oeuvres. If she's willing to bury the hatchet by proffering crab cakes, I can accept that, I decide, summoning a gracious smile.

"Wipe that silly smile off your face and offer these around," she says. "Remember, we all pitch in around here."

Shaking my head, I hoist the tray and plunge into the crowd. Fortunately, good things come to those who waitress: I overhear glowing reviews of my speech as I work the crowd. Gratified, I pop a whole crab cake into my mouth. I can serve *and* chew; I am multitalented.

"Waitress!" a man's voice say. "How about leaving some food for the guests?"

I spin on my sensible heels to find Tim grinning at me. Too bad I've barely kicked off the McIssac Reno Project.

"Look, I've earned this," I mumble through a mouthful of crab cake.

"Well, it's nice to see you working a crowd without flowers and purse for once."

"Where's the orchestra?"

"I'm here on my own. The music camp for underprivileged kids I support just won an award. I volunteer every summer."

Of course you do, Mr. Selfless. How does the guy find the time and energy for these good works? The closest I've ever come to a charitable act was resisting the urge to frame a "Cigarettes Kill" poster as a birthday present for Lola. I'm a selfish git.

"So," Tim continues, "are things going better?"

"A little. The Minister is actually letting me write speeches."

"That's great! Did you write today's?" I nod reluctantly. "It was terrific!"

"Thanks," I say, beaming. "God knows I won't get any praise around here."

"In my experience with Clarice, you only know you're doing okay by the absence of complaints."

Once again, he's managed to make me feel good about myself. Maybe he sees me as another one of his charities. I can't imagine he's interested in me. In fact, he's probably already seeing some do-gooder he met at a fund-raiser—a Big Sister, or a Girl Scout leader. They'll spend their weekends working in soup kitchens, wearing matching sweaters knit by South American peasants.

I'm not feeling so good about myself anymore.

"Libby!" Margo is signaling me from across the room where she is pitching in by schmoozing the dignitaries. "We're hungry over here!"

For once I'm grateful for Margo's intrusion. My tray of crab cakes has developed a noticeable tremor: it's the damn pheromones again.

"A speechwriter's work is never done," I say, smiling at Tim, "I'll see you."

I'm carving a path through the hungry masses when I hear him call after me, "Congrats on a great speech, Flower Girl!" Somehow it's bearable when he says it, so I turn and smile. Then I pan down and confirm that he's wearing black socks with his suit tonight.

14

To: Romanobean@torlives.ca
From: Mclib@hotmail.ca
Subject: Blubber Alert

Lola,
   Just wanted to warn you that I've gotten as big as a house so
that you won't be shocked when you see me at the café tomorrow.
I fear I'm already "starting to show." Don't say I'm imagining it,
because my clothes are telling the real story. The stress of the job
is turning me into a compulsive eater—I've even dedicated a desk
drawer to emergency rations. Mind you, I've behaved better since
bumping into Tim. Can't wait to tell you about that!
Lib

To: Mclib@hotmail.ca
From: Romanobean@torlives.ca
Subject: A Solution to your problems

Hi Lib,
   Actually, I noticed at Emma's party that you've put on a few—

the drawstring pants were a dead giveaway. I have a suggestion: instead of meeting for fancy coffees, why don't we start a running program? Although my weight doesn't yo-yo like yours, I could definitely afford to tone up. What do you say?
Lola

The Internet truly does make people bold. Even Lola wouldn't dare say in person that I've "put on a few." What a bitch! Her job as a friend is to tell me I look great, regardless. Why do I keep this woman around, anyway? Oh right, because Roxanne is thousands of miles away and Emma is caught up with new husband and homestead. Even a beleaguered speechwriter needs a social life.

The nerve of her suggesting we take up running as if it's something I don't do all the time—or at least occasionally, which is more than I can say for that little smokestack. Nature may have blessed her with an hourglass figure, but she can't climb a flight of stairs without hacking up a lung. Put your sports bra where your mouth is, my friend.

With this thought, I shoot off an e-mail agreeing to her suggestion and start scheming. Lola is known for dragging her stiletto heels, so I've probably got a few weeks before she gets around to embracing this new fitness regime. Meanwhile, unbeknownst to her, I've already run three times since I saw her last, and I've mostly given up whipped cream on my mochaccino. If I can just sneak in a few more runs before we officially kick off the program, I'll leave Lola in the dust.

I'm thinking about buying myself state-of-the-art running shoes when the phone rings.

"Hey, it's Lola. Let's start running tomorrow—strike while the iron is hot, I always say."

Since this is something Lola *never* says, I realize there's a man behind the fitness craze. There's usually a man behind any change of this magnitude—I should know. Michael must be transcending his tech nerd beginnings.

"Excellent," I say. "Why don't you come to my place at 6:00 tomorrow morning?" Lola is a notoriously late riser.

"You're on," she says. Michael is definitely a contender.

Lola arrives at 5:55 a.m. in a steady drizzle. Left to my own devices, I would certainly have crawled back into bed, but the spirit of competition stirs. Lola's feeling it too, judging by her new Lycra leotard and matching Skechers. She looks fabulous.

"I've got pockets," I say, slapping my sweatpants. "Want me to carry your smokes?"

"Very funny. Cinch that drawstring a little tighter and let's hit the road."

Soon we're trotting along Bloor Street and Lola is turning heads, even at that ungodly hour. Her hair is pulled back in a careless ponytail with fetching tendrils framing her face. Mine is in a ponytail too, but the layers are busting out all over and curling into horns at the temple. Worse, I'm actually struggling to keep up with Barbie, although I suspect her energy stems from the new rubber she's wearing. When we hit a red light, she continues to jog back and forth, while I gratefully seize the opportunity to stand on the spot. Suddenly I see why everyone is staring: "Lola, for God's sake, get a sports bra."

"You don't need one with these Lycra outfits. The guy at the sports store said so."

"Since when did guys offer reliable advice on support?"

"Like I always say, if you've got 'em, flaunt 'em." (This she does always say.)

"Well, if you want to avoid tucking them into your socks after a few runs, wear a bra. In fact, wear *two.*"

"Why, thank you! Did you hear that, girls?" she says to her boobs.

Fortunately, the elastic in Lola's getup soon starts to give and she slows down considerably. Great. Now that I can breathe, I'll tell her about my seeing Tim. I open my mouth, and—

"Isn't Michael *fabulous?*"

Or we could talk about Michael.

"I wouldn't know, you held him prisoner on the porch at Emma's party—after deserting me, I might add."

"Sorry about that, we just really hit it off. He called me the next day and invited me to drive to the country in his Audi TT."

"That must have been nice."

"Not half as nice as his new penthouse! He's had the whole thing professionally decorated and let me tell you, that man knows the meaning of luxury. I spent the next couple of days there, as a matter of fact."

"That luxurious, huh?"

"Oh yeah."

"Hot tub?"

"Yup."

"Steam bath?"

"Check."

"Egyptian cotton sheets?"

"Four-hundred-thread count."

"Slut."

"Look, it's not a pickup truck, but what can I say, I'm easy."

We both laugh, which is remarkable, considering we've passed the twenty-minute mark in our run. Finally, I try broaching the subject of Tim again.

"So, I saw Tim last week."

"Really? Where?"

"At the office. He was—"

"Michael took me for a tour of *his* office. It's this renovated warehouse space full of art deco furniture and Italian leather." She glances over at me to see if I'm absorbing the splendor of it all and detects my frustration. "Sorry, Lib. You were trying to say something about Tim. Why was he at your office?"

"Supporting yet another of his good causes. He—"

"Michael's company donated over 10 grand to the Hospital for Sick Children last year. He must be doing *very* well!"

I give up on trying to share the nuances of my encounter with Tim, since it all pales in comparison, and encourage her to babble on for the remainder of the run, taking comfort from her wheezing. By the time I usher her to her car, she's about to keel over. I, meanwhile, have enough gas to run up the street to the Second Cup, waving merrily to her as she sinks behind the steering wheel.

I've actually given some thought to what I'm wearing, but when I see the crowd at Storm, I realize that no matter how I try, I will never be cool enough. My black pants are classic and my cashmere blend sweater casually elegant, but cool they are not. And then there's the matter of footwear: since I walked from my place, I made the sensible choice and am wearing my Blundstones. It's not like my parents ever notice what I wear.

They're already at our table and shifting uncomfortably in steel mesh chairs when I arrive. I kiss them, sit down and take a look around. Elliot had said the place is trendy but I wasn't prepared for this. There's a waterfall dividing the dining room from the cocktail lounge. In the latter, blue light dances off a gleaming silver bar. The barstools are covered with lime-green fun fur, and white plastic egg chairs are suspended from the ceiling with chains. Macy Gray is blaring from the speakers and my mother winces when she realizes the backup singer is chanting, "Fucky for you."

I'm going to kill Elliot. He never batted an eye when I told him I was planning to bring my parents here. He's *met* my parents: it's not like he could think that this is their kind of place. Obviously, it's one of his little jokes on the suburbanites.

"What an *unusual* place, dear—so imaginative!" As usual, the nicest woman in the world is trying to be positive. She's squinting at her menu, where the shiny blue lettering fades into the aqua background. My father is tilting his to catch the light.

"Can I get you drinks to start?" the waiter asks, gazing blankly at us through pale blue aviator glasses. He's wearing floral bell-bottoms, and a tight, ribbed T-shirt.

I place an order for drinks before my father can say anything embarrassing about the purple polish on the waiter's fingernails: "A pint of domestic beer, a glass of house white, and a Maker's Mark on ice, please."

We all lean out to check the waiter's shoes as he leaves and sure enough, they're platforms. Then we lapse into silence as my parents return to deciphering the menus. Head to head under the single blue halogen bulb lighting our table, they squint at the restaurant's offerings.

"Listen to this one, Marjie: *Crispy salmon with green capon sauce.* Green capons! Now I've heard of everything."

"Well, they've come a long way with hybrids, Reg. You liked the broccoflower casserole I made last week."

"I'll eat any vegetable covered in cheese, Marj, but that doesn't mean I'll try green poultry. Especially on salmon."

Incredulously, I check my own menu and roll my eyes. "That's crispy salmon with a green *caper* sauce, Dad."

"Oh. What's a caper?"

"It's a seed, I think. Or maybe a vegetable. I'm not sure, but I know it's small and round."

"If you're not sure, maybe it would be safer to stick to capon."

Huggy Bear soon returns with our drinks and I ask him to recite the specials, hoping something will appeal to my parents and end the menu torture. Much to my relief, each chooses a special and I'm able to engage them in pleasant conversation until the food arrives.

"What's this?" Dad asks Huggy when he slides an oversized plate in front of him.

"Indigo Thai rice with citrus marinated shrimp, just as you ordered, sir."

"All I see is a branch. Has a hurricane struck the restaurant?" Then he turns to me and says in a loud stage whisper, "Maybe that's why they call it 'Storm,' eh, Lib? Probably blew in over that waterfall."

I smile apologetically at Huggy.

"It's a banana leaf, sir," the waiter says with a patient smile.

"The food is nestled inside." I feel myself tensing up. Reg is not a man to let a word like *nestled* go by without comment.

"Oh, I see. Well, you should change the name of the dish to 'Nestled Shrimp in a Leaf.' Then people might know what to expect."

It's obvious that the waiter is not impressed with my father's humor and my mother shoots him a look as she tucks into her tuna. At least she's getting into the spirit of it, loading wasabi onto her fish. I had no idea she even knew what it was.

"Lib, grab that cutlery off the table behind you," Dad directs, as he clumsily pokes at his banana leaf with a chopstick. "It makes sense that they'd expect you to tackle foliage with a couple of twigs, but I like a good old-fashioned knife and—"

A whimper from across the table cuts him off. My mother's face is scarlet, her eyes are watering and she's waving her hand in front of her mouth. I pass her a glass of water and after a moment, she's able to speak.

"What in the name of God is that green stuff?" She's lost a bit of her perky optimism.

"Wasabi—a kind of horseradish. I figured you knew that, the way you were loading it onto your tuna."

"I thought it was avocado."

"Well, at least your rice is the right color, Marjie. Look at this! I think some of that poofter's nail polish got into mine!"

*"Dad/Reg!"* My mother and I reprimand my father in unison. Not that it will do any good.

"Just as well you didn't bring that priest boyfriend of yours along, eh, Lib? What would he make of all this?"

"He's not my boyfriend, Dad. We only went out a couple of times and it didn't work out."

"You know, your mother and I have been thinking. How is it that an attractive girl like you has such trouble finding a man? Have you ever considered that it might be the way you dress?"

I take a big swig of bourbon before answering. Then, in my calmest voice, I ask: "What's wrong with the way I dress?"

"Well, it's not exactly *feminine.*"

"So what are you saying—that it's masculine?"

"More like androgynous." How does a man who doesn't know what a caper is use *androgynous* in a sentence? "For example, look at what you're wearing tonight: black pants, a shapeless sweater and those clunky boots! When was the last time you wore a *skirt?*"

I look to my mother for support but the traitor actually agrees with my father.

"Well, with your height, dear, it probably wouldn't be a bad idea."

"What are you trying to say, Mom?"

"We just worry that you might be sending out the wrong message, dear."

"That I prefer girls?" They both cringe.

"Don't even joke about *that,*" Reg says.

"No need to get defensive, dear," Mom offers, soothingly. "We're just trying to help."

"You two have never given me a hard time about being single before. What gives?"

"Well, you're not getting any younger, Libby," Dad offers.

"Nor shorter, for that matter. Listen, next time you feel inclined to help me out like this, can you warn me in advance? I'll reserve at Pizza Hut."

"Suits me," my father says, smiling.

"But this was delicious," my mother hastens to add, as I pick up the four-hundred-dollar tab and bid Huggy a fond good-night.

The Minister charges down the aisle of the school auditorium, giving me a nod as she passes that says "Follow me, kid." Or more specifically, "My Louis Vuitton had better appear the second I crack the door to the staff powder room or your ass is grass." I scuttle along behind Her Grace but am cut off twice by the flow of children headed to the cafeteria. By the time I arrive in the washroom, the door to the only cubicle is closed and I can hear a steady stream of water hitting the porcelain bowl. I know it's Mrs. Cleary because her perfume is slowly choking off my air supply.

"Is that you, Lily?" The Princess's voice rings out over the Pee.

"Yes, I have your bag," I reply, marveling at her stamina. The eight glasses of water a day rule is gospel to her, but how does she fit such a capable bladder into that compact body? Maybe her husband the surgeon has removed part of her stomach to accommodate it.

Eventually the stream tapers off and the Minister emerges. She takes her purse and rummages through her cosmetics bag. While applying the finishing touches with an eyebrow pencil, she examines me in the mirror.

"Margo could do wonders with those eyebrows, Lily."

Having seen the Minister without benefit of makeup, I'm aware that her eyebrows have all but disappeared under Margo's care. Still, I don't want to ruin the moment.

"That's very kind, Minister. I'll set something up when I have a little more time." Like when hell freezes over. God gave us big brows for a reason—although I have no idea what it is.

"You know, I used to have unkempt brows myself, back in junior high." I let the insult slide since she rarely speaks to me about anything personal. "I wanted to tweeze, but my mother was dead set against it. She wouldn't let me pierce my ears either, although all my friends were doing it." I'm bewildered by her sudden familiarity. Have my unruly brows tipped her off to the fact that I'm actually human?

"That must have been *horrible* for you," I say, oozing sympathy.

"It *was* horrible, Lily. In fact, it was a very difficult time in my life. That was the year when my ballet instructor, Madame Boulier, dismissed me from class—permanently."

"What happened?"

"Madame was not a woman of refined tastes and she failed to appreciate my style. In fact, she advised my mother that *I had no talent.* Her exact words were, 'There's nothing more I can do for Clarice. She is holding back the class.'"

"That's a terrible thing to do to a child." For once I am sincere.

"I feel the humiliation to this day, Lily."

I'm amazed: Mrs. Cleary is not only human herself, but almost likable. Suddenly, I have an idea.

"You know, Minister, sharing stories like this one would really help you connect with your audiences, just as humor does. I'd like to use more personal anecdotes in your speeches if you agree."

"I suppose so, Lily, although I'd want to review them well in advance. I'll see what else I can come up with."

She snaps her cosmetic pouch shut, drops it back in the Louis Vuitton and hands the bag over to me. I'm already wondering if I just imagined the last five minutes when she pauses at the door and turns to me.

"Just after I took office, Madame Boulier was selected for an Ontario Diamond Award for her contributions to dance. Her name mysteriously disappeared from the list before the ceremony. It was the strangest thing."

"You *didn't*," I gasp.

"It's a joke, Lily. You take everything so seriously. But quite frankly, what *would* Madame do with a Diamond Award in a retirement home anyway?"

She smiles and raises a penciled-on brow in a sinister arch as she walks out the door.

15

Running with Lola has inspired a snack drawer makeover. When I open it now in search of sweet inspiration, a box of low-fat granola bars is sitting front and center. I'm crunching virtuously as the phone rings.

"Libby, it's the Minister. Come to my office right away. I have an idea for one of my speeches."

I toss the granola bar on the desk, pick up a notepad and make my way down the hall. Ten minutes later I'm back, cursing my own big mouth. The Minister has been pondering what I said during our moment of washroom bonding and wants to get "more personal" with her audiences. For starters, she wants to quote a favorite poem from her childhood at next week's fund-raiser for the Canadian Opera Company. She can't remember title or author—just that it's in praise of song. All I have to work with is a Post-it note upon which she's scribbled a few lines. Although they're hardly operatic, I hate to discourage her, so I start searching Web sites on poetry.

Half an hour later, I remember the half-eaten granola bar: it's disappeared. Strange, I think, rifling through the papers on my desk. Then I remember the rattrap under my desk. Surely the rodents aren't making midday rounds? Last time I checked, I was still at the top of the food chain and I'm not prepared to share.

I open the drawer and pull out the box of granola bars to discover it's almost empty. Didn't I just open it yesterday? Or has my compulsive snacking reached the point where I forget what I've eaten? I shake a premakeover bag of fruit cream cookies. It's as light as air, yet there's no sign of forced entry. This rat is either extremely dexterous or it's of the redheaded variety.

"Locking up your secrets?" Laurie asks, when she finds me searching for a padlock from the supply cupboard.

"Locking out the vermin, actually."

Rat Girl is on a diet.

BEEP—"Lib, it's Emma. Give me a call, I've got something to tell you—*Bob, stop it, she's not there*—" Click. Tell me what? Why didn't she just leave details?

BEEP—"Hey, Lib, just making sure we're still on to run to-morrow morning." Jesus! Why doesn't she give it up?

BEEP—"Libby…hi, it's Tim Kennedy." *Oh my God!* "I hope you don't mind, but I asked Bob for your number. I know it's short notice but I just got pressured into buying a couple of tickets for a benefit concert tomorrow night and wondered if there's any chance that you might join me? Give me a call."

BEEP—"Lib, it's Bob." He's whispering. "Look, Emma's in the other room so I have to make this fast… She wanted to tell you herself, but he called *me* after all. Tim, that is. He asked for your number. Yeah, I know I vowed not to get involved, but what can I say, I— *Oh, Emma, I'm just*—" Click.

Cornelius watches me dance around the apartment with an expression of disgust on his face. When my heart rate returns to normal I pick up the phone and leave Tim a message ac-cepting his invitation.

★ ★ ★

"Thanks, Janet," I tell the Legislative Librarian. "I really appreciate this. I spent most of yesterday searching for this poem and I don't know where else to look."

I feel a weight lift from my shoulders as I pass my burden to her. I've had a surprisingly productive morning, considering how excited I am about the fact that Tim Kennedy will be knocking at my door in six hours. There should be time for deep breathing and affirmations this afternoon. The Minister is speaking to Grade 11 students at the Royal Ontario Museum but I didn't write the speech and with any luck, I'll be able to get away early and hit the MAC boutique on my way home. The occasion warrants a new lipstick.

Margo appears at my partition: "Hurry up, Libby." Her eyes light on the padlock and linger. I believe it's the first time I've seen her look directly at anything. There's a twitch in her left eyelid.

"Margo—" the Minister pounces as we enter her office "—don't you vet the draft speeches before I see them?"

"Yes, always."

"Then I must say I am dismayed you would let such *drivel* land on my desk." She's shaking a handful of papers in Margo's direction.

"What can I do if Libby sneaks drafts of her speeches to you?"

"Lily didn't author this insult to my intelligence, it's what's-her-name."

"Who, Christine?"

"No, not Christine, the forgettable one."

Ah, yes, Forgettable. Her muse must have strayed.

"It wasn't *that* bad, Minister. I can help you salvage it," Margo offers.

"You can't salvage trash, Margo." To illustrate her point, the Minister turns and feeds the speech into her paper shredder. Margo and I watch in disbelief as the speech she's supposed to recite in half an hour emerges from one end of the machine in long, thin strips.

"Lily, throw a few points together for me and I'll ad lib the rest. Maybe I'll even tell a joke or two."

I charge back to my office, type a few fragments in size 36 font, then race through the halls of the Pink Palace and launch myself into Bill's car. I make a few handwritten additions during the five-minute drive and pass the notes off to the Minister with only moments to spare. Her delivery is choppy and her jokes a little lame but she manages to convey the points I've given her and the audience seems engaged. With the exception of one ad-libbed—and long-winded—digression about her very first trip to the ROM, I'd say the speech went very well, all things considered. I must be getting the hang of this speechwriting gig. Maybe I've found my calling at last.

Rat Girl scents hubris in the air and brings me crashing back to earth: "I hope that speech for the Opera Company is finished, Elizabeth. I expect to see it on my desk tomorrow."

I'll be damned if I miss my date with Tim to work on something that isn't due for a week.

"That isn't possible, Margo, but you'll have a draft first thing Monday."

I expect her to put up a fight but the caterers are rolling out appetizers and her head snaps around so fast the vertebrae in her neck crackle like Rice Krispies.

"Libby, we take deadlines seriously here. I hope this isn't going to become a pattern."

I don't bother to answer since she's already halfway to the trough.

Recalling my father's comments about my wardrobe, I slip into a short skirt and high heels before my date with Tim. The skirt is still a little tight across the butt, but the overall effect isn't bad at all—and it certainly isn't androgynous.

Tim's expression when I open the door suggests that my father is right, for once.

"Wow, you're a girl," he says.

"Remember *The Crying Game*? Besides, I was wearing a dress when we met."

"Long and yellow, as I recall. Hoped you'd wear it tonight."

"I thought about it, but it doesn't work without a bouquet, and for once I don't have one."

Cornelius waddles out of the bedroom and stares balefully at Tim.

"My God! That's the biggest cat I've ever seen," he exclaims.

"And the meanest—keep your distance."

"You need a dog to give him a workout."

"Let me guess, a Jack Russell?"

"The only breed worth having."

We head out to his Jeep and drive west along Bloor.

"So where's the concert?" I ask.

"High Park."

"*High Park?* Is it in a tent?" My voice is squeaky.

"No, open-air. Don't worry, I brought a blanket."

"I assumed we'd be inside. I'm a little overdressed for a park, Tim."

"Nah, you'll be fine. It's a beautiful night." Spoken like a guy who's never worn a skirt or high heels.

I stumble into a pothole before we're even out of the parking lot and when we hit the grass, I teeter along on my toes to avoid aerating the turf with my heels. In short, I've become one of those girly-girls I mock. My annoyance at my father peaks about the time I have to lower myself gracefully onto Tim's blanket and find a comfortable position that doesn't offer the people in front of us a show they didn't pay for.

During the intermission, a posse of Tim's teenage orchestra students descends on us—six girls who show a decided disinterest in meeting me. Since eight is definitely a crowd, I clamber to my feet and ask an event organizer to point me in the direction of a washroom. Finding myself before a long line of Porta Potti's, it crosses my mind that this date is on the skids.

I'm choosing the least vile among the potties, when Tim's admirers appear.

"It's Mr. Kennedy's *girl*friend!"

"I guess she has to pee."

"Nice skirt, lady!"

They've surrounded me now and I'm momentarily grateful for the heels. Were it not for my extreme height advantage, I might be intimidated. These girls have about thirty visible tattoos and piercings between them and they seem aggressive.

"How long have you and Mr. Kennedy been going out?"

"Where did you meet?"

"Do you teach music, too?"

Fortunately, there's no need to respond. They're all talking at once and seemingly for their own amusement.

"She probably teaches *choir,*" the ringleader says, as if nothing could be lamer.

"Or the recorder."

"No, the piccolo. Picture it, she's a *giant.*"

"I am *not* a giant," I retort.

"You're taller than Mr. Kennedy."

"He's got an inch on me," I say, taking the bait, which is exactly what I advise the Minister against.

"Are you kidding?"

"You *towered* over him."

"It must be the heels," one says to appreciative snickers all around.

In a feeble attempt to recover some ground, I ask, "So, you're all musical, ladies?"

*"So, you're all musical, ladies?"* They echo in unison.

"Six-part harmony—I'm impressed," I say. "A choir unto yourselves."

Snorts and eye-rolling. Then Alpha Teen speaks up: "What do you do, ma'am?"

*Ma'am!* "Why do you want to know?"

"We want to know if you're good enough for Mr. Kennedy. Duh."

"Probably not, but to satisfy your curiosity, I'm a speech-writer."

"Yeah? For who?"

"For *whom*," I say. Oops. More eye-rolling. "For the Minister of Culture."

"Whatever."

"Boring."

"Do you ever stop talking about yourself?"

Recognizing I have no hope of winning this battle, I try to cut my losses: "I'd love to stick around and chat, but..."

"We'll wait for you," Alpha thug offers.

"Look, you should go keep Mr. Kennedy company."

They shuffle off a few yards and pause, whispering and gig-gling. If this were a movie, I'd be able to make a dignified exit about now, but because it's real life—or at least, *my* real life—the only option is to open the door of the nearest Porta Potti and step inside.

The smell is almost overwhelming, but I lock the door and start breathing through my mouth. "Don't look down, don't look down," I chant to myself. I look down: it's inevitable. Somehow, I manage to do my business without stumbling off my heels or touching anything. There's a rattle at the door as I'm peeing: the girls must be trying to catch me in the act. Like I'm stupid enough to leave the door unlocked!

The stench is starting to turn my stomach by the time I turn to unlatch the door. It won't open. I jiggle it, then push on it but it's clearly jammed. Panic rises in my throat as I realize that the girls have locked me in. Oh God. I can already feel the bac-teria eating at my skin but I try to relax: the concert is only half over. There are hundreds of people in the park and some of them will need to pee. At the moment, however, all is silent.

"Hello? I'm stuck here! Hello!"

When I pause to listen for a response, I hear the band start again in the distance and my heart sinks. Traffic around here is likely to be slow until the concert is over. I could suffocate before anyone finds me.

"HELP! HELP!"

I'm banging vigorously on the door when it occurs to me that things could get a whole lot worse if I tip the place over. Better to chill out. In fact, the air doesn't seem quite so foul now; I must be getting used to it. My feet are killing me, though, so I lower the lid of the toilet, cover it with strips of tissue and take a seat. Every so often, I offer up a plaintive "help" and finally I start to cry, chafing my nose with low-grade toilet tissue. This is definitely the worst date I've ever had.

Darkness is falling on my humble retreat when I finally hear footsteps.

"HELP!" I yell.

"Libby?" It's Tim.

"Over here!" I shout.

The door swings open and Tim reaches in to help me escape. "Are you okay?"

"I'm fine," I say, sniffling. I'd blow my nose, but I've got my purse in one hand and he's still holding the other.

"There was a stick jammed in the handle," he says. "Someone deliberately locked you in."

"*Someone!* It was your students. Those thugs."

"Libby, I'm sorry, they're a handful sometimes. All of them have difficult home lives and they act out."

"I can't feel any sympathy for them at the moment," I say, sounding as sulky as I feel. "Would you mind if we just went home now?"

"Come on, Libby, where's that notorious sense of humor?"

"It corroded in there."

Tim is clearly disappointed but I just want to get out of this ridiculous outfit and into a warm tub with plenty of perfumed bubble bath. I have never felt less sexy in my life.

"I'll talk to them on Monday, don't worry."

"*Talk* to them? This calls for corporal punishment!"

He schticks to cheer me up on the drive home but I can't rise to the occasion. Convinced that potty fumes are clinging to me, I roll down my window. Tim opens his too. I must really stink. When we finally pull up in front of my place, I jump out of the car mumbling, "Thanks." He calls out after me.

"Let me make this up to you, Libby. Could we try again next week?" I don't see the point when we're clearly jinxed. As he gives me a hopeful smile, he adds, "Please." I relent.

"Well, okay."

"I'll call you!"

He won't call.

The phone is ringing but I decide to let voice mail take care of business. My shoes are propped on the desk and I'm savoring the last morsel of a chocolate bar. It's the first I've allowed myself in two weeks and I resent the intrusion. Who could blame me for the indulgence, given my recent trauma? The phone rings again a few minutes later and my professionalism wins out.

"Libby McIssac."

"Hi, Libby, it's Janet from the Legislative Library. I've solved your mystery."

"Thank you so much, Janet. I've almost finished the speech and there's a perfect spot for the Minister to recite this poem."

"Don't thank me yet." Something in her tone tells me there's a rewrite ahead of me. "The lines she gave you aren't from a poem."

"No? What are they from?"

"A song, actually."

"A song? Well, that could work."

"Probably not for the Opera Company: it's by Sawdust."

"Not the brother/sister duo from the '70s?"

"Allow me," Janet begins: "As a girl I listened to the radio, Belting out my favorite songs…. I think they knew I sang along, It made them smile…"

"It's schmaltzy, but pleasant enough," I say. "And the Minister likes it."

"I'm just getting started: Every la-la-la, every Dosie-do-do, sunshine… Maybe you're right, Libby—it is perfect for the Opera Company."

"Okay, I get your point."

But Janet is enjoying herself too much to stop: "Every ting-a-ding-ding, the bells are starting to ring…."

"All right, already!" She sneaks in a swooping "Good times" before I cut her off. "Look, how was I to know? Sawdust was a '70s band. I was like, five."

"Every dosie-do-do…"

"Janet, librarians are supposed to be quiet and shy."

"I'll fax over the lyric sheet so the whole audience can sing along."

I hear one last wo-wo-wo before the line goes dead.

## 16

"As promised!" I announce dramatically to the shadowy form behind Margo's desk.

It takes my eyes a moment to adjust to the gloom. No wonder she prefers to raid my stash of snacks—she'd need night-vision goggles to find her own in here. Using the glow from the computer monitor to guide me to her desk, I present the speech for the Opera Company with a bow and a flourish.

"It took me most of the weekend, but I think the Minister is going to be pleased," I say. I actually finished in time to meet Emma for a late lunch on Saturday, but I'm not about to share that with the Dungeon Master.

Ignoring both speech and amateur dramatics, Margo looks up from her computer.

"The Minister has hired a private political consultant who's flying in from London tomorrow to advise all of you on how to improve our image."

I'm not fooled by her apparent nonchalance. There's a chocolate chip cookie sitting uneaten on her desk—she's plenty worried. I just hope the consultant is a guy: we could use some testosterone on the executive team.

"Is there a reason you're still here, Libby?"

"Yes, actually. The speech…?"

"What speech?"

"The one I just put on your desk—for the Opera Company?"

She looks down at the speech as though wondering how it got there.

"Oh, that. I'll look at it when I have the time."

I beat a hasty retreat before she snaps out of her daze and questions me about the state of the reference shelf. On the way back to my desk, I bump into Bill and ask if he's heard the news about the new consultant.

"Yeah, I heard, all right. It's Richard Neale. I can't believe she's hiring that arrogant son of a bitch."

"You know him?"

"He's a friend of the Clearys' and I've driven him around when he's been in town. Thinks he's better than the rest of us just because of that posh British accent. It's phony, if you ask me. He's from Yorkshire, for God's sake—farm country—but he acts like he was to the manor born."

"A real snob, huh?"

"Take it from me, Libby, the man's a pain in the arse."

I'm waiting by the microwave for my soup to heat up when I learn that the Ego has landed. Two female admin staff spill into the kitchen, abuzz with the news.

"Who was *that?*" one asks, fanning herself with a Lean Cuisine box.

"I don't know, but I'd sure like to! What a hunk! And that accent!" The woman extends her hand to her friend in an imitation of Richard: "Good Aufternoon. That's an absolutely *charming* jumper you have on."

Please. So the man has an accent and a little polish. Big deal. In my experience, the private sector consultants are always smooth. They arrive wearing expensive navy-blue suits and expressions of bemused tolerance—Big Business riding into town to clean up the Bungling Bureaucracy. Yet, time and again I've watched them crumble under the red tape, delays and mixed messages of government. The strain begins to show when the suits are replaced by bad casual wear. Their hours get shorter, their meetings get longer and all thoughts of reforming us vanish. By the time they're fully assimilated, you couldn't pick them out of a crowd of civil servants, except for their bulging wallets. I give this guy six weeks.

The women's twittering is making my head ache so I collect my soup and head down the hall to dine in the relative peace of my cubicle. Rounding a corner, I nearly run into Margo, who's leading a very tall, well-built man in a navy suit toward the boardroom. This must be Richard Neale but he doesn't seem like such hot stuff to me. Margo hurries past without a glance, but Richard, who accidentally clips me in the shoulder, stops to apologize.

"I'm dreadfully sorry," he says, squeezing my arm gently before rushing after Margo.

Whoa! The hairs on my arms are all standing at attention and as I turn to watch Richard's broad shoulders disappear into the boardroom, I feel my brain roll over, kick a few times and die. Surely Bill is mistaken about this guy; he seems perfectly delightful. But perhaps a fatal blast of pheromones has disengaged my usually stellar capacity for reasoning.

Back at my desk, I'm very much aware of Richard's presence in the boardroom nearby. The Minister is giggling and even Margo's voice has a breathless quality. There's also a constant stream of women passing my cubicle to stroll by the boardroom. Evidently, the pheromones have already penetrated the building's ventilation system.

"How can you sit there so calmly?" Laurie says, peeking around my partition. The fast, high tone of her voice betrays that she too has been affected by Richard's magic—and this is a woman who is so happily married I usually want to slap her.

"Don't tell me you're on your way past the boardroom too?"

"You bet I am. Richard is hot! Haven't you met him yet?"

"Well, we haven't been formally introduced, but I've seen him."

"And...?"

"And I suppose he's attractive enough."

"Playing it cool, huh? Well, then I won't bother to share what I've learned about him."

I pull a Mars bar out of my drawer and surrender half of it to her. "Spill it, sister."

Laurie laughs and perches on the corner of my desk and tells me that Richard is divorced, currently single and living in Chelsea, an upscale London neighborhood. Although he's a renowned political consultant, the stock market is behind his great wealth. He received a modest inheritance as a teen and parlayed it into a small fortune by the time he was twenty-five. He met Mrs. Cleary and her husband, Julian, at an alumni event at Cambridge and despite the difference in their ages, they've been close friends ever since. The Minister is particularly fond of him.

"So," Laurie concludes, "I'm heading down to the coffee machine. Care to join me?"

From the coffee machine, one can enjoy an unobstructed view into the boardroom. "I could use a coffee."

I steal a good look at Richard as we pass the open door. His suit looks expensive, as does his shirt and tie, but when my eyes slide south, I'm surprised to discover that he's wearing fancy, fringed loafers with a pointy toe.

"Did you check out the shoes?" I whisper to Laurie when we reach the coffee machine. "He's wearing party pumps."

"Maybe that's the height of fashion in London."

"Or maybe it's a big mistake."

"Are you saying you'd reject him on the basis of his footwear?" Laurie asks.

"I'm saying he'll need the services of a friendly native to help him get dressed in the morning."

"It looks like Mrs. Cleary is already applying for that position." Laurie nods in the direction of the boardroom where the Minister is currently straightening Richard's tie. "Not that Richard seems to mind," she adds.

"He's probably just being polite," I say. "Do you think he realizes how attractive he is to women?"

"I'd say he's pretty confident of his appeal, yes."

"He's awfully manly for a civilized Brit. Maybe he was blessed with two Y chromosomes."

"Well, if you ask me, two Y's spell trouble."

What's a little excessive masculinity between colleagues? I could help him find more constructive uses for that testosterone.

Richard has rearranged the furniture in his office so that his desk now faces the door. I know this because I've been devising lame excuses to stroll down the hall past his office. For example, I'm catching up on my photocopying, what with the copy room being near his office. I also take the long way round to the washroom and back. It's pathetic, but I'm in good company: who knew so many women worked in the building?

Ashamed, I consult with my self-help library and discover a volume entitled, *Flirt Now, Marry Later*. It confirms that the parade is a time-honored courtship ritual and offers the following guidelines:

• Preen before setting off; fluff hair and apply lipstick;
• Invent feasible excuse for mission;
• Walk briskly and with purpose toward destination;
• Look straight ahead, shoulders back, hips swaying;
• Smile ever so slightly so as to look caught up in fascinating life, yet still attainable.

If I tried all that, I'd blow a circuit, but fortunately, even my feeble attempts are generating good results: I'm almost certain Richard looks up as I'm passing and tracks me with his eyes. The book doesn't indicate whether it's allowable to laugh once you're out of sight, but I do—I can't take the game that seriously. Just the same, I find myself pondering the relative merits of thong underwear. If he's going to monitor my backside, perhaps I should give him less to look at. On the other hand, given my expanding girth, I'm better off with something more binding.

I'm still tabulating the pros and cons of various undergarments when I overhear Richard's deep voice greeting our receptionist on the other side of my partition:

"Good morning, Nancy. Where might I get a decent cup of tea around here?"

"I'm fine, thanks!" Nancy replies, before adding, "I love tea."

What is it about Richard that is reducing all of the women—and some of the men—on our floor to idiocy? I'd love to set up a few cameras around the office to study the phenomenon—maybe do a little in-house reality television show.

*We open with a view from the Ladies' Bathroom Camera where the audience witnesses a dozen women jockeying for a position in front of the mirror. They're fluffing and preening and turning to examine their profiles. Some are describing what they'd do if they got Richard alone for a night—or even for twenty minutes in the office boardroom. Several discuss sharing him. The giggling is deafening. After a final adjustment of panty hose and bras, they sashay out the door one by one.*

*We cut to Hall Camera, which picks up Richard swaggering past the ladies' room, seemingly oblivious to the steady stream of well-groomed women—all staring straight ahead with expressions of studied nonchalance. The audience is wowed by Richard's cool demeanor in the face of such temptation, but wait! What's Hall Cam picking up now? As the women pass, Richard waits a beat, then cranes his neck around to do an ass check. No human has ever before shown such flexibility of the cranial vertebrae. It's almost reptilian.*

*Let's cut to Cubicle Cam for a closer look at the action. There's our hero now, stopping at a few desks as he collects the informa-*

*tion he needs to do his job. He's charming his way from desk to desk while women stare agog like schoolgirls. Under Desk Cam reveals nervous trembling and crossed fingers. Special sensors pick up an increase of perspiration and blood flow to the privates.*

*Finally, Richard makes his way to his office and closes the door. Office Cam provides an insider's view of primal man in his habitat. Viewers may be startled, and even horrified, as Richard belches (where's that British polish now?). Under Desk Cam zooms in on the man's crotch just as his large, well-manicured hand comes to rest upon it. The cameras will linger there, simultaneously titillating and repelling the viewer. The credits roll to end this week's episode and the voiceover asks, "Will the Minister's girls have their nasty way with Richard? Or will our hero choose self-love over a foursome on a boardroom table? Tune in next week to* Much Ado about Dick *to find out!"*

The phone rings, shattering my fantasy.

"Hi, Libby, it's Tim."

For the first time in three days, all thoughts of Richard have vanished from my head. My heart starts pounding. I'm a woman of simple tastes after all. Why waste a moment's thought on an unattainable businessman when a very pleasant high-school music teacher is actually on the line?

Tim apologizes again for the Porta Potti incident and explains that the girls mistakenly believed one of their own pals to be in the potty when they jammed the latch. It was just a harmless joke that got out of hand because they forgot to come back for her, he says. I don't believe this for a second, but why dispel his kindhearted delusions? Instead, I graciously accept his apology. And when he invites me to join him for a movie, I happily agree.

After hanging up, my concentration immediately improves and I take full advantage by tackling one of the two new speeches the Minister has assigned. I haven't been able to focus since Richard's arrival. At checkout time, I take the shortest route to the elevator. I don't give Richard a thought all evening and even forget to mention his arrival to Lola when she calls to complain that Michael canceled dinner plans at the last minute again. For a change, I'm blissfully content as I climb into bed. My second date with Tim is going to be terrific. I will carry cologne in my purse, though, just in case.

I awaken with a vague sense of guilt. Then my dream about Richard comes flooding back to me. I let the man have his way with me. No, worse, I had my way with him. The details are sketchy, but clothes were flying and he was talking dirty to me with that lovely English accent. The sex, if I may say, was incredible.

I go heavy on the cold water in the shower to erase the feeling and am soon able to appreciate just how uncomfortable the boardroom table would be for a real life shagging. I'm not eighteen anymore and Richard and I are both very tall. And how about those party pumps? I must cleanse my mind of illicit thoughts of Richard and replace them with images of Tim. Tim is just as handsome as Richard and his footwear—with the exception of the sports sock episode at the Governor General's—is far superior.

A trip to the photocopier is my first priority upon reaching the office, despite my good intentions. I still haven't been formally introduced to Richard. Admittedly, the opportunities have been few because the Minister and Margo keep him in back-to-back meetings. Still, you'd think they'd stop by my cubicle and make an introduction. Or you'd think he'd make an effort himself. He may even be going out of his way *not* to notice me. Given my frequent visits to the Xerox machine, he probably has me pegged as the office lackey and Bill did say he's a snob.

I manage to live through the day without seeing him. Laurie says the Minister has taken him to a policy seminar. At least it leaves me free to focus on my other speech and by 6:00 p.m.

I'm able to drop both of them on Margo's desk. I have just enough time to hit the ladies' room to prep for my date and take one last, slow pass by Richard's office on my way out to see if he's returned. I made quite an effort with my appearance today and I'd like Richard to benefit from Tim's good fortune.

I'm loitering by the bulletin board near Richard's door when Margo appears.

"Thinking of buying a boat?" she asks.

"What?" I look at her incredulously.

"Well, you're staring at that ad for a sixteen-foot power boat."

"Not at all. I'm looking at this ad for the dog walker," I say, pointing to it.

"You don't have a dog."

"How do you know that?"

"You're obviously a cat person."

"I am not," I say, bristling. I hate being labeled a "cat person," as if I'm some old spinster living in a Victorian house that reeks of cat pee.

"My mistake. No need to get defensive," Margo says, grinning.

A simple elbow to the temple, and she'd be down for the count. It's ridiculous to have to rein in my brute strength like this day after day.

"I'm not defensive," I say, defensively. "I like cats—and I'm getting a dog."

"Yeah, what breed?" She looks skeptical.

"A Jack Russell—they're bred to hunt rats, and I could use the protection around here. Anyway, is there something you want from me, Margo?"

"I noticed that the reference shelf is *still* in disarray."

"Did you notice the two speeches I put on your desk?"

"Perhaps I failed to explain how important these reference texts are to the Minister."

"You've explained. I've just been busy."

"Maybe you could look into it when you're done with these ads."

She scuttles off and I'm turning to leave myself when Richard pokes his head out of his office with a curious smile. Evidently, he's overheard our petty conversation. That's what I get for trolling.

Thanks to my unexpected run-in with Margo, I arrive at the theater a few minutes late. Tim has already bought the tickets and the trailers are starting as we sit down. A group of people move into the row behind us, knocking into my seat repeatedly as they pass. I turn around to glare and find it's the six juvenile delinquents from the concert.

"Hi, Mr. Kennedy!" they chorus.

Tim looks around in surprise. "Well, girls, this is a coincidence! You remember Miss McIssac? In fact, I think you have something to say to her."

The ringleader, who is directly behind me, speaks up: "Sorry about locking you in the Porta Potti last week, Miss McIssac. It was an accident."

"An accident?" I say, raising my eyebrows.

"Yeah, we thought it was Shelley in there and we were just joking with her. Right, Shelley?" Alpha Teen turns to a girl farther down the row, who blows a bubble and cracks it before nodding at me.

I can't see their faces very well in the darkened theater but I sense a row of smirks. Tim is oblivious to mockery and smiles proudly at his students. He's fallen for their bullshit, hook, line and sinker. He finds them hard to ignore during the movie, however. Every few minutes, one or another asks him to explain the plot. They laugh overly loudly at the jokes and make kissing noises during the love scenes. About halfway through, Alpha Teen leans forward and says,

"How do you feel about the recorder, Mr. Kennedy?" He shushes her, but moments later, she inquires, "How tall are you, Mr. Kennedy?"

"Six foot three. Now, be quiet."

I smile smugly in the darkness, but then they start whispering for my benefit.

"What's that perfume?" Shelley asks Alpha.

"It's called Outhouse," Alpha replies.

"Man, it reeks."

Somehow I manage not to rise to the bait. The fact that Tim has taken my hand gives me strength. Later, the girls simmer down and settle for pelting me with popcorn and kicking the back of the chair in a restrained way, so as not to attract Tim's attention.

I've never been so glad to see credits roll. Tim quietly suggests we give our entourage the slip and find a quiet coffee shop. I'm all for it, but when I stand to leave, my feet won't move. They're stuck to the floor and my efforts to free them tip me sideways onto Tim. He pushes me upright and stands himself. The girls have moved out into the aisle, and are standing there, snickering. My feet, it turns out, are glued to the floor with a soft drink that the Ruffians deliberately spilled behind me. A struggle reminiscent of the chicken dance finally frees me to stalk out of the theater ahead of Tim. He catches up to me in the lobby and sheepishly points to the paper napkins stuck to my shoes. The girls advance again while I'm peeling them off, but Tim stops them in their tracks with a severe "Good *night,* girls."

Realizing they've worn out their welcome, the girls disappear down Yonge Street amid much laughter. We head in the opposite direction and find a quiet café in Yorkville. Tim plucks kernels of popcorn from my hair as we sit down.

"Sorry," he says. "I seem to have to say that to you a lot."

"Well, you can't help it if you're a hit with younger women."

"They don't have your sophistication."

"True. You saw the way I handled the soft-drink-and-napkin crisis."

"Grace under pressure."

"I've had a lot of practice lately."

We order Spanish coffees and Tim is soon regaling me with stories of his work. His passion for teaching is obvious.

"You're lucky to have found your calling," I say. "Until I started writing speeches, every job I've ever had was just that— a way to pay down the Visa bill."

"And now?"

"Now, I know the fulfillment that comes of carrying designer handbags."

"Don't sell yourself short, Libby," Tim says, "you're also a great waitress. And you're not half-bad at speechwriting. At least it's something to fall back on."

"As long as I never have to teach. Those girls of yours scare the hell out of me."

"Their bark is worse than their bite," he says, smiling. Then he turns serious. "They've *had* to be tough, Libby. All of them have overcome serious problems to get where they are. Brianne, for example, was a homeless kid who I met when she was busking on Queen Street. I got her into a shelter, then into a technical school and finally she auditioned for the Youth Orchestra. You wouldn't believe how far she's come."

My God, the man is some sort of musical missionary, cruising the streets of Toronto for opportunities to change lives. He really cares about these kids. No wonder they adore him. Whereas, in my spare time, I pay Elliot to tell Me more about Me. Not that Tim is trying to make me feel small. On the contrary, he's leaning across the table and his arm is touching mine. He doesn't seem nearly as repelled by my shallowness as he should be. Clearly, I need to help him fathom my complete lack of depth.

"Tim, it's amazing the way you support these kids. I have to confess, the closest I've come to helping humanity was when I considered smothering Margo in a motel room last month— and even then, I was too lazy to follow through. All I seem to want to do on weekends is chill out and it's never occurred to me to volunteer. I guess that's pretty selfish."

"There are plenty of weekends where all I do is hang out with my dog," Tim says. "Besides, I'm sure you put a lot of energy into writing your book."

Damn that book, I curse the moment I invented it! Since we're sharing this confessional moment, I should come clean right now. But he looks so earnest and kind that I hate to disappoint him. Surely I've humbled myself enough for one night.

"Well, I haven't made a lot of progress lately…so busy…"

"That must be frustrating, when it's your creative outlet."

Why can't I be like other girls and choose flawed men who allow me to feel good about myself? Instead I'm sitting with the nicest man in the room and lying to him. Really, I'm despicable.

"How do *you* find the time to juggle so many things?" I ask.

"I'm just used to it. These days, it's only stressful when someone throws a curveball."

"Like what?"

"Well, a few months ago, one of my guys from music camp showed up at my door with a black eye and a dislocated shoulder. His mother's boyfriend has been roughing him up. My life became a series of court dates and meetings with the Children's Aid Society. It was brutal, but I'm grateful he could confide in me."

"I don't know how you handle it."

"You just do, Libby. You'd do the same if it were you."

I'd never let it stand between me and a mochaccino, that's for sure. The man refuses to accept just how frivolous I am. The same blind eye he turns on his students' bad behavior is now benefiting me. Tim's life seems terribly grown up, whereas mine is all about petty battles with Margo.

The combination of shame and Spanish coffee is bringing me down. I sit back in my seat and withdraw my arm from the table. By the time Tim drops me off at my house, I'm wondering why on earth he'd want to spend a minute with me. He's as sweet and charming as ever when we say good-night, but I jump out of his Jeep before he can kiss me—or worse, avoid kissing me. No sense in becoming too attached to a guy who's bound to see through me anyway. I'll save him the trouble of spurning me: the self-dump has long been my preferred method of saving face.

★ ★ ★

The phone is already ringing when I reach my cubicle the next morning. As I pick up, I notice that nothing is on my desk as I'd left it: Margo has been rifling through my things again.

"Hey, Lib, it's Lola. Remember Julie Redding, from journalism school?"

"How could I forget? She's the one who told me I should get my teeth done."

"Yeah, well, she told me that smoking was aging me," Lola replies.

"Smoking *is* aging you."

"And you *should* get your teeth done. Cosmetic dental work is far more advanced than when we were in college."

"When you get your first face-lift, I'll do my teeth and we can write a book about it," I suggest. "So, why are you calling?"

"To tell you that Julie has just published her second book."

"Jesus." I feel like the wind has been kicked out of me.

"I know. Her first one sucked."

"A total piece of crap."

"I paid full price for it, too," Lola adds.

"I got it out of the library, but at least you were able to deface yours."

"True. I wrote profanity in the margins and sold it to a secondhand book dealer."

"Yet they've set her loose on the page again. It's so wrong. *We* should be writing books, you know. Julie Redding has nothing on us."

"Except that she actually *does* it, instead of just talking about it, you mean."

"Exactly, but if we were to write, we'd be far better than she is."

"That goes without saying."

"So, thanks for ruining my day."

"My pleasure," Lola laughs.

When I get home, I pick up the latest compelling addition

to my woo-woo self-help library, *Write it Down, Make it Happen,* and vow to work through every exercise. I don't have a lot of hope though, because I've kept a journal for twenty years and nothing much has come of writing it all down. At least I'm consistent, having listed writing a book as my goal for the past decade.

Despite a brisk round of affirmations, I feel demoralized as I climb into bed. Talentless Julie Redding is writing books full-time whereas I'm best known for carrying someone's handbag. Furthermore, I'm dating a man who is too good for me. I should give him Julie's number.

There's been a lot of press on "sick building syndrome," but Queen's Park is probably the first case of "horny building syndrome." On my way in today, the security guard told me he's patrolling hourly, because a couple keeps coming in off the street to have sex in the women's washrooms. He's caught them in the act three times in two days. This never happened before Richard arrived. Fortunately, he won't be with us on a full-time basis or no one would get any work done. Margo just informed me that he'll be flying in from London as his schedule permits. I'm wondering if I'll get to meet him before he leaves, when Margo adds, "By the way, the Minister expects you to attend the Opera Company event tonight. Richard and I will be there, of course. It's black tie, so please make an effort."

Thanks for the advance notice, Marg. I have no choice but to resurrect Roxanne's lucky dress. To my relief it fits better than it did a month ago. With the aid of two dozen bobby pins and heavy-duty hair spray, I anchor my hair in an elaborate up-do and still make it out the door in record time.

Forty minutes later, I'm watching a soprano perform a painfully long piece. Literally. Every time she warbles the high notes, I feel an invisible stake driving into my gut. The control-top panty hose must be squeezing my spleen against my kidneys. Not that I had any choice about wearing them tonight—without them, I wouldn't have the courage to meet Richard.

The Minister finally takes the stage to address the crowd and for the first time, I'm thankful for her habit of racing through her speeches. She's had a glass or three of champagne and keeps giggling over her own (i.e., my) jokes. Fortunately, the crowd seems to find this endearing. They even laugh warmly at the reference to the Sawdust's song—not that the Minister intended this to get a laugh but I couldn't see any way to work it into the speech other than to make a gently self-deprecating joke at her own expense. I trusted that she would not read it in advance, and I was right. Her champagne consumption is an unexpected bonus. Although momentarily taken aback by the laughter, she soon joins in and when the speech is over, she floats off the stage and across the room with Richard in tow.

"Richard," she says, "I want to introduce you to Lily. She helps me prepare my speeches."

*Helps me?!*

"It's a pleasure to meet you—" he takes my hand, and I'm overcome by an urge to bury my head against his chest "—Lily."

Did he just call me Lily? Better address that right away. I don't want him screaming that into my pillow. I give myself a mental slap and release his hand.

"Hello, Richard. The name is *Libby.*"

"Libby?" he repeats, turning quizzically to the Minister.

"Will you excuse me for a moment?" she says. "I see Monique LeClerc." She leaves me alone with Richard and my burgeoning hormones.

"So," he says, "you help the Minister with her speeches."

"Uh…yes, yes I do."

What am I supposed to say? That I write every last word of them and she isn't involved in any way, other than to deliver them poorly?

"I believe I've seen you at the copy machine," he says. "You must be lining up facts for Clarice."

So he *does* think I'm the office minion. This has gone far enough.

"Actually, I've been very busy—".

"—researching and formatting the Minister's speeches," Margo interrupts smoothly, materializing with her usual stealth.

So that's it: the Minister doesn't like to admit that she never writes her own speeches. No wonder I get so many mixed messages about my job—it doesn't really exist! It's crazy. Very few Ministers write their own speeches, although now that I think about it, I believe Monique LeClerc, Minister of Recreation and friend of Mrs. Cleary, does write hers.

"Well, tonight's speech hit the mark," Richard says, "although Clarice spoke much too quickly. And the reference to that '70s song was a bit odd."

What a discerning fellow he is! My knees are buckling, so I tip half a glass of bourbon down my throat to steady myself.

"The Minister has good instincts about an audience like this," Margo pipes up again. "She offered strong direction to Libby in preparing the text."

"She did indeed, Margo," I say, smiling. "Every dosie-do-do…" The booze is going to my head and I can't resist.

Margo looks at me as though I've lost my mind, then turns abruptly to Richard and changes the subject.

"Are you a fan of the opera, Richard?"

"Not at all," he replies. "I find it exquisitely painful and attend only under duress."

I stifle a guffaw and am rewarded by a steady gaze from the most hypnotic green eyes I've ever seen. Suddenly the room feels extremely warm and I use my copy of the Minister's speech as a fan. Then, recalling that fans just move the pheromones around, I judge it safer to remove myself.

Call it women's intuition, but I sense that Richard is watching me go. While I stand at the bar waiting for my drink, I chance a look over my shoulder and sure enough, he's swiveled right around to stare at my butt! He catches my eye and has the audacity to *grin* at me! I should feel harassed, I suppose, but I'm harassed only by doubts about the quality of my rear view.

After a few casual sips of my drink, I look around a second time. Mrs. Cleary is at Richard's side, chattering up at him vivaciously, but he's looking over her head at me. I suspect he's been matching the Minister glass for glass of champagne. I have consumed more alcohol than usual myself, but there's no mistaking the expression on his face. Red alert, Libby! You got away with professional misconduct last month, but do you want to tempt fate again? You're not *that* lucky. Richard is still gazing at me and my face is flushing. If he comes over, resistance will be futile. So, I gather my strength, set my unfinished drink on the bar and head out the door. I am not too drunk to know when I'm way out of my league.

I once switched coffee brands simply because the television commercial for the one I was using featured a woman springing out of bed and singing into the rising sun with a steaming cup of coffee in her hand. The beauty of a sunrise is quite lost on me.

There are two alarm clocks on my bedside table; a third sits on the dresser across the room. I set the first clock—the one where the snooze button has taken such a beating that the first two letters have worn off—fifteen minutes fast. The second and third display the correct time. Each night, I set the first clock to wake me an hour and a half before I have to be at work. That's how long it actually takes me to shower, get dressed, blow dry my hair, put on makeup, eat breakfast and walk to Queen's Park (singing into the morning skies). I set the second clock, the backup, for thirty minutes before I need to be at work. The third alarm, the coma-buster, I set for fifteen minutes later still.

A morning in the Libby McIssac household might play out as follows.

6:30 a.m.: First alarm goes off. I hit the "ooze" button.

Though far from awake, I still register that this clock is fast and that I therefore have fifteen minutes to doze.

6:45 a.m.: Alarm rings a second time. I hit the ooze button again. I can still spare a few minutes.

7:00 a.m.: Alarm buzzes a third time. Time for some choices: breakfast can go. Hit ooze again.

7:15 a.m.: Alarm goes a fourth time. I cut it short with another press of the magic button. I don't need much time to get ready. I'm very efficient.

7:30 a.m.: Not really, it's only 7:15. Plenty of time. I feel wide awake, so I turn off the alarm. I'll just lie here for a second and collect myself.

7:30 a.m.: Real time kicks in as the second alarm clock rings. Okay, no breakfast, no makeup, my hair can air-dry during the walk. I'll rest my eyes as I plan my attack on the day.

7:45 a.m.: A quick shower will suffice. I can recoup a few minutes by taking the bus.

7:50 a.m.: Third alarm rings. Panic catapults me out of bed and across the room to silence it. My hair is more manageable dirty anyway.

The advent of Richard hasn't helped as much as one might expect, although I generally regret my failings with respect to personal grooming once the pheromones assail my nostrils.

Last week, I consulted my doctor about my lack of energy. As usual, she says there's nothing wrong with me.

"Any chance you're depressed?" she asks.

I briefly consider telling her about Margo and the Minister, about the handbags and the bouquets, about my boy troubles, about the fact that I have to stoop to walk through the doorway at Queen's Park—a building clearly constructed for the little people of the previous century. But I shake my head: better to keep that between Cornelius and me.

"Check my iron again," I say.

The truth is, I can get up when sufficiently motivated. For example, I give the ooze button a well-earned rest the following Sunday, and am stretching by the door when Lola arrives for a run. I figure I can always doze during the jog as she delivers the next in the series of Michael Monologues.

"So how's everything going with Tim?" she asks as soon as our feet are moving.

Just when I think I've got Lola's number, she surprises me. "You actually want to hear about *my* life? Is this a new technique for undermining my athletic performance?"

"Can't a friend be interested in another friend's life?"

"Sure, but you're usually not that kind of friend, Lola."

"That would probably hurt if Michael hadn't more or less killed me already."

Here we go. Michael has been treating Lola poorly from the start. One minute he's all over her, the next he virtually ignores her. I don't understand why she puts up with it. This is the woman who once dumped a guy simply because he didn't always shave before seeing her. Lola's philosophy has always been that guys are like buses—another will come along in five minutes. Yet, when Michael pulled up to her stop, she suddenly felt blessed to be offered a ride.

"So what's he done now?" I ask, planning to shift my brain into Neutral.

"It's what he *hasn't* done. He doesn't call enough and he cancels half the time because of work—or at least he *says* it's because of work. I'm starting to worry that he's seeing other women."

"Oh, Lola, when would he find the time? He didn't make millions working nine to five." But I'm wondering myself. It's so early in the relationship.

"I guess you're right, but it's depressing. How about distracting me with the details of your movie night with Tim?"

"Distraction I can provide," I say, recounting the story of Tim's students at the theater.

"He sounds interested to me. Tim's a good guy."

"He *is* a good guy. Too good."

"Bad boys have never been your thing, Lib. I'm the one who likes an air of mystery. Even now, I find it sort of sexy that I can't figure Michael out. It's that 'dangerous guy' appeal."

"He's a computer whiz, Lola, not a secret agent."

"Don't let the geeky exterior fool you. The man is complicated."

"You can keep your men of mystery, Agatha, I like to know where I stand with a guy. I can't see why Tim isn't pursuing someone as serious about life as he is."

"You'd be surprised how many men find superficial woman appealing," Lola says grinning. "It makes them feel good about themselves."

"Lola!"

"I'm kidding, Libby, lighten up. You may not be deep, but you're usually fun. Why else would I bother with you?"

We're passing Dooney's and Jeff, Master of the Mochaccino, waves from the window. Lola grabs my arm and pulls me toward the door.

"Enough of this foolishness, Libby. I declare this run officially over!"

"We've barely started," I protest, but only enough to appear the more dedicated runner.

Lola flops into a chair and reaches into her new sports bra to produce her emergency cash. "We've both had a rough week," she says. "Coffee's on me."

A few minutes later, Jeff sets two bowls of nonfat mochaccino with extra whipping cream in front of us. Then he pulls a pack of cigarettes from his pocket, hands one to Lola and lights it for her.

"You are *so* getting a tip," she says, smiling appreciatively at him.

If Jeff had a tail, it would be wagging. This is the effect Lola usually has on guys.

"You are *so* getting a fine from the antismoking police," I tell him. Smoking is banned in Toronto restaurants.

"You're the first customers of the day," Jeff says. "She'll be finished before anyone else comes in. Smoke fast, beautiful!"

After Jeff is out of earshot, Lola says, "Obviously, it's only Michael who's immune to my charms."

"This is how most of us feel early in a relationship, Lola. You're usually spared the agonies of doubt common people experience. Some of us even exaggerate our assets to impress the object of our affections."

"Stuffing your bra again?" she says, drawing the last of the smoke into her lungs and stubbing the cigarette out in the espresso cup Jeff delivered for that purpose. "Or is the lie a little bigger?"

"It started off as a joke," I explain. "When we met at Emma's wedding, I was embarrassed about my lame government job, so I told Tim I was writing a book about my experience with weddings. I didn't realize he believed me until I saw him at a Ministry event, where I was carrying the Minister's purse and flowers."

"And you didn't confess because you wanted to look like you've got a lot going on in your life."

"Exactly." I thought Lola might understand. She's been known to stretch the truth herself on occasion. "Look, please don't tell Emma, I feel like an idiot. Now I've left it so long it's going to be humiliating to admit the truth to Tim."

"Maybe you don't have to confess to Tim that you *aren't* writing a book about weddings."

"Please don't tell me I *should* write a book about weddings."

"Actually, I think *we* should write a book about weddings."

"Because we're such experts in the field?"

"Remember the column I wrote for *Toronto Lives* last month, 'The Anatomy of a Modern Wedding'? A publisher left me a message asking if I'd be interested in writing a book about the Canadian wedding in the new millennium. I didn't even return the call, but maybe it's not so ridiculous an idea if we tackle it together. I don't want to be a copy editor forever and I suspect you want to do more than put words in Clarice Cleary's mouth."

"I don't know, Lola. The only one who hates weddings as much as I do is you."

"Look, it's a start. Once we've proven ourselves, we can move on to more exciting projects."

"But I want to write about something I enjoy. There's nothing enjoyable about a wedding."

"What about the free food and booze?"

"I get that at work. Besides, even if we could suspend our disbelief about the subject, do you really think we could work together? Let's be honest, Lola, we're competitive. Aren't you afraid we'll kill each other?"

"Aren't you afraid that Julie Redding is at a book-signing this very moment?"

I pause to picture Julie autographing a big stack of books at Indigo. "Well…as long as we're competing with Julie and not each other, I guess it would be okay. What the hell, why not?"

We order another mochaccino to toast our new partnership, as well as a slab of chocolate cheesecake. Halfway through the cake, I'm already having regrets about my impulsiveness. How am I going to work with Lola? Worse, how am I ever going to take the subject as seriously as the publisher will? I have wedding issues and the fact that some of my friends are already undoing their "I do's" has done little to diminish my cynicism. Leanne, for example, married last May and was separated by December. What became of my tasteful wedding gift? Why, it's ensconced in Leanne's smart condo, which was in turn financed by cash wedding gifts. It's not like I want the ceramic bowl back, nor the hand mixer from the kitchen shower, nor the gardening set from the Jack and Jill. What I want—*what I deserve*—is an antishower where people bring gifts to celebrate my single status.

Lola waves at me and asks, "You're not chickening out on me, are you?"

"No, but I'm indulging in some mental nuptial bashing. I was thinking about how much I resent dishing out wedding gifts. 'My turn' may never come and I still have to eat, drink, sleep and entertain in my home. I deserve some nice things, too, damn it!"

"Hear! Hear! I could tell the publisher that we want to write a book that encourages single women to celebrate single bliss through antiwedding events."

"Yeah! It's time to avenge those $120 designer bowls, to demand payback for every wineglass that cost you more than you'd spend on an entire set for yourself. We could call it *The Counterfeit Wedding: A Guide for the Thoroughly Modern Spinster.*"

Since it's nearly noon, we call Jeff over and order Irish coffees.

"We'll take Martha Stewart's lead and offer step-by-step instructions for holding the Counterfeit Wedding," Lola continues. "It's a matter of turning the traditional wedding script on its ear and adapting it to fit our unique premise."

"Naturally, we'll start with a chapter on engagement," I jump in, "including advice on proposing to oneself and a thorough discussion of self-love." At this, Jeff's ears perk up. "Of the spiritual variety," I assure him, turning back to Lola. "Let's come out of the gate with a 'single and proud' message. What's so bad about being able to do what you want when you want and spending every cent you earn on yourself?"

"Right on, sister! Those surveys we run in *Toronto Lives* always show that single women report being happier than both married women and single men."

"I think we'd get plenty of support. Most people can do the math around how much single women fork over in gifts through the years." I illustrate the basic calculation on a napkin. "Volume of friends/colleagues/acquaintances/relatives times two shower gifts @ $40 plus one stagette @ $40 plus one wedding gift @ $120. And if you're part of the wedding party, add several hundred more for bridesmaid dresses, additional shower gifts and gift upgrades."

"Libby, this is so bent. It's politically incorrect, it's offensive...what's not to like?"

"Let me write the bridesmaid chapter. I have dresses in every shade of pastel and every style from 'wench' to 'toga.' Hey, let's wear them for book-signings."

Lola checks the clock and leaps to her feet. "Shit, I've gotta go! Michael is taking me to Storm for dinner and I'm getting my hair done to look spectacular." She hands her bra money to me and asks me to take care of the bill.

"Say hi to Huggy Bear for me—my dad is still talking about him!" I call after Lola as she sprints toward the door.

Back at my apartment, I check my voice mail, hoping against fading hope for a message from Tim. There's nothing, so I climb into the shower, dejected. Although Richard has been a welcome diversion in the office, Tim is in the realm of the real and I like him. I've checked my messages five times a day since I saw him last week. But it's probably time to face the facts: it's Sunday afternoon, and if he were going to call, he'd have done it by now.

By way of distraction, I flick on the computer and fire off an e-mail to Lola:

To: Romanobean@torlives.ca
From: Mclib@hotmail.ca
Subject: The Announcement

Lola,

For reasons that shall remain nameless (Tim), I'm still pondering The Counterfeit Wedding. In Chapter 2, Sally NoSpouse, our heroine, could proclaim to her community that she loves the single life. Okay, so maybe she doesn't love it, but she knows she's a hell of a lot happier than a lot of her married friends. She's committed to getting on with her life and getting the most out of it, man or no music teacher. We'll walk her through taking out a classified ad in the local paper, hiring a blimp or even renting the pixel board at the SkyDome—whatever it takes to get her message out there! Some sample announcements:

*Ms. Sally NoSpouse wishes to announce that she is joyfully flying solo. She will not be wedded to Mr. Almost Right anytime soon.*

*She is not dysfunctional, nor is she suffering from commitment issues.
And no, she's not a lesbian (not that there's anything wrong with that).*

Or the blimp-size,
*I'm single...get over it.*

The possibilities for this book are endless, Lola. We'll be hailed as the champions of the unattached underdog, supporters of single women everywhere to celebrate the power of one!
Who needs men, anyway?
Lib

P.S. How was your date with Michael?

## 18

With Tim seemingly out of the picture, I've decided to dust off my fishing pole. I even cut short my morning ritual by several presses of the "ooze" button, simply to have time to polish my lures. I'm wearing the lowest-cut blouse I own—hardly risqué, but a little daring for the civil service—as well as my favorite black skirt and knee-high boots.

At my desk, I apply lip gloss, grab an empty water bottle as a prop, and sail off to the water cooler, a course that takes me past Richard's office. I slow down to dangle the bait as I troll by his doorway. He looks up from his desk, sees me, then looks back at his work without so much as a nibble. No "good morning," no smile, no glimmer of recognition. I'm clearly using the wrong lure. Strange, because these boots rarely fail. Sure, they bring me up to six-five, but Richard has an inch on that. Did I imagine interest last Friday night? I could have sworn he was giving me the eye.

Demoralized, I clip back to my desk. The boots are already killing me, but maybe I can take advantage of the added height by menacing Margo a bit.

★ ★ ★

My forehead almost crashes into the keyboard as I input the Minister's revisions to Wiggy's latest speech. This is by far the dullest thing Wiggy has ever produced and not something I should be tackling with only three extra snoozes this morning. I make a mental note to ask Laurie to ply the audience with coffee in advance of the Minister's speech at the Textile Museum.

Desperate for a diversion, I log on to my e-mail.

To: Mclib@hotmail.ca
From: Romanobean@torlives.ca
Subject: The Announcement

Lib,

My date with Michael was so good it ended only an hour ago! I may not need to host a Counterfeit Wedding after all. But don't worry, I'm still sympathetic to the cause. There are plenty of women out there like you, who have trouble hanging on to a man. I've even come up with an idea for your invitation:

*Together with her disappointed parents,*
*Miss Elizabeth Anne McIssac (yes, still single)*
*Requests the honor of your presence (and we do mean presents)*
*On...*
*Regrets will definitely not be accepted*
*Nor will donations to the Society for the Prevention of Cruelty to Spinsters.*
*Ludicrously expensive gifts, however, are most welcome.*

Libby, this is so much fun. What do you think about serving each guest a nuked Lean Cuisine dinner for one?
Your co-author in crimes against the traditional wedding,
Lola

*There are plenty of women out there like you, who have trouble hanging on to a man.* That, dear Lola, is because some of us consider a choke hold inelegant. Seems like every time I let my guard down with that woman, she takes a shot at me. How can I write a book with her? I should call right now and tell her I've had a change of heart. Picking up the phone, I punch in the first few digits of Lola's number, then hesitate. She's a pain in the ass, all right, but this is still a good opportunity to get published. I dial my voice mail instead.

BEEP—"Hi, Libby, it's Tim. It's Sunday afternoon and I thought you'd be home working on your book. I meant to call sooner but it's been a crazy week. Listen, I'd love to take you for dinner Friday night if you're free. I know the perfect place— the food's amazing, the bar has good bourbon and best of all, none of my students can afford it! Let me know."

BEEP—"Hi, Flower Girl, it's Elliot on Monday morning and I want to say I'm picking up some very interesting vibes about you. I could swear you're off your rock again without my consent. Have fun, but absolutely no pickup trucks. You have way too much class for that—and if you don't I'm ashamed for you. Let's get together. Günther's band is going on a six-city tour next week—in a tacky little van, if you can believe it, which leaves me alone, boo-hoo, but available to my devoted clients and—" Click.

BEEP—"Libby, we discussed this answering service. I cannot communicate all I need to in three minutes. By the way, are you wearing your boots right now? You feel extra-tall today—and extra-sexy. I'd do you myself if it weren't for that unfortunate second X chromosome of yours. Call me, doll."

I go back and listen to Tim's message twice, check the time it was sent, and save it for my future listening pleasure. He must have called while I was in the shower yesterday. I dial his number and leave a message accepting his dinner invitation. If all goes well when Lola contacts the publisher this week, I may not even have to lie to him about writing a book.

"There's a meeting in two minutes and your presence is requested."

I look up to see Laurie standing at my cubicle "door." "Requested by whom?"

"Margo wants the entire staff in the boardroom, pronto."

"What now?" I sigh, getting up and following Laurie down the hall.

Five minutes later, I am standing with Laurie at the back of the boardroom as Margo lectures us about the new office rules.

"The Minister would like to instill the office with a more *formal* atmosphere. She asks that everyone stand as she enters a room and wait to be seated until she is seated herself. Then, as she leaves the room, all will rise again."

"You've got to be kidding." The words are out of my mouth before I can stop them. My filtering device must have shorted out.

"Have you known me to kid, Libby?"

Come to think of it, never.

I have a chance to experience the new formality within hours. I'm in the front passenger seat beside Bill, waiting for Margo and the Minister. Mrs. Cleary is scheduled to open the new Power Plant Gallery installation today. When they finally emerge, Margo opens the door, then closes it again abruptly when the Minister, still standing outside the vehicle, mutters something in her ear. Margo steps over to my window. Glancing dubiously at Bill, I roll it down.

"What's wrong?"

"The Minister wants you and Bill to get out of the car while she gets in."

"Pardon me?"

"You heard me, Libby," she snaps. "Remember the new formality."

I lean toward Bill, whispering, "Wasn't there an HBO special about the royal family this weekend?"

We both climb out of the car and close the doors. The Minister declines to meet my eyes as she slides into the back seat. Bill closes the door gently and we get back in.

Unbelievable.

When we return to Queen's Park, Bill cuts the engine and we disembark while the Minister remains seated in the back with Margo. Bill opens her door and she sweeps past me without acknowledgment. Margo emerges a second later and informs me that the Minister would like to see me right away. Muttering obscenities about the "new formality," I follow the trail of perfume through the hallways.

"Yes, come in Lily," the Minister says as I arrive at the door. My butt is already halfway into the leather chair when she adds, "You may sit down." I spring back up again and then settle back into the chair, as if for the first time. "I'll get straight to the point. What did you think of this?"

She's holding Christine's latest speech, the one I revised earlier. Fearing this is a test to find out whether I'm willing to bad-mouth a fellow writer, I play it safe.

"Well, it's not the most dynamic speech you've delivered, Minister, but textiles aren't a very lively subject."

"The speech is duller than the complexion of a woman who doesn't exfoliate. Have you noticed Christine's face?" Not being an exfoliator myself, I remain silent. "Very dull, indeed, Lily. However, her dullness is well-timed. I want to become more 'hands-on' with my speeches. I could spice them up by adding personal anecdotes."

She seems to think the personal anecdotes are her idea, but I'm so chuffed she's consulting with me at all that I don't mind. I want to encourage her to confide in me.

"Casual ad-libbing could add some interest to this speech, Minister."

"I knew I could count on your support, Lily."

Bill and I are lounging in the car when the Minister emerges from Queen's Park. We wait until the last possible second, and then hoist ourselves from the car while she takes her place in the back seat. We're off to the Textile Museum and I'm nervous. I can't imagine what the Minister plans to add to her speech by way of personal anecdotes, but perhaps she knows more about the textile arts than I do. During the drive, I offer to rehearse with her, but Margo promptly reminds me that I should not address the Minister unless she addresses me first. I hazard an uninvited glance over my shoulder to find the Minister gazing out the window and smiling.

I'm disappointed at the small turnout at the museum—until I hear the Minister deliver her speech, that is. And I do mean, *her* speech: Wiggy's words have all but disappeared. They were boring, yes, but at least they made sense and drew a link to the Ministry's work. The Minister, on the other hand, is rambling on disjointedly about textiles in the fashion industry. In fact, it appears she's speaking on the fascinating subject of "dresses I have owned and loved." And—wait for it—there's a nugget of wisdom people can take away: "As I always say, Lycra is a woman's best friend." The audience responds with a polite chuckle.

Praying that she won't ask for my opinion on the speech, I head over to the Minister to surrender her purse.

"Well, Lily, I'm not one to toot my own horn, but I must say, I saved that speech! The audience *loved* it. Just think, if it weren't for your encouragement, I might not have attempted this. I must do it more often!"

I am wracked with the kind of guilt and worry that only a trip to the refreshment table can cure.

I've just discovered something else to like about Tim—the man knows a good restaurant. As I savor the last bite of his white-chocolate mousse cake, I tell him so.

"I'm glad you were able to make it," he replies. "After the trouble I had with some students last weekend, I needed something to look forward to."

"Don't tell me Mr. Kennedy has bad days."

"Occasionally. It builds character."

"More character you don't need. What did they do this time?"

"Three boys in the orchestra got their hands on a bottle of vodka and after our concert at Nathan Phillips Square Saturday night, they got shit-faced on public property."

"Oh no."

"A couple of police officers patrolled the area as Curly, Larry and Moe got into a pissing contest—literally—against the Mayor's reelection banner. They were hauled in for drinking underage and destroying public property. Naturally, they called me and it took me the rest of the night to convince the cops to drop the charges and release them."

And I've been having such a good time up till now. Any minute he'll ask what I did last weekend and I'll have to conceal that I spent most of it bone idle, worrying about whether he'd call.

"I'd never have the patience to work with teenagers," I say, suddenly glum.

"Libby, relax. I didn't tell that story to prove I'm a long-suffering saint. Besides, you've already confessed your dark secret to me." I must have a puzzled expression on my face because he says, "You know, the one about how you like to take it easy on the weekend?" Oh, that dark secret. "I want you to know that I've thought a lot about that."

His tone is unexpectedly serious and my mouth suddenly dries out. If there's one thing I've acquired from my vast collection of self-help books, it's finely-tuned intuition. It's so obvious: Tim has invited me out tonight with the sole purpose of dumping me face-to-face. Which is more evidence of his excellent character, because a phone dump is quite acceptable after only two dates. He's leaning across the table now and I sense the bullet hurtling toward me.

"Am I coming across as some boring martyr, Libby?"

"Boring, definitely not," I reply, taken aback. "But I do have this vision of you combing the streets of Toronto searching for youths to save."

"That's unfair. I also search out seniors and indigents. There aren't enough lost youth in this city to keep me challenged." Tim's eyes are twinkling with mischief.

"All I am saying is, your heroic tendencies could make *some* people—not me, of course—feel a little unworthy."

"That's crazy. I'm just following my own interests and doing what I like to do. At any rate, I certainly don't want anyone else—particularly speechwriters entirely lacking a social conscience—to feel bad about how they spend their time."

"Don't knock the life of the morally depraved until you've tried it, pal. You could use a rest from your mission work."

"I'd love to lighten up a little. Maybe you could give the teacher a lesson or two on relaxing?"

He's taken my hand and for a second I wonder if my sleeve has caught fire on the candle, because I feel heat racing up my arm. Obviously my intuition needs tweaking.

"Anyway, Lib," he continues as we leave the restaurant and stroll down the street, "I don't know how you can comment on my patience when you put up with Clarice and Margo all week."

"Margo has never locked me in a Porta Potti. Mind you, I do spend a lot of time in the ladies' room with Mrs. Cleary."

"I suppose those purses you haul around contain a lot of makeup?"

"Bingo."

"Just think of the muscle mass you're acquiring," he says. "I guess you need it for taking out the competition when you're fighting for bridesmaid bouquets."

"Or taking on music teachers," I counter, flexing my biceps.

"I dare you to try," he says, slipping an arm around me.

"Tough talk for a man who waves a baton for a living. By the way, I've been meaning to ask you, do the white socks you wear while conducting keep you grounded?"

"I don't know what you're talking about," he says, but a slightly defiant grin suggests otherwise.

"I'd be talking about the white athletic socks you wore with a black suit at Rideau Hall last month."

"How much bourbon did you have tonight?"

"I know what I saw."

"Look, it was that or nothing. I only had a few minutes to pack for the trip and I forgot my black socks."

"Let me guess: you were at a 'save the whales' fund-raiser and rushed home with seconds to spare before taking on further good works." What the hell, if you can't join 'em, beat on 'em.

"Actually, I was shooting hoops with the guys."

"More likely you were tied to a frog during a standoff with developers over the Rouge Valley Marshland."

"Listen up, Miss I-Don't-Do-Charity," Tim says as he hails a cab, "if you have a problem with my attire, maybe you should volunteer to help single guys dress." He pulls open the door of the taxi, then adds, "Or undress."

"Where to?" the cabbie asks.

Tim gives the driver his Harbourfront address, then looks at me questioningly. "But we might stop in the Annex first."

"Are you crazy?" I say. "There's a five-dollar charge for extra stops—it says so on the guy's rate card. Think about the people you could help with that money." I tell the driver to head straight to Harbourfront. "Don't worry," I reassure Tim. "We'll give the cash to a good cause."

## 19

I awake to the muffled clattering of pots and pans and wonder for a moment where I am. Then I notice the covers thrown back on the other side of the bed and panic swells in my chest. What possessed me to commandeer that cab last night? I practically threw myself at Tim! And on our third date, too. I'm a god-damned cliché. Soon the clattering downstairs stops and the smell of pancakes wafts into the room. He's cooking breakfast for me.

Before I can ponder a discreet exit out the window, some-thing brown and white streaks into the room and lands square on my chest—a very fat, very exuberant Jack Russell terrier. She licks my face, throws herself onto her back, jumps up and licks my face again in an abasement of joy. I laugh in spite of myself.

"Get down," I say and she promptly rolls onto her back again. Then she seizes the sheet I'm clutching to my chest and starts pulling. This isn't the well-trained canine I expected of "dog trainer" Tim. Maybe I'm not the only one who lied at Emma's wedding.

There will be no peace here, I quickly surmise, and get out of bed. The dog bounds around as I retrieve my clothes from various points in the room. Steps ahead of me, she seizes my bra and races out of the room trailing it behind her. She's flattering herself: that Jack Russell is no 36B. I'm not about to chase her naked, however, so I head to the en suite bathroom and climb into the shower. A few minutes later, the foggy shower doors reveal a small, spotted missile leaping repeatedly into the air and scratching the doors on the way down. I left the bathroom door ajar in case she wanted to bring the bra back, but there's no sign of it as I emerge. She launches herself against my bare legs. Yelping myself, I struggle to towel dry my hair and get dressed while fighting interference. Then I rummage in Tim's medicine cabinet for toothpaste and scrub my teeth with my index finger—the worst aspect of the morning-after "walk of shame."

I'm about to head downstairs to join Tim when I notice the framed photographs on his dresser. Although it feels like spying, I examine the pictures of Tim with friends, family and students. There's a black-and-white of a beautiful woman tucked way in the back. This must be the ex who moved to Vancouver. Fair and petite—everything I am not. It looks like the Hospital for Sick Children in the background. I expect she volunteered there while earning her many degrees. Beautiful, brainy and selfless...he's probably still in love with her.

"Good morning!" Tim says, as I enter the kitchen. He hugs me and sets a bottle of maple syrup on the kitchen table. "There's fresh coffee brewing and blueberry pancakes in the oven. I hope you're hungry."

"Always," I say, managing a weak smile.

Actually, my stomach is in knots, but he went to such trouble that I sit down and work my way through a couple of pancakes and mug of coffee. I can't shake the uneasy feeling I had when I awoke; seeing Florence Nightingale's photo on his dresser only made it worse. I don't belong here, having Tim fuss over me like this.

We make small talk about the weather and current events.

Tim pours far too much syrup on his pancakes and keeps reaching for the coffee to fill our mugs. He must be as uncomfortable as I am. Nevertheless, after breakfast he suggests we go for a walk. I decline, saying I need to head into the office to work on a speech I promised for Monday. When he reaches for his car keys, I insist on taking a cab. I know I'm being an idiot but I've already hurled myself over that particular cliff and there's no clawing my way back. I can't tell if Tim is confused, or angry—or relieved.

"Where's the dog?" I ask, jiggling in all my B-cup glory toward the front door.

"Around here somewhere, why?"

"She's purloined something of mine."

He heads into the living room calling "Stella" and returns holding the remains of my bra.

"I'm so sorry. She's usually so good."

"No problem," I assure him, trying to smile. "Really."

Stella, having partaken of my special "date" bra, a lacy hundred-dollar confection, wags her stump of a tail furiously and smiles.

Margo is right about one thing: I am a cat person.

In the sanctity of my apartment, I feed Cornelius before picking up the phone to dial Roxanne's hotel on the Isle of Man.

"Hello?"

"Help."

"Uh-oh, what have you done this time?"

"How do you know I've done something? Maybe somebody's done something to me."

"You'd have e-mailed if *you'd* been wronged, so let's have it. What happened with Tim?"

"Who said anything about Tim?"

"Your last e-mail said you were seeing him for dinner last night and now you're upset. Call me Sherlock."

"I went home with him."

"So what?"

"Whattaya mean, 'so what'? I slept with Tim Kennedy!"

"If it's shock you're after, maybe you should tell Marjory and Reg instead. What's the big deal? It was your third date and you know what they say…"

"Yes, I know what they say." I hear the brittle edge to my voice and scale back my annoyance a notch; Roxanne isn't Lola. "The big deal is, he's too good for me, he isn't over his beautiful ex-girlfriend yet—he still has her picture on his dresser—and I practically threw myself at him!"

"First, just because he teaches and volunteers doesn't mean he's too good for you. Second, how do you know the picture was of his ex? And third, what do you mean you threw yourself at him?"

"After we left the restaurant, I *demanded* that the cabdriver take us to Tim's."

"And Tim was trussed up in the trunk?"

"Well, no."

"But he was fighting you off and screaming for help?"

"Not exactly."

"In the morning, he practically pushed you out?"

"He made me pancakes, actually."

"He called Aunt Jemima in to help… You're right, he definitely wanted you outta there."

"Maybe he feels guilty for using me to get over his ex. Or maybe it's a crusade to enlist me to help my fellow man."

"There was only one man he was interested in helping last night—and that's Tim."

"Yeah, for all you know, he was playing subliminal recruitment tapes while I slept. Anyway, the guy was clearly uncomfortable with me this morning."

"The guy was uncomfortable because you clearly wanted to bolt from his home after having sex with him. Personally, I think you're afraid to get too close because he might just be *The One.*"

"The sea air is corroding your brain. How can you, of all people, talk to me about soul mates?"

"It doesn't matter that my longest relationship can be measured in seconds, because we're talking about you here. You're destined to settle down."

"Please."

"If you won't listen to me, why don't you seek psychic counsel?"

"I already called Elliot. We're getting together next week."

"I look forward to hearing what he says."

"He'll agree that you're off your rocker."

"Listen, Lib," Rox says, suddenly serious. "Whatever you do, treat Tim decently—for the sake of your relationship with Emma and Bob, at the very least. Don't back yourself into a corner here."

I hang up the phone and am still standing beside it pondering Roxanne's words when it rings. I check my call display and see it's Tim's number. Already? It's only been two hours! Since I haven't prepared my apology for my hasty retreat, I let the machine pick up. I'll call a bit later, when I've calmed down.

By the end of the weekend, however, Tim has left three messages and I haven't returned his calls. The real mistake was avoiding his first call and allowing this to become a big deal. Now I'm both awkward and ashamed of my adolescent behavior.

This might be the corner Roxanne mentioned.

I unlock my snack drawer and reach for the new bag of fruit creams. I've been trying to write the Minister's speech to promote Club 3:30, another new arts initiative where volunteer instructors will lead sessions at high schools on everything from dance to glassblowing to fashion design. Unfortunately, writing about schools just reminds me of Tim and my inexcusable behavior. These cookies are medicinal: boosting my serotonin levels will help me relax.

I'm hoisting a third cookie into my mouth when Margo appears. No doubt she heard the padlock snap open from down the hall.

"Hard at work, I see," she says, eyeing the cookie.

"You can't rush genius." I make a show of savoring every bite.

"I'll need the Club 3:30 speech on my desk by early afternoon." She appears to be speaking directly to the bag of cookies, which is sitting, open and inviting, on my desk.

"You'll have it by two." I pluck the last cookie from the row and pop it, whole, into my mouth. Then I slide the remaining biscuits into the package and make a big show of resealing it. I look up at Margo as if surprised she's still there. "I guess I'd better get back to work then," I mumble through a fine mist of cookie dust.

Messing with Margo's head has revived me more than the sugar.

Message number four from Tim is charm personified. It's Tuesday and he's concerned that he hasn't heard from me. Is everything okay? Surely shopping for a new bra couldn't be taking up so much time that I can't call him back?

What I'm experiencing is beyond shame. I am a horrible person. And yet, I still feel the two walls of my corner firmly behind me. So I calculate carefully and call.

"Hi, Tim, it's Libby. Thought you might be in by now. Sorry I haven't gotten back to you sooner. It's been *crazy* here in the office. I have all these speeches to write, but so many events scheduled I'm hardly ever at my desk. Anyway, I honestly don't mind about the bra—I'm glad Stella enjoyed it. I'd have given it to her if I weren't afraid you'd get laughed out of the dog park. Okay, I've gotta run to a meeting with Margo—wish me luck. I'll call you again when I get a chance. Thanks for a great time Friday."

There. Just the right mix of breezy, busy career woman and friendly pal. I think. Well, I'd rather not think about it because

I still feel guilty. What would Marjory, the nicest woman in the world, have to say about this?

"Lily, I think you're going to enjoy the changes I made to your speech." The Minister deigns to address me as I stand at attention beside the car.

Recalling how the Minister enhanced Wiggy's speech for the Textile Museum, I'm filled with dread. We're heading off to Central Tech, the first—and roughest—of the high schools to receive the new Club 3:30 program. This audience won't be nearly as charitable as the patrons of the museum were.

"What are you planning to add?" I ask anxiously as Bill pulls into traffic.

"Don't worry, I haven't changed the substance of the speech. I've just included some personal anecdotes."

"I'd love to hear them," I say, hoping to limit the damage.

"Well, I hate to spoil the surprise for you, but all right. I'm going to tell the kids about being the captain of my high-school Fun Squad."

*Fun Squad?* The students will write Mrs. Cleary off as a dinosaur! Her Fun Squad memories have nothing to do with this new program and she could discourage kids from participating by making it seem lame by association. I must subtly dissuade her, because Margo clearly doesn't intend to.

"Good idea, Minister, but keep in mind that the school asked us to keep the speech short. It's hard to hold a teen's attention these days—we're dealing with the sound bite generation, you know. I timed the speech at exactly eight minutes, which is the maximum this audience could stand."

"If I see that the kids are getting bored, I'll trim a little from the speech. Trust me, they're going to love this!"

I stand at the side of the auditorium, watching the kids file in for the assembly. They look like a pretty tough crew and I'd bet a bottle of Maker's Mark that none would ever consider participating in anything resembling a fun squad. It would be a shame if the Minister lost them today, because Club 3:30 is a good program.

The principal is introducing the Minister now and I hold my breath. Please don't let her wing this....

"Good afternoon, everyone. My name is Clarice Cleary and I am the Minister of Culture for the Government of Ontario. I'm here today to introduce a program I'm very excited about."

So far, she's sticking to the script. As she continues to read the words I penned, I start to breathe again. The kids look moderately interested, although one girl in the third row is applying makeup and two others are checking their cell phone messages.

"—my days as leader of the Fun Squad."

Huh? I let my attention wander for a moment and there it is. The kids are already sneering.

"I wish I had a program like this when I was young, but at least I had the Fun Squad. We spent so many wonderful hours organizing bake sales and raffles to raise funds for club sweaters. This may not be your *bag* today, but you will never regret participating in the Club 3:30 after-school arts program. I urge you to get involved and pursue your interests, whether you play a little tune, create an objet d'art or move those feet to the beat. To conclude, I've invented my own Fun Squad cheer: *Listen up all you kids in the 'hood! After-school arts is so 'baaad' it's good!*"

Her arms are at shoulder level in an apparent attempt to bust a hip-hop move—in her Jackie O suit. This is way beyond lame. My face burns for her. Margo, too, is scarlet with embarrassment.

The kids are pissing themselves laughing. The Minister leaves the stage looking dead pleased with herself because she actually thinks they're laughing *with* her!

"Hi, Miss McIssac!" Where have I heard this singsong falsetto before? I turn to see several of Tim's ruffian orchestra members.

"Didn't you say you're the Minister's *speechwriter?*" Alpha Teen asks.

"Nice speech, Miss: it was really baaaad!" Cue the sniggering.

"Tiffany! Come and meet the Minister's speechwriter!"

"Hey, no way! What brings you to our *'hood?*"

I have to admit that Tiffany is doing a pretty good imitation of Mrs. Cleary's pathetic dance move.

"Were you in the glee club too, Miss McIssac?"

"The tallest member in glee club history!"

"That's probably where she learned to play the recorder!"

More laughter. I haven't had a chance to get a word in edgewise.

"It was the Fun Squad, not the glee club," I finally squawk and before I can think of a witty follow-up, the Minister rushes past with Margo on her heels.

"The Minister needs to freshen up, Libby. Stop your chatting and bring her purse."

My humiliation is now complete.

The girls call after me.

"Hurry up with that purse, Miss McIssac!"

"You're *bad,* Miss McIssac, the Minister needs to freshen up *now.*"

"Write a speech about that, why dontcha?"

I want to die, I want to die, I want to die.

The Minister is still on a high when we return to Queen's Park.

"Well, Lily, I really reached those kids today, didn't I? I told you my speech wouldn't bore them. I hope you see how effective a personal touch can be."

What can I say? If I tell her that they think she's totally out of touch, she'll never ask my opinion again. On the other hand, it's my job to make her look good and it wouldn't be fair to let her continue delivering speeches like this when I know she's falling well short of the mark. Speak truth to power is thy motto, Libby. She'll thank you for it later.

"Yes, Minister, they ate it up."

I'll call the hospital tomorrow to schedule another spine transplant.

★ ★ ★

I visit Indigo on my way home to do some preliminary research for the book project. Lola's publisher contact has suggested we pull together an outline. Feeling like a fraud, I take up residence in the wedding-book aisle and am flipping through *A Tiffany Wedding* when a deep voice asks, "Are you getting married?"

Startled, I drop the book and look up to find Richard smiling flirtatiously at me. "No," I reply with more force than necessary. "It's an engagement gift for a friend."

He says he's staying down the street at the Sutton Place Hotel and comes here when he's bored at night. He takes one of the books from the stack under his arm and holds out: "Look at this one: *Timepieces*. I have a thing for watches."

I take it and flip through it: "So many gorgeous watches... Let's see yours."

He holds out his wrist and I examine his watch: a Cartier. It appears to be solid gold.

"Now you show me yours," he says, with the merest trace of a leer.

"Not in public," I reply playfully, putting my hand behind me. He takes my wrist and looks at my Seiko. I didn't even know it was a Cartier knockoff until I saw his.

"Clarice isn't paying you enough for the real thing?" he jokes, still holding on to my wrist.

"There's no Cartier in my future—not on a bureaucrat's salary."

"Well, you never know—depends on who you're marrying," he says, pointing to *A Tiffany Wedding,* which lies where I dropped it. "So, how do you like working for Clarice?"

"She's quite easy to write for," I offer tactfully, recovering my hand.

It's more or less true, but thank God Richard didn't hear the school speech today. He wouldn't be impressed by my talents—and I do want to impress him. I search my memory for tips from

*Flirt Now, Marry Later* and come up with, "always be the first to leave." Well, that I can do.

"My faux Cartier tells me it's time to be going," I say.

He insists on walking me to the cash, which means I feel obliged to buy the damned *A Tiffany Wedding*. An early birthday gift for Lola.

There's a spring in my step as I walk home. Something about Richard makes me want to lay down my arms and collapse into his. I'm unsettled by his overt sexuality, but thrilled by it at the same time. It must be the appeal of the dangerous man that Lola talks about. Compared to Richard, Tim seems very tame. Sure, he's funny, and nice and cute, but he's a little...*vanilla:* pleasant and homey, but boring. It's a Ben & Jerry's world out there and I'm eager to sink my teeth into an exotic flavor like Richard Nealeapolitan.

This feels like the beginning of a serious crush. I christen it with a stop at a bookstore closer to home, where I pick up a helpful tome called, *Why Men Don't Listen and Women Can't Read Maps.* Learning more about how Richard's mind works might allow me to court him more effectively. While I'm there, I also buy an exercise video to help me tone and a yoga tape to keep me calm.

To: Roxnrhead@interlog.ca
From: Mclib@hotmail.ca
Subject: Hot Stuff

Hi Rox,

Thanks for the pep talk the other day, but I don't think Tim is my type. It would seem that my type is dangerous after all—or at least big, British and brazen. Richard Neale is the new consultant I mentioned and let me tell you, this guy is the business. Last night, I bumped into him at Indigo, and sparks were flying all over the place. They ignited a major crush.

He was supposed to be in the office today but didn't show up. Which is annoying because I actually went to the trouble of washing my hair on an "off" day simply for the sake of looking desirable. I resented having the effort go to waste. Just the same, I think I'll give myself a hot oil conditioning treatment tonight. It's an investment of only $3—no grand statement.

I know what you're thinking, Rox—that for me, no crush is official until the spending spree begins. You've seen it all before and you know I'm gearing up for a full-on beauty assault. It starts with a trifling $3 investment. Next, I'm throwing good money after bad in a frenzied effort to look young and attractive. But I've grown, Rox, I've learned from past mistakes and I promise I'll take it easy. I've got a drawer full of sexy lingerie I've never worn to remind me if I falter.

Just the same, I've booked an appointment for expensive dental veneers. You know I've wanted to fix my ugly front teeth for a decade and what's a couple of grand when you're talking about a smile that will dazzle for a lifetime? I'm not quite sure what's involved, but there'll soon be a toothy beauty strolling the halls of Queen's Park. Lib

"I'm just going to rough up the surface of your teeth a bit so that the veneers will adhere," Dr. Hollywell says as I jump into his chair.

He puts on protective eyewear, freezes my mouth and fits me with a rubber dental dam, before I can protest.

"It's a two-step process, as you know," he says, firing up his drill. When my eyes bulge, he asks, "You didn't read the brochure? Well, today I'll remove the enamel from your teeth. When that's done, I'll cover them all temporarily—they'll be sensitive without enamel, of course—and send you off to a special clinic to have your teeth custom matched. When the veneers are done in two weeks, I'll glue them on and you'll have a beautiful smile."

My brain is vibrating from the drilling, but it dawns on me

that removing the enamel is pretty permanent. Which means I am compromising perfectly good teeth for the sake of vanity.

"I've outdone myself," he announces proudly, handing me a mirror.

I smile to inspect the temporary plastic covering—basically a hockey mouth guard: a yellowy, shapeless mould tucked around my upper front teeth. I burst into tears and Dr. Hollywell flees the room. The word gets out through the clinic: "A sister is down! Close ranks." Soon every woman on staff has gathered by my side.

"It doesn't look bad at all," they reassure me. "No one will even notice."

It's not as if I can retreat to my bedroom for two weeks; I serve at the pleasure of the Minister. So I return to the office after my appointment and discover the sisters were lying.

"Lily," says the Minister during our afternoon meeting, "what happened to your teeth?" This from a woman who barely registers a life-form reading when I am in the room.

"It's a mouth guard," I reply. "I've been grinding my teeth because of stress. I need to wear it 24 hours a day for two weeks."

I've been getting pretty good at spinning the yarn lately, but who knew I could do it with such speed and ease?

To: Roxnrhead@interlog.ca
From: Mclib@hotmail.ca
Subject: Facial Renovations

Rox,

As I'm sure Bridget Wilkinson can tell you, personal enhancement is not for the faint-hearted—nor the tight-fisted (does she really have butt implants?). I'm going to have to factor the cost of personal therapy into the dental work. No wonder the dentist squeezed me in right away. I wouldn't have gone through with it if I'd had time to read the brochure.

There's a plastic hockey mouth guard temporarily covering my front teeth. I'm still getting over the shock, but I suppose it's good to get a taste, as it were, for the great Canadian pastime. Remember your toothless NHL player of 1990? Now that his career's on ice, I hope he's looked into implants.

There's no sign of Richard around the office, which is just as well, considering the state of my smile. Nonetheless, my crush slipped into first gear sometime around noon today. That's when I walked to Holts in the rain to buy a new pair of hoop earrings.
Lib

## 20

Tim leaves his last message on Friday. I can tell it's his last message from the finality in his tone. There's a hint of wounded pride in it, too, but what he says is perfectly civil.

BEEP—"Hi, Libby, it's Tim. You're obviously too busy to meet right now, but I just want to say I really enjoyed last weekend and I hope we'll be able to catch up sometime—at least at Emma and Bob's. Take care."

It would only make me feel more inadequate to get involved with someone who has that much class, I conclude, curling up on the couch with a Black Russian, my comfort drink. I'm surprisingly morose for someone who has engineered her own fate. After all, there's nothing to stop me from picking up the phone, calling Tim and telling him I've been a goof. It's only been a week and the situation could certainly be salvaged. But I can't call.

Instead, I fetch a square of cooking chocolate from the cupboard and risk breaking my mouth guard on it. I don't have anything finer—and I don't deserve it.

The next day, I officially begin penance by visiting my parents in Scarborough. The drive past the factories and strip malls is enough to drag me into the valley of despair.

"What's wrong?" my mother asks as I walk up the front stairs.

"Nothing, why?" I say, brightly.

"Something's bothering you, I can tell."

"My stomach is upset, that's all."

"Ah, so you're stressed."

"No, I ate a lot of cooking chocolate last night, that's all."

"If you're settling for cooking chocolate, you must feel guilty about something."

"What is it with you and Rox? You think you can read my mind."

"A mother has a sense about these things."

She gives up and takes the passive approach, darting glances my way and hovering too close, as if trying to absorb the cause of my angst from the air. I back into her as I'm closing the cookie cupboard.

"Mom, for God's sake! Are you trying to get a look at my aura?"

"Your color is off, dear," she says. Then she tests a new theory. "So, what's happening with Lola and the book?"

"We're expecting an offer this week."

"Wonderful! And how about work… Are things going a little better?"

"Look, everything is fine. Turn off the radar."

I flounce down the hall to my bedroom and slam the door. No, wait, that was 1984. Today, I don't flounce and I don't slam because I recall just in time that I am thirty-three years old. My room, however, hasn't aged a bit. Marjory has maintained it as a shrine. I'd blast some Springsteen if I could remember how to use my old turntable. I settle for flopping dramatically onto the twin bed and staring at the ceiling.

I'm not confessing to her about Tim. I won't yield no matter what she bakes. The woman does not need another reason to look at me in pained disappointment. When I was a teen, she wouldn't even lie to guys for me the way other mothers did. Not Marjory, the nicest woman in the world. I wonder if she has any idea how much pressure she puts on me. Fortunately, there are constructive ways to deal with it. I emerge from my room and pull out the vacuum cleaner. Then I clean the bathroom tub and sink. Dad arrives just in time to save me from starting on the litter box.

Mom is in the kitchen baking but I fear she is losing her touch. Does she really think I'll cough up details for a *coffee cake*—especially one as dry as this? Not a chance. There's a hint of a smile on her face as I choke on cake dust; she doesn't offer me a beverage to wash it down. She's on to me.

Richard is back in the office. Recognizing the impossibility of being coquettish with a mouth full of plastic, I quietly absorb his pheromones from the safety of my own cubicle. I manage to avoid him all day, but as I'm gathering my things to leave, he appears.

"So, Ms. McIssac, when's that wedding?"

"Get a date, then set the date, I always say."

I'm nervous that Margo might come by and rain protocol lectures down on my head. Richard clearly isn't bothered by the specter of Margo—nor by my mouthpiece for that matter. He's so busy telling me about himself that it hasn't even registered something has changed. Normally, I'd find this self-absorption infuriating. Have I lowered my standards simply because he's a rich and powerful man? That's never been my MO before. Still, I contemplate investing in a quality watch.

Margo is out of the office for two glorious days scouting a potential excursion to northern Ontario. I pray each night that this trip will not come to pass. I pray that Richard will use his power over the Minister to convince her it's a bad idea. I pray that if the trip does happen, that Richard and I will be left behind at Queen's Park to do something about the pheromones.

To: Roxnrhead@interlog.ca
From: Mclib@hotmail.ca
Subject: The Crush Continues

Rox,

I thought you'd like to know that I am fanning the flames of my office crush. In fact, the "season" of Richard opened today with a trip to Banana Republic. I tried on over 20 outfits and wore out two perky young sales clerks. Though familiar with the common crush, they're used to helping younger girls through it—girls who look good in everything. At my age, it takes work. I finally settled on two silk sweaters, one of which I'll likely return once I've seen it in my own mirror. As you've discovered yourself, the mirrors in Banana Republic are enchanted.

I've decided that certain protocols must govern my spending during a crush. In first gear, I will stick to tame purchases, including clothing, hair care products and earrings. While it's justifiable to buy almost anything in the name of infatuation, timing is the issue. Remember when I bought the Pink Floyd boxed set after two dates with that pothead, Dave Weir? Where is he now?

Richard is likely to be an expensive and embarrassing diversion. He's the kind of guy that drives a girl to buy something ridiculous, like a pricey watch—or a Jet Ski. The problem is that, despite his boorish habits, I somehow feel he's out of my league. The more outclassed I feel, the more I'll spend to even up the odds. He's older, he's worldly, he's bright, he's rich and he's connected. And he's incredibly sexy. So what if he's a bit of a pig? He still outranks me. You know what I mean, Rox. Tim was too good for me, but he was still in the realm of possibility. With Richard, I am at a loss as to what I would bring to the match.
Lib

★ ★ ★

With Margo blighting the northern wastelands, I'm making good progress on several speeches. In fact, I'm focusing so intently that when Mrs. Cleary's perfectly groomed head peeks around my cubicle wall I jump.

"So this is where you hide, Lily," she says, as I scramble to my feet. "I just stopped by to see how you're doing with the speeches for the Culture Vulture Festival."

The festival is two weeks away and I haven't even gathered material yet. "I'm sorry, Minister, I'm not working that far ahead. I have five other speeches to write first."

"That's fine, Lily, but I'd like to share my ideas while they're fresh, if I may."

"Shall I come to your office?"

"No, no, I'll sit down here," she says, looking around. "Don't you have a chair?"

"I'm afraid not. Margo took it."

"*Really.* Well, I'll just get one from another office."

She sets off to do just that—with her own two hands—hands that never carry so much as a handbag!

"No, let me get it," I say, bustling after her. She's already heading into an office several doors down.

"Whose office is this?" she asks.

"No one's used it since I arrived."

"Then why aren't you using it?"

"Pardon me?"

"Why aren't you using this office instead of that dreadful *box* you sit in?" It's a Linda Blair moment: I expect her head to start spinning on her shoulders. "I don't know how you concentrate. You're practically sitting in the hallway."

"I've noticed."

"*I* wouldn't be able to work in that environment." More importantly, she wouldn't have the desk space for her toiletries.

"It is hard to focus."

"Well, why don't you just move in here right now? We can talk about the speeches tomorrow."

"Uh—okay." I stand, frozen, waiting for the other glass slipper to drop. "I guess I'll start packing."

"Off you go, then!" she says gaily. "Don't break a nail!"

It crosses my mind to grab a chair and bash her over the head until the spirit possessing her flies out, but I want the office too badly to stall over this service to humanity. Instead, I run back to my office and start grabbing files before she can change her mind. An hour later, I pin Cornelius's photo on my new bulletin board and sit down to enjoy my office while I can.

I might find myself stuffed into the supply cupboard tomorrow.

The posters at the entry to Crews clear up the mystery of why Elliot asked to meet here instead of his beloved Manhole. It's the Wednesday Night Drag Show. I silently curse Elliot because I've come straight from the office and I'm actually wearing a skirt. On the bright side, Cher is working the door and waves me in without collecting the cover charge.

Elliot is at the bar flirting with the handsome bartender.

"Where's Günter, the love of your life?" I ask, pulling up a stool. The bartender gives Elliot a disgusted glance before beating a hasty retreat.

"On tour, as I told you," Elliot replies, unfazed. "Besides, he never comes along when I'm working."

"Is that what you call it?"

Elliot cranes after the bartender and smiles. "Just because I like to window shop doesn't mean I'll pull out my…wallet."

"Speaking of wallets," I say, hauling out my own, "what's it gonna cost me tonight?"

"A double espresso and a shot of the best cognac the place has to offer. If I'm reading the signs correctly, you'll soon be able to buy me the entire bottle."

"Cash on delivery," I tease, withholding the cognac when it arrives.

"I'm not going to miss you," Elliot says, reaching for the glass.

"Am I going somewhere, or just finding a new psychic?"

"Hope you're still laughing when I tell you about the upcoming road trip." I groan. "Pack up your glue stick, doll, there's another scrapbook in your future."

Depressed, I scoop a handful of peanuts from the bowl on the bar and dump them into my mouth.

"My God, don't eat those, Libby!" Elliot says, horrified.

"Whph?"

"Haven't you read the studies about bar nuts?" Siphoning nut bits from the edges of my mouth guard, I raise a quizzical eyebrow. "They're crawling with bacteria, because of people who don't wash their hands after going to the washroom."

"Thank you, Dr. Hygiene." I take a swig of bourbon and slosh it around my mouth to kill the germs. "Can we get back to how my life in the civil service is going to finance premium booze?"

"I didn't say it has anything to do with the civil service. On the contrary, I sense you are currently quite *powerless* on that front. What I see is a lucrative creative project on the horizon. It's strange, though. I see you working on it, but you're hidden behind a veil."

"Have you been talking to Lola?" I ask, suspiciously.

"No, I've been avoiding her because I'm sick of hearing about Michael when we could be talking about Günter. Why?"

Elliot is surprised to hear Lola and I are collaborating on a book—even more so when he hears the topic. "Not a *serious* book on weddings?" he asks.

"I know it's awful, but it's not our idea. Lola knows this publisher and he wants us to explore how women are struggling to modernize their weddings despite pressure to stick to the traditional 'script.' We met the guy for lunch on Monday and tried to talk him into something funnier, but he didn't buy it. We're desperate enough to sign the contract anyway."

"Congratulations—I think. Hey, if it's unique stories you're after, you should come to my sister's wedding. She and her idiot boyfriend are druids and they're getting married in a forest near Cobourg. Thank God my father stipulated he'd only pay for the reception if it were held at his golf club. Being broke, the druids saw reason."

"If your sister wouldn't mind, I'd love to come. Maybe I'll meet the druid of my dreams."

"I doubt it," he says, narrowing his eyes. Uh-oh.

"I'm in no mood for the rock-and-sign crap, Elliot. And for your information, I'm practically irresistible to men these days."

As if on cue, the bartender slides another Maker's Mark toward me. "Compliments of Mimi," he says, gesturing toward Cher at the door.

"I see what you mean," Elliot says, smirking.

"Oh, shut up." I smile at Mimi and raise my glass in thanks. Elliot watches, amazed. "Look," I explain, "if a guy who looks like a girl wants to buy a drink for another girl who apparently looks like a guy trying to look like a girl, then, as I see it, it would be rude and hurtful for the real girl to decline."

Elliot laughs, but he says, "You're misleading him. And please forgive me for saying so, but Mimi isn't the only one you've misled. You always send conflicting signals, Lib." I glower at him silently. "Fine, I'll say no more about the two men I see. Retract your claws."

"Okay, tell me," I say hastily. The guy can read me like a cheap dimestore novel. "What do you see?"

"I see a thirsty psychic." Rolling my eyes, I order him another round. He closes his eyes and continues. "I see two men, both smart, both funny, both utterly charming, if I may say. But one is a true diamond, while the other is a lump of coal."

"And?"

"And nothing—that's all I've got. You don't need me to tell you what you should do."

"That wasn't worth the price of another double Remy, you scammer."

"You buys yer rounds, you takes yer chances."

Next morning, I ponder my session with Elliot as I climb the stairs of the Pink Palace. I don't need him to tell me that Tim is a diamond and Richard is coal. Besides, I don't put any stock in this psychic stuff. Like anyone else, I'll see the sparkle where I want to. Richard might be arrogant, but he isn't that bad.

I open the door—ah, a real door at last—and behold my new office. The oak paneling on the walls is my dream come true. The place is dim, though, and unlike my cave-dwelling colleague Margo, I'm diurnal. I flick on my desk lamp and nothing happens. Ditto for my computer, which is plugged into a separate outlet. Dead. Other than the weak overhead light, I am powerless in my new office—exactly as Elliot predicted!

I am pondering the situation when Margo's voice floats down the hall: "Where on earth is Libby? Her things are gone!" She sounds more hopeful than alarmed.

Richard's voice answers: "I think she moved down the hall."

Thump thump of rapid footsteps. For a change, she doesn't try to conceal her approach. "What are you doing in here, Libby?"

"It was the Minister's idea," I babble nervously. "She wanted to sit down in my cubicle and there wasn't a chair. When we came to this office to borrow one, she said I should move because it's so much quieter."

"I have plans for this office."

"Well, there are other empty offices, and I'm here now. I have a problem though: there's no electricity."

"That *is* a problem. I don't see how you're going to do your work."

"I'll manage somehow until it's fixed. I'll ask Laurie to look into it."

"No, I'll call Maintenance, but they're always very slow to respond."

Which means she'll drag it out as long as she can. I can out-wait her; I'm not going to lose this prize. No, when the going gets tough, the tough get extension cords, and so I enlist Laurie to help me run one out of my office and into the office next door.

I pour my mochaccino into my "Life Sucks" mug, because it usually does. This is my fourth morning in the luxury suite and I still have no power. Nor has the phone line been changed. I can't even forward my calls from my old office because the phone is an historical artifact.

I am wondering if I dare call Maintenance myself when I hear rapid footsteps approaching. Sensing it's the Minister, I push my chair back to stand—just as a flying form in a chartreuse suit hurtles into view. She's actually airborne for a moment before crashing to the floor with a scream! The Minister has apparently caught the heel of her favorite Manolo Blahniks on one of the extension cords. Richard and I both race to help her. As we lean over her prostrate form, our faces are nearly touching and our eyes lock for one fleeting but decidedly meaningful moment.

"Are you two planning to leave me down here all day?"

The electricity disappears so quickly at the sound of the Minister's voice that I wonder if I only imagined it. We hastily place her on her feet and she lurches and staggers into Richard, as if injured. It turns out that the heel of one shoe has snapped off. Richard puts his arm around her for support.

"Are you all right, Clarice?"

"I think so. What happened?"

"I'm sorry, Minister," I pipe up. "I'm afraid you tripped over an extension cord."

"Why is it there?" she asks, eerily calm.

"The outlets don't work in my office so I had to run cords into the office next door."

Margo and Laurie arrive at this moment.

"Maintenance hasn't responded to my call," Margo says. "I've already suggested that Libby return to her own office, but I didn't realize she'd created this health and safety hazard."

"Must I do *everything* myself to ensure it's done properly?" snaps the Minister. "Laurie, get an electrician in here before someone breaks more than a heel. Richard, I'm shaken. Please help me to my office."

She limps off, leaning on Richard's arm. Margo follows, carrying the heel from the Minister's shoe. Richard glances back at me and grins. I wonder if I could stage a little wipeout myself so he can rush to my aid. Mind you, even if I could snap the heel off my Hush Puppies, he'd pop a hernia trying to lift me.

All in all, though, I'm happy to have come out of this incident so well. Even a month ago, the Minister would have fired me for causing that header. With Richard on her arm, she's almost a pleasure to have around.

Margo's attempt to starve me out of my new office has failed. With Laurie on the case, the matter was resolved in hours.

"The building manager said it was the first he'd heard of your electrical problem," Laurie says when she stops by to deliver the good news. "Margo lied about calling."

"Margo *lies?* Now there's a shocker!"

The Minister's sudden appearance startles us both. "Lily, I've been calling and calling you. Why aren't you picking up your phone?"

"My phone line still hasn't been transferred from my cubicle, Minister."

She scowls and stalks off without another word. Laurie and I tiptoe to the door in time to see her enter Margo's office.

"Margo, I have had just about enough of this," she screeches as she's closing the door.

Richard pokes his head out of his office to see what's going on. When he sees us, he smiles, cups a hand to his ear and winks. I shoot him a smile before ducking back inside.

"What was that all about?" Laurie asks, following me inside.

"I suppose the Minister has had enough of Margo's power pranks."

"That much I got. I mean, what's going on with you and Richard?"

"Nothing," I squeak. Laurie raises a skeptical eyebrow. "Honestly, nothing's going on," I repeat in a calmer tone.

"Yeah, a whole lotta nuthin' if you ask me."

The next morning, my office phone rings for the first time.

"Libby, it's Margo." Figures, the woman who resisted hooking it up is the first to use it. "The Minister expects you at Casa Loma tonight for the Culture Vulture black-tie."

"She told me I don't have to attend," I protest.

"I reminded her that someone must tend to her needs while I'm making contacts for future program support." In other words, she needs me to hold the Minister's purse while she networks with the cheese tray. "Be there at seven sharp," she says, slamming down the phone.

The nerve of her, ordering me to attend an event outside of work hours and at the last minute—as if I have no life. I have a life, I just don't have anything to wear. I'm tired of Roxanne's lucky dress and in my current crush-weakened state, I fear finding myself with a dozen new ball gowns and only creditors to appreciate them.

Richard walks past my door and doubles back when he catches me staring into space.

"Trying to decide which party dress to wear tonight?" he asks, leaning against my door frame. "I liked the little black number you wore to the Opera Company affair."

The guy has more talent for mind reading than Elliot, but he's awfully forward, especially for a consultant. I should probably display a little righteous indignation, but I don't waste my energy.

"I'm still waiting to see what Versace has lined up for me," I say.

"Say, have you checked CNN's Web site today? There's a

piece on Chicago's Culture Vulture Week, which I presume is what we're copying here." He approaches my desk, comes around and leans over my shoulder to grab my mouse. "Allow me."

"Libby."

I jump at the sound of Margo's voice. Richard jumps too, but recovers instantly.

"Hi, there!" he says cheerily. "What's up?"

"I'd like to have a word with Libby, if you don't mind," she replies, stiffly.

"Not at all." Seemingly undaunted, he adds, "Listen, when are we going to have a one-on-one about the trip to the north?"

"It seems like you're booked solid with one-on-ones these days."

"I'll always make time to chat with a beautiful woman," Richard says, turning on the charm. Margo flushes and looks down. With her personality, she probably doesn't get compliments that often. Winking at me as he leaves, Richard says, "I think you'll find that article very interesting."

"Libby," Margo whispers as soon as he's out of earshot, "is he bothering you?"

"No, he was directing me to a review on the CNN Web site."

"Well, you let me know if he's bothering you and I'll take it up with the Minister."

"I appreciate his help, Margo."

Since she didn't have a reason to drop by in the first place, she leaves without further discussion.

To: Roxnrhead@interlog.ca
From: Mclib@hotmail.ca
Subject: Gathering momentum

Rox,
    Just thought you'd like to know that the geologic disturbance you felt on the European continent last night was not an earthquake,

but the aftershock of my crush shifting into third gear. Richard has turned up the heat on the flirting. Today, he told me he likes your lucky dress! You were right about its powers!

What a relief. Third gear means I can acquire candles and perfume without guilt. I booked an appointment at the Aveda spa for a facial and eyebrow waxing—time to surrender my simian ridge for a provocative arch!

Third gear protocol also permits the purchase of a new ball gown. Now, don't give me a hard time, Rox. I've got a formal event this evening and Richard has taken too much notice of your frock for me to wear it again so soon. Besides, I need to show more skin to offset the mouth guard. I so wish it came off today instead of tomorrow. Lola recommended a place in Yorkville that sells used designer cast-offs from the city's jet set. I picked up a silver-gray strapless Ralph Lauren for a mere $200! It's a little big around the bust and since there's no time to alter it before tonight's event, I plan to use double-sided tape to anchor it in place. If it works for Jennifer Lopez, it will work for me.

Thank God I'm triple the Minister's size. Imagine if I showed up in one of her cast-off frocks? Gotta run. It's almost 4:30 and I'm sneaking away early to tape my dress on!
Lib

It's a miracle that I'm only twenty minutes late arriving at Casa Loma. Margo caught me just as I was leaving and demanded I reformat the Minister's remarks a font size larger. By the time I sweet-talked the balky printer, there was no time to buy double-sided tape. Instead, I secured the dress with loops of ordinary transparent tape, which should do the trick. Soon I'll be so burdened with bouquets and clutches that no one will even see my dress.

Laurie, who also received a last-minute decree to attend, greets me at the castle door.

"Hey, Cinderella, is that a new gown?"

"Well, new to me."

"Trying to impress the Big Dick?"

"Laurie!" I exclaim, looking around quickly. "That's *Prince Charming,* if you don't mind."

We're still giggling a few minutes later when the Minister makes her grand entrance, dazzling in a silver, sequined, strapless dress.

"Libby," Margo calls, "we could use a little help over here."

As I take her coat and wrap, the Minister favors me with a look of such intense loathing I fear I've stepped back through a time warp. What have I done now?

"You're wearing *silver,*" she snaps. "We look like the Doublemint twins. Stand away from me, please."

"I can't imagine anyone will confuse us, Minister," I reply, drawing myself up to full party height of six foot five. "My gown is gray and yours has sequins."

"They're virtually identical! Put my wrap on," the Minister commands, as she pushes Margo, in her sensible navy taffeta, between us.

"I am not wearing a wrap all night, Minister—it's warm in here. If my dress bothers you that much, I'll keep to the other side of the room."

"I don't think so," Margo says. "We need your support. Put the wrap on."

She stands on her tiptoes and tries to slip the Minister's shawl over my shoulders. I shrug and it slides off onto Margo's head. Tousled but undefeated, she tries again.

"Stop it, you two," the Minister whispers, before calling out, "Why, Tim! What a pleasure to see you!"

Tim Kennedy is standing at the entrance, apparently transfixed by the sight of Margo and me wrestling with the wrap. At his side is a stunning woman with sleek blond hair. A wave of nausea rolls over me as I look from Tim to his date. I let my hands drop to my side and Margo seizes the moment to hoist the wrap onto my shoulders. Tim eyes me coldly, then turns his gaze on the Minister and signals that he'll be right over. He turns to help his companion with her coat.

"Minister, let's invite Tim and his girlfriend to sit at our table," Margo says.

I glance down to see Margo watching me watch Tim. She may not know the source of tension between us, but she instinctually recognizes an opportunity to make me suffer. I snatch the Minister's wrap from my shoulders, roll it and shove it under my arm.

"Lily, be careful, that's cashmere," the Minister says. "By the way, your dress looks very familiar… Is it Lauren?"

Richard's arrival saves me from responding. He strides across the hall and plants a kiss on the Minister's mouth.

"Clarice, you're absolutely enchanting," he booms. "And Margo," he adds, stooping to buss the wretched one's cheek, "Aren't you smashing?" Margo blushes to her rosy roots.

"Richard," Mrs. Cleary pouts, "don't you think Lily's dress is too similar to mine?"

"Of course not, Clarice, you're in a league all your own. I promise all eyes will be on you. But," he adds, winking at me, "Libby does scrub up well."

He puts a warm hand on my bare shoulder and I almost drop the cashmere wrap. When I look up, I find Tim watching me swoon. In retaliation, perhaps, he places his hand in the small of his date's back to guide her across the room toward our table. To my relief, however, they sit at the other end, leaving me flanked by two painfully boring bankers.

The Minister is the first speaker of the evening and despite a hurried belt of champagne, she delivers my toast brilliantly. I'm elated with the audience's warm response. Tim speaks next. I'm impressed with his ease and his humor, but my enjoyment is ruined by his date's overly enthusiastic applause. Look at her showing off those big white teeth, the shameless hussy.

Speeches over, the waiters begin circulating with trays of food. Most guests are free to mingle, but I'm on a short leash, never more than ten feet from the Minister as I wrangle her purse and her wrap. Not that I miss out on the refreshments. I have learned to stake out a spot where I can place my drink and goodie plate, which allows me to indulge with one hand. In fact, I'm enjoying a plate of shrimp when Richard approaches.

"You did a nice job with that speech," he says, spearing two of my shrimp.

"I've got my hands full, but somehow I manage."

He leans over to wipe a tiny speck of cocktail sauce from my arm. "You can dress a girl up…"

"Careful of the cashmere. I can't even afford the dry cleaning."

"Richard," Margo's piping voice shatters the moment. "I don't believe you've met Tim Kennedy." She has Tim and date in tow and I suspect her timing is deliberate. "Tim runs the Ontario Youth Orchestra and this is Melanie."

Tim ignores me as he shakes Richard's hand. No one introduces me to Melanie so I stand by awkwardly, until Margo instructs me to fetch Tim and Melanie a drink from the bar. This is a particularly humiliating move and even Tim seems embarrassed.

"No need, Margo," he says. "We'll head over to the bar in a minute."

"I'd be happy to get you a drink," I say, eager not only to avoid another scene, but to avoid having Tim detect my mouth guard. I hand Margo the Minister's things and set off.

"Pick up a tray of snacks, too, Libby," she calls after me.

Having noted earlier that Melanie, like Tim, is a red wine drinker, I request two glasses of white. I take my sweet time about delivering them, too. I am duly punished, however, when I find Tim sitting alone at our table, making it impossible for us to avoid each other. The Minister and Melanie have disappeared, while Margo and Richard have moved a few steps away and are speaking in hushed tones. At first, I assume they're discussing the northern tour, but then, to my shock, Margo actually laughs—a sound I've rarely heard. Richard raises his wine and they clink glasses.

As much as I'd like to observe them longer, Tim's presence is too distracting. I set the drinks on the table in front of him; he simply nods his thanks.

"So, how are you? I hope Stella is well," I say.

"Fine," he replies, icily.

"Great! Well, I suppose I should see to the Minister…"

I'm about to bolt when I notice Margo has left the Minister's purse and wrap beside Tim. Reaching for them abruptly, I topple the table's floral centerpiece, which rolls toward Tim. As I lunge across the table for it, my right breast blasts through the tape loops and over the top of my dress.

"I wouldn't leave that out where Clarice can see it," Tim says smiling, as I clumsily stuff everything back where it belongs. My face is so hot it feels as if my head could explode. "Relax, Libby," Tim says, thawing marginally. "I've seen it before, remember?"

Finding my tongue at last, I say, "It's all Stella's fault. She ate my best party bra." When he laughs, I seize the moment to say, "Listen, Tim, I really want to—"

"What's going on?" Margo interrupts, arriving with Richard.

"Libby is taking her frustrations out on the flowers, as usual," Tim says, retrieving the centerpiece from the floor. "Aren't you chilly, Libby? Maybe you should put this wrap on." He stands and arranges the Minister's wrap around my shoulders; I clamp it to my sides with my elbows.

Margo is suspicious and she toys with me further when Melanie returns to the table.

"So, Libby," she says, with false chumminess, "Melanie writes for *Maclean's* magazine. Isn't that exciting? You went to journalism school too, didn't you? I was just telling Melanie that you often help the Minister with her speeches."

Melanie gives me a puzzled smile, but Tim appears to enjoy

the abuse. (Maybe I just imagined a thaw?) Richard, however, steps forward chivalrously and hands me a glass of white wine.

"She drinks red," Tim says.

"You do?" Richard asks me.

"This is fine," I say quickly, "although I often drink red."

"I'll get you a glass of red, then."

"No, I'll get it," Tim says. "I have to get some red for Melanie and me, anyway."

While Tim gets the wine, I ponder whether he is trying to make me feel small for the white wine stunt, or is jealous of Richard. He soon returns and hands me a glass, but I'm afraid to raise it to my lips, lest a boob escape.

"So, Libby, Margo's been keeping you chained to your desk?" Tim asks, with a trace of bitterness.

"Very busy, yes," I mumble.

Margo says nothing, but watches closely, alert for clues.

"Oh, she gets out," Richard says. "We met at a bookstore recently."

Both Margo and Tim look annoyed at this—and Richard has only begun peeing around me.

"That was shortly after I arrived from London. Of course, I still go back every other week to consult with two major British corporations. So, remind me what you do, Tim?"

"I teach."

"University?"

"High-school music."

"Oh, an *artiste*," Richard says, condescendingly. "I suppose you're also quite an accomplished musician?"

"Quite."

"I see. What a rewarding career—although not financially, I'm sure, unless they pay teachers better here than they do in Britain."

Suspecting that Richard will only stop posturing if I leave, I call out to the Minister, who's across the room chatting up the Chair of the Art Gallery of Ontario: "On my way, Minister! Please excuse me," I say to the others, "the Minister waved me over."

"She didn't," says the ever-helpful Margo.

"She did. I don't expect you can get a good view from your position. I do have the height advantage," I say sweetly.

Tim, Richard and Melanie all laugh. I'll pay for my impudence tomorrow, but at least I've lifted the mood. I bid a polite good-night to Melanie and Tim and nod curtly at Richard before I leave. How dare he suggest there's something between us? And how dare he mark his territory by diminishing Tim?

I spend the rest of the evening avoiding them all. As much as I'd like to follow through on my earlier attempt to apologize to Tim, I keep out of harm's way, huddling behind a pillar, swathed in the Minister's wrap. Tim and Melanie certainly seem very comfortable with each other. How could he be that comfortable with someone else so soon? It's only been a few weeks since our last date. Maybe he was already seeing her, the cad!

Meanwhile, Richard cuts a dashing figure as he works the room. He may be a pig, but he's the sexiest pig I've ever met.

"Lily, for heaven's sake, give me that wrap. I am catching a chill."

Dr. Hollywell completes the final work on my veneers and hands me a mirror. At this point, I hardly care how they look, but to my relief, they're great! I flash my new teeth to the women in the office, then hurry off to the MAC boutique to select four new shades of lipstick. Now that it's done there's nothing to do but enjoy my own beauty!

Not one colleague notices my new choppers—not even Richard, who's been holed up in his office. It's rumored he's working on a campaign to bring order to this office and the first step will be shooting down Margo's idea of a road trip through the northern constituencies. The Minister has called a meeting to discuss Richard's preliminary observations and for a change, Laurie and I are invited.

The Minister is in a good mood when we arrive in the boardroom. She's sitting beside Richard and keeps touching his arm. Dour Margo, who has a coffee stain over her left breast and red jam on her sleeve, is on the Minister's other side. Laurie and I take seats at the end of the table, where the air circulation is a little better. I'm worried my pheromone receptors might overload, even though I'm still annoyed over the way Richard treated Tim.

Richard begins by delivering a short presentation that deftly congratulates us on past successes while pointing out areas for improvement.

"My media analysis revealed a great deal of favorable coverage, due in no small part to Margo's efforts," he says, smiling at her. "I would like to hear more about your plans with respect to traveling to northern Ontario."

Margo says that the trip would give the Minister a chance to promote Club 3:30 in a region she hasn't yet visited. In response, Richard suggests, in the nicest possible way, that she's a complete idiot. He says that the trip is unnecessary, given the heavy media coverage that program has already received across the province. After our recent adventures on the road, we'd be better to focus on generating press through a series of positive announcements about our upcoming programs. We're far more likely to get good press about the arts in the big city. In fact, we've been getting consistently good coverage of local events, he notes, "thanks to some excellent speeches from Libby." The Minister beams at me.

Richard concludes by saying that he'd welcome further discussion with Margo, who has turned an unusual color. She must be beside herself, because she storms out of the boardroom without so much as touching the tray of perfectly good pastries.

A battle is heating up between Richard and Margo. They've been ignoring each other all week, speaking only when absolutely necessary. The Minister has called another meeting to discuss Richard's findings.

I am making my muffin selection when Richard and Margo file into the boardroom. Wasting no time on pleasantries, they start throwing punches. Apparently, Margo has continued to plan the trip to the north, despite Richard's disapproval.

"Minister," says Richard in a rare show of protocol, "I want to remind you of the words of Albert Einstein: 'We cannot solve problems with the same thinking that created the problem.' We must try something different."

"With all due respect to Richard, Minister, I believe I understand the political environment in Ontario a little better than he does."

"I'm sure you have an *excellent* understanding of Ontario's unique perspective, Margo," Richard says, "but I have nearly two decades of experience in anticipating the reactions of average voters—of Ma and Pa Backporch, as it were."

"And how many back porches do they have in London, Richard?" Margo retorts, holding her own.

Richard glares at her. The Minister, on the other hand, appears amused. I suspect she rather enjoys bringing combustible people together to create a little drama in her life.

"Margo, Richard, please… I am open to being convinced either way on this, but we won't get anywhere with you sniping at each other. What do *you* think, Lily?"

Lily is in a bit of a bind: her heart pounds for Richard, but her brain remembers that Margo currently controls her career. On the other hand, she'd rather endure another round with Dr. Hollywell than sleep in the same room as Margo again. So Lily hops onto the fence.

"Minister, I see Richard's point and I see Margo's point. Since we have nothing new to promote on a road trip, why don't we try Richard's way first? Perhaps we could travel to the north sometime down the road."

Margo and Richard are clearly unimpressed.

"Well, I'll need to think about it," the Minister concludes, adding with a tinkling laugh, "I hear Wawa is lovely this time of year."

"Minister," says Margo, with a smug smile, "perhaps our new consultant could give us an unbiased opinion."

"New consultant!" Mrs. Cleary and Richard exclaim in unison.

"Yes, we've hired Mark O'Brien from Sanders and Stevenson to provide the Ministry with advice."

"On what?" the Minister asks, furiously. "How could you hire another consultant without asking me first?"

"Actually, the Deputy Minister made the decision. I've been trying to brief you on this for over a week, but you've canceled our meetings. The Deputy wants strategic advice on introducing the new programs we're planning."

"I will speak to him about this directly. It's ridiculous! How many consultants do we need around here? I *do* apologize, Richard."

"Not at all, Clarice," he replies. "I welcome Mark's input."

The Minister adjourns the meeting and as Margo stands to leave, she tears the tops from two muffins and stashes them in her briefcase. I'm not sure how she convinced the Deputy Minister to buy it, but it was a masterful stroke. With Mark as her mouthpiece, she'll be far better able to counter Richard's Rasputin-like influence on the Minister. I have no doubt at all that she'll manipulate Mark so thoroughly that he won't have an opinion to call his own. Richard will recommend one thing, Mark another and the two will effectively cancel each other out. A government dream come true!

22

Elliot's psychic ship has finally run aground. After an extended course of smooth sailing during which he correctly predicted the major events of my life, he's been proven wrong about the road trip. The Minister, perhaps punishing Margo for bringing Mark on board without her approval, has declined to tour the hot spots of northern Ontario.

I couldn't be happier. I can't share the moment with Richard, however, because he's been giving me the cold shoulder since the Minister's last meeting. His arrogant male mind has somehow translated my failure to side with him against Margo as a betrayal and a sign of disinterest. Elliot probably has a point about the mixed signals I send, but it's unfair of Richard to hold a grudge over this. He's a consultant with other clients and a fancy London refuge, whereas I could only escape Margo's wrath through an express ticket back to the education policy shop—a slim portfolio under one arm and the standard framed photo of the Minister (signed) under the other.

I refuse to fret too much about the current chill in the office air because the latest issue of *O* magazine advises giving up the "disease to please." Time to stop taking things personally, Oprah says. It's not all about me. Besides, there's a bright side: if my crush never kicks into fourth gear, I'll save a bundle. No lingerie shopping, no filling the refrigerator with food he likes, no new bed linens, no bikini waxes. And I do hate bikini waxes. If God meant for people to be hairless, he'd have begun our evolution from the reptile line.

"Daydreaming, I see," Margo says, materializing at my side in the kitchen, where I am staring at the coffee machine after a fruitless stroll past Richard's office. "What's on your mind?"

"Evolution...and bikini waxes." She winces. "Well, you asked."

"When you're finished musing, I'd like to introduce you to Mark."

Mark O'Brien is the consultant she'll be manipulating shortly. He's very nice—polite, mild-mannered and seemingly untroubled by extra testosterone.

Richard will take him down in a week.

In the three days since his arrival, Mark has spent a lot of time in my office "consulting" with me. I haven't a clue what I've done to deserve my newfound popularity. Maybe it's the dazzling smile. Or maybe those bridal bouquets are finally taking effect. I'm glad something is working, but Mark, I regret to say, has absolutely no impact on my hormones—and he's awfully dull. Even now, he's in the hall outside my office talking to Laurie about carpenter ants:

"In August, they become *nocturnal* and no one knows why!" he's saying. "Just when you think 'thank God they've moved on,' you discover they're actually devouring your cottage by night. One morning, you get out of bed and BOOM!—you fall through the floorboards."

Laurie has neither a cottage nor a particular interest in entomology, and judging by her glazed eyes, she's given up all hope of escape.

"Laurie," I call out from my desk, "Margo needs you." She mouths "thanks" and departs at a run. Only a very dull man could make a summons from Margo good news.

Mark steps to my door: "Hi, Libby! How's it going today?"

Fearing a pop quiz on insects, I rustle some papers and complain about deadline pressure. He takes the hint and leaves, but moments later, the elusive Richard arrives. True to form, he's decided to acknowledge my existence now that there's competition.

"What did Professor Snore want?" he asks.

"Mark isn't so bad."

"If you've got insomnia, you mean."

"You just have to get him on the right topic."

"Really? You're telling me that you actually find Mark stimulating?"

"Well…"

"That's what I thought."

Uncomfortable with this line of questioning, I use the time-honored feminine ploy of requesting Richard's help (*Flirt Now*, Chapter 12). He's a whiz at all things electronic (or so he boasts), so I ask him to show me how to change my screen saver to feature Cornelius in a fetching pose. Immediately forgetting all about Mark, he takes control of my mouse and leans in very close. I promptly lose all powers of articulation, repeating the words "cool" and "amazing" until I want to slam my own head into the computer screen. In fact, the only thing I learn from this demo is that he still has the hormonal upper hand. To ensure my complete surrender, he strokes my hair as he turns away. I suck back another lungful of pheromones and *purr*.

To: Roxnrhead@interlog.ca
From: Mclib@hotmail.ca
Subject: LUST

Hi Rox,

Remind me how we survived adolescence? Thanks to Richard, I spent another lunch hour shopping. This time, I bought two new bras, one in an impractical jade-green. I also got some suck-it-in underwear and a pair of fishnet tights. I expect you'll recognize the signs of a crush thudding into fourth? Gather the girls for an intervention before I cash in my retirement savings! Lib

I've barely hit Send when Richard strolls into my office again.

"What's so special about Sotto Sotto? I hear that celebrities like it."

"It's close to the major hotels and I've been told the food is great."

"You haven't sampled it personally?"

"No."

"Well, let's have dinner there tonight."

I'm struck by the same feeling I get when a job I've been pursuing relentlessly drops into my hand—the joy tempered by terror because now I'm expected to deliver the goods.

"Aren't you going to say something?" he asks.

"Uh—well, I'll need to think about it."

"What's to think about? We go out, we eat, we drink, we talk. Nothing to it."

"It sounds like a date."

"And…?"

"And dating you would make my life miserable."

"Ouch!"

"You know what I mean. These sandstone walls couldn't contain Margo's wrath."

"She wouldn't find out."

"She would, she *always* knows."

"Always? How many guys have you dated around here?"

"Never mind, but thanks to her, I've adopted a no-dating-colleagues policy."

"Well, my job is to recommend changes to current policy. And in case you haven't noticed, I'm on a roll lately."

"It's not that I wouldn't like to…"

"I can see that," he says, reaching toward the lingerie bag beside my desk.

I snatch the bag away from him and point to the door. He swaggers out, seemingly *encouraged* by this exchange. Infuriating man!

I'm devouring an Oh Henry! bar and watching my Lean Cuisine manicotti revolve in the microwave oven. Chocolate isn't my usual appetizer; its purpose tonight is to distract me from thoughts about how much better the manicotti would be at Sotto Sotto. Now that I'm home, I can't quite remember why I passed up dinner at a fabulous restaurant with a hot guy. Do I want to spend my life alone, sharing frozen dinners with my cat?

Maybe I should call the Sutton Place to see if Richard has gone straight home like a good boy. If he's there, I could suggest dinner in the west end of the city, where Margo is less likely to have spies on the ground. There's a little Italian place near High Park....

BEEP—BEEP—BEEP. The microwave brings me back to earth. I put the phone down and tear the cellophane from the manicotti. I wouldn't be Marjory's daughter if I allowed a perfectly good frozen dinner to go to waste. On the other hand, it's because I'm Marjory's daughter that I'm not gazing across a candlelit table at Richard right now.

"Richard is a mistake you shouldn't make," Mom would say, "he probably has a fling in every town." "Don't soil the bed you lie in," Dad would add. And they'd be right. Look at how awkward it is with Tim. Even Joe the Priest bolts when he sees me in the halls. But still, it's the rare guy who makes one's arm hair stand on end... A *really good* fling might just be worth the awkwardness and the career risk.

I can handle it. It's not as if I haven't dated a few bad boys in my time. Okay, make that one bad boy, but what a blast that was... The wining, the dining, the dirty weekends... Then he dumped me—via voice mail—just as I was falling for him. The trick is to enjoy the ride and avoid the emotional attachment. Lots of women do it. I read about them in *Cosmo,*

I see them on TV. If they can do it, I can do it. Marjory is not the boss of me.

If I'm going for it, however, there's work ahead to turn this place into a love shack. I certainly can't invite him over without going through the pre-boff cleansing ritual, where anything remotely embarrassing is hidden or vanquished. Hard to believe I've accumulated so much since last year's sort-and-dump for gorgeous Glen Taylor. Before *he* came to dinner, my parents came by with the truck to haul away boxes for their garage sale—CDs, framed posters, old sheets and towels, stuffed animals. The bookshelves always cause me the most trouble. I'd love to keep every book, but clever guys like Richard inevitably think they can figure you out by assessing what you read. My strategy is to intimidate them with the classics. I display works of literature prominently and stack anything embarrassing in secret rows behind them. No guy (and I've never been wrong about this) is so desperate to discover the real you that he'll pull *Pride and Prejudice* off the shelf. If a male hand even hovers near the classics, one need only redirect attention to the interesting array of magazines on the coffee table—magazines like *The New Yorker* or anything with cars on the cover.

Good magazines are useful for another reason: if a lady should ever fight with her gentleman caller, she can hurl *Harper's* at him instead of *Cosmopolitan*. I'm not saying this happened to me, but it's true that one fellow did leave with a slight bruise over his heart and the January "bedside astrologer" edition of *Cosmo* lay open on the floor. Libra and Scorpio were indeed destined to part that year. Spooky.

The diet books are just where I left them, behind the great Russians. Only Tolstoy and Dostoyevsky have the heft to conceal such a collection. Richard's potential ridicule in mind, I cull a couple of the least plausible (e.g., *The Five-Day Miracle Diet*) before moving on to the self-development section, located behind the complete works of Dickens. Finally, it's on to the worst of my little bookshelf secrets: the woo-woo spiritual section, well hidden on the bottom shelf, behind massive volumes of Shakespeare and Chaucer. I sacrifice one book on exploring my chakras and another on summoning my guardian angels.

I'm rearranging a small modern fiction collection to disguise several books on dream analysis when the phone rings. Hoping it's Richard, I rush into the kitchen.

"Hi, honey!" It's Mom, sounding offensively perky.

"Mom," I say, trying to keep the disappointment out of my voice, "it's after eleven, you know."

"Yes, Scarborough is in the same time zone, dear," she burbles merrily. "You sound a little winded. Is everything all right?"

Since Mom is normally asleep by 10:00, she must sense I'm up to no good.

"Of course everything's all right," I answer, defensively enough to confirm her suspicions. "I just finished cleaning my apartment, that's all."

"Cleaning at this time of night?" She sounds skeptical.

"I'm not expecting company, I just find cleaning therapeutic. You know that."

"How about some deep-breathing exercises instead?"

"Have you been meditating again?" I ask, suspiciously.

"I've started a yoga class with Joan from down the street," she says, serenely. While we chat, I pull my best wineglasses off a shelf and wipe them with a cloth. "Anyway, dear, I just wanted to make sure you're behaving yourself. I'll let you get back to your dusting."

I stick out my tongue at the phone and immediately feel guilty. After all, the woman's calling because she cares about me.

"No need to worry, Mom," I assure her. "Margo's promo trip to the northern constituencies is a no-go and I've got some quiet days ahead."

Elliot leads me past a long lineup and into the crowded night-club. I had no idea Günter's band Glam Session was so popular.

"They're a huge hit on the university circuit," Elliot confirms proudly, seemingly oblivious to the fact that we're the oldest people in the room. He slings his arm around my shoulders as we weave through the crowd. "By the way, Flower Girl, I had a strange vision yesterday morning. A tall man and a short woman were playing tug-of-war with a map and you were sitting in an enormous empty suitcase watching them."

"And there I was thinking that love had clouded your psychic abilities. As it happens, the Ministry sideshow you forecast has been averted. Honestly—"

"There he is!" Elliot cuts me off, his face aglow. I follow his gaze to see two men near the stage shouting at each other.

"Ve told you ve only vanted Beck beer in our dressing room, yah? Vat is zis Molzonz scheisse?"

"His accent is very strong," I whisper to Elliot. "Didn't you say Günter left Germany as a child?"

"Yeah, sometimes he puts it on for effect. Isn't it great?"

So this is the man who's tamed Elliot's roamin' ways.... Somehow I didn't expect the long, curly platinum hair, nor glittery blue shadow and opalescent lipstick. Conservative Elliot with a man in a mauve angora cardigan and purple vinyl pants tucked into silver platform boots? Unthinkable. And then there's the hot-pink feather boa.

"Günter, I'd like to introduce you to—" Elliot begins as the club manager leaves to sort out the beer problem.

"Vy can't zay ever get it schtrait?" Günter interrupts petulantly. "Every club ve play, zer iz alvays problems. Who is zis?" he asks, tossing his dyed yellow mane in my direction.

"This is my friend, Libby. I've told you about her."

"Ze von on ze rock?" Günter says, taking my hand. "Guten abend, Libby." And then to Elliot, without a trace of an accent, "You never told me she was so tall."

"Vat—I mean, *what*—difference does that make?" I ask, testily.

"Relax, darling." Günter wraps his boa around my neck. "I find tall women sssssexy. Rahrrr! Now tell me, sweet Amazon," he says, pulling me closer with the string of pink feathers, "why do I always get shitty beer at these gigs?" When I hesitate for a moment, he adds suspiciously, "You *do* drink beer, don't you?"

"I much prefer bourbon, I'm afraid," I say, raising my glass sheepishly.

"Ooh, you like the *hard* stuff..." He slides the boa slowly from my neck.

Before I can question Günter's allegiance to men, Lola arrives, attracting all eyes with her black suede miniskirt, fishnet stockings and knee-high boots. She tows Michael over to introduce him. Michael gapes openly at Günter's ensemble as he extends his hand and Günter, in turn gapes openly at Lola's. Then the muffled strains of "La Cucaracha" issue from Michael's coat. He immediately retracts his hand, leaving Günter's dangling in the air. As Michael pulls his cell phone out of his jacket, "La Cucaracha" increases in volume.

"Hello," he barks into the phone. "Am I the only one with a brain in this company…? This is unbelievable… Do I have to come down there and sort this out myself?"

He steps into the middle of our little group, seemingly to provide optimal viewing of *The Michael Show*. Günter rolls his eyes dramatically at Elliot and stomps off to join the band. I sense Michael will be on the receiving end of a thick German accent when they finally meet.

Lola seems embarrassed by Michael's behavior, because she attempts to divert our attention from him.

"Libby, I've discovered a whole new category of brides—the 'Ultimatum Girl.' My colleague badgered her boyfriend to marry her for a year before issuing the ultimatum: ask me before my thirtieth birthday or I'm gone."

"I gather he relented."

"He held out almost till the stroke of midnight on her birthday before proposing. She had the hall booked the next day."

"That's pathetic," I say.

"Very sad," Elliot agrees with me for once.

"We could write a sequel," I suggest, "called *Ultimatum Girls: Ten Years After*. I can't imagine these marriages work out."

"Well, my boss is an Ultimatum Girl who's had twelve glorious years with her husband."

"God, I hope I don't have to harass anyone into proposing. It's so degrading."

"Yeah, well pride doesn't keep you warm at night," Lola says.

Thoughts of a cold bed prompt Lola to take Michael's arm proprietarily the second he puts his cell phone away. He reaches out and gives her ass a squeeze. She grabs his and suddenly they're all over each other. Elliot looks at me, eyebrows rising, but before he can comment the announcer introduces Glam Session and we turn to the stage. The lights go down, except for a tiny pink spotlight that shines on one of Günter's silver platform boots. His foot taps out a few beats, then the spot widens out to reveal the entire band as they start playing.

*"Well you're a dirty sweet flirt, in that skirt, I think that I love you…"*

Even with the band, I can hear slurping as Michael works away on Lola's neck. I try not to look but they're like a bad accident—terrible, but riveting.

*"Well you're strong and you're meek, your curves make me weak. You're a dirty flirt and you're my girl."*

Michael's hand is crawling up Lola's sweater.

*"Get it on, make love till dawn, get it on…"*

The crowd is pushing toward the stage and carrying us before it on a wave. Michael breaks Elliot's trance by clipping him in the head while throwing an arm around Lola's neck. In retaliation, Elliot attracts Günter's attention and points to the happy couple. Günter, in turn, signals the spot operator, who focuses his bright beam on the tangle of limbs.

Lola's suede skirt has flipped up in the back, exposing her thong and the crowd whoops enthusiastically above the sound of the band. Eventually, the noise brings Michael up for air and the two stare around, dazed. If I were in Lola's boots, I'd die of embarrassment, but she simply yanks down her skirt and gives the crowd a sassy little curtsy. Günter pulls her up onto the stage, where she proceeds to bump and grind.

Glam Session is really very good and just as they strike up a favorite David Bowie tune, a faint, annoying noise interrupts my listening pleasure. "La Cucaracha." Michael is reaching into his pocket for his phone. He glances at the incoming number, before turning away from the stage to answer it. Something about his secretive stance prompts me to step closer.

"…I'm at a concert with a friend of mine…it'll probably be a late night…he's going through a rough time…promise I'll come by and see you tomorrow."

As he slides his phone back into his pocket, Michael catches me watching and shrugs apologetically.

"The world of technology never sleeps," he says.

That conversation had nothing to do with technology. I've

heard that tone before—it's the one a guy uses when he's placating a demanding woman. I'm still speculating when his phone rings again. This time, he moves a couple of yards away. Straining, I manage to pick up a few words: "Okay, okay, I'll stop by later."

I may not have Elliot's gift, but I can smell a cheating boyfriend a mile off.

Lola steps down from the stage and hugs Michael. Again his phone rings. This time he checks the incoming number, clicks off the ringer and puts the phone in his pocket.

"Work again, damn it," he says. "Listen, I've got to get down there and sort these guys out." He gives Lola an apologetic kiss on the cheek. "Sorry, babe."

"It's midnight, Michael. Surely they can manage without you?"

"No can do, sweetheart. I am the boss. But don't worry, I'll call you as soon as things calm down."

Lola mutters something about walking Michael to the car and as she trails after him, Elliot dances up to me.

"The girl has 'desperate' stamped all over her," he says. I nod ruefully. If I'm wrong about Michael's playing around, he's obviously a workaholic. Either way, Lola is not first on his list. "You know," Elliot continues, smiling at me, "it's amazing how many women are determined to see a lamb when it's clearly a wolf at the door."

In other words, cleaning my apartment was probably a waste of time. I hope I can still rescue the book on guardian angels from the trash.

Walking home past Sotto Sotto, I nearly jump out of my skin when a voice drifts out of the shadows.

"Shouldn't you be tucked into bed, little girl?" Panic races through me before I recognize Richard's burly form on the restaurant's steps.

"Richard, you scared me. What are you doing here?"

"Having dinner, of course." I can tell from his voice that he's also had a few drinks. "Since you refused to try it with me, I invited Clarice instead. Julian's out of town and the lady is lonely."

The lady doesn't have girlfriends to keep her company? Sometimes I wonder if there's more between these two than an old friendship.

"And where's the lady now?" I ask, wondering if I can escape without seeing her.

"Powdering her nose. Tell me what brings you to these parts."

"I live near here—on Bernard," I say. I can see Mrs. Cleary through the window, shaking hands with patrons as she makes her way to the door. I turn to go with a hasty "good night."

"Just a second," Richard says, grabbing my arm and pulling me close. His mouth practically on my ear, he whispers, "You *are* going to go out with me, you know."

The alcohol on his breath isn't enough to stop my heart from picking up the pace.

"Actually, I'm not. I've made my decision." Be strong, Libby, be strong. The man obviously needs constant female companionship and anyone will do. I am not special. And Lola is not the only one who got hit with the "desperate" stamp at the entrance to the bar tonight.

"You'll change your mind," he says, practically nuzzling my neck. "And you will show me what was in that lingerie bag I saw. Are you wearing it right now?"

"I'm surprised you have to ask," I say, disentangling myself from his clutches and moving to a safe distance. "I thought a superhero could see through clothes."

It's almost 3:00 a.m. when the doorbell awakens me. I creep to my bedroom window and peer out at the porch. Richard is leaning on my buzzer. Before I can figure out what to do, he looks up and catches me.

"Libby... Open up! Issme, Clark Kent!" Extending his arms

like Superman, he takes a little leap, loses his balance and topples into the recycling bins.

He's totally smashed and at my door in the middle of the night. I was wrong, I am special.

Clambering to his feet, he starts hammering on the door. I grab my bathrobe, run a brush through my hair and rush to the door, worried that he'll wake Mrs. Murdock.

"I came to tuck you in," he says, staggering toward me.

"How did you find out where I live?"

"You tol' me the street, so I looked you up."

"So you're not too drunk to use a phone book."

"I'm jus' a lil' tipsy, but you should see Clarishe! I had to put 'er in a cab after we closed down the piano bar at th' Windsor Arms. You shoulda bin there, Lib, we were great."

"The two of you *performed?*"

"Oh yeah, we were hhhhhot!" Richard says proudly.

This can't be good. If anyone recognized Mrs. Cleary, it's bound to get a mention in the gossip columns. Seeing the worried look on my face, Richard adds, "Oh, don' worry your pretty head. There weren't any reporters around—I can smell 'em."

"Was she really that drunk?"

"Drunk enough to tuck her skirt into her panty hose. I had to pull her off the piano to straighten her out."

"Tell me you're kidding. Please."

"Would you relax, Libby? Ish a shecret between me and the piano man."

"Have you left anything out?"

"Invite me in an' I'll *de-brief* you in full." He winks sloppily at me.

Although I hate myself for it, I find the offer vaguely tempting. Still, I say, "I don't think so, I have to get up for work in a few hours."

"But you haff some lingerie you want to model for me." He leans in closer and belches, which has a distinctly sobering effect on my hormones.

"In your dreams, Dick," I say, shutting him down.

"Hey, enough with the coy routine," he says, suddenly harsh—and surprisingly articulate. "You've wanted me since the day I arrived and you still do, or you wouldn't be standing here now."

"I'm standing here because you rang my doorbell in the middle of the night."

"But you took the time to brush your hair." Grrrrrr! "Don't tell me you're holding out for that pathetic Mark? Is a dull consultant more your speed?"

"*You're* a consultant!"

"Don't be naive. I took this job as a favor to Julian. He begged me to give Clarice a hand, but I've got my own political career waiting for me in London. I just fancied a nice bit of Canadian crumpet while I'm here. To go out with a bang, so to speak."

I step back into the hall and slam the door in his face and lean against it, stunned. Richard's true character just emerged in that exchange: he's a vicious and egotistical drunk.

But he's also seen right through me, damn him, and that thought keeps me awake the rest of the night. In fact, I spring out of bed at 5:30, unaided by an alarm and fire up my espresso machine.

The phone rings at 6:00. "Libby," Margo says, "I need your help."

"What's the problem?" I ask, closing the hissing steam valve.

"I'm at the hospital with the Minister. We need you to go to her house and collect some of her toiletries and a change of clothes. The housekeeper will have them ready for you."

The paper arrives as I leave the house. To my relief, there's no mention of last night's piano bar antics in its pages, although the *About Town* column notes that the Minister dined with a handsome colleague at Sotto Sotto.

Looking more dishevelled than ever, Margo is kicking a candy machine in the waiting room of the emergency ward when I arrive.

"Is everything all right, Margo?" I ask anxiously, setting down the Minister's Louis Vuitton bags.

"No, the machine robbed me." There are rings under her eyes and her hair is in knots.

"I mean with the Minister. You look like you've been here all night."

"I didn't get much sleep, that's for sure, but Mrs. Cleary will be fine." She looks around carefully before continuing. "It's alcohol poisoning. Richard got her drunk. I could kill him."

"Do you want me to cancel today's events?"

"Laurie is already taking care of that. Let's deliver the Minister's things."

She leads me to a private room where Mrs. Cleary is reclining in a mint-green hospital gown. She's drawn and pale, her hair hanging around her face in dirty strings.

"It's about time you got here, Lily," she snaps, "I'm beginning to chafe in this gown." Wincing, she hoists herself onto one elbow, and with obvious difficulty, swings her legs off the bed. "Help me to the bathroom, Margo. I'll have a quick shower, then you can style my hair."

They're shuffling across the room when a stout nurse comes in pushing a wheelchair.

"I'm glad you're up," the nurse says. "We need to take you down to radiology."

"Radiology? Why?" Margo asks.

"Mrs. Cleary's wrist is swollen and we need to see if it's broken."

"It isn't broken," the Minister says. "Even if it is, I won't wear a cast."

"I think you will," the nurse says, glowering.

"I think you've forgotten who I am," the Minister retorts, drawing herself up regally.

"I think you've forgotten rank doesn't matter around here," the nurse counters. "But if you'd prefer to sign a waiver saying you refuse treatment, I'll see what I can do.

We need to protect the hospital in case your wrist heals poorly."

The Minister stops to consider this. "What do you mean by 'poorly'?"

"If it isn't set properly the wrist could become deformed. Nothing you couldn't hide with a long sleeve, though and if it doesn't worry you, it doesn't worry me."

"I'll be down after I'm showered and dressed," the Minister says, seeing reason.

"The technician is ready for you now."

The Minister sighs. "I'm not taking the chair."

"It's hospital policy."

"I could introduce a few policies around here you won't like."

"We'd welcome some culture around here, Minister. Do your worst."

Whipped, but not broken, Mrs. Cleary looks the nurse in the eye and says, "Look, I will submit to your X-ray, I will submit to your cast, but I will not submit to your wheelchair."

"Suit yourself, then," the nurse relents, shrugging. "It's for your own safety."

The Minister steps out of the room in her standard-issue gown and starts the long shuffle down the hall, pushing her I.V. pole in front of her.

"Well, don't just stand there, help me!" The Minister turns on Margo savagely. "And you, Lily, get my brush and bring it down to radiology so that Margo can back-comb my hair."

I take a moment to enjoy the sight of Margo scuttling behind the Minister.

"I need a smoke," the Minister's voice echoes in the empty hallway.

"You don't smoke," Margo says.

"I'm starting. Did Lily bring my pashmina? This green is terrible on me."

Mark is helping me to upload a new program onto my computer when I glance up and see Richard walking past my door.

When he notices Mark bent over my screen, he backs up and throws a kiss at me before carrying on down the hall. How could someone so immature have a political career in the offing? Mind you, Mrs. Cleary's continues to flourish.

Margo arrives at the door waving a news clipping. "You said the paper only mentioned a restaurant sighting."

Mark takes it from her hand. "It's a photo of you pawing at the back of the Minister's dress."

"It's not a dress, you idiot, it's a hospital gown and I'm holding it closed."

"I checked yesterday's paper, Margo. I thought we were in the clear." I take the clipping from Mark and examine it. "I didn't see any photographers."

"With a telephoto lens a photographer could have taken this from a long way off," Mark offers eagerly. "Today's faster film speeds mean you don't even need a flash."

"Don't worry, Margo," I reassure her. "The article only says the Minister has food poisoning and is canceling her appearances for the rest of the week."

Margo turns and huffs back down the hall to her office.

"What's eating her?" I ask. "This could have been so much worse. If anything, it will garner public sympathy for the Minister. She can wave her cast around while soldiering on with her duties."

"Check out the caption," Mark says.

*Minister Cleary In Bayview General, Attended By Unidentified Child.*

Smiling, I slip the clipping into my filing cabinet. It will have pride of place in my next scrapbook.

24

Elliot's sister is getting married in Port Hope in less than three hours. I'm cutting it close: the drive will take at least two and I'm still standing paralyzed in front of my closet. I can't imagine what Emily Post would recommend wearing to a wedding in a wooded glade, followed by a reception at a golf-and-country club. Certainly nothing in my wardrobe seems appropriate. To complicate matters further, I need to look professional, because it's my first gig as a roving wedding reporter. Settling on a navy suit, a sequined tank top and strappy heels, I teeter toward the door. "Oh, shut up," I tell Cornelius, who is watching me with a Cheshire smirk. Nonetheless, I change into my sneakers for the drive. Better safe than sexy.

I arrive in Port Hope with half an hour to spare and set out to explore the town. Wandering in and out of shops filled with folk art, I feel quite safe from temptation. Roxanne would be vulnerable here, but I am not the folk art type. Nonetheless, I emerge from a shop with a coatrack that features eight foot-long whales jutting out from a central post, their mouths agape to hold the coats. What a prize! It

has a strong whiff of the Maritimes about it. It was not, however, designed to travel in a Cavalier. With some effort, I
manage to wedge it into the car crosswise, leaving several
humpbacks protruding from the open front window on the
passenger side.

By the time I reach the conservation area, I have only ten
minutes to hike into the woods to the site of the ceremony. The
trail, though well-marked by balloons and signs, is overgrown
and muddy, so I decide not to change my shoes. Leaving the
coat rack jutting out of the car, I lope down the trail. Elliot and
Günter are cowering behind a squat spruce when I enter the
matrimonial clearing. At least, the bushy blond ponytail suggests
it's Günter; without the glitter, he's almost unrecognizable.

"Forget your party shoes?" Günter asks, in perfect English.

"Left them in the parking lot with your boa."

"She's feisty," he remarks to Elliot.

"It's annoying at first, but it grows on you," Elliot replies.

The guests are forming a circle at the direction of the bride,
who, regardless of the muck near the babbling brook, is wearing the most elaborate wedding gown I have ever seen.

"I've stumbled into the wrong fairy tale," I whisper to the
guys. "Isn't that Little Bo Peep?"

Half a dozen bridesmaids in pink chiffon are flitting through
the conifers; the ring bearer is threatening to push the flower
girl into the creek and an usher is showing off by climbing a
tree in his tux. The guests, meanwhile, are casting covert glances
at everyone else's apparel. One couple is in Tilly Endurables
from head to toe. Others are in black tie.

"The whole thing is insane," Elliot complains. "We're trying
to stay out of harm's way."

"What happened?"

"Regan crumbled as the big day approached and decided to
go for the traditional deal."

"Yah, it's been crazy trying to pull it all togeser," Günter adds,
a slight accent betraying his disgruntlement.

"Moss—and no one knows his real name—gave in on everything except Regan's last-minute request for a Catholic wedding," Elliot says, swatting a spider off Günter's arm, while the latter bleats in terror. "And so we await the druids."

Moments later, a pale man with a long red beard and a white, hooded cape enters the clearing. "Welcome, honored guests. Please join hands."

"What are we doing?" I ask, taking Elliot's hand.

"Forming the ring of friendship and love—*obviously*." Elliot's lip is twitching.

"Don't get me laughing," I warn him.

The ceremony is shorter than I feared. Red Beard honors the four directions (north, south, east and west) for the good of all beings, invokes some gods and goddesses to join the party and briskly recites the sacred vows. Regan and Moss repeat the vows, accept the blessings of the four elements, and swear upon the Sword of Justice to keep their vows. To conclude, Bo Peep gathers her crinoline and jumps over a branch with her groom. Two bridesmaids lunge forward to free the heels of the bride's Jimmy Choos from the mud as the happy couple kisses. We're back in the parking lot within twenty minutes.

The whale coat rack is still in the Cavalier and when Elliot spies it, he simply shakes his head and walks on by. I'm not sure what to do with it when I get to the club. I can't risk having it stolen from the car, but I can't carry it with me and look professional. The best choice, I decide, is to leave it at the club's coat check. So, after changing my shoes in the parking lot, I pull the coatrack out of the car and wobble up the cobblestone path with it.

"Oi, Girlie! If it's Moby's Dick ye'er after, ye'er in look— I'm Moby!"

A stocky, rumpled man of Irish origin is standing in the front entrance, leering at me with his few remaining teeth. He follows me to the coat check, but by the time I've convinced the staff to store my treasure, Moby has breached somewhere else, leaving me to take my place in the long receiving line.

"You're poetry in motion, Flower Girl," Elliot quips as I lurch unsteadily toward him. He leans over to kiss my cheek.

"Maybe you'd rather kiss my ass?"

"Actually, I would," he says, bending over.

*"Elliot!"* I leap backward and Günter, laughing uproariously, grabs my arm to steady me.

"Just kidding," Elliot says, but I doubt that. "I've hooked you up with the bartender."

"Thanks, but I already hit it off with Moby."

"Moby? Oh, the groom's cousin!" He turns to the vacant space beside Günter in the receiving line. "He was here a minute ago."

"Don't tell me he's in the wedding party!"

"He arrived unannounced from Ireland yesterday and Moss's mother felt obliged to include him."

The toothless Irish wit splashes into sight carrying three overflowing pints of Guinness.

"All this kissin' and hand-shakin' can make yer man tirsty!" Moby announces, surrendering two of the pints to Elliot and Günter. "And look who's here! Have ye come to take me up on me offer, long legs?"

He stands on his toes and plants a sloppy kiss on my cheek, giving my butt a squeeze.

"I'm warning you, Moby," I say, slapping his hand away, "there's a harpoon in my purse."

"There's nuthin' I loike better' a big foisty lass," he comments delightedly to Günter, as Elliot wisely departs to collect my bourbon from the bar.

After that, the evening is pure formula, from the meal of rubber chicken and mixed veg—interrupted by glass-tapping and kissing—to the awkward speeches. Regan and Moss sway through a sappy first dance before cutting into an elaborate cake. Then, inevitably, the D.J. calls upon single women to assemble on the dance floor. I gratefully use my role as observer to abstain from the bouquet toss. Regan fires it over her shoulder and it sails past many outstretched hands to land—whump!—in my lap, only to rebound onto the floor. Moby surfaces nearby, shoves several ladies out of the way and seizes the bouquet. He returns it to my lap with a gallant bow.

"Come on, long legs—ye know ye canna' resist me charms much longer."

He's dragging me toward the dance floor when the D.J. cues the dreaded "Chicken Dance." The crowd parts to accommodate Moby's flapping arms and wriggling butt and soon we are in the middle of a cheering circle. He pulls me close for a moment and rests his head against my bosom, grinning lustily at the crowd. Then he flings me around the dance floor in a frightening round of combat polka. He's surprisingly powerful for such a small man. The crowd applauds as the song ends and Moby and I take a bow.

When I hear the first strains of "Hey Jude," however, I bolt for the ladies' room, where I find Elliot's mother alone, smoking. She stubs out her cigarette in a coffee cup with a sheepish smile. Though in her late fifties, Grace is surprisingly hip in her black leather pants. Still, it's an odd choice for mother of the bride. I've noticed throughout the evening that she seems oddly detached. I explain about the book and ask Grace if she'd be willing to chat about the wedding.

"Sure," she replies, leading me out of the washroom and into the club's bar area, "as long as you promise not to blame any of this on me."

"Blame any of *what* on you?" I settle in beside her on a couch and take out my notepad and pen.

"Regan's change of heart about the big splashy wedding. The original plan was so much simpler."

"But this is all pretty standard."

"Exactly, and it's ridiculous, all this white-dress-and-flowers-bullshit." I cough, choking. "Oh, you know what I mean," she continues, "and it's costing her father and me nearly thirty grand."

"Isn't it usually the mother who pressures a bride to do the traditional thing?"

"With Regan, it's a backlash against a mother who *isn't* traditional. I fought her every step of the way—the worst strategy a mother can take, I suppose." She stops a passing waiter with a tray and snags a glass of red. Sipping, she adds thoughtfully, "Regan has been angry since I left her father two years ago."

"Oh?"

"Elliot didn't tell you? He's been very supportive of my decision, of course, but Regan hasn't forgiven me. I understand how she feels, but she is thirty, after all. She wouldn't let me bring a date—yet her father is here with his girlfriend."

Grace and I chat for nearly an hour, at which point she suggests visiting the courtyard. Lighting a cigarette in front of the ice sculptures of Cinderella and Prince Charming, she shakes her head in disgust.

"Why on earth do you want to write about weddings?"

Suddenly, I'm not sure. The only thing I'm sure about is that her hand is resting in the small of my back. This is odd, but there's no need for panic. It's the mother of the bride, after all. She's probably just an affectionate woman. Since I feel a trifle awkward, however, I start to babble about weddings being a fascinating topic, about the book being a way to break into the market, about needing an escape from my job. Grace's hand doesn't move. So I set off on a mad ramble about my job. It's quite hellish, I tell her, but at least it has allowed me to meet some pleasant men and I have a crush on one now. (Richard may be a goof, but he has enough testosterone to bring an ice sculpture of Cinderella to her frozen knees.)

"Relax," Grace says, withdrawing her hand. "I hear you. And I appreciate your candor—although it wouldn't hurt to be a little more direct." She takes her business card out of her purse and hands it to me. "Call me if you change your mind."

It's the first time I've ever been hit on by a woman and I wish I'd handled it with a little more…*grace.* Especially since it's Elliot's mother.

"Leaving so soon, Flower Girl?" Elliot asks when I track him down. "Moby will be disappointed."

"He's not the only one," I say, collecting my whale coatrack and heading for the door. "Why didn't you tell me your mother is gay?"

"You never asked," he says, in a matter-of-fact tone as he follows me down the front stairs. "Why, did she make a move?"

"Well, yes," I confess. "Maybe I should consider it—she's an attractive woman."

"Then you'd be my stepmother—*that* would be weird!"

"Give me a hand with this, *son,*" I say, beginning to wedge the whale coatrack back into the Cavalier.

"I'm not touching that monstrosity."

"It's folk art. You have no taste—except in men, I suppose. I like Günter."

"Isn't he great?" Elliot gushes.

"Yah!" I reply. "You seem good together." I must sound pensive, because he leans over and hugs me.

"Your turn will come—just as soon as you accept what's good for you."

"I suppose you think that's Tim."

"Well, he does have a nice ass."

"There are other nice asses in the world."

"True, but few men amount to more than that and I should know. You'd be better off with Mom than the guy you're chasing."

"Good thing I took her card, then!" I climb into the car and turn the key in the ignition. "Bye, Elliot."

"Don't come crying to me when he breaks your heart," he says.

"Can't hear you," I yell through the closed window, but he's already walking back across the parking lot toward Günter, who is silhouetted in the light of the club's doorway talking to Moby. The German accent is likely very dense indeed.

## 25

The Minister and Margo are chatting in the hall outside the boardroom when I arrive. Richard strides toward them, a smile stretching across his face.

"Hello, Richard." Margo is surprisingly civil, considering he's behind some bad press.

Ignoring Margo, he presses his lips to Mrs. Cleary's cheek. "How are you feeling, Clarice?"

"Much better," she replies. "Thank you so much for the flowers, Richard. You have some explaining to do with Julian though," she adds playfully.

"And the wrist?"

"Healing beautifully, I'm told."

At that, they both burst out laughing. Clearly, there's a story behind the broken wrist, but they're not sharing it.

The smile leaves Richard's face when he notices me. As if *he* has any reason to be annoyed! Well, as long as I can keep the image in my mind of his arriving drunk at my apartment door, I should have no trouble killing off this crush.

★ ★ ★

I'm trying to find my yogurt in the staff refrigerator when Mark appears, carrying two gourmet sandwiches.

"Goat cheese with roasted peppers," he says, offering them up for inspection. "Would you like one?"

"I can't take your lunch, Mark. Besides, my tasty fat-free yogurt is in here somewhere."

"I can guarantee it won't be as good as one of Vessuvio's sandwiches. Really, take one."

"Are you sure?" I ask, ripping the foil off and sinking my teeth into the sandwich before he can change his mind.

We're savoring the last bites when Richard arrives and goes through the motions of making tea. Since he always buys it from the shop downstairs, I sense there's more than tea brewing.

"Thanks again for the sandwich, Mark," I say, making a quick exit before Richard can insult either of us.

Moments later, Richard appears at my office door—without tea. The spirit of competition must be easing him over his snit.

"So, you're falling for the old sandwich ploy," he says.

"So, you're passing through puberty in reverse."

"I'm just trying to protect you. Mark seems to be playing some kind of game."

"I'm all for a game that involves food."

"He's been wracking up a lot of billable hours with you. Is he fascinated by the speechwriting process, or is there something less cerebral at play?"

"Proceed directly to the apology, then go bill the Ministry for *your* time."

"Apology for what?"

"For being a jerk. For coming to my house in the middle of the night, drunk. For insulting me. Take your pick."

"I believe it is *Dick* who is owed an apology."

"I was provoked."

"Maybe I was upset that you rejected me," he says, changing

tactics. "Maybe I'm hurt that you prefer what's-his-name's company to mine."

"Mark and I are pals."

"Well, I guarantee you he's hoping for more."

"He's a nice guy, we're pals, end of story. If you gave him half a chance, you might like him."

"I have enough *pals* already, thanks."

"Your loss. Now, if you don't mind, I have a speech to write."

He sulks in his office for the rest of the afternoon but returns around 8:00 p.m., offering to show me how to find "classic" speeches on the web. I find myself accepting and the pheromones heal our rift in no time. In fact, we're soaking in them when Mark comes by to see if I am leaving. Richard eyes him sullenly as I hastily reply that I have hours of work ahead. Turning to leave, Mark crashes into Margo, who's materialized behind him.

Sounding more flustered than the situation warrants, Margo smoothes her suit and says, "Richard, I suggest you leave Libby to her speech. The Minister has already asked for a draft."

Richard makes a show of taking his sweet time before leaving. Margo follows him, but returns a short time later.

"Libby, do you think you're spending too much time with Richard? We've noticed you're falling behind with your speeches."

"If I'm slowing down it's because I'm exhausted, Margo. In case you haven't noticed, I've been churning out a lot of speeches lately—including two for last Friday that were never used."

"Are you interested in him?"

"Margo, we've been over this before. I'm not involved with Richard—not that it's anyone's business but mine."

"Well, that's a relief. I expect the Minister would consider it a 'career limiting move.' You know," she adds, lowering her voice conspiratorially, "I don't know how anyone could find that man attractive."

"I've got to get back to work, Margo," I reply wearily.

Like I'd ever fall for her faux gal-pal routine! Besides, were I not so convinced she's immune to normal human desires, I'd say Margo is attracted to Richard herself. She's been acting weirder than usual around him lately. This morning, I caught her staring at him during a planning meeting. Maybe she's heard about his political aspirations and it turns her on. At any rate, few seem able to resist his raw sexuality. He has a habit of standing too close and whispering, as if the most mundane statement is a secret you're sharing. Margo seems as enthralled as the rest of us.

I'd recover from my obsession with Richard much sooner if he'd just stop *touching* me. He's always coming up behind me and putting his hand on my shoulder and yesterday, he actually put his arm around me. For one short, blissful moment I gave myself up to it and leaned on him. Then I remembered I must be aloof, like a cat, and moved away. It was all I could do not to weave around his ankles and jump into his lap—figuratively speaking, of course.

Which isn't to say I've forgotten what he's really like. Even my subconscious reminds me. Last night, I dreamed Richard and I were having dinner in a nice restaurant. During dessert, his cell phone rang and he informed his caller that he'd be right over. Then he offered me a thin excuse about having to resolve some crisis at work—even though it was past midnight. Enraged, I accused him of running to another woman. He didn't even have the decency to deny it. "Libby," the dream Richard told me, "you and I are just good pals. But I promise I'll bring you a nice sandwich next time I see you."

It was just a dream, I tell myself, inspired no doubt by my

suspicions about Lola's beau, Michael. Just the same, it's left me with a bad feeling all day. I can't afford to let this crush slip into fifth gear. Fortunately, I know exactly what I need to do to slow down the runaway train.

To: Roxnrhead@interlog.ca
From: Mclib@hotmail.ca
Subject: Brake Lights

Hey Rox,

All signs indicate that my crush on Richard must come to a screeching halt. He can't possibly be the man for me. He has the E.Q. of a 12-year-old, whereas I am at least 15. Although I swear his appeal isn't linked to his cash flow, I can't account for where it does lie. Somehow, he's as irresistible to women as a free makeup bonus.

Since the night he showed up at my door, he's been working much harder to impress me. I've been receiving helpful tips on everything from handling my computer to investing my considerable wealth. I try to remain aloof, but then he whispers in my ear or touches me, and I crumble. He probably thinks I'm playing games, but I'm really just trying to resist.

Obviously, the problem is my own weakness, so I must bolster myself with a show of strength on the home front. Today I collected all my crush-related purchases to see what could be returned. I started with one of the sweaters I bought at Banana Republic, which was really too tight anyway. The tags were still on, but since it's now on sale I was only able to recover half its value. I stopped at Aveda on the way home and got a full refund on two scented candles and a bottle of body oil. I delivered some bath bombs to a delighted Mrs. Murdock upstairs, and called Dad to pick up the box of frozen filet mignon (no wonder he doesn't believe I'm vegetarian). The bras, underwear and fishnets I can't return, but that's okay. They've migrated to the back of my underwear drawer, where they will stay until my hormones awaken for some other guy.

My cleansing efforts did not kill the crush, but they delivered a disabling blow. The downshift into third gear almost threw me to my knees. Still I managed to stagger toward chocolate.
Lib

The Minister is in excellent spirits this morning when she drops by my office first thing.

"Why look, Lily, a guest chair! Things have changed, haven't they?"

"They have, Minister," I smile. "Would you care to use it?"

"I would," she replies, perching gracefully on the edge. "You haven't seemed yourself, lately, Lily, if you don't mind my saying so."

"I'm a bit tired, Minister—nothing serious. It's been an intense period of writing, as you know." It's also been an intense period of research on the book front, but I'm careful not to let *that* drop at the office. My Lady would not tolerate divided loyalties.

"Everyone seems a little down this week," she continues, which is the closest she's come to acknowledging that she inconvenienced a lot of people with her drunken escapade. "Do you know what I think we need?"

"Medication?"

*"Lily!"*

"All right, a vacation?"

"No, a party! I'll host it."

"A party?" Since when does she care so much about office morale?

"We've been working very hard and we deserve to cut loose."

"Cut loose?" I echo, dubiously.

"Don't be a spoilsport. I'm having a party and that's all there is to it. All we need is a theme!"

"You mean like 'come as your favorite pop star'?"

"That's the spirit! I'll work out the details and get back to you."

I'm a little stunned by this exchange, but Richard isn't surprised when I tell him.

"Clarice loves a theme party," he says. "She has one every year. There are two possibilities: Disco Fever or Talent Night. Last year we performed, so I'd start polishing my platforms if I were you. I'll have my housekeeper ship my disco gear from London. Incidentally, Clarice has her own disco ball."

Sure enough, an hour later Margo anxiously assembles the full staff for a special announcement. Mrs. Cleary is pacing briskly up and down in the boardroom.

"People," she begins, "I'm throwing a party next Thursday night at my home to cheer you up. All refreshments will be provided. The theme is 'Disco Night' and you are required to dress accordingly. And by the way…" She stops pacing to glare at us. "Attendance is mandatory."

Margo's stunned expression suggests she hasn't held on to her tube tops. She watches, frozen in dismay, as the Minister hurries over to me.

"Thanks so much for the idea, Lily! This is going to be *great!*"

She giggles and whirls off, leaving me to shrug sheepishly at Margo and slink back to my office, where I find Richard lying in wait.

"If you're a good girl at the party," he whispers in my ear, "I might just let you *ring my bell.*"

I roll my eyes, but when he rests his hand on my shoulder, I find myself regretting the return of the tight sweater. I'm no longer reluctant to see my colleagues (Richard) in a social setting. I've been working like a slave and could use a little distraction (Richard) from the grind. My current malaise is nothing a little dancing (with Richard) couldn't fix. Long live the Hustle.


Tim Kennedy emerges from the Minister's office just as I arrive to deliver a draft speech. It's been weeks since I've seen him. He's grown a beard and it looks great.

"Thanks for coming in, Tim," the Minister says, walking him out. "I appreciate your advice on my new program ideas." She sees me cowering in the next doorway and says, "Lily, you've met Tim, haven't you?"

"Yes, of course. How are you?"

"Very well, thanks," he says, summoning a stiff smile.

"Oh, I have a marvelous idea!" the Minister exclaims. "Tim, I am having a little party for my staff on Thursday and you must join us."

A fleeting expression of panic crosses Tim's face, but he responds calmly: "Thank you for the invitation, Clarice, but I'm afraid I already have plans."

"You must try to reschedule them, Tim. This will be the event of the season. It's a disco theme."

"Disco? Well, that does sound like fun. I wish I could make it, but I'm afraid it's impossible."

"What a shame," the Minister pouts. "Are you quite sure?"

"Quite sure, but thanks again." As he passes me, he permits himself a grin and mutters, "Boogie on down."

I hope Tim isn't passing up an opportunity to make Mrs. Cleary happy simply because he hates me. Let's face it, the budget for his orchestra depends very much on the Minister's whim. He could probably finance new uniforms simply by suffering through a short Abba number. Just the same, I'm relieved he declined. With Richard attending, it would only become a Ballroom Blitz.

Elliot and Günter pull me along Baldwin Street and into their favorite vintage-clothing store. Apparently Günter gets most of his Glam Session costumes here.

"It's a '70s theme, remember," I say, steering them away from a rack of debutante dresses. "And the point is to look totally fuckable!"

"Well, it's *your* heart, Lib," Elliot cautions, knowing full well that I have Richard in mind. "If you're determined to have it crushed, who am I to stop you?"

Which is rich, coming from the man who has deliberately crushed scores of hearts. But I am not about to pick a fight when I need them to help me get ready for the Minister's party, so I meekly try on every outfit they toss my way. We're all partial to the orange off-the-shoulder dress with frills, but it seems unlikely to provide good coverage during a frenzied boogie. Next, there's a mint green wrap skirt with a rose blouse featuring French cuffs and a detachable tie. Too sedate, we decide. We almost have to dial 911 for the old lady who runs the store when she sees me in the tube top/elephant pant combo. Far too funny to carry me into the fuckable range. Besides, I failed the pencil test a decade ago.

In the end, we all vote for a red polyester jumpsuit with a wide silver belt. It has the best shock value—particularly because it's a size (or two) too small. Günter assures me it's nothing a good sturdy girdle can't handle; I don't question how he knows this. Then he offers to lend me his glitter platforms with the real block-of-wood soles. For once, these size 12 pontoons have come in handy!

"All we need to do is style your hair like the Charlie's Angel of your choice and you'll be perfect," Günter says, pushing me toward the cash register.

"Yeah, and if that ain't the way your heartbreaker likes it— *uh-huh, uh-huh*—you better give it up for lost, Flower Girl."

To: Roxnrhead@interlog.ca
From: Mclib@hotmail.ca
Subject: Body sculpting

Dear Roxy,

What's in a name? Let me tell you, when they started calling the common girdle a "foundation garment," they revolutionized the whole notion of support. We curvaceous gals have been crazy to let it all hang loose in the mistaken belief that girdles are for geezers. The Minister was right when she said Lycra is a woman's best friend!

I walked into the department store yesterday wearing dark glasses. Heaven forbid I reveal my secret need. You wouldn't believe the range of options. There are big Lycra tubes, bicycle shorts, miniskirts and some that go almost head to toe. I carried several different items into the change room, and with the help of a good slathering of body butter, slid into each like a greased pig.

Curious minds want to know, where does the fat go when it's squeezed into serious Lycra? Does it well up around the neck and down around the calves? It's gotta go somewhere, right? Well, my little experiment shows that it doesn't become a spare tire in an unlikely locale. The flab is actually squeezed inward. Damage to internal organs may result from prolonged usage.

Anyway, I found one that lifts and separates, and packs the rest neatly away. When I got my rubber treasure home, I squished myself into it and slipped the jumpsuit over top. It was like computerized "before and after" magic: I looked as though I shaved off 10 pounds without giving up chocolate! So what if I have treadmarks all over when I take it off?

By the way, it occurred to me today that my crush may have geared up to fourth again without my noticing. I only figured it out while girdle shopping, when I found myself in the fitting room with a black garter belt in my hand; I don't recall picking it up. For someone who doesn't even like wearing panty hose, that's surely the sign of a crush at its peak. My thoughts are clearly disordered. Lib

P.S. I didn't actually buy the garter belt.

## 26

The foundation garment is a wondrous invention, but it is not built for comfort. Once I'm into it, I can neither expand my lungs fully, nor bend in the usual places. In fact, I have to throw myself sideways into a cab en route to the Minister's party. It's worth the pain, however, because the cabbie's sidelong glances confirm I look surprisingly fetching. At any rate, my hair looks better than it could have in the seventies, thanks to the excellent products of the new millennium. Günter introduced a perfect Farrah flip to it and blasted it into a helmet. Then he dusted my face with so much glitter that it's tough to see the wrinkles.

When I walk through the door of the Minister's Forest Hill home, my ratings soar.

"Lily," the Minister squeals, "you look fantastic!"

She's so thrilled she actually embraces me, which is how I discover her turquoise wrap dress is silk; it was designed to *look* vintage. My stretch polyester jumpsuit, on the other hand, is thirty years old and could go up in flames at any moment.

Richard lounges across the room in a perfectly tailored white three-piece suit and platform shoes that take him up to about six-nine. He looks oddly at ease in the ensemble.

"If it isn't the long-lost Gibb brother," I say.

Margo is lurking behind the Minister, in her usual navy suit and white shirt. She looks sullen, despite the "happy face" kerchief tied around her head.

"What do you think of Margo's outfit, Lily?" the Minister inquires.

"Corporate disco at its finest," I say. "The bandanna works, though."

"See?" Mrs. Cleary says to Margo. "Lily, when Margo arrived without a costume, I went though my closet and found this kerchief."

The Minister takes my arm and leads me to the living room, where a disco ball is showering sparkling light over Mark. His orange shirt, open to the navel, showcases several gold medallions.

"You look amazing, Libby," Mark says and out of the corner of my eye, I see Richard watching. "Can I get you a cocktail?"

"I advise you to stay sober," Margo whispers.

"Yeah, tell it to the Minister," I whisper back. But, tempted as I am by the sight of the full bar where two bartenders are serving up colorful concoctions, I tell Mark to get me a club soda.

I avoid alcohol for a full hour—until the Minister rolls out the karaoke machine, saying that each guest will be required to perform a disco hit of her choosing. At this point I head straight for the bar where I hastily knock the parasol out of a Singapore Sling and chug it down, maraschino cherries and all.

The Minister delivers a surprisingly raunchy version of "Lady Marmalade." As a mark of favor, she asks me to perform next and I manage a fair rendition of "I Will Survive." After this, karaoke hour becomes a lot more fun. Richard then takes to the makeshift stage next and belts out "She's a Lady," gyrating with such enthusiasm that the Minister takes off her Hermès scarf and throws it at the stage. Finally, when everyone else has performed, Margo stands and grimly *speaks* the words to "Born to be Alive," unintentionally bringing down the house.

By the time the dancing begins, I'm having a great time, sipping my third cocktail and glorying in the Minister's newfound fondness for me. Clarice is a fine lady, I decide. How wrong I've been about her! She and Richard execute the Hustle and the Bump with precision, while Bill, Laurie, Mark and I dance together. Eventually, Richard grabs Margo's hand and twirls her into Mark, causing them to crash into the wall. Brushing roughly past Mark, Richard collects Margo just seconds before the pace of the music slows. Peaches and Herb start singing "Reunited" and before he can escape, Margo wraps her arms around his waist. She's either ignoring her own rule about sobriety or I was right about her interest in Richard.

Mark has wisely removed himself from the scene of the crime and I follow him to the food table, eager to examine the glazed Spam centerpiece. Besides, the Singapore Slings have overcome my good sense and I'm burning like a "Disco Inferno" over the fact that Richard hasn't asked me to dance. He eventually joins us, with the Minister now close on his platform heels. With Julian away at a conference, she's been free to flirt with Richard all night. Now, when he sits down in a huge leather club chair, she drops gracefully into his lap and begins feeding him maraschino cherries from a crystal bowl. One by one, she pops them into his mouth and he washes them down with great swigs of Long Island Iced Tea.

"Okay, Clarice, enough," Richard says, when she's half emptied the bowl.

She giggles, snuggles into his shoulder and unbuttons his white vest, leaving sticky red fingerprints all over it. Moments later, she's asleep. Richard gets up and deposits her on a velvet divan and Margo covers her with a chenille throw. I recognize my cue to leave, but no, I'm trapped in the middle of Mark's rambling monologue about the chemical content of maraschino cherries.

"You wouldn't believe how long it takes them to break down in a landfill site," he says earnestly. "Longer even than wieners!"

"Mark," Richard interrupts.

"Yeah?"

"You're boring."

"Yeah, well, you're drunk," Mark retorts. "And you're probably the only one bored."

"Hardly," Richard says. "Look what you've done to Clarice. And Libby is struggling to stay conscious, aren't you Lib?"

I ignore Richard and turn to Mark. "I've got to get going. Do you want to share a cab?"

"I'll come with you," Richard says.

The three of us walk to the end of the Minister's driveway and the two guys almost rumble over hailing a cab. Each tries to slip an arm around me, only to rebound off my Lycra/polyester combination. Margo is watching from the door and I can imagine what she's thinking. By the time a cab pulls up, I'm so disgusted that I jump in and slam the door in their faces while they're still jostling each other out of the way.

"Since you two can't keep your hands off each other, why don't you share one?"

I fully intended to come home alone anyway: watching a woman bust her way out of a foundation garment would surely kill the mood.


Richard is seriously hung over when he arrives at work two hours late. I had him pegged as the type of guy who'd make it a point of honor never to acknowledge a hangover, but when I offer a chipper good morning, all he can manage is a weak twitch of his lip as he pops half a dozen mints into his mouth.

Half an hour later, I find him with his head on his desk, a muffled snore rising into the air with the smell of stale alcohol and breath mints. Sensing slumbering prey, Margo has crept out of her web and is dancing down the hall on eight hairy legs.

She squeezes past me and sends Richard's door into the wall with a deliberate crash.

"What the...?!" Richard sits up, dazed.

"We're not paying you $2000 a day to snore!" she screeches. "The taxpayers of Ontario deserve better than this!"

"Get to the point," Richard grumbles, "I'm not feeling well."

"Maraschino cherries must disagree with you."

"Please, Margo," he says. His voice betrays his weakness.

"I've had it with you. Your behavior has been unprofessional since the day you arrived."

"Clarice is no better. She didn't even make it in today."

"Mrs. Cleary is an elected official and she can serve as she chooses. Your behavior, on the other hand, is fair game."

I can't watch anymore. The screaming is hurting my head. Besides, it will probably be my turn next and I'd rather be sitting down when she starts. The truth is, Margo is right that Richard's behavior is unprofessional. So is hers, so is the Minister's, and so, I daresay, is mine. It's the most dysfunctional organization I've ever encountered. I've been so caught up in the action that I've almost lost my objectivity. I'd be wise to cut short my contract and return to the Education Ministry while I still can, but from the perspective of my speechwriting career, it's still too early. Although I've written a dozen speeches, that's not enough to launch me in this profession. A few more months would put me in a much better position.

As long as I haven't been corrupted beyond redemption, that is. In recent weeks, I've almost started enjoying myself here, and that's dangerous. There will come a point where my assimilation will be so thorough that I am no longer fit for normal government life. Will I recognize this point before I reach it?

I'm still musing when Richard, pale and bleary-eyed, steps into my office to say he's heading back to the U.K. to lie low for a week. It's strange that he wouldn't return for good, given his higher aspirations. Then again, he hasn't mentioned the subject since the night on my doorstep. Maybe it was just champagne talking. Surely someone planning a career in the public forum wouldn't allow himself to drift into this vortex of lunacy, favors to old friends notwithstanding.

## 27

Some people collect frivolous decorative objects like china dolls or Beanie Babies. Me, I prefer functional pieces—specifically coffeemakers and related gadgetry. I've installed shelves in my kitchen to hold my collection and have come to consider it art. Which is a superb example of cognitive dissonance, I admit, but when you've invested as much in the pursuit of the perfect home-brewed mochaccino as I have, rationalizing is inevitable.

The mission began after a quick calculation revealed how much I'd been spending on espresso, café latté, cappuccino and, my favorite, mochaccino. Actually, it was my ever-helpful brother Brian who did the math.

"Christ, Lib," he said, "if you gave up those cash-guzzlers, you could buy a house in a year."

An exaggeration, but he had a point. At three bucks a pop, fancy coffee is a pricey indulgence—and hardly my only one. Making my coffee at home could be a good way to save for a new car, I decided. How hard could it be?

Three years later, I am still driving the Cavalier. I bought two espresso makers, each of which produces a bitter brew. I bought two different frothers, neither of which produces a decent foam. And I bought several hybrids, some of which produce an adequate espresso, others an adequate foam, none both. Even the gorgeous chrome number taking up half my counter generates a noxious blend.

I consulted experts. The problem is the coffee beans, some advised, so I ran around the city to locate Colombia's finest. No, it's an issue of grinding those beans fresh, others said, so I bought a coffee grinder. I tried filtering my water, using a stainless steel pot for steaming the milk and tracking down Belgian chocolate syrup. And when none of it worked, I cleaned my machines and started all over. Eventually, I became capable of firing up several different machines and turning out a respectable mocha. It took nearly an hour and it was cold long before I cleaned up.

Finally, my interviews with the best coffee wranglers in the city uncovered the truth. Producing a stellar cappuccino requires two things I will never have: a $5,000 machine (which would finance a lot of Cavalier) and the right technique. Apparently the talent is inborn and those of Scottish descent are at an evolutionary disadvantage. Better to try my hand at distilling whisky, they advised.

Once I learned that it wasn't in my genes to brew a decent cup of coffee, I turned my appliances into art and abandoned myself to the joys of Dooney's once again. After all, it's not just the coffee I love, it's the whole café environment. Sitting at my usual table by the window, I hold the mug against my cheek for a moment before taking that first divine sip, basking in the warmth and the aroma of chocolate and coffee. I savor every mouthful, watching the world go by and eavesdropping on the people around me. In short, it's a full sensory experience for three lousy bucks.

When Jeff slides my coffee in front of me this morning, I'm relieved to see that I'm practically alone because I've come to work. I turn on my Walkman and start reviewing my tapes from Regan's wedding. Listening to her wax on about the "biggest day of her life" soon saps the pleasure from my mochaccino and I find myself wondering why I allowed Lola to talk me into this book. The only wedding I've enjoyed in a decade was Emma's—and that was only because of Tim.

"What are you smiling about?" Jeff's voice penetrates Moss's discourse on druid symbolism and I pull the headset from my ears.

"I'm smiling?"

"You are. You must be thinking about your boyfriend."

I feel the smile fade. I'm actually thinking about the boyfriend I might have had were I not such an idiot. As the caffeine rush hits me I realize that Tim is to Richard as a fine mochaccino is to one of those fizzy instant packets. The latter might have flash and convenience, but the *soul* is missing— and there's a nasty chemical aftertaste. I have been led astray by my own laziness and cowardice, coupled with some clever advertising.

*This epiphany brought to you by the Coffee and Cacao Exporters of South America!*

What a shame I can't live my whole life with a constant slow drip of high-quality mochaccino into my body. I'd have a lot fewer regrets.

I brood a little more during the drive to Sunday dinner.

*Richard and Tim are central characters in Libby's life story: compare and contrast.*

The exercise distracts me quite nicely, but when I get stuck in a traffic jam outside Wal-Mart, I go a step further and start imagining I'm taking Richard home to meet the family. This works so well that before I know it, I'm pulling in behind my parents' battered Taurus and am somehow seeing my life as if looking through the windshield of Richard's Porsche. His snobby English nose would be hoisted at the sight of this modest house.

The smell of burnt lima beans greets me as I open the front door. Mom must be cooking them especially for me, legumes being an excellent protein substitute for deluded vegetarians. Dad waves from the maroon leather La-Z-Boy recliner, where he's watching football on TV. The sound is muted and Supertramp is blaring out of the stereo—the same stereo he bought the year I was born, which is built into an oak cabinet so long it looks like a coffin. On the custom made shelves above it are hundreds of LPs. Every three months, he removes each record from its sleeve and cleans it, whether he's played it or not.

Time has almost stood still here. When I help Mom set the table, I retrieve the tall glasses Dad collected 30 years ago when a local garage gave one away with each tank of gas. We use them for everything, including wine, which they'll hold tonight. Mom gets the purple glass, Dad the green, I take yellow and since he's home for a visit, Brian will have his blue glass.

"Where's Bri?" I ask Mom.

"Playing basketball with the boys."

The "boys" are Brian's high-school pals, who are all thirty-one. My brother left for university in Vancouver a decade ago but he and the guys remain close. They all live for sports. In fact, Bri is a high-school gym teacher who spends his free time teaching either snowboarding or sailing, depending on the season. He has yet to meet his ideal woman—the brainy beauty who can make clever repartee while swooping down a mountain slope.

"Killing time until all the work is done, as usual," I snort.

My brother, like his father before him, is a stranger to domestic drudgery. True to form, the front door opens just as the last bowl of food lands on the table.

"Lib! Give your baby brother a hug!" Brian jogs over and tries to pull me against his sweaty body in a big bear hug. At six-four and two hundred pounds, he has the upper hand.

I struggle to free myself. "Get away from me, you pig!"

"Don't call your brother a pig," Mom says.

"Yeah, you're breaking my heart!" He snickers as he ducks into the bathroom for a quick shower.

Dinner is getting cold, but of course we wait for Brian to

take his place at the table. His butt is barely in the chair when he and Dad simultaneously spear the largest pork chop. There's a turkey patty on my plate. It's not *red* meat, ergo—to my mother—it is virtually vegetarian.

"Another fad diet?" Brian asks, eyeing my pale dry turkey patty while sawing away at his pork.

"Well, you know what they say, you are what you eat, little piggie."

"Are you saying I'm fat?"

"If the trough fits…" How nice to have him home!

"So, what is it this time, high-cardboard/no-flavor? Or did Mom grill the box by mistake?"

"If you must know," I say with dignity, "it's a turkey burger."

"Then you're right, you are what you eat."

Walked right into that one—must have poured a little too much wine into my yellow tumbler.

"Touché—*Sparky*." Adding Granddad's nickname for Brian to any statement automatically guarantees a win. I don't like to play the card too often, but it feels like the right moment to remind him who's boss.

"Shut up," he starts, but Dad intervenes before further regression occurs.

"Good news, son, your mother finally agreed to the GX85."

Brian falls for it: "Awesome! What's the starting system like?"

"Manual recoil, dual path hydrostatic transmission and zero-turn radius steering."

"Fifteen HPs?"

"Fourteen-five."

"What are you two talking about?" I interrupt.

"Lawn mowers!" they chime in unison.

"Your father's bought a yard cruiser, dear," Mom explains.

"A yard cruiser?"

"You know, a lawn mower you drive," Brian says enthusiastically.

I roll my eyes at my mother. Theirs is one of the bigger yards on the block, but it hardly warrants a rider mower. Mr. Whitmore is probably behind this. He and Dad have competed for years and last winter, the Whitmores got a snowblower.

As Brian and Dad ramble on about the GX85, I shudder at the thought of Richard's witnessing this visit. It's not as if my family isn't capable of more interesting conversation. I'll prove it by steering them on to a more cultural topic.

"So, I saw the new Dutch 'masters' exhibit at the art gallery."

"Cool," Brian says encouragingly. "The guy who cut his ear off was Dutch, right?"

"Van Gogh," I offer, warily.

"What did he chop it off with?"

"I have no idea."

"A razor," Dad states. Like he would know.

"Messy—should have used a knife."

"That wouldn't be messy?" Mom asks.

The art world isn't ready for the McIssac clan, I realize, redirecting the conversation to something a little more mainstream: "Hey Dad, are you going to take Mom to see the *Lion King?*"

"Why would I shell out two hundred bucks, when she can watch the video from the comfort of her own home for five?"

"But that's *Disney.*"

"So? Beats that movie you told us to rent last month."

"What, *Life is Beautiful?*"

"You never said it was foreign!"

"Don't tell me it was *subtitled,*" Brian guffaws. "Jesus."

"Your father couldn't read the subtitles with his bifocals," Mom says, "so he turned on the stereo and ruined it for me."

"I was bored."

By the time my mom serves the apple crisp, the conversation has turned to the adventures of Luther, Mr. Whitmore's raggedy mutt, who escapes periodically to terrorize the neighborhood. Last week, he chased a fox onto the Rosings' porch. Dad, now the neighborhood hero, tempted Luther away with a frozen steak.

"But what if the fox went for the steak instead?" I ask.

"Foxes don't eat steak, Libby," Dad replies witheringly, "they eat rodents."

No point debating, he's clearly the authority on that too. At any rate, he's moved on to describe Luther's latest. Yesterday, Mrs. Bingham came out to find Luther unearthing the sprinkler system from her front lawn. She threatened to call animal control, but her twin grandsons, aged six, adore Luther and went into hysterics. By the time my dad left, the boys and Luther were working their way through a tin of homemade cookies on the wrecked lawn.

After dinner, Dad and Brian perform their usual disappearing act and I help Mom clear up.

"So, are things going a little better?" she inquires, no doubt referring to my last visit, where I retreated to my old bedroom in a sulk.

"I guess so, although I've been stewing over a few regrets lately."

"Don't waste time on that, dear. We all make bad decisions now and then—especially when our heads are turned by grander things."

"It's spooky how you do that. You're Elliot's nicer twin."

"Mothers have a sixth sense when it comes to their daughters. Anyway, you'd do better to swallow your pride and try to rectify the situation."

I'm saved from responding by the cuckoo clock on the kitchen wall that announces it's time to leave. There's still no sign of Dad and Brian.

"Try the backyard," Mom suggests.

"But it's dark, surely they're not…"

"Your father's rigged the yard cruiser with headlights," she sighs.

I hear the purr of an engine as I step out the back door. My parents' lawn is freshly cut and they've moved on to Mr. Whitmore's yard. Brian and Dad are taking turns on the yard cruiser while Mr. Whitmore stands by with a flashlight and Luther races around, barking crazily.

"Wanna take her for a spin, Lib?" Dad says, pulling up beside me.

"No thanks," I yell above the 14.5 horses. "Just came to say good-night."

"See ya at Christmas!" Brian says, giving me another hug. Then he shouts far louder than necessary: "You're looking good, Lib—you must be getting laid!"

"*Brian!* There are some things a father doesn't need to hear."

"Sorry Dad. But speaking of sex, how's Lola?" Brian's unrequited crush on Lola has endured for a decade.

"Loser boyfriend, long story."

"What you're saying is, she'd be better off with me."

"Who wouldn't, brother?"

"Back at ya!"

I smile through most of the drive home, the empty coffee cups rolling around on the floor of the Cavalier.

"I assume you've read *Anne of Green Gables*," Laurie says, dropping into the chair beside my desk.

"Oh, about ten times."

"L. M. Montgomery's other novels?"

"Every one, like a good Canadian girl."

"And the published journals?"

"All four volumes—plus a couple of biographies."

"Excellent, I backed the right horse. You know I've been organizing the press conferences to announce the new mentoring program."

"Yes, of course, the Minister's pretty charged up about it."

This is an understatement. The mentoring program is Mrs. Cleary's darling and it's taken a fleet of analysts several months to bring it to life. Next week she will finally launch "Tomorrow's Talent," which encourages leaders in the cultural community to mentor students. Some of Ontario's finest musicians, artists and dancers have already agreed to participate and the program may well become a hit.

I've had a terrible time with the speech for the launch. Mrs.

Cleary has called me daily to share personal anecdotes about the various mentors in her life and would like to pay tribute to each and every one. I keep telling her there's only so much gratitude one can cram into a ten-minute speech without sounding like an Academy Award winner.

"She's charged up, all right, *and* she's still on a high from the success of her little costume party."

She raises her eyebrows at me and sits back to wait for dim light to dawn. Realization hits me like a rush of cold to the head.

"Laurie...tell me the Minister isn't planning to dress up as one of her mentors."

"I couldn't lie to you about that. You'd punish me for it later."

"And Margo will also be in costume?"

"Yes, indeed."

I close my eyes and sigh. "I suppose I'll be attending as Lucy Maud Montgomery."

"Bingo."

"Why does she want to torment me? We've been getting along so well lately."

"To her, it's an *opportunity*. She really believes that dressing as Canadian cultural icons will attract attention to the program and encourage artists to get involved. Unfortunately, Richard isn't here to tell her otherwise."

"So, who are the Minister and Margo going as?"

"I can't spoil the surprise," Laurie says, shaking her head and standing to leave.

"Wait!" I yell after her, but she has already disappeared down the hall.

The launch of the mentoring program is scheduled for 11:00 a.m., but the Minister has decreed that Margo and I will arrive in her office at eight to get into costume. I end up sprinting across Queen's Park to make it on time. It's Lola's birthday and I stopped at her place to leave a gift in the mailbox. Michael is taking her to dinner tonight so I won't see her in person.

When I arrive at the Minister's doorway, I have to swallow a yelp of laughter. She's already wearing a pink tutu, tights and pointe shoes. There's a short, brunette gamine wig under her tiara.

"Karen Kain, I presume?" I say, offering a silent prayer of thanks for Victorian modesty. I put up with a lot of abuse around here, but I draw the line at wearing a pink tutu in public.

"Bien sûr, Lily. Madame Boulier is a guest of honor at today's event. I told you about her, remember?" She executes a clumsy pirouette.

"Your ballet teacher? The one who kicked you out of class?"

"Correct. And she thought she could keep me off the stage!" She hoists a leg onto her desk and stretches awkwardly over it. "I want her to see me in pointe shoes before she dies."

She directs me to the closet for my costume—a floor-length navy-blue skirt, a petticoat and a high-necked white blouse with enormous puff sleeves and a million tiny buttons. I pick up the granny boots from the floor: Size 12. *How did she know?*

"Lucy Maud, the early years," I say.

"This will complete the look," she replies, handing me a cameo brooch and a pair of wire-rimmed spectacles. "Margo will be out in a second to do your hair."

"What's wrong with my hair?"

"L. M. Montgomery did not have a wild mane, Lily. She'd have had no time to write if she'd been wrestling with *that*."

"Now wait just a minute…"

Before my lip gets the better of me, the door to the Minister's private bathroom opens and Margo appears, wearing a black turtleneck, bell-bottoms and a black tam over a long blond wig. Strapped to her back is an enormous acoustic guitar. As she steps into the room, the instrument swings forward and the momentum nearly takes her down.

"Anne Murray?" I snigger.

"Joni Mitchell," she gasps, adjusting the guitar strap that's now choking off her air supply.

I'm not laughing half an hour later, after Margo and Mrs. Cleary have harnessed me into my costume. Bushy hair would have been the least of Maud's worries. This lace collar is so itchy, I'm getting hives.

Twang, twang, twang. The guitar slaps against Margo's butt as we hurry down the front stairs. We've used up all our lead time and have only twenty minutes to get to the west end of the city. Bill jumps out of the car as we approach and somehow manages to keep a straight face as he opens the rear door for the Minister. He closes it quickly behind her, leaving a flutter of pink tulle protruding from the door. I'm about to point this out when the Minister rolls down her window.

"Get in, Lily," she snaps. "We don't have all day."

Fine, if she's reverting to that tone, she's on her own. I wrestle my petticoats into the front passenger seat. Bill pulls into traffic and drives silently through the muddy streets of Toronto. I notice he keeps glancing at the rearview mirror and eventually Margo notices too.

"What's on your mind, Bill?" she asks.

"I was just thinking you should be arriving in a Big Yellow Taxi."

"Very funny."

It is, though, and the Minister, laughing so hard her tulle rustles, apparently agrees.

When Karen Kain takes to the stage at the Etobicoke School of the Arts, one side of her tutu is crushed and mud-splattered. The students are already snickering, but the Minister is too revved up to notice.

"I'm here today to launch my Ministry's new mentoring program. Tomorrow's Talent is very dear to my heart, because it is *my* mentors who made me what I am today. I will mention just a few of them…"

She reels off the entire list of people who inspired her to greatness, none of whom happen to be ballerinas. Clearly, the point of the tutu is to stick it to her former teacher—a point that appears to be lost on Madame Boulier, whose head is lolling forward as she dozes in her wheelchair.

"Nice do," Laurie says, gazing at my tight topknot.

"Now I know how I'll look after a face-lift. Margo stuck about fifty bobby pins straight into my head—and she looked like she was enjoying it. Either that, or she was amused by my Dumbo ears."

"Your ears are fine, but that bustle is not so flattering."

"Laurie?"

"Yeah?"

"I'm not wearing a bustle."

"Oh. Excuse me while I see if the caterers need a hand."

More aware than ever about how ridiculous I look, I scan the crowd to make sure Tim Kennedy isn't here. Mercifully, there's no sign of him. The last thing I need is to parade my bustle before him looking like Prince Charles in drag.

"Hold this!" Margo says, thrusting her guitar into my hands. I'm already juggling Mrs. Cleary's purse and my own, but there's no time to protest. Margo is heading toward the stage at a brisk trot, carrying an enormous bouquet of red roses.

The Minister, having returned at some point to the script I penned, now finishes with a deep curtsy. Although the crowd applauds politely, she doesn't straighten up immediately. Instead, she holds her pose and casts a sideways glance at Margo, who's standing in the wings. From where I stand, I can see that Margo has been momentarily distracted by a student. She collects herself and rushes onto the stage to present the Minister with the bouquet—just as if Clarice were a real prima ballerina. The Minister straightens up and accepts the flowers graciously. Her wig has slipped askew during the extended curtsy. Clutching it to her head with one hand, she races off the stage and storms down the stairs toward me, Margo in hot pursuit.

"Bring my bag," the Minister says, tossing the bouquet at me.

It hits me in the chest and drops to the floor because my hands are too full to catch it. Before I can lean over to pick it up, Margo stampedes past and tramples it. I sling the guitar over my shoulder, pick up the crushed blooms and follow them over to Madame Boulier, who is wide awake now that the speech is over.

"Of course I remember you, Clarice," she is saying, her voice surprisingly strong for one so frail. "I am surprised to see you in such a costume, my dear. Dare I hope I was your greatest role model?"

After hesitating briefly, the Minister rises to the occasion: "Why yes, of course, Madame Boulier, it goes without saying."

"I *was* a fine dancer in my day," Madame says, smiling at the memory. "It's a shame *you* didn't have the gift, Clarice."

At this, the Minister visibly deflates to the dimensions of a wounded seven-year-old and looks over at me in dismay. Suspecting that Madame Boulier can't see very well, I signal the Minister to take her best shot by clenching my fist and jabbing it ever so slightly toward the old woman. Mrs. Cleary straightens up and says, "Madame, I realized at some point that it was far better to *control* the ballet than perform in it. It's so much easier on the knees!" I give her the thumbs-up and point toward the door. "It was *so* nice to see you," the Minister continues, before the old lady can respond. "My assistant Lily will wheel you to the door." As she brushes past me, the Minister whispers, "If you were to stumble near the front stairs, no one would blame you."

When I've hoisted Madame Boulier into her cab, I hurry to the car. Margo is fixing the Minister's wig in the back seat and there's a lecture in progress.

"I told you to rush the stage with that bouquet the exact second I curtsy—not twenty minutes later," the Minister is saying. "And what happened to the bravos? I specifically asked you to have everyone scream 'bravo' at the end of my speech."

"I'm sorry, Minister, I forgot about the bravos."

"You should be sorry. I had a great finale planned and you ruined it. It would have been so *perfect*."

It would have been so *humiliating*. My job description is already stretched to its limit without playing an unpaid extra in the Minister's fantasy life.

My phone is ringing as I enter the apartment and I sprint over to answer it.

"Lib, it's Emma. We've got a 911."

"Lola?"

"Yeah. Michael didn't show for their date tonight and when she called his house, she heard a woman giggling in the background."

"The bastard! And on her birthday of all days! Okay, what's the plan?"

"The usual. She picked a new bar at Yonge and Eglinton."

"But it's a meat market up there," I whine.

"That's the point. Anyway, Bob's offered to chauffeur. We'll swing by your place in half an hour and then collect Lola. You know your role."

I hang up the phone and bid goodbye to the weekend. Lola, Emma and I initiated the 911 party during university. Each time one of us was wronged by the hairier sex, the others took her out for a who-needs-'em-anyway girl's night out. The 911s are rarer these days, and thank God, because it takes so much longer to recover.

I race into the kitchen and pull out a cocktail shaker and a thermos. After measuring vodka and Triple Sec into the shaker, I squeeze several limes with a practiced hand. I'm shaking the ingredients over ice when Bob toots the horn outside. Pouring the liquor into the thermos, I throw three shot glasses into my purse and head for the door. My wicked Kamikaze shots are a 911 tradition.

We've already got a decent buzz by the time Bob pulls up in front of Magnolia.

"Fuck, there's a lineup," Emma says.

My sentiments exactly. Lineups weren't so bad at age twenty-three, but at thirty-three, it's demoralizing. What if the muscle-bound wanker with the headset passes me over for some young babe who looks better in Lycra?

"Why don't we just head down the street to the wine bar?" I suggest, hopefully.

"No way!" Lola protests. "It's *my* 911 and it's *my* birthday. We're staying here."

She gets out of the car and joins the queue.

"No arguing with that," Emma says, dividing the last of the Kamikazes between our shot glasses.

"Here's to humiliation." I clink my glass against hers before draining the contents.

"It's not looking good, ladies," Emma observes as we join Lola in the line. She's referring to our chances of being allowed in when we're surrounded by scantily clad women who appear—to my trained eye—to be under legal drinking age. Much to our surprise, however, the beefy bouncer immediately points to the three of us, unhooks the velvet rope, and waves us inside.

"We've still got it, Lib," Emma whispers happily to me as we pay the cover and hurry after Lola to the bar.

"A bottle of your cheapest champagne and three tequila slammers!" Lola calls to the bartender. "Look at all the yummy guys!" she says, as we fight our way to seats at the end of the bar. "I feel better already."

"Yeah," I agree, scanning the crowd, "but they still have their baby teeth."

"Oh, come on, Lib, we're not *that* old."

Emma shoots me a look and I know what she is thinking. Lola's 911s usually end with Emma and me catching a cab home without her. I notice a young man who appears to be checking me out. I turn around to see if there's a gorgeous twenty-year-old woman standing behind me, but no. When I look back, the guy is smiling at me and his buddies are nudging him.

"Looks like you've already got a fan," Emma says.

"Well, he may be young and cute, but he's no Tim Kennedy."

"Tim!" Lola exclaims, gulping champagne. "You ran that guy right out of town."

"I did not run him out of town, I just didn't return his call."

"*Calls,* as in plural. You slammed the brakes so hard your forehead is still dented. Having second thoughts?"

"Maybe," I confess.

"He'll only break your heart," she says, pushing two tequila slammers toward us. She raises hers and proposes a toast: "Here's to Michael—may his penis shrivel, rot and drop off!"

"To eunuchs," I cheer.

We tip the tequila down our throats and Lola orders a round of B52s. Emma has been silent since I mentioned Tim's name and it's making me uneasy.

"Emma?"

"Mmm?"

"He's seeing someone, isn't he?" She nods. "It's that tiny journalist he took to the Culture Vulture opening, isn't it?" I can't hide the disappointment in my voice.

"Sorry, Lib, I'd have mentioned it sooner, but I didn't think you cared who he dated."

"I didn't think so either, but I guess I do. How long have they been going out?"

"Not long. The Casa Loma thing was their first date."

"I told you so," says Lola, handing me a test tube of layered liqueurs. "They're all two-timing scumbags. Except for Bob, of course," she adds, handing Emma a test tube. Then she offers another toast: "Here's to Michael—may he discover he's had ovaries all along."

"To hermaphrodites!" I cheer. Before I can interrogate Emma further about Tim, we're swarmed by a group of baby-faced cuties who drag us to the dance floor. Among our assailants is Brendan, the guy who was smiling at me earlier.

"What do you do?" I ask.

"I'm in college—studying to be a golf course technician."

You need a degree for everything these days. Brendan assures me that he has a part-time job as well, and it happens to come with a company car. He leads me to the front window and proudly points to a beaten-up Tercel at the meter, which has a mammoth slice of plastic pizza on the roof. I am meant to be impressed. And I am impressed—by his pecs, showing to such good effect in a ribbed T-shirt. We dance for close to an hour, but when the D.J. starts spinning house music, Lola, Emma and I retreat to our seats. Lola immediately orders another bottle of champagne.

"Obviously, I'm far too hot for Michael anyway. Josh is barely twenty-one and he's absolutely *gagging* for it." This isn't an idle boast. Josh, now sitting down the bar a stretch, is quite obviously fixated on Lola. She crosses her legs to flash him a little more thigh.

"You don't have to do something crazy just because Michael is a jerk," Emma warns.

"What better reason?"

She hops off her bar stool and leads Josh to the dance floor. Moments later, their pelvises are locked together in a spicy little salsa number. I pour the champagne and when I look back, their lips are also locked. Brendan, meanwhile, is trying hard to get my attention, perhaps eager to meet the same fate as his buddy.

"Help me out here," I say to Emma, who's busy scrutinizing the crowd. "We need to look like we're in the middle of a serious conversation. I'm trying to discourage a Boy Scout from coming over here to earn his make-out badge. You can tell me all you know about Tim and *Melody*."

"It's *Melanie*—and I honestly don't know much about her. I'll see if I can weasel more details out of Bob, but he'll suspect it's for you, and he thinks you've done poor Tim wrong, re-member." She finishes scoping the room and turns to me. "Lib, have you noticed that there are a lot of older women with younger guys here?"

I take a good look around and see that Emma is right. "That's weird. It must be a new trend."

"It's Cougar Night, ladies, what did you expect?" the bar-tender asks with a smile.

*"Cougar Night!"* we exclaim in unison.

"I'm too young to be a cougar!" I say, deliberately suppress-ing the memory of Danny and the pickup truck.

"And I'm married!" Emma adds.

"Surely you have to be over thirty-five to be considered a cougar?" I say to Emma. "I have never been more insulted in my life. They didn't even 'card' us to see if we're old enough."

"Care to Merengue?" Brendan asks.

"Sorry, I don't know how."

"I'll teach you," he says, practically drooling as he watches Josh and Lola grind away on the dance floor. "Besides, it's the last dance."

"Oh my stars, is it that late already? Why Miss Emma, it's closing time. I need my beauty sleep. I'm up so early to feed my ten cats!"

Brendan departs in a hurry and Lola soon returns trailing Josh.

"Send the boy back to the playground," Emma tells her. "It's time to go."

"Oh, please, can't I keep him?" she wails, trying to pinch Josh's ass when his back is turned. "He's much more fun than boring old Michael."

"Easy, grandma," Emma says, reaching out to intercept the play. "We've had a lot to drink tonight and you'll regret it to-morrow if you take him home. And then you'll call me and ask why I didn't stop you."

"I won't, I promise!"

"You will—you always do. So this time, I'm stopping you."

We can only convince her to leave Josh by agreeing to accompany her to an after-hours club down on College Street. I'd rather crawl home to bed, but stumble gamely into the cab. Soon we're weaving our way into another crowded club. My head is starting to ache and I'm grateful that booze is not an option here. Emma orders a round of Cokes, while Lola disappears into the washroom; she returns with a mickey of rum in her purse.

Daylight is pushing its way around the blind in my bedroom window by the time I get home. And today was the day I promised myself I'd do some research on wedding traditions. Before I throw myself into bed, I set my alarm for noon. Plenty of time to hit the library then—if I'm mobile.

*I'm standing near the bar in the after-hours club trying to order another round of Cokes to mix with my rum. There's a couple in my way and they're making out, completely oblivious to everyone around them.*

*"Don't worry, babe, I'll take care of this," a male voice says. I turn to see a teenage boy beside me, with bad skin and limp orange hair. He gives my ass a reassuring squeeze before deliberately banging into the amorous couple. When they come up for air, I'm horrified to see that it's Tim and Melanie.*

*"Excuse me, ma'am," Tim says to me. "Could you ask your son to be a little more careful? He just spilled my wife's drink."*

*"Your wife?!"*

*"Do I know you?" he asks.*

*"It's Libby McIssac."*

*"Oh, yes! Didn't we go out once? Sorry I didn't recognize you, but you look…older. Besides, I thought you moved to England with that rich, horny guy."*

*"She did," pipes the kid, "but she found out he'd been having an affair with another client all along. Lucky for me, eh pal, because I'm not her son, I'm her boyfriend." The Cokes arrive and*

*he turns to me. "Can ya lend me ten bucks, babe? I'll pay you back when I get my allowance!"*

*Tim turns to leave and I hear Melanie ask, "Who's the cougar?" The boy snorts and pulls out his Game Boy. Beep, beep, beep. The noise makes me crazy.*

*"Do you have to play with that thing now?"*

*"It's the last gift my mother bought me before her accident with Minister Cleary's curling iron. She said, 'Libby will love this.' She was thinking of you right up to the end."*

Beep, beep, beep.

I reach out and cuff the alarm clock to the floor, but there's no danger of my sliding back into sleep. I can't risk returning to that dream. Instead, I lie there, head pounding, trying not to read too much into it. Dreams have no meaning. This one does not hold the key to my troubled psyche. And Margo, sadly, is very much alive.

I have to get to the donuts before Margo does. Bill brings in a box every Monday morning, but timing is critical. I can't even slow down to say hello to Richard, who has just returned from London, although I do notice that he's wearing a suit. I haven't seen him in "uniform" in ages.

"Slow down, it's too late," Bill says, stepping into my path.

"Damn, damn, damn."

"I know, I'm sorry. She got in early today. I promise I'll bring some tomorrow and keep them in my office." Then he nods in the direction of Richard's office and whispers, "I hear the Brit dried out enough in London to finalize his new strategy for the Minister."

"Oh yeah? Margo's lecture after the party must have lit a fire under his ass. This is going to be great: every line in the report will be crafted to cause Margo pain."

After a few minutes of gleeful speculation, I head down the hall toward my office. Margo's door is open and she hails me with a loud, but muffled grunt.

"Good morning," I venture uncertainly.

"You mean good *afternoon,*" she says, swallowing. "Obviously, we aren't keeping you busy enough if you can afford to show up this late. Mind you, I walked past the reference shelf this morning and noticed it's in worse shape than ever. If I didn't know better, I'd say you've never reorganized it."

"I don't know what you mean, Margo," I say, trying to look righteous.

"I mean that you've been taking liberties around here lately and it's time I cracked down on you." Margo must sense that Richard is about to destroy her and wants to remind me of her power while she still has it. "When you're finished with the reference shelf, I want you to start a new scrapbook celebrating Tomorrow's Talent."

Margo's blouse is covered in crumbs. Craning, I see a large open box of donuts on her desk.

"Hey, are those Bill's?" I ask.

"What?"

"The donuts—aren't they the ones Bill brings in for *everyone?*"

"I brought these for my own personal consumption, if you must know." She pops a part of one in her mouth and chews defiantly. "Look, you've got a lot on your agenda so you'd better get going." At least I assume that's what she's saying: all I hear is oinking.

I stalk back to my office and find Richard's butt in my guest chair and his tasseled party pumps on my desk.

"Make yourself at home," I say.

"Just here to warn you that I've given Clarice a lot to think about and I'm going to lay low for a couple of days while she mulls things over."

"Can you give me any hints?"

"Well, for starters, I told her to fire Margo and that sap, Mark."

"Mark isn't a sap." I can't help but defend him, even though I agree that his presence isn't really necessary.

"Whatever. He needs to go."

"Do you think she'll turf Margo?"

"Don't hold your breath. What other assistant has Margo's unique skill set? How are *you* with a blow-dryer?"

"Get real." I indicate my unkempt mane. "So, what else are you recommending?"

"A couple of political changes to generate some positive attention from the public and media. I shouldn't say anything until Clarice considers them. But I *can* tell you that I advised her to call off the midget and let you focus on what you were hired to do. She can get a skilled Public Relations consultant on retainer to handle the other work Margo assigns you."

"Or a trained monkey—but I thank you."

"No need, it just makes sense. Clarice knows you're good at your job, but she didn't realize how much time you waste on grunt work."

"It sounds like you're wrapping things up here. I guess it's time to launch your new career in politics?"

"What are you on about?" he asks, giving me a puzzled look. I guess his earlier boasts on my doorstep were all hot air and bubbles. He was probably too drunk to remember mentioning it.

"Oh, nothing." No point rehashing that drunken night again. I didn't come off so well in that story either.

He stands and comes around the desk to rub my shoulder. "Feel free to pine for me while I'm away," he says, before turning to leave.

After he's gone, I feel out of sorts. Something isn't as it should be, but I can't quite put my finger on it. Then it hits me: he squeezed my shoulder and I barely noticed. The hairs on my arm did not prickle. My pulse did not quicken. The crush is finally, indisputably dead.

To: Roxnrhead@interlog.ca
From: Mclib@hotmail.ca
Subject: Requiem for a Crush

Obituary:
Libby's Crush on Richard

July 24/02—Oct. 15/02

The Crush lived a short and unfulfilled life and its timely demise was a mercy to all. It is survived by its owner, Libby McIssac. It will not be missed.

Funeral services will be held this evening at Ms. McIssac's apartment, presided over by Ms. McIssac herself, who will dispose of The Crush's remains as she sees fit. Her devoted cat, Cornelius, will be in attendance.

The wake follows. Maker's Mark and chocolate will be served.

In lieu of flowers, please send donations to the Toronto Chapter of the Society of Bitter Spinsters.

I expect the Minister to be gone by the time I deliver the first draft for the Canada Stage speech. It's nearly seven and she has a dinner engagement with the Premier. As I approach her door, however, I hear something that sounds like a jet preparing for takeoff but is more likely a salon-quality blow-dryer at full rev. I rap sharply on the door.

"Come!" the Minister's voice commands above the din.

Margo is round-brushing the crown of the Minister's hair for maximum height.

"Close the door behind you, Lily. One has a reputation to maintain, you know." She's smiling, though. There's nothing she enjoys more than a private audience with the most powerful man in the province.

Margo switches to styling the Minister's bangs while I cross the room, jerking on the dryer as she repositions it. I nearly trip over the cord, which is no doubt her intent. Looking down, I see a rat's nest of cables, all coming from the same extension cord. It appears that hot rollers, curling tongs, a paraffin wax heater and a foot massager are all being powered by the same source.

"That's a bit of a fire hazard, Margo. The building's wiring is ancient."

"It's fine," she barks over the noise of the blow-dryer. "I do it all the time."

I drop the subject and Margo, showing off, takes the curling iron in her right hand and slides it over the Minister's bangs while continuing to use the dryer with her left.

"Wow, ambidextrous," I say.

"Don't provoke Margo while she's styling," the Minister intervenes. "I need to look my best tonight. Lily, you really ought to let her have a go—"

The Minister's voice is cut off by a thunderous crack, followed by a scream and a thud as the office plunges into darkness.

"Is everyone all right?" I ask. I stumble to the door to let in light from the hallway, but it too is in darkness.

"Oh, Lily," the Minister's voice quavers, "I'm afraid something has happened to Margo. I felt a breeze beside me and the curling iron was yanked out of my hair."

"Were you burned?"

"No, but please see to Margo. I'm afraid to get up in case I tread on her."

I shuffle toward the sound of the Minister's voice. As my eyes adjust, the light from the street lamps on University Avenue is sufficient to make out Margo's prone form on the floor. I lean over her and place a finger beneath her nose.

"She's breathing, Mrs. Cleary. Probably got a shock. I'll call for an ambulance."

I try to sound calm despite noticing the similarity the situation bears to my recent dream about Margo's death by electrocution. Groping for the Minister's phone, I call 911.

A flashlight's beam cuts across the room and Laurie's voice says, "Minister? Are you all right? I was just leaving when the lights went out."

"We're fine, but Margo's out cold," she responds. "There must have been a power surge when she was styling my hair."

Laurie shines her flashlight on Margo and spies the tangle of electrical cable beside her. "No wonder there was a surge! We're lucky it didn't cause a fire!" She kneels and shakes Margo by the shoulder until she groans and stirs. "Libby, we'd better un-plug all of this stuff before the backup generator kicks in."

A few minutes later, a security guard leads the paramedics into Mrs. Cleary's office just as the lights come on. All eyes are on Margo as the paramedics revive her with a shot of oxygen and a few judicious slaps. By the time they wheel her out on the stretcher, she's answering their questions in a dazed way. When they ask what she does here at Queen's Park, she says "hair, makeup, waxing."

After they're gone, I notice the Minister's hair. When Margo collapsed, she took the Minister's bangs with her. All that re-mains is a jagged fringe and the smell of burned hair hangs in the air. Laurie obviously isn't inclined to deliver the bad news either, but she does suggest canceling dinner with the Premier.

"I'll call him myself on the way to the hospital," the Minis-ter says. "I want to check on Margo."

"I'm afraid Bill has left, Minister," Laurie says. "I'll have to call you a cab."

"Nonsense, I'll drive myself. I coped very well before I had a fleet of staff, you know."

"Yes, of course, Minister. It's just that Bill took the Ministry car because the Premier's driver was to pick you up and drop you at home."

"Oh. Well, fine, call a cab then."

Fortunately she'll be surrounded by medical professionals when she discovers what's happened to her hair.


Laurie steps into the boardroom for the impromptu staff meeting carrying two large mochaccinos. "I'm out of the of-fice tomorrow so this is in honor of your birthday."

"How did you know?"

"You forget I have access to the HR files."

"Well, thanks, but don't tell anyone else," I caution her as Richard walks in.

Twenty minutes later, the Minister finally arrives and she's wearing a wig. It's quite a good one and no doubt very expensive, but it doesn't fool Laurie and me. Obviously, there was no salvaging the bangs.

After assuring us that Margo has made a full recovery and will be back in a few days, the Minister explains that Richard has submitted a report recommending a reform of the way we do business. She reels off a list of minor changes, working up to the major policy news.

"I'm very excited to announce that we will soon introduce a new policy initiative that will become a key priority for the Ministry. It's called 'Contact Culture' and it will be better than anything we've offered to students in this province before. Young people from every social and economic background will soon have equal access to the arts, thanks to Contact Culture. A slick marketing campaign will make sure that both students and their parents hear all about it. In fact, we're turning to an outside agency to ensure we're talking to kids in their own language. Naturally, our programs are no good to anyone if people don't hear about them and use them."

This sounds very much like a speech and the fact that she's actually rehearsed something means the Minister is taking this new initiative very seriously.

"Pardon my ignorance, Minister," Mark says, "but doesn't the current After the Bell program do more or less the same thing? And wasn't the Premier behind its creation?"

The Minister shoots Mark a disapproving look. After the Bell predates all of us, including Mrs. Cleary and it doesn't get much attention anymore. Designed to expose students of middle- and low-income brackets to the arts, the program's mandate is to provide subsidized access to local arts organizations. Funding is distributed according to the average family income in each community, thereby ensuring that financially underprivileged students have the same opportunities as their peers.

Richard takes control by responding to Mark in his most patronizing manner.

"If you understood this Ministry better, you'd know that the Minister is committed to meeting the Premier's agenda. After the Bell won't be canceled. In fact, we'll dust it off and polish it up. Contact Culture will offer even more to the young people of this province. The Premier is excited about the new program too—at least, he said so during dinner last night."

Margo will be steaming figuratively as well as literally when she learns her accident allowed Richard a one-on-one with the Premier!

The Minister hastily adjourns the meeting before anyone else can ask questions.

"What's the deal?" I ask Laurie.

"After the Bell runs smoothly but it's been around so long that only the people who use it know about it. I guess they figure we can offer it up to the public in shiny new packaging and receive the accolades."

"But we're relaunching a program that already exists. Why would the Minister agree to that?"

"Because it's good publicity. And I'm sure she believes it's a good opportunity to improve services to kids in need. That's politics, Libby."

We finish our mochas, commiserating over the fact that the Minister can hardly fire Margo now. No one else would be so willing to die for the cause.

I'm a year older and I feel it. Just hours ago I was thirty-three—a fun number with curvy good looks that's easy to say, and cool to write. At thirty-three, I was young enough to look good, yet old enough to have some cash to blow on life's finer things. Thirty-four sounds dreary and looks dull; it has an air of responsibility about it. Thirty-three spends its last dime on a skirt to wear to a new restaurant that's so expensive, the meal has to be paid off over several months. Thirty-four wears last year's skirt (still perfectly good) to the reliable and affordable bistro around the corner. Thirty-three rushes to the liquor store to buy a case of Beaujolais Nouveau. Thirty-four knows it's overpriced, overrated, underripe grape juice and bottles her own. Thirty-three seduces bartenders during a business trip. Thirty-four waits for someone safe to come along. Thirty-four is sensible. Thirty-four is mature. Thirty-four thinks long-term.

"Happy birthday to you." The sound of someone singing startles me out of my reverie. "Happy birthday to you." Richard creeps into my office. Closing the door behind him, he walks toward me, singing breathlessly, à la Marilyn Monroe. "Happy birthday dear Libby, happy birthday to you." The last two words are little more than warm breath on my cheek as he leans down to kiss me. I quickly push my chair a safe distance away.

"Uh, thanks."

"Here," he says, putting a small, wrapped box on the desk.

"You bought me a gift?" I'm surprised by the gesture. We've hardly been the best of friends lately.

"Maybe."

I unwrap the box and open it. "A watch!" I say, astonished. "It's beautiful." I realize immediately that I can't accept it and snap the box closed. It's too extravagant a gift. When I look up, he's beaming at me.

"You're welcome!"

"Richard, I love it, but I can't." I hand the box back to him.

"Why not?"

"It wouldn't be right—you know, because we work together. Others would wonder about our relationship and we're not exactly involved."

"I've noticed. Why *is* that?"

"It's such an awkward situation. I can't afford to give those two anything on me."

"We're talking about a *fling,* Libby, not Romeo and Juliet. Lighten up a little."

"Richard, I don't have the luxury of being your *Canadian crumpet.* You get to fly home anytime you like, but I have to take my career here seriously."

"So you've been leading me on all this time?"

"Look, this job has been good for me and I want to keep it. If you and I got together, Margo and Mrs. Cleary would show me the door."

"So it's not worth the risk," he says.

"Not for a fling. I'm sorry."

"You know, McIssac," he says, his face now inches from mine, "you're not getting any younger. All work and no play make *Lily* a very dull girl." He strides across the room and flings the door back against the wall.

I rest my forehead in my hand. Yesterday, I'd have sworn Richard had no more interest in me than he has for anyone with a uterus. He flirts with everyone. So what is he thinking, giving me a gift like that? The man doesn't need to spend that kind of cash to have company. And surely I don't come across as the type of woman who would fold for a pretty bauble?

To: Roxnrhead@interlog.ca
From: Mclib@hotmail.ca
Subject: Gifts from the Grave

Thanks for your birthday card and your note of condolence on the demise of the crush. The weirdest thing just happened. Richard came into my office, sang Happy Birthday and presented me with a watch. I don't know what brand because I snapped the box shut quickly (so as not to be tempted) and gave it back to him. It definitely resembled a TAG.

Now, I'm just as turned on by extravagant gifts as the next girl, but when they come from a guy like Richard, I can't help looking for strings. In any case, I'm over him. The proof: he kissed me on the cheek and it didn't even start my heart racing. I've accepted that he's not the type of guy for me and a fancy watch isn't going to change that.

I hate to confess it, Rox, but this has just made me pine for Tim. I've got the birthday blues—you know, another year older and no relationship.

But I refuse to be maudlin. No, I am going to finish this speech and meet the gang for dinner and have a good time in spite of myself.
Lib

P.S. I'm glad to hear you've picked up the torch I laid down. Does Gavin know he's been replaced by a sexy Spanish director? Good luck finding lingerie on that tiny island. If you run into problems, let me know and I'll ship you a selection from my enormous inventory.

At the end of the day, I am cheered to find seven new voice-mail messages, all wishing me happy birthday. Curiously, there's no word from my parents although Brian remembered to call from Vancouver. The phone rings as soon as I put it down.

"Happy birthday to you, happy birthday to you…" It's Mom and Dad.

"Thanks! I thought you'd forgotten."

"Don't be ridiculous!" says my father, who'd never remember were it not for Mom. After a brief pause, he adds, "Well, I'll let you talk to your mother now. I've promised to mow Mrs. Hadley's lawn." My mother covers the receiver and yells something to him. "Uh, right. So, Libby, have a great time tonight and, uh, we love you." He hangs up and my mother picks up the ball.

"So how was your day?"

"It was kind of weird. I don't think I like being thirty-four."

"Well, in my opinion, everything gets better at thirty-five."

"Easy for you to say. You were never a cougar."

"A cougar?"

"Nothing. Did Mrs. Hadley move?"

"No, why?"

"Her place is a mile from yours. How is Dad—?"

"Don't ask, dear," Mom cuts me off. "Let's just say it's a source of embarrassment to me."

The thought of my father cruising along the back streets of Scarborough on his lawn mower makes me smile.

"We want to take you for dinner," my mother continues. "How does next Sunday sound? We'll let you pick the place."

"There's a pizza bistro that just opened in my neighborhood. Why don't we try that?"

"Lovely. Have fun tonight. And Libby, it really does get better after thirty-five."

"Thanks, Mom."

I'm only a few minutes late when I arrive at Canoe, but the noise from the corner indicates my friends have already assembled. They've taken over the bar's prime real estate—a little sitting area beside the window. The view from the fifty-second floor of this downtown office tower is spectacular at night.

"Happy birthday!" they chorus as I join them.

"Thanks, guys." I'm cheering up already. What great friends I have!

Then, as I settle into one of the leather chairs, they all start growling and snarling while presenting me with a case of Wildcat beer.

"Only the best for our cougar," Elliot says. I glower at Lola.

"Don't look at me!" she says, "I wasn't the only one there."

"Emma! I didn't expect *you* to spill the beans."

"What can I say? I was traumatized and needed to share the details with my devoted husband."

"I guess I'm sensitive now that I'm officially in my mid-thirties," I say, sighing.

"You're hardly in a position to complain," says Elliot, who turned forty last year.

"You're all a bunch of old farts," Günter comments, "but it's nothing a little makeup can't hide." I notice he's wearing liquid eyeliner and mascara.

"Keep your glitter to yourself, thanks," says Bob, who likes Günter but feels obliged to keep up the heterosexual front.

The waitress arrives with a tray of drinks. They've already ordered all six of the bar menu's specialty cocktails for me. Wonderful—two weekends in a row of painful detox. But I start in on the cranberry cobbler martini without complaint, biding my time until I have the nerve to corner Bob. I'm spooning up the fruit at the bottom of cocktail number three before I conclude that subtlety is overrated.

"So, Bob," I say, leaning across the table and rudely interrupting his conversation with Günter and Elliot. "What's the deal with Tim and Melanie?"

"Who are Tim and Melanie?" Günter asks.

"Tim's the guy Libby is meant to be with," Elliot explains.

"Then who is Melanie?"

"Melanie's the slag he's been dating," Lola offers.

"Melanie's no slag," Bob says. "Ouch!" Emma has hoofed him under the table. "Not that I *like* her or anything, but Libby had her chance."

"It's okay, Bob," I say. "I know I blew it." Cocktail number four is bringing me down.

"Tell her about Melanie," Emma prods Bob.

"I'm not talking about this," Bob retorts.

"Fine, I'll tell her," Emma says. "Apparently, Tim isn't that interested in Melanie. He knows her from the fund-raising circuit and she asked *him* out. He told Bob there are no major sparks. Right?" she asks her husband.

"I'm still not talking about this."

"Anyway, she's been chasing him for all she's worth, the slag."

"Emma!" Bob is outraged.

"Look, I offered to let you tell the story and you declined, so I get to tell it my way. Anyway, Libby, if he's not mad about Melly, why don't you just call him and claw her right out of the picture?"

Everyone laughs, but I say, "I don't think it will be so easy to win him back." Bob's silence confirms I'm right.

"The man is a pig!" Lola exclaims.

"He is not!" Bob defends Tim. "Libby dumped him so why shouldn't he—"

"Not Tim—*Michael!*" Lola points to the entrance where Michael is making an entrance with a gorgeous young blonde. He nuzzles her neck as they wait for the hostess. "That's his admin assistant," Lola gasps. "He hired her just after we started going out. He was probably two-timing me all along!"

"I hate to say it, but you're probably right," Elliot agrees ruefully.

"He was an asshole the night you brought him to my concert," Günter says. "I'd love to take him down a notch."

"If you really mean that, honey, I think there's something we could do," Elliot says to Günter, who picks up on the unspoken plan and nods gleefully.

"Lola, would you mind?" Elliot asks.

"Be my guest, fellas," she says, settling back with the rest of us to watch the show.

"MICHAEL? DARRRRRRLING!" Elliot carols, in his most effeminate voice.

Michael looks over and the color drains from his face. He lunges for the hostess but Elliot and Günter are already speeding toward him. Each seizes one of Michael's arms affectionately.

"Hi, Elliot," he says awkwardly. "And uh, you are——?"

"Excuse me?" Elliot says. "I can't imagine you've forgotten Günter, after all that happened. Mikey, don't be coy. And who's your friend?" he adds, giving her the once-over.

"This is Jenny," Michael says cautiously.

"Yenny, Liebling," Günter jumps in, "vat is zat cheap perfume you are verring? Vas it a gift from Mikey? He alvays had terrible taste, didn't he, Elly?"

"Yeah, but he didn't taste terrible, did he?"

"Vell, no, actually," Günter giggles, "but ve shouldn't discuss zis in front of poor Yenny."

Michael tries to protest, but Elliot jumps in quickly. "I'm sure she knows all about his sordid past, don't you?" Jenny looks bewildered and she's edging away from Michael.

"Did you tell her about ze night ve met, Mikey?" Günter asks.

"Why would I tell her about that?" Michael says, irritated.

"You ver so sweet, coming backstage vith ze roses. My little groupie! How could I help falling for you?"

Some of the customers at the bar are starting to tune in now and Michael flushes with embarrassment. He tries to walk away but Elliot tightens his grip.

"Aw, look, he's blushing," Elliot says to Günter, "he misses you."

"This is bullshit!" Michael explodes. "I barely know you and I was certainly never your groupie. I don't even *like* your music."

"Ouch!" Günter says, looking hurt. "Zat's not vat you said ven you were trying to get into my plether pants."

"Shut the fuck up!"

"You said you loved me."

"I did not! Jenny, he's lying."

"Vell, maybe I yust hoped for that," Günter concedes. "But I wrote a zong for you, Mikey. Shall I sing it now?"

"I am going to shut you up, you prancing——"

"*Michael!*" Jenny interrupts. "Clearly you two have some unresolved business."

"We do not. They're just trying to get back at me for—"

"For what?"

"For breaking Günter's heart, you asshole," Elliot says. Günter's eyes well up with tears. "He really cared about you, and here you are, Mr. Gay-when-it-suits-me, strutting around with your dolly pretending you're straight. There's nothing wrong with being bisexual—as long as you're honest about it. Jenny, he hurts people. You need to know."

Günter takes out a tissue and honks noisily into it. His eyeliner is running. Michael, now crimson, glares over at Lola, who raises her glass to him and smiles. Jenny, meanwhile, looks from Günter to Lola to Michael, then says, "Give the bartender your credit card, Michael. You've upset these people. The least you can do is pick up their tab."

Michael hesitates for a moment, but everyone at the bar is watching and waiting. When he finally hands his credit card to the bartender, there's a loud cheer. Jenny turns on her heel and walks out. Michael follows at a run.

Elliot and Günter make their way back to our table to joyous applause. Moments later, another round of cocktails arrives, this time courtesy of the bartender, who has enjoyed the show.

"Hell hath no fury like the friends of a woman scorned!" Bob says, raising his glass. Lola hugs Elliot and then Günter.

Maybe Mom was right about things improving with age.

The battle rages on. Although the Minister hasn't disclosed the entire contents of Richard's report, I get the feeling Margo knows about his recommendation to fire her because her hostility toward him has skyrocketed. Richard isn't taking her abuse lying down, so it's open warfare.

Margo is reluctantly supporting the Minister's plan to introduce Contact Culture but disagrees with Richard about how to do it. They're arguing about the allocation of funds and how the new program should be announced. Richard wants to use an outside firm to design the entire launch at significant cost. He's chosen Loud Mouth Productions, a hip young company, to develop a strategy that will appeal to kids. He also wants to keep a lid on the initiative until every detail is finalized so that we get the best mileage out of the announcement. Margo is complaining that the firm is far too expensive and has no proven track record. She says that the money we're already forking out to our consultant (i.e. Richard) should buy us a great campaign, particularly with people on staff who have experience launching new programs. She also wants to consult broadly as we develop the program.

Richard and Margo are already holding meetings with policy analysts, lawyers, assistant deputy Ministers, the deputy and the Minister. I attend some of them simply to observe their efforts to outstrategize each other. Neither is stupid. Each proposes different policy approaches, funding approaches and public relations tactics. The Minister's head is spinning and it will be a miracle if nothing falls through the cracks—particularly since all of her energies at the moment are going toward the mentoring program, Tomorrow's Talent. A month ago, in my then-undefined role as communications generalist, I would have considered it my duty to take it up with her. Fortunately, Richard has clarified that I am a speechwriter, no more, no less, and as long as I can get factual information about the initiatives in time to write the Contact Culture speeches, I'll be fine. I'm free to enjoy the show.

Normally, I'd put my money on Margo. She's devious, manipulative, omnipresent and largely without scruple. However, she's lacking the one thing Richard has in abundance: testosterone. Sure, he has skill, but the testosterone gives him the competitive edge. Yesterday, when they were arguing in the hall, Richard moved closer and closer in a deliberate attempt to intimidate her—he's a foot and a half taller than she is, after all. Then he stepped back and raked her over with his eyes until they came to rest on her chest—a sexual power dynamic if I've ever seen one.

Now that my lust blinders are off, I wonder what I ever saw in him. I feel as though I picked up a pretty rock only to discover nasty critters running around underneath.

"Hey, Libby." Mark pops his head around my office door and holds up a paper shopping bag. "Can I tempt you with lunch?"

"If that's a Vessuvio's bag, I'll meet you in the kitchen in five minutes."

"Actually, I was hoping we could eat at your desk today."

"Sure," I say, dragging my guest chair closer to the desk. Mark takes sandwiches, brio and a brownie out of the bag. "Quite a spread."

"Let's call it the last supper. The axe came down this morning: the Minister says my services are no longer required."

"I'm sorry, Mark."

"Don't be, I expected it. Richard didn't want me here and his word carries a lot of weight with the Minister. I started looking for work weeks ago and landed a contract with the Ministry of Education."

"That's great! I'll hook you up with a couple of my old colleagues."

Mark smiles and chews thoughtfully for a minute. "Listen, Libby, keep an eye out for Richard. Call it consultant's intuition, but I think there's more going on with him than meets the eye and the Minister is naive."

"You think he's up to something?" Hearing Mark voice his concerns makes me realize that I have a few doubts of my own. I've been too numbed by desire to take them seriously before now.

"I don't have any proof, but I think so. I know you don't like Margo, but she is loyal. And as for the Minister, sure she's flighty and high maintenance—"

"You got that right," I snort.

"—but she's bright and when the pressure is on, she's capable. She's even got charm. I think she's committed in her own way to seeing the arts flourish. Unfortunately, she has a blind spot for Richard and I worry about that."

I finish my sandwich and pick at the brownie. "I appreciate the advice, Mark, and I promise I'll keep my eyes open."

"Just looking out for my favorite colleague," Mark says, smiling. "Of course, we won't be colleagues for much longer…" I can tell by his tone where this is going but before I can throw up a roadblock, Mark plunges forward. "I was wondering if we might get together socially?"

He means more than a casual coffee and I don't want to mislead him, so I say, "I'd love to keep in touch, Mark, but it's only fair to tell you that there's someone special in my life right now."

It's not a complete lie: Tim is special. Getting him into my life is a minor detail.

"I'm not surprised, but I had to ask." He stands to collect the remnants of our meal.

"But let's have lunch when you've settled in at Education."

"I'd like that," he says graciously, shaking my hand before he leaves. A gentleman.

Today, the Minister sends both Margo and me to Richard's office to debate the order of events for the Contact Culture launch.

"Richard," she begins.

He doesn't look up from his computer or acknowledge us in any way.

"Excuse me, we need to talk to you about the announcement."

No reaction at all from Richard. It's as if we've entered another dimension. He's so fascinated by the images on his screen that he can neither hear Margo nor feel her evil presence.

*"Richard!"* she barks. "The Minister sent us to talk to you about the launch agenda. I'd appreciate a moment of your time."

Still nothing. It's the old I'll-ignore-you-until-you-spontaneously-combust-and-then-I-win maneuver. Brian and I played this game often in our youth but Margo apparently never learned the rules of engagement because Richard is gaining control of the situation simply by feigning deafness.

"Would you like me to tell the Minister that you're unwilling to help?"

By way of a response, he dredges a load of phlegm from his sinuses and swallows loudly.

"Will you listen to me?!"

He reaches into his mouth with a forefinger and explores a molar.

"ARE YOU *DEAF?!*" she shrieks.

Richard leans forward to inspect his computer screen, seemingly oblivious to Margo's dance of rage at the door.

"His eyesight must be going too," I tell Margo in a stage whisper.

He pushes his chair back from the computer abruptly and turns to give me a scathing glance.

"Oh, hi Margo," he says calmly. "Did you say something?"

Margo has lost her voice. I follow her gaze to Richard's hand, which is resting in his crotch. He gives himself a casual scratch.

"Margo?" he asks again with a faint smile. "What can I do for you?" He adjusts his grip as he makes the offer.

I expect Margo to bolt, but she surprises me.

"You can review my suggestions for the launch. I'll tell the Minister that you're—" she pauses for effect "—caught up with a *small matter* and will share your comments shortly."

"Whatever you like," he replies, blandly, but I can tell Margo has scored a minor victory.

I hurry back to my office with Margo shadowing me.

"Did you see what Richard did?" she asks.

"Ignore you? Yeah, I noticed."

"*No,* the other thing."

"What other thing?" I may admire her for standing up to Richard, but I can't pass up an opportunity to mess with her head. Can she bring herself to say the words *fondle,* or *grope?*

"*You* know." (She can't!)

"Sorry, Margo, I'm not sure what you're saying." Somehow, I keep a straight face.

She stares at me for a long moment before muttering, "Never mind." Maybe I should own up. I have no interest in protecting the man, yet I don't want to get dragged into a discussion with the Minister of Richard's nether parts. Still, it wouldn't kill me to toss her a bone: "Margo, don't let him know he's getting to you."

She sniffs and stomps out, leaving me to ponder my lifeless crush with quiet bemusement. It's been six feet under for days and if I ever had any fears of its resurrection, they've certainly been laid to rest today.

★ ★ ★

I'm getting plenty of work done while Margo and Richard pursue their own agendas. There are other benefits, too: no surprise visits by Margo; no assignment of menial tasks like booking the Minister's reflexology sessions; no boring events; no carrying the damn handbag. Richard, my antiprince, at least gave me this gift. But I also feel sidelined. Margo is busy protecting her turf from Richard and Richard is busy trying to look like he's above scheming. The Minister is getting crotchety and finally explodes.

"Why can't I get a straight answer out of either one of you? Are these initiatives under control or not?"

"Minister, he—"

"Clarice, she—"

"Enough!" she bellows. "Kiss and make up, you two! If your relationship doesn't improve immediately, I'm hiring a baby-sitter. For now, I'm separating you. Margo, you will go to your room and handle the funding announcement. Richard, you will go to *your* room and manage the regulation changes. I am holding both of you accountable. Margo—call Leon and rebook my massage. I'm *very* tense."

I feel guilty that I'm not helping, but staying out of the game means I keep my sanity. I need it to handle both my speech load and the work with Lola on the wedding book, which is proceeding well despite the many distractions.

I doubt the Minister meant it literally when she ordered Richard and Margo to kiss and make up, but he's been positively *courtly* toward Margo ever since. Poor Margo has been disoriented by the about-face. When Richard attempts to guide her into the boardroom with a hand on her back, she flinches as if he's struck her. When he gives her a cup of coffee, she leaves it untouched, perhaps fearing he's poisoned it.

*And the Oscar for best performance of sincerity by a self-serving lead actor goes to Richard Neale!*

I still have the mentoring program's press conference to worry about. I'm putting the last touches on the new speech when I hear shuffling in the hall, followed by clattering in the stairwell and muffled obscenities. Venturing out to investigate, I find Laurie in the stairwell, cursing like a trooper while she picks up an odd assortment of clothes, sports equipment and art supplies.

"Sorry," she says, "I didn't realize anyone was still here."

I help her gather up the items on the stairs. "When's the rummage sale?" I ask.

"These are your costumes for tomorrow."

"Can you explain to me why we're playing dress-up again when the costumes weren't a hit the first time?"

"The Minister still has faith in her idea, although she's decided to mix it up a bit."

"So I don't have to strap myself into that corset?"

"Nope, and your new costume is *much* roomier."

"Uh-oh, who am I this time?"

"Roberta Bondar."

"The astronaut? Hey, not bad."

"Let's see what you think when you're suited up."

Something glittery catches my eye and I stoop to pick up a skimpy, sequined halter top. Twirling it on my index finger, I ask, "And who's wearing *this* little number?"

"Fortunately, it isn't Richard, although he's agreed to join you. He's trying to suck up to Mrs. Cleary."

"Can't he be the astronaut so that I can be a sex symbol?"

"You'll have to settle for having a beautiful mind—we don't breed a lot of sex symbols in Canada. Anyway, I promise you'll enjoy Richard's costume."


"Beam me up, Jim," the Minister says, giggling in the back seat.

"Love to, Shania, but my uniform is too tight to move!"

"Oooh, *that don't impress me much!*" she says, quoting a song from Shania Twain, the sexy country singer she's impersonating today.

Richard is dressed as Captain James T. Kirk of the U.S.S. Enterprise, circa 1965. It's nice that William Shatner has so inspired the Minister, but I'm not sure today's students will see it. They will, however, see far more of Richard than necessary. Laurie got the largest trekkie suit in the costume shop, but it's still too small for him. The pants end at his shins, the sleeves far short of his wrists. While following him to the car earlier, I couldn't help but notice his underwear migrating north beneath the rust-and-black polyester.

The Minister is quite fetching in a long brown wig, the midriff-baring halter top I picked up in the stairway yesterday and tight, stretch-velvet pants. I've got to hand it to the woman, she looks damn good for fifty.

"Ouch!" Margo yelps suddenly. "The rat is biting me!"

I crane around to see her fighting off an energetic Pomeranian. She's dressed as Emily Carr, the eccentric artist and author. To keep the costume "authentic and recognizable," Mrs. Cleary insisted Margo wear a fat suit under the shapeless caftan. There's a bowler cap on her head and she's juggling an artist's palette in addition to the dog. The Minister borrowed Goliath from her sister because Emily Carr, a noted animal lover, was often photographed with her dogs.

Richard is sitting between Margo and the Minister, his legs splayed. Margo glances nervously toward his crotch. And no wonder: the man is either far better endowed than he appeared to be earlier this week, or he's wearing a generous codpiece. When he catches me staring, he smiles and looks me straight in the eye. I shake my head.

While Captain Kirk and Shania resume flirting, I reach over and turn down the heat in the car. It's jacked sky-high to keep the Minister's exposed flesh warm, but steam is issuing from the neck of my heavy space suit.

"Bill," Shania's voice rings out, "it's chilly back here. Could you turn up the heat?"

By the time we reach the North York Civic Centre, I'm poached and open the door to gasp for fresh air.

"Lily, close that door! People need to know who we're representing today. Put your helmet on."

"Minister, this suit is very warm and the helmet makes me claustrophobic."

"We all make sacrifices for the job, Lily," she says. "Look at how ridiculous Margo and Richard look, but you don't hear them complaining."

Sighing, I scrunch down in the seat and slip the round orb over my head. It bangs against the roof as I get out of the car and the clear plastic visor steams up immediately, but I dutifully follow the others toward the main doors.

"What is this about? Richard? Margo?" The Minister's voice is muffled by the helmet, but she sounds upset.

"I had no idea this was happening, Minister," Margo apologizes, while Richard argues unintelligibly with another man.

Through the mist on my visor, I make out a crowd of people around the front door of the civic center. The Minister is sufficiently distracted that I risk pulling off my helmet and see she's standing beside Tim Kennedy. Behind him is a crowd of teachers, parents and students, all waving placards reading STUDENTS NEED ACCESS TO ARTS. Among them is the posse of girls who locked me in the Porta Potti.

"Richard," the Minister steps forward, "stop shouting and let Tim speak."

"Thank you," Tim says. "We're here today to protest your Ministry's proposed changes to arts funding."

Margo takes a step back and whispers, "What have you told him?"

"I haven't spoken to Tim since the last time he visited the Minister."

Tim, meanwhile, calmly explains to the Minister. "I brought my students here today because they need to learn that they have a voice. Your Ministry's changes may deny them access to the arts and they need to speak up about that."

"My Ministry is committed to ensuring all students have access to the arts. The new program won't change that. No one knows better than I how important it is to expose young people to the arts early, Tim."

"But Minister, you usually consult with stakeholders when developing new programs and we're concerned about your silence regarding After the Bell. How else will we understand your plans?"

"You're absolutely right, Tim but this isn't the time to discuss it. I'm hardly dressed for formal consultation!" She laughs disarmingly and everyone smiles. "I'll have Margo set up a meeting where I can get your input." Tim lowers his placard. "Since you're already here," Shania says, tossing her shiny mane, "why don't you all come on inside? I'd love to tell you more about my new mentoring program, Tomorrow's Talent." She flashes an engaging smile at the teachers and parents. "I know a group of role models when I see it. We could really use your support."

Occasionally I catch a glimpse of why Mrs. Cleary has succeeded in politics. With a few well-chosen words, she's defused an ugly situation and pitched another project. Mark is right, the woman has charm.

"Helmet, Lily," she says, her smile contracting slightly. Then she takes Tim's arm to proceed into the Civic Centre.

"Hi, Rocket Girl," Tim greets me as I replace my headgear.

Any smart reply I could devise would be swallowed by my visor, so I save my strength. Besides, I'm more inclined to grovel at the moment. I'm more ashamed than ever of the way I treated him. To underscore the point, Richard passes me and plucks his briefs from his ass.

Little Goliath is standing against my boots, yipping. Realizing the helmet is scaring him, I take it off again and pick him up. He's licking my face when Margo swings back through the double doors.

"There you are, you little beast." She snatches the dog from my arms. "If he didn't belong to the Minister's sister, I'd dump him in the trash."

Goliath bares his teeth and growls at her as she carries him off.

"I think she's gotten meaner since the electric shock," Laurie says, helping me put the helmet on and guiding me into the rotunda.

During the reception following the speech, I judge it safe to remove the helmet, the crowd having had ample opportunity to appreciate the full ensemble. Gulping two bottles of water in quick succession, I help Laurie hand out printed material about Tomorrow's Talent. I'm planning my descent on Tim when two gentlemen from the banking industry approach me for information about participating in the program. By the time I escape their clutches, Tim is talking to the Minister.

Heading to the ladies' room, I find it's been commandeered by Brianne, the Alpha Teen, and her demonic sisterhood. They're applying lip gloss at the mirror. Before I can back out the door, Shelley sees my reflection and says, "Look, Brianne, it's Mr. Kennedy's friend. Haven't seen you in a while, Miss McIssac. Have you been *lost in space* all this time?"

Their sniggering demolishes what's left of my patience. "Look, ladies," I say, slamming my helmet on the counter so hard the contents of Brianne's makeup bag rattle, "let's just cut the crap, shall we? If you have something constructive to say, say it fast, because I have a challenge ahead of me to get out of this suit. If you don't, I'll thank you to excuse me."

The girls stare back at me in stunned silence so I push past them and squeeze into a cubicle. At least I'll be able to crawl under the door if they lock me in again.

Over the noise of a steady stream of water hitting the bowl, I hear the girls whispering. I'm sure they're planning a counterattack or they'd have left by now. Struggling back into uniform, I exit the cubicle and head for the sink, where they're standing in a half circle eyeing me warily. They're trying to psyche me out, I figure, so I make a show of lathering up my hands and washing them slowly. I'm reaching for the paper towels when the bathroom door opens and Margo appears.

"There you are, Libby. Where's that wretched Pomeranian?"

"Check the last cubicle. I think I heard barking."

"I don't appreciate flippancy, Elizabeth. You've obviously spent too much time with these teens."

"Don't give them credit for my attitude."

"Well, get out here and help me find the dog."

"In a minute. You've interrupted a mentoring moment."

She snorts in disgust and leaves.

"What a bitch!" Brianne exclaims.

"Just the tip of the iceberg," I say, shaking my head. "My job isn't all funny costumes, you know."

"How can you stand it?"

"When things get rough, I just put on the helmet—it's virtually soundproof. But it's hell on my hair."

There's a moment's pause and then they all laugh—*with* me, and not *at* me, for a change. They look at each other, then Shelley pushes Brianne forward.

"Listen, Miss McIssac, we're sorry for giving you such a hard time," Brianne blurts out.

"Is this a trick? Have you stuck something to the back of my spacesuit?"

"No, really, we're sorry," she insists. "We were just having some fun because Mr. Kennedy is our favorite teacher." She lowers her head and mutters at the floor, "Some of us kind of have a crush on him."

A chorus of denials follows.

"Speak for yourself!"

"I already have a boyfriend!"

"Gross—he's old."

"Relax!" I say. "Believe it or not, I understand. So, you really like Mr. Kennedy?"

"Oh yeah!"

"He's really cool!"

"The best teacher we've ever had!"

"What's so great about him?"

"He doesn't make us feel stupid like some teachers have and he makes music fun. Everyone wants to be in his class."

I nod my head, remembering what Tim said about their difficult backgrounds. "He told me you're a talented bunch."

"I want to be a teacher just like him one day," Shelley offers shyly.

"Not an astronaut?" I ask. "I'm hurt."

"Hey," says Brianne, "who's the guy with the big bulge? You know, in the *Star Trek* suit?"

I feel my face start to burn. "Uh, that's Richard, otherwise known as Captain James T. Kirk. He's a consultant who works with the Minister."

"Did you go out with him?" Shelley asks.

"No," I turn to the mirror to fluff my helmet head.

"I bet she did," Shelley says to the others. "Is he nicer than Mr. Kennedy?"

"No one is nicer than Mr. Kennedy—am I right?"

"Right!" they all chime.

"But I bet Mr. Kennedy doesn't look like *that* in a space suit," Brianne offers.

"I doubt we'll have a chance to find out," I say.

"So is it real?"

"What?"

"The bulge."

"Brianne!"

"What? He's *your* friend."

"Trust me, we're not that close."

"Anyway," Brianne concludes, "we didn't mean to break you two up."

"Who?" I ask, honestly baffled at this point.

"You and Mr. Kennedy."

"You aren't responsible for that."

"You could give him another chance," she says, offering me her lip gloss. "Try this, it would look good on you."

It's not the time to worry about hygiene, so I take it and put some on. "Will it show through my visor?"

"Libby!" Margo is back at the door. "What do I have to do to get some help out here?"

I hand the lip gloss back to Brianne. "Listen, girls, let's fan out and locate the Pomeranian."

Shelley soon entices Goliath out from under a display case with a cocktail wiener from the snack table. Tim watches from across the room as they gather around me and the dog. He doesn't come over. Finally, the girls say goodbye and by the time I've taken another trip to the washroom to collect my helmet, the whole group has disappeared.

"Roxanne's help line."

"How did you know it was me?" I ask.

"I recognize your ring. Besides, you're the only one who forgets about the time difference." I look at my watch and make a quick calculation.

"Shit. Sorry, Rox, did I wake you up?"

"Nah, I'm still at work—on lunch actually."

"But isn't it 2:00 a.m. there?"

"Yup."

"Hey, is Miguel with you?"

"Yup."

"Is he still sexy?"

"Yup."

"Are you still sneaking to his room every night?" I can't resist teasing Roxanne when she's at work and can't divulge any personal information.

"Yup."

"Is he beginning to suspect that you're talking about him?"

"Yup. So when are you going to tell me what's up? Are you having regrets about the Brit?"

"Oh yes, but only that I ever gave him a passing thought. The man is willing to do whatever it takes to get what he wants. Thank God I never cracked. He'd be tossing me aside by now without a second thought about my reputation. I was an idiot!"

"You're hardly the first girl to sacrifice logic to lust."

"Rox, I think I used him as an excuse to avoid getting involved with Tim."

"If you're still having regrets about that, why don't you just call him?"

"He won't even talk to me when he sees me. Besides, he's seeing someone else."

"Is it serious?"

"I don't think so."

"Well, it ain't over till the fat lady says 'I do'."

"She's blond, five-two and skeletal."

"Yeah, but can she write like you?"

"Actually, she writes for *Maclean's*."

"Jesus. Well, what's the worst that can happen?"

"He could tell me to fuck off."

"And if he does, it'll ruin your life? Look, you've gotta move before he gets serious with the bone rack. You must save him from a life of misery with the wrong woman."

"So, by stealing him back, I'll be doing them both a favor."

"Now you've got it."

By the time I put down the phone, Rox has me pumped, so before I can talk myself out of it, I dial Tim's number. His machine clicks on after one ring and I'm paralyzed by the thought that he's on the phone with Melanie this very moment. She's probably filling him in on the big news story she's breaking. I hang up.

**32**

*"When the moon hits your eye like a big pizza pie, it's your birth-day,"* my father croons as we wait in line at the new Wood Oven Pizza Bistro.

After my parents' reaction to the new fusion cuisine a few months back, I'm taking no chances: pizza is paternally sanctioned. Besides, this place is ideally located midway between my apartment and Queen's Park and I want to check it out.

"Dad, my birthday was last week."

He grins at me before launching back in: *"When the world seems to shine, like you've had too much wine, it's your birthday."*

"Can you make him stop?" I ask my mother. She shakes her head helplessly.

*"Bells will ring, ting-a-ling-a-ling, ting-a-ling-a-ling, veeta bella…"*

Fortunately, the hostess arrives in time to spare me the big fin-ish and leads us to a corner table. After this, dinner progresses qui-etly enough until a waiter arrives carrying a piece of tiramisu with a sparkler jutting out of it and begins singing "Happy Birthday." My father and half the diners join in enthusiastically. My humil-iation is cut short by a commotion at the front of the restaurant.

"What do you mean it's not bloody ready?" a man's voice is

demanding. "It's bad enough that you don't deliver. Now I've left my hotel and traipsed over here and you have the gall to tell me my order isn't ready. This is unacceptable!"

I know that voice. The imperious British accent is a dead giveaway. A glance over my shoulder reveals Richard leaning over the bar in an attempt to intimidate the manager. There's a nearly inaudible response from the manager and then, "No, I don't want a bloody drink while I wait! I want the meal I ordered, thank you very much. I have work to do this evening. Oh never mind. Forget it. Just give me whatever is quickest." After another calm response from the manager, Richard barks, "You're damned right I'm not paying for it. I've never experienced such poor service in my life!"

I can't believe how rude he is. If I'd seen this side of him three months ago, I'd have kept my hormones to myself, like a proper lady.

"Get a load of the limey," my father snorts. "The accent's given him delusions of royalty. He's damn lucky *I'm* not the manager here. I'd shove a pizza up his crumpet-eating ass—teach him some manners." I sink down in my chair.

*"Reg!"* My mother is scandalized. "Keep your voice down!"

"I've never met a Brit I liked and I don't care who knows it." Dad's arm shoots into the air to summon the waiter.

"There are plenty of fine Englishmen around, Dad."

"Nah, they're all pale and uptight. The dampness rots their brains." He's baiting me now. "And look at the crap they eat. If it isn't fish and chips, it's steak-and-kidney pie."

"You love fish and chips," my mother says.

"You're missing the point, Marjory, which is that I am Scottish: I'm supposed to hate the British."

"*Grampa* was Scottish, Dad. You've never left this continent."

"The blood of the Highlanders still courses through these veins, lassie."

"Italian wine is coursing through your veins, Rob Roy," Mom says.

I glance again toward the door in time to see Richard striding out with his meal. Dad watches him go, then turns back to pay our bill: "All I can say is, thank God you and Brian never dragged home a Brit."

"Well, I'm not promising a man in a kilt," I tell him as we get our coats.

I am sitting with the Minister while she reviews a draft speech when I hear it: a high-pitched giggle. It sounds like Margo's voice, but it can't be. She's incapable of giggling. I hear Richard's voice murmuring something just outside the door and there it is again. It's definitely Margo, and Richard is inducing that freakish sound. I almost seize the pencil from the Minister's hand and drive it into my ear.

"Do you think that's meant to impress me?" the Minister asks, nodding toward the door.

"I believe that's the point, yes. Is it working?"

"The performances aren't very convincing." She looks at me over her glasses and smiles.

"You're supposed to suspend your disbelief," I advise.

"Better to suspend the staff, perhaps?"

I silently marvel over the fact that I've actually come to like Mrs. Cleary—at least most of the time. Despite the pleasant exchange, however, I leave her office feeling uneasy. For some reason, I'm still worried about the upcoming policy changes. Richard and Margo are far too caught up with their personal agendas to pay attention to the details and when it comes to government, I've learned that the devil is always in the details. I'd like to stay on the sidelines and let the chips fall where they may. It's not my job to prevent Richard and Margo from embarrassing the Ministry. Unfortunately, the Minister will take the bullet if something goes wrong and I don't really want to see that happen. She may be naive, vain and annoying, but she doesn't deserve to be dragged down by scheming opportunists.

I suppose it wouldn't kill me to do a little digging and see if there's any basis to my suspicions. Marjory would say it's the right thing to do.

* * *

"I don't see why we can't meet somewhere nice for once," I grumble, as Elliot and I slide onto a bench at the Queen's Head beside eight strangers. Normally it's not this busy on a Wednesday, but it happens to be fetish night.

"I do my best work in these places, you know that. Things just flow better..." His voice trails off as a man in a wet suit passes. The rear of the suit has been cut away to expose the guy's waxed butt.

"Elliot? Hello? A little focus would be nice."

"Sorry, what were you saying?"

"How does Günter put up with you?" I sigh.

"He doesn't appreciate the humor of it all as you do," Elliot concedes.

A buxom woman in a black leather bikini, thigh-high boots and an executioner-style face mask tickles the back of my neck with the tip of her whip. "You shopping, honey?" she asks, in a surprisingly feminine voice.

"Just looking, thanks." I wave the whip away, while Elliot laughs. "That's the real reason you bring me to these places—to mock me."

"It's been good for you—you're only half as uptight as you used to be."

"I'm not uptight."

"Trust me, your bolts still need loosening. I've never met such a worrywart."

"I am not!"

"Self-knowledge is a wonderful thing, Lib." Elliot signals the waiter to bring another martini. "But let's not ruin the evening by arguing. Tell me what's happening in Flower Girl's love life?"

"Before you corner me on that, could we talk about work? I sense something is going wrong with a new Ministry initiative, but I don't know what to do about it."

"Thought you didn't worry," he says, smiling.

"Fine, I worry—and in some cases it's justified."

"Well, I'm seeing the image of a chessboard. I sense someone is being played."

"I knew it!" I say, remembering Richard's recent behavior with Margo. Maybe he's trying to put her off the trail of a secret plot. "What else do you see?" I ask eagerly.

"Well, it doesn't seem to make much sense in this context, but I see a crucifix."

"Really? Maybe someone is going to be crucified at work. I hope it isn't me."

Elliot's interest evaporates as a police officer walks toward us. I'm convinced it's a real cop until I notice the velvet thong he's wearing over his uniform pants. Only after the cop makes a mock arrest of the woman with the whip can Elliot concentrate long enough to confirm there's still hope with Tim—but only if I'm willing to make the first move.

As we walk to the subway, Elliot invites me to attend a wedding with Lola as research for our book. One of the guys in Günter's band is formalizing his union with his longtime boyfriend. I suspect this might raise a few eyebrows with our publisher, but agree anyway. Knowing the two grooms, this is likely to be the event of the season.

Joe Connolly is sitting at his desk as I stroll down the hall of the policy branch. I've barely seen him since the Gay Pride parade, and each time we've passed in the hall, we've looked carefully in opposite directions. Today he catches me watching him and waves me over.

"So, how have you been?" I ask, leaning against the door frame and surveying his office. Its sparseness reminds me of his condo: no certificates on the wall, no calendars, no personal photographs—nothing but the essentials of work. Still living the monastic lifestyle.

"Great, you?" The man is surprisingly gracious, considering the terms of our parting.

I'm about to ramble on casually when I notice the crucifix hanging over his computer monitor. My throat dries out as I recall Elliot's vision. It must be a sign. Since being on staff, Joe has gained the reputation of being one of the best policy analysts in the Ministry. "Listen, Joe, I wonder if you could give me some advice about our new policy initiative."

"Contact Culture? Actually, I'm not really in the loop. I'm working on other initiatives."

"I just want to know if you get the sense everything is under control."

"You're worried?"

"I can't help thinking that Margo might be missing an important detail. She's still reasonably new to policy work and you know how complicated it is."

"But Richard Neale is working closely with one of my policy colleagues on the changes. You don't think he's withholding information from Margo?"

I shrug. "All I'm saying is that I have a hunch something is being overlooked."

"Look, I've got a meeting right now, but let me do some digging. Why don't you swing by my office tomorrow?"

I nod gratefully and head back to my office. Joe is known to be very thorough and he's certainly a man of honor. If there is any dirt clinging to this launch, he'll find it.

The door to Joe's office is closed and I wonder if I've left it too late to visit. After all, it's almost five on Friday afternoon.

"Hi, Libby," I turn to see him walking toward me. "I hope you haven't been waiting long."

"Just got here."

"I've just come from the comptroller's office and it looks like your instincts were right on the money."

I sigh. I didn't want to be right about this. After all, I spent three months fantasizing about Richard. Do I need more evidence of my poor judgment?

Joe invites me into his office and I see that a framed eight-by-ten glamour shot of a woman has arrived on his desk since yesterday. Joe positions his guest chair to offer me optimal viewing.

"How bad is it?" I ask, ignoring the blue-eyed beauty in her cheap pine frame.

Joe explains that Richard appears to be paying a company called Loud Mouth Publicity far above the amount he originally quoted to the Minister. The additional funds have been siphoned out of the After the Bell budget, since Contact Culture's budget is already much smaller than that of its predecessor. The restricted funding will obviously have an impact on the support currently offered to students. Worse, Joe says the scheduled changes are likely to impact the students from lower income families the most.

He has more to say, but I've heard enough. The Minister should hear this directly from Joe and fortunately, she's still in the office. I sneak him up the emergency staircase to the Minister's office. Margo and Richard are working together in the boardroom and I don't want to raise any suspicions on their part by walking past them with Joe.

Mrs. Cleary beckons us in and I explain that Joe has identified some potential problems with Contact Culture. She listens impassively as Joe speaks until he reaches the part about the reduction in student access to the arts.

"I don't understand," she interrupts. "Richard and Margo both know that guaranteeing the poorest kids access to the arts is extremely important to both me and the Premier. How could this happen?"

I offer no explanation.

"I'm afraid there's more," Joe says. "Minister, I hope you don't mind, but I took the liberty of researching Loud Mouth Publicity and discovered something interesting." He pauses and waits for her assent to continue. When she nods, he says, "It's a new company, owned by a twenty-seven-year-old named Maxwell Peel—the son of the wealthy London financier James Peel, who has strong ties to the Labor party. Max apparently had trouble holding down a job and when his idleness started causing trouble in the U.K., Daddy shipped him off to the colonies and set him up in business here."

"So Margo was right in saying the company had no track record," the Minister says. "I've been so wrapped up in Tomorrow's Talent that I obviously haven't paid enough attention to this project. But why is Richard so anxious to give this Maxwell our business?"

"I have it on good authority that Richard plans to run as a member of British parliament when a senior MP retires this year. James Peel has a lot of political clout and he's promised to back Richard if he keeps up his end and helps Junior Peel get his business off the ground. A government contract would go a long way to help."

"Julian and I had no idea!" Mrs. Cleary is dumbfounded. "How did you learn all this?" she asks Joe.

"As Libby knows, Minister, I have friends in high places." He looks at me and raises his eyes skyward in a joking reference to his previous career.

"Does Margo know?" the Minister asks. In need of comfort, perhaps, she opens her drawer and runs her index finger along a row of gleaming gold lipstick tubes.

"I doubt it, and I doubt she understands the impact Richard's scheming is having on either Contact Culture or After the Bell. It was hard enough for me to uncover these details and I had to call in a lot of favors. Plus, I was tipped off that there might be a problem." Joe gives a pointed nod in my direction.

The Minister pauses in her lipstick application and lowers her compact to look at me. "Libby, how did you know something was going on?" It's the first time she's ever used my correct name.

"I didn't. It was just a hunch, which is why I went to Joe first."

"Well, I'm grateful that you raised your concerns," she says. "And now, if you two will excuse me, I have some investigating of my own to do." She reaches into her drawer, pulls out her curling iron and hands it to me. "Plug this in before you go, would you?" I hesitate for a moment and she adds, "Don't worry, the office has been rewired." I notice that her hand is trembling.

I thank Joe on the way out and offer to buy him a beer at the pub around the corner. He declines, saying he already has a date "with a special lady." Sensing I'm supposed to eat my heart out, I summon a disappointed expression. I owe him that much.

Later, walking home I feel relieved. Whatever happens now, I've done what I can and it's out of my hands. Hopefully, it isn't too late for the Minister to straighten this mess out.

Lola is outside, honking the horn impatiently. I throw some food down for Cornelius, kiss him on the head (a mistake, since I'm wearing sticky lip gloss) and hurry out of my apartment. I almost careen into Mrs. Murdock, although the scent of lavender should have alerted me to her presence. Obviously she's been using the bath bombs I gave her.

"Better hurry," she says, "your ride is leaving without you."

I run down the walk toward Mindy, Lola's beloved 1965 Ford Mustang, named in tribute to her favorite TV series of all time, *Mork and Mindy.* Lola dropped a ton of cash rebuilding and painting Mindy's chassis but she ran out of funds before she could get Mindy's engine overhauled, so it's always a roll of the dice as to whether you'll get where you need to go. Mindy is sensitive to changes in the weather and it's been damp all week. I could have offered to drive, but I've long suspected Lola keeps the old wreck simply to avoid taking her turn as the designated driver.

Lola allows Mindy to creep forward along the curb. I open the door, take a few running footsteps and launch myself into the moving vehicle. Lola presses down on the accelerator the moment my butt is in the seat and we chug away.

"What's wrong with Mindy?" I ask, as the car shakes with deep, sputtering gasps.

"PMS." Lola raises her voice over the whine as the engine catches and guns it through an amber traffic light. "She isn't in the mood for idling today but as long as I keep her moving, we'll get to the wedding on time."

Lola guides Mindy through a series of side streets, turning onto a main road now and then. When there's a red light in the distance, we peel off to a side street again, or cut through a parking lot or gas station—anything to keep Mindy moving in the general direction of the Capitol Theatre. When Lola pulls into a parking spot and cuts the engine, Mindy coughs twice and dies.

"Poor Mindy," I say.

"She'll be fine," Lola assures me, "but we'll need to call the motor league half an hour before we want to leave."

The Capitol Theatre, a beautifully renovated old movie house, is the perfect venue for Decker and Jordie's wedding. They aren't having a formal meal, just tapas and sushi and fancy cocktails.

Lola and I head straight to the main bar, a beautiful mix of stainless steel and gleaming dark wood, and settle onto bar stools to take in the view. And it's quite a view. Jordie is a set decorator for films and he has a skilled eye. Rows of tiny votive candles line the upper balcony, which has been strewn with garlands of greenery and hot pink and orange gerbera daisies. Wrought-iron candelabras light the main floor where enormous urns burst with spring blooms. The rear wall of the theater is covered in a rich, midnight-blue velvet with holes punched throughout. Behind the curtain, strings of twinkle lights make the wall look like an expanse of stars.

"Wow, Jordie has a gift," I tell Elliot and Günter when they arrive. "It's magical."

"There was a lot of hard work behind the magic," Elliot says. "We spent most of yesterday helping them set up. But we didn't work half as hard as this guy," he adds, pulling over a short, stocky, balding man. "Libby, Lola, allow me to introduce Paul, floral artiste extraordinaire—the man behind those gorgeous arrangements. Paul, Libby and Lola are researching their book on the modern Canadian wedding."

Paul shakes hands with us, saying, "The next few hours should give you two plenty to write about." He seemed like a pretty ordinary guy at first glance but now that he's grinning, his blue eyes twinkle with mischief. It has a magical effect on Lola, who strikes up an animated conversation and by the time Paul leaves to assist the grooms, Elliot and I are suspicious.

"He isn't loaded, Lola," Elliot cautions. "He owns a flower shop in the Beaches."

"You're telling me this *why?* It's not like I only date people who are rich," she says.

"True, you'll usually date them if they're gorgeous," I offer helpfully.

"Could someone give me a little credit here?" she says. "You're making me sound *shallow!*"

"Many have risked spinal injury diving into Lola, but we love you anyway," Elliot says, slipping an arm around her.

Before the conversation can get ugly, the leader of the five-piece band steps to the mike at the edge of the stage.

"Ladies and gentlemen," he begins, as the percussionist gives a drum roll, "it gives me great pleasure to welcome you to the wedding of Jordie and Decker!"

An enormous movie screen descends behind the band and

the opening credits of the *Sound of Music* fill the screen. While Julie Andrews spins her way across the Alps, two figures appear on stage, dressed as Captain von Trapp and Maria. Cheers erupt as people realize it's the grooms. Decker cuts a fine figure in the Captain's dress uniform and Jordie looks fresh and pretty in Maria's pinafore. The latter is holding an acoustic guitar in one hand and a bouquet of plastic edelweiss in the other. The bridal party, consisting of three nuns in full habit, appears behind them. The ring bearer and flower girl arrive next, in outfits similar to those Maria made from curtains for the von Trapp children.

The bandleader, who has stepped behind the curtain, reappears dressed in liederhosen and a fake moustache: We have our Uncle Max.

"That's Oliver Blake," Günter explains, "a pal from the music circuit. He married *his* boyfriend last year and encouraged the guys to make it official."

"Dearly beloved," Uncle Max begins. "We are gathered here today to honor Decker and Jordie. As many of you know, they were very young when they met and they knew in an instant that they were meant for each other. But let us hear the story from the grooms themselves, shall we?"

The grooms step to the mike and begin the duet, "Sixteen Going on Seventeen."

By the time they finish, the audience is convulsed with laughter. Jordie curtsies as Decker bows. They gesture for silence and the two repeat their vows. Afterward, Günter gets on stage, takes the acoustic guitar and accompanies himself to "Edelweiss," complete with German accent. The grooms dance. Many of the guests rush the stage and join in a lively rendition of "The Lonely Goatherd," yodelling enthusiastically.

Elliot and I rush the sushi bar instead but we both keep our eye on Lola, who is bounding around the stage in a mad polka with Paul, the florist. It's not like her to completely abandon her dignity.

"Interesting," Elliot notes, "but it'll never last. Paul's far too normal and nice." I nod in agreement. Nice-and-normal has never commanded Lola's attention for long.

Elliot and I carry our overflowing plates to the balcony and sit by the rail to watch the show. Günter and Decker have joined the band, kicking things up a notch with an energetic cover of the Ramones'"I Wanna be Sedated." Lola and Paul are slam dancing the nuns, which reminds me to tell Elliot about how his vision of a crucifix played out at work.

"I'm glad I could help," he says. "But since you're in the mood to acknowledge my remarkable gift, why haven't you followed my advice about Tim?"

"Who says I haven't?"

He looks at me steadily. "Remember who you're talking to. Look, in the words of the Reverend Mother, 'When God closes a door, he opens a window.' Your window is about to close and you, my friend, are going to get your fingers squashed if you don't act soon."

"Roxanne said almost the same thing."

"So who else needs to tell you? Are you afraid to surrender your title as the Girl with the most Secondhand Bouquets?"

"Give it a rest, Elliot. It's one thing to know what you should do and another to do it."

An hour later, Uncle Max summons everyone to gather before the stage for the tossing of the bouquet.

"You're up, Flower Girl," Elliot says. "Don't break a nail."

"No danger," I answer, waving my fingers at him, "I've gone acrylic."

The band strikes up "Edelweiss" again, only this time Günter sings the lyrics in the mode of Sid Vicious. There's a long drum roll as Jordie takes center stage and limbers up with some shoulder rolls. He turns his back to the crowd and heaves the plastic bouquet over his shoulder. The nuns surge forward, nearly trampling the von Trapp children, but the bouquet sails over their outstretched fingers toward me. I consider reaching up and snatching it dramatically out of the air. With this crowd, there's pressure to put on a bit of a show. I could even do a little leap. Before I can do anything, someone deliberately steps in front of me and shoves me roughly aside. When I regain my footing, my hands are raised over my head—empty. The bouquet is in the hands of the man beside me: Elliot.

"I don't believe it!" I exclaim. "The curse is broken!"

"I did it for you," Elliot says, examining a bleeding gash on his hand from the impact of the plastic stems.

"How does it feel, Flower Boy?"

"Like I need a drink," he replies, but he's grinning.

Günter hurries over, carrying two glasses of champagne and gives one to each of us. "Oh, liebling, let me be your bride," he burbles happily, daubing Elliot's hand with a napkin.

"I did it for you," Elliot tells him, winking at me.

"Come on, Lib," Lola grabs my arm and pulls me toward the dessert table, "let's celebrate your deflowering with wedding cake."

After the cake is cut and distributed, the two of us fan out to interview guests. In what seems like no time at all, the band-leader announces the last dance: "So Long, Farewell."

Jordie's dad waltzes me around with relative ease, consider-ing my two-left-size-12s. Lola, meanwhile, is cheek-to-cheek with Paul the florist and when the song is over, they step to the bar and exchange phone numbers. Then Lola and I bid the grooms good-night, and make our way to the door, where we're given a small package.

I unwrap mine in the parking lot as we wait for the motor league to resuscitate Mindy. It's a Jesus night-light with the grooms' names and the date at our Saviour's feet.

Lola lights a cigarette, takes a long pull and blows a smoke ring into the chilly air. "That," she says, "was a fucking great wedding."

"Amazing," I agree, stuffing Jesus back into the box. "Give me one of those, will you?" I take the pack of DuMaurier Lights from her hand.

"Are you kidding?"

"Nope, I'm celebrating. Can you believe Elliot caught the bouquet for me?"

"Hmmmm? He's fantastic, isn't he?"

"I assume you mean Paul, not Elliot. Are you sure he's single?"

"There were too many of his friends around for him to lie."

"True. So, is he rich and famous?"

She shoots me a look, "Yeah, I hear he did the boutonnieres for the Oscars."

"He's not even that cute," I say, then catch myself. "I'm sorry, Lola, I didn't mean that. It's just that you normally go for guys who are movie-star gorgeous."

"Or, rich, as you noted. That's the second time this evening you've accused me of being a gold digger and I'm not too thrilled about it."

"*Gold digger* is far too strong a term," I assure her. We're silent for a minute as the motor league truck pulls into the lot. "You're sure he's not gay?"

"Libby," she says, exasperated.

"I'm sorry, but I'm missing something. You've never been interested in a guy like Paul before."

"You mean a decent guy with no agenda?" she asks, flicking her cigarette onto the asphalt and grinding it out with her foot. "Well, I'm a pragmatic woman and it's becoming painfully obvious that my old ways aren't working. I've decided to give 'normal' a try."

She pops the hood and the guy with the jumper cables gives her an appreciative once-over. On his signal, she turns the key in the ignition and Mindy springs to life. We drive home in silence, each of us lost in thought. I jump out in front of my place while Lola keeps Mindy rolling forward.

"Thanks for the ride," I say as she sputters away from the curb. I run alongside the car for a few paces. "Look, Paul seems great. Good luck!"

Her confident smile suggests she had only to make a decision for everything to fall into place. Walking back toward my door, I wonder if I have the courage to make the same decision so gracefully.

**33**

Alarm clock number four, which I so cleverly placed across the room last night, is buzzing incessantly. The first pillow I toss misses, but the second is a direct hit. The clock slides off the dresser with a crash, sending Cornelius skittering out of the bedroom. Still, the damned clock buzzes and now I am without pillows to block the sound.

It's all Mindy's fault. If I'd driven my own car to the wedding last night, I wouldn't have drunk so much bourbon. And if I hadn't drunk so much bourbon, I wouldn't have set my clocks for the ungodly hour of 9:00 a.m. on a Sunday. Nor would I have sprained my ankle jumping out of Mindy and chasing her half a block. I'd have known my limits.

I'm still contemplating those limits when the phone rings. Limping to the phone, I wave weakly to my new roommate, Jesus, who shines his light from the outlet near the stove.

"Libby, it's Margo."

"Margo! It's Sunday."

"I noticed. The Minister's called an emergency meeting because of the problem with Contact Culture. I hear you already know about it."

"Yeah. I'm on my way." Sighing, I hang up the phone and head for the shower. I can hardly complain about having to work on Sunday when I'm the one who sounded the alarm.

An hour later, I poke my head into Margo's lair to find it empty except for her coat and briefcase. I start down the hall toward Mrs. Cleary's office just in time to see Laurie disappear into the stairwell. She's on the first landing before I can catch her.

"Hey, where's the fire?" I call. It's been our favorite line since the fateful power surge that almost rid the world of Margo.

"Pretty close, if the heat on my ass is any sign. The boss is cracking the whip."

"I'm sure she wants to get everyone home to enjoy what's left of our weekend."

"The sooner you abandon that notion, the better, my friend. We'll be lucky to get home before Tuesday."

"Why, what's happened?"

"The shit's hit the proverbial fan and we're on clean-up duty. The Premier heard about our little problem yesterday and hauled the Minister onto the carpet."

"How did he find out?"

"Richard told him that Mrs. Cleary fired him."

*"Fired him!"* I knew it was a possibility but it still surprises me. "But why was Richard speaking to the Premier?"

"I guess they had time to chat between innings at the hockey game."

"Periods. There are no innings in hockey."

"Whatever. The point is, Richard took the Premier to a Leaves game last night and shared his tale of woe."

*"Leafs!* And Richard knows even less about hockey than you do."

"Ah, but the Premier is very fond of the game and Richard is very fond of the Premier, if you catch my drift."

"Of course." Perhaps the Premier would also fancy a new

watch. "But if Richard's sucking up to the Premier, why would he admit he's been canned?"

"Trying to tell his side of the story first, I suppose and suggest Mrs. Cleary has dropped the ball on this initiative. The Premier called Mrs. Cleary in a rage and demanded an explanation."

Apparently Richard underestimated the Minister's power to think on her Manolo Blahniks. She convinced the Premier that Contact Culture will give all students better access to the arts—and that it will provide benefits that After the Bell never had, such as opportunities to "shadow" artists at work. She also guaranteed everything would be in place by Tuesday's launch, which means there's a lot of work ahead to make sure the program will do what it needs to do. What's more, the financing needs to be reworked because the money paid out to Loud Mouth Productions can't be reclaimed.

The launch itself has been jeopardized by Loud Mouth's bumbling. For starters, they distributed not one, but two media advisories, each providing different times and dates for the press conference. Since she has no confidence in the firm, the Minister has asked Laurie to take over.

The hubbub coming from the Minister's office surprises me as I enter. It seems like half the Ministry has reported for duty. I squeeze into a corner at the back and immediately notice Tim Kennedy sitting to the right of the Minister. I suppose she'll portray his involvement as "consultation" with stakeholders. Anxious as I am, I feel a little thrill at seeing him. He looks great in his faded jeans, but I wish he looked a little happier to see me.

"Libby!" Margo's voice rings out above the din and I brace myself. Margo has never yet missed an opportunity to diminish me in front of Tim. "Thank God you're here," she says. "You'll need to get started on the speech right away."

What, no insults? It's almost disappointing. At the moment, however, she's intent on bringing me up to speed on the highlights of the reworked policy for Contact Culture. She's informative, polite, and patient. Obviously her guilt over missing the screw-up is overpowering her normal personality. She ushers Joe over to walk me through the regulations, then calls on the Minister to discuss the overall tone for the speech.

Finally, after receiving far more help than I need, I retreat to my office to write. Margo calls me hourly to offer assistance. She brings me coffee, and, incredibly, pastries. If I didn't know better, I'd say she's groveling. The Minister also drops by twice to see how I'm faring. It's the first time I've really felt like a valued member of this team...the first time I've felt needed.

Despite their frequent interruptions, I soon become so absorbed in the work that I have little time to wonder what Tim is doing. I barely notice when Laurie stops by to tell me there's Chinese food on the boardroom table. By the time I finish a draft it's already dark outside. I've been hunched over my computer for seven hours; Tim is probably long gone.

The boardroom is empty when I arrive but the table is still covered in takeout containers. I fill a paper plate with a little of everything until it's sagging ominously in the middle. Using a second plate as reinforcement, I add a little more chow mein. Then I set my plate on the table and reach for the fortune cookies. I don't much like the taste, but I love cracking them open and prying out the message—especially since I adopted Lola's habit of reading them aloud and adding the words *in bed* to the end of every fortune, as in *"Success in life must be earned with earnest efforts...in bed."* I pry one open and read to the empty boardroom: *"You will be blessed beyond your wildest dreams...in bed."*

"Lucky you!" Startled, I drop the cookie fragments on the floor. Tim is standing in the doorway with his empty plate.

"The cookies never lie," I mutter, a flush surging from my feet toward my face like a rogue wave.

"You've taken five," he notes. "Maybe that one was meant for Margo."

"Well, it's mine now and I read it out loud, which means it will come true. Lola says so."

He glances at my overloaded plate. "What does she say about testing the weight limits of disposable dinnerware?" Finally, he's really smiling and I'm so relieved I forget to take offense at the reference to my gluttony.

"My creativity improves on a full stomach."

"I'll tell Clarice there's a work of genius underway."

Voices drift down the hall. Suspecting we may not be alone for long, I take the plunge: "Will you have dinner with me?"

"Ah, so that's why you've taken enough for two," he says.

"Not *now*, I mean some other time."

Tim's smile fades and he considers for a moment. "I don't know, Libby. What's changed?"

"*I've* changed."

"People don't change much at thirty-three."

"I'm thirty-four now. I've matured."

He shrugs and says, "Let's consult with the cookies." He selects one from the carton and cracks it open. *"The time is right for second chances…in bed."*

"Let me see that!"

Tim crushes the slip of paper and puts it in his pocket. "The cookie has spoken—but I'm only committing to dinner."

Most people leave over the next hour, but the Minister, Margo, Joe and I burn the midnight oil. While Mrs. Cleary rehearses the speech, I draft fact sheets, hypothetical media questions and responses. By the time sunlight begins to stream through the leaded glass windows, we're ready for one last runthrough. The flow of traffic along University Avenue picks up outside and the noise of the rush hour provides a backdrop to our mock media scrum. When the Minister is confident we've examined Contact Culture from every possible angle, she calls Bill to drive Laurie, Margo and me home.

Bill walks into her office moments later with the morning papers. On the front page of *The Star* is a story about Contact Culture. After all this work, our news has been leaked. It must have happened overnight because the facts, hammered out only hours ago, are accurate. Interestingly, the story has the byline not of the paper's Queen's Park reporter, but of beauty editor Lynn Seward, who has been a staunch supporter of Mrs. Cleary's since they ended up in a mud bath together at a Mexican spa a few years back. Today's article practically qualifies as a puff piece, it's so positive about the new program.

The Minister seems genuinely shocked about the leak. "It's the Premier's doing, I'm sure of it. You sent our materials to him last night, didn't you Margo?"

Nodding, Margo says, "I suppose he thought it best to get the true story into friendly hands."

"Well, we can always count on Lynn, but unfortunately, this leak has stolen my thunder. What's the point of a press conference now? The other papers will run the story on the back page because it's already old news." Her disgruntlement eases quickly, however, as she notes the extremely flattering stock photo they've used.

I'm too tired by this point to care much about this latest twist, but as we're heading for the car, I notice that Margo is smiling in a self-satisfied way. I suspect the Premier isn't to blame for the leak after all. It was a ballsy move on Margo's part, but she gambled and won. We couldn't get better press if we paid for it and she's set the tone for tomorrow.

The press conference is going off without a hitch and enough reporters have shown up to make it legitimate. The Minister has rehearsed enough that the speech sounds natural and sincere and she performs beautifully in the Q-and-A that follows. Lynn Seward is glued to the Minister's side. I overhear her ask Mrs. Cleary—on the record—about her beauty regimen. Taking the question seriously, the Minister describes, in painstaking detail, her approach to cleansing and toning.

The rest of the reporters focus on the benefits of Contact Culture. No one mentions our connection to Loud Mouth Productions, nor the recent dismissal of a high-profile political consultant. Perhaps these details will follow, but the positive coverage will continue to buoy Contact Culture through any rough waters ahead.

The Premier calls as the news conference ends and we can hear the Minister tittering on the phone in her office. Evidently he, too, is pleased. She emerges shortly to share his congratulations and propose an impromptu celebration at the local pub. I'm the only one to decline, but then, I'm the only one who has a date with Tim. Mrs. Cleary stops by my office on the way out.

"Libby, thank you." For the second time in a week, she's addressing me by my given name. "Everyone came through in this crisis, but without your intuition, I doubt we'd have anything to celebrate."

"That's nice of you to say, Minister. I'm happy it all worked out."

"I did well at the press conference, didn't I?" she says, smiling broadly.

"You did."

"And…?"

"And you looked *fabulous* doing it," I reply, picking up on my cue.

"Oh, stop," she laughs. "Are you sure you won't come with us?"

"I'm afraid I have other plans."

"Well, you'll be missed." When she reaches the door she turns and eyes me cagily. "Do give Tim my regards."

"Cheers," Tim raises his wineglass to mine, "and congratulations."

"Congratulations yourself. You share the credit on this one."

"Yeah, but rumor has it that it was you who saved the day."

"You know better than to believe in rumors. Anyway, all I did was follow a hunch."

"Do you get a lot of those?"

"I've got a book on developing my intuition."

"What's your intuition telling you right now?" He's leaning toward me and I think he's flirting, but I don't want to presume too much too soon.

"I have a very strong hunch…that you'll order the chicken." While he's laughing, I summon my nerve and stampede toward my opening with the subtlety of a hormonally-challenged rhino. "And as for rumors, I heard you've been seeing someone."

"Well, what did you expect?" he asks, his voice chilling as he leans back in his chair. "Did you think I'd sit at home and pine? We only went out a few times, Libby—it was hardly a relationship."

The conversation has taken a dangerous turn and I scurry back to cover. "I know that, but I like to think it might have been if one of us weren't an idiot."

"I hope you're referring to yourself?" he says, obviously more hurt by my past performance than I'd imagined.

"Don't hold back, now."

"I'm only agreeing with you."

Examining my cutlery with interest, I decide I am an idiot— for thinking he'd really give me a second chance. I'm tempted to bolt, but indulging that instinct is what got me into this bind in the first place. I have to stick it out this time.

"May I take your order?" the waiter asks, interrupting the awkward silence.

"The lady is still deciding," Tim tells him, "but I'll definitely have the chicken."

It isn't much, but I take it as encouragement. I promptly order the chicken too. Once the waiter disappears, I say, "Relationships have never been my forte, Tim—but a girl can't be good at everything. I got spooked last time, but I promise to try harder if you'll give me another chance."

He sips his wine for a moment and ponders. "You know, Melanie didn't have a sense of humor."

"Past tense?"

"Well, she may have one now, but I haven't seen her in weeks, so I wouldn't know."

"She seemed very nice, though," I offer magnanimously, confident that poor Melanie will find much solace in her excellent journalism career.

"Who needs nice? I like a woman with an edge."

"Really? Well, in that case, Melanie's a bag of bones and way too blond."

"Not *that* much edge," he laughs.

I find myself wanting to jump over the table and into his lap, but the chicken hasn't even arrived. Besides, the chairs look fragile and between us, we're twelve-and-a-half feet and well over three hundred pounds of burgeoning relationship.

When dinner arrives, Tim tells me about his students and I am full of new fondness for them. I tell him about the progress Lola and I are making with the book. After a moment's hesitation, I confess that I lied to him at Emma's wedding by implying I was writing a book many months before I actually was. It's another mistake I learned from, I say. The guilt actually drove me to agree to work on a book I never wanted to write—and now I'm enjoying it.

"I'm glad you're over your need to impress me," Tim jokes, unfazed. Then he adds, "You're fine just the way you are."

Both of us are taken aback when the waiter tells us it's last call. Tim holds my hand as he drives me home and walks me to my door. When I invite him in, however, he asks for a rain check.

"One of the kids from my orchestra is crashing at my place this week. Both of his parents are drunks and the mother just took off. So—"

"—you want to set a good example." I interrupt. "I understand." But the doubt must be showing in my face.

"Do not, I repeat, do not read anything into this. I want to stay, Libby, but the kid needs to know he can count on one adult in his life."

"It's okay, really, I understand." And I do, but the fifteen-year-old inside is wondering if this is just an excuse. Sensing she's resurfaced, Tim leans over and kisses me, a lingering, lusty kiss that blows my doubts into the street with the rustling leaves.

"The kid moves in with his aunt on Saturday."

"What are you doing Saturday night?"

"Bringing my dog over to your place. If we're welcome, that is."

"I'll lock up my best bras."

"You won't be needing them."

He kisses me again and heads back to his Jeep. "By the way," he says, stopping halfway down the walk, "What did you say to the girls from my orchestra? Suddenly, they're big Roberta Bondar fans."

I'm thrilled at this, but try to look cool. "Oh, you know—girl talk. They think you're the world's greatest teacher, but you didn't hear it from me." He's smiling as he opens the car door and I call out, "Listen, can I ask you something?"

"Yeah, but you're asking the whole neighborhood right now."

"I was just wondering if you have any Scots ancestry."

"There might have been an Angus on my mother's side, why?"

"How do you feel about kilts?"

"Can we talk about this on Saturday?"

"Sure, I'm serving haggis." He shakes his head and gets into the car.

Far too wired to sleep, I break the news about Stella to Cornelius and sit down to comfort him, remote control in hand. I flip through every channel, but nothing holds my interest. It's too late to call Roxanne and I'm too full of wine and chicken to go for a run. But a walk, I could manage. It's well after midnight when I set out. Mom would be horrified, but my neighborhood is still busy. The cafés are full of students. I stride briskly along Bloor Street to Bay, turn south to Queen's Park and walk back through the university grounds.

My route takes me right past the Sutton Place Hotel where

Richard stayed for months at the taxpayers' expense. I expect he's left for London already, tail between his legs. It sure looks like his six-foot-six form in the hotel's entrance as I pass, however. Crossing the street to get a closer look, I confirm it's Richard. He's wearing a denim shirt, open nearly to the waist, and sweatpants. He turns toward a petite woman and blocks her from my view. Even in my state of bliss, I can put two and two together: he is seeing someone to the door after a shagging.

Curious, I stop to watch. Could it be the Minister? Whoever she is, she's bold because she reaches around and squeezes Richard's ass proprietarily. He leans over and kisses her, and from the incline of his head, I can tell he's aiming for the cheek. This speaks volumes; the lady is obviously the keener of the two. Finally Richard struts back into the lobby and the woman starts down the short driveway toward me, silhouetted against the hotel lights. She's about the right size for the Minister, but the hair is definitely longer. And redder. I grab a hydro pole for support: it's Margo, looking more disheveled than ever, with her shirt buttoned wrong and her suit jacket trailing.

At first I can't quite take it in. Margo and Richard? How could she sleep with him after all that's happened? How could he sleep with her, when he apparently liked me? And how could the thought of it be bothering me so much when my crush burned out a month ago? Tim is twice the man Richard is, I have no doubt of that, but my inner 15-year-old is rising again. It seems that the further I get from high school, the more I regress. I don't want Richard, but I don't want anyone else to have him either—especially not *her.*

Margo is barely three yards away when she sees me. Even in my shock, I realize it's one of those rare golden moments in life. It looks as though she may faint as she weaves unsteadily toward me. By the time she's standing in front of me, however, the old, calculating look is back on her face: she's wondering if she can talk me out of believing what I'm seeing.

"What are you doing here?" she asks casually.

"Just getting some air. You?"

"We all went out to celebrate. You were invited…"

"Not to Richard's room, I wasn't. Private party?"

"*Libby!* What are you saying?" But she hasn't denied it. In fact, the truth is written all over her flushed face.

"I'm saying the 'optics' here aren't good." I'm remembering her reproach when I was dating Joe.

"I can explain—"

"No need. The razor burn tells the whole story." I reach out and pluck one of Richard's hairs from her shirt. "My question is, what does Richard have to celebrate? He was fired only three days ago for scamming the Ministry. Or have you forgotten that already? At least this explains how he was able to get away with as much as he did."

"I had no idea about his relationship with Loud Mouth," she protests.

I believe her, but can't bear to end the game just yet. Furrowing my brow in mock confusion, I ask, "So you're punishing his bad behavior by sleeping with him?"

"Look," she says, "I only learned what he was up to this weekend and by then it was too late." She claps her hand over her mouth, realizing she's revealed more than she intended.

"Ah, so you've been at it for a while now."

"It's only been a few weeks. Not that it's any of your business," she adds, defensively.

"You're sleeping with the enemy, so it is my business. How could you still see him tonight after what's he's done?"

She stares down Bay Street in silence, then mutters, "I don't know."

"Margo, you're not in love with him!" I exclaim, light suddenly dawning.

"Of course not," she says irritably, "how could I be?" But her expression tells a different story. "Libby, you can't mention this to the Minister."

"She wasn't with you?" I ask, just to see her expression.

"Don't be ridiculous! She went home hours ago!"

"Just checking. She had a thing for Richard herself, you know. Remember the maraschino cherries? My guess is, she'd want to hear all about it." I'm tempted to prolong the game indefinitely, since revenge is sweeter than I anticipated, but I do the decent thing and hail her a cab. I even help her into it with a little more force than necessary and slam the door.

"Look, Libby—" she says, rolling down the window.

"You should wear a turtleneck tomorrow, Margo," I interrupt rudely, pointing to the hickey on her neck. "Where's Buffy when you need her, eh!"

Waving as the taxi pulls out, I set off for home, my euphoria now replaced by faint nausea at the thought of Richard sucking on Margo's neck like a great horny vacuum cleaner. He had sex with her, but wouldn't kiss her on the lips afterward. Hell, he didn't even hail her a cab, the pig. And how poor is her self-esteem if she'll invest thirty-six hours into repairing the damage he caused and still run to his bed?

I can excuse a lot of foolish moves in the name of lust, but betrayal isn't one of them.

Margo is sitting in my guest chair, swinging her short legs. "You're late," she announces, calmly pulling apart an enormous cinnamon bun.

I expected shame, perhaps even some groveling from her this morning, not unruffled complacency. Indeed, if it weren't for the Minister's happy-face kerchief tied around Margo's neck to hide the hickey, I'd wonder if I dreamed last night's encounter. Obviously, bouncing back from disgrace isn't tough when you're built so low to the ground.

"Gosh, you'd better fire me if you're such a stickler for rules," I snort, sitting down at my desk. "Mind you, the Minister might complain when she sees Lily packing her boxes. She's grown fond of me lately. But as always, Margo, I defer to your expert knowledge of office protocol. Tell me, what's the proper procedure for letting the Minister know you boffed the man who nearly ruined her career?"

Popping a piece of cinnamon bun into her mouth, she smiles at me. "You won't tell her."

"Won't I? You don't know me."

"I know you. Righteous Libby wouldn't stoop so low."

"Margo, when you're my height, stooping is nothing new. Besides, I've learned a thing or two about lowering myself from you. You're quite a role model."

She's right, though. I'd love nothing more than to see her exposed and punished, but I don't want to be the one who turns her in. My mother, the nicest woman in the world, has made it impossible for me to savor revenge like a normal person. Instead I remind myself that what goes around, comes around, even here in the Pink Palace.

Margo has decided not to take any chances. "Okay, I'm *asking* you not to tell her."

"What's the magic word?"

Her eyes narrow, but she chokes out a *"Please."*

No need to capitulate too soon. It's not as if Mom's bugged the office. "I'll think about it and get back to you."

Putting down her bun, she slaps my desk with a sticky hand. "No, I want your assurance now."

"I don't think you're in a position to make any demands." How nice to have the power for once.

She sneers. "Look, you *owe* me. You've had the chance of a lifetime in this job."

This is like fire to gunpowder. Hold on to your spatula, Marjory, because I'm fed up with "nice."

"Let me make this perfectly clear. I owe you nothing, Margo. You didn't hire me and you've treated me like crap since the day I arrived. You've sabotaged my work and undermined my confidence. Frankly, I'd be *thrilled* if the Minister turfed you out on your sorry ass."

There's no sign of complacency on her face now. In fact, she's become so pale that the cinnamon slick on her mouth stands out in a muddy ring. Coming around the desk, she puts a claw on my shoulder and when she speaks, her tone is pleading.

"Libby, you need to understand that I love my job. Things

haven't gone very well for me lately and I've just regained the Minster's respect." With her free hand, she fiddles nervously with the happy-face kerchief. "I don't want to lose it again."

Plucking her fingers from my shoulder one by one, I stand to have the pleasure of towering over her. "Margo, *you* need to understand that the sooner you shove off, the sooner I'll get a chance to love *my* job. Why not head to London? Surely Richard will need your help on his political campaign. A good hair-and-makeup person is hard to find."

"Oh, *I* get it. This isn't about loyalty to the Minister at all. It's about your bitterness that Richard chose me over you."

"You're welcome to him, Margo, if you think he's such a great catch. I wish you luck."

"Sounds like sour grapes to me. I saw the way you flirted with him, in your short skirts and high heels. You know what your problem is, Libby? You're just not feminine enough. You have bushy eyebrows and an aggressive personality."

For a second, my vision blurs. I lean on the desk to steady myself and take a deep breath. Finally I say, "If you're so confident of your girlish charms, Margo, I suggest you ask Richard about the watch."

"What watch?" She's eyeing me suspiciously.

"Go call him."

"I guess I can hardly blame you for being jealous of me."

I take a menacing step toward her. I'll knock her down and tell the cops I was just reaching for the cinnamon bun. She'll have a mannish size-twelve tread mark on her face to remember me by.

"Ladies, *what* is going on?" The Minister's voice startles us both. She's standing in the doorway in her red Armani suit, the one she always wears when she wants to look invincible. "I could hear you arguing about Richard down the hall. Is there something more I need to know?"

For a moment, neither of us says anything. Margo glares up at me and I glare down just as fiercely, trying to force a confession. Mrs. Cleary clacks her fingernails impatiently against my door frame until Margo clears her throat.

"Yes, there is something else you should know, Minister. I, uh, sort of fell for Richard—"

"—for Richard's *shtick*, she means," I interrupt, stepping away from the midget. "Margo feels guilty for missing the signs of trouble."

Why couldn't I just let her hang herself? She deserves it. But the truth is, I don't believe Margo would intentionally harm Mrs. Cleary. She may be petty and mean, but her whole identity is tied up in being EA to the Minister. She'd fall apart if Mrs. Cleary ever cut her loose. And the Minister, in her own way, is also dependent on Margo. With Richard out of the picture, there's no reason they shouldn't continue to bask in their dysfunctional relationship.

The Minister looks doubtfully from Margo to me. "I expect we all feel a little foolish for being taken in by that con man, but let's try to move on, shall we? Now I really must go, girls, I can't be late for my meeting." She departs at an unusually brisk trot for a woman who normally prides herself on making the world wait for her.

"I *knew* you couldn't tell her." Margo's smug expression creeps back as she scrapes the icing from the cinnamon bun box with a forefinger.

"Sure you did. And you're welcome, by the way."

She shrugs. "The Minister would have forgiven me eventually. As you say, a good hair-and-makeup person is hard to find."

Shaking my head, I reach for my purse. There's nothing left to say here, and I have earned a mochaccino.

"Where do you think you're going?" She moves, raining crumbs onto the carpet.

"For coffee."

"Not before you clean up the boardroom, you don't. There's Chinese food left over from Sunday and the janitors are on strike. Remember the rats, Libby."

In other words, we're back to business as usual, which is comforting in a strange sort of way. Just for fun, I abruptly stop walking so that she plows into me. "Fix your hickey rag, Margo. Your trophy is showing."

When I return with my mochaccino, I prop my feet on the desk and listen to my voice mails.

BEEP—"Hi, Lib, it's Emma. Congratulations! Bob played squash with Tim today and heard the good news. I am so thrilled for you! I can't wait to hear all the details—" *"Tell her not to screw it up this time!"* Bob yells in the background. "Bob! Ssshhh. That's no way to talk—" Click.

BEEP—"Hey, it's Lola. Heard the news about Tim from Emma. What did I tell you—normal is the way to go. Not that this is a competition, but Paul likes me more than Tim likes you: he's called me every night this week. Doubt you can top that! Besides, I'm sure Tim has no talent with flowers and Paul sent me the most beautiful bouquet today. It's almost enough to make me change my mind about weddings. Call me."

BEEP—"Libby, it's Elliot. I've been haunted all day by this image of you and Tim in a little restaurant... Okay, I actually heard about your date from Emma. I take full credit for your current happiness because of my sacrifice with the edelweiss. Günter keeps creating these opportunities for me to propose! What's going on at work, by the way? I see you in the eye of a hurricane, chaos swirling around you. Make sure you stay there, where it's calm. Look at me, giving out free advice. Günter's making me soft."

BEEP—"Hi, Lib, Emma again. Sorry about my earlier message. Bob is thrilled for you too—he was just kidding." *"I'm a funny man!"* "You're a *sad* man. Anyway, Lib, I mentioned your date to Elliot when I ran into him. Hope you don't mind."

BEEP—"Hey, Lib, Rox here. Lola just sent me an e-mail about Tim. I can't believe I had to hear the news from her. Of course, she was mainly writing to tell me how much nicer Paul is than Tim, but you'd never last with a florist anyway after all the trouble you've had with bouquets. Anyway, fill me in—it's the least you can do when you complain to me all the time. My movie wraps in two weeks and then I'm going to tour Ireland with Miguel. Let's toast to new beginnings when I get home."

BEEP—"McIssac! Richard Neale here. I'm at the airport and hoped to speak to you before boarding. We have unfinished business. I'd like to explain a few things, so give me a ring in the U.K., would you? My number is—"

I press the buttons to skip to the end of the message and delete. The man is welcome to finish his business with Ratgirl if he likes, but I never want to hear from him again.

Laurie races into my office. "Come on, Libby, the Minister has a big announcement."

Outside the boardroom, Margo intercepts me and clutches my arm. Her eyes are bloodshot. "Libby, I've been such a fool," she blurts. "Richard's left for England without saying goodbye. I had to hear it from the hotel concierge."

I reluctantly pat her shoulder, but the Minister's arrival prevents me from actually having to say anything. Leading us inside, Mrs. Cleary claps her hands for attention.

"There's been a Cabinet shuffle, everyone, and I'm pleased to say that the Premier has given me responsibility for the Ministry of Education." She beams at all of us. Education is the largest Ministry after Health and has a huge budget. In other words, she's been promoted far beyond her abilities. She may suspect this herself, because she continues, "The opportunity comes as something of a surprise.

Our recent success with Contact Culture must have sealed the deal."

Success! Narrowly averted disaster is more like it.

"Over the next couple of days, I'll be making decisions about staffing and inviting some of you to share this new adventure with me. I wish I could take everyone, but the new Minister of Culture will need experienced staff."

Laurie grabs my arm as we leave. "Can you believe it?" she whispers. "Cleary was barely a match for arts advocates and now she's going up against the teachers' unions. They'll eat her alive!"

I have an odd, un-Lily-like surge of loyalty for the Minister, but I suppress it. I spent three years in Education and Laurie is probably right.

The Minister is arranging fabric swatches and paint chips on her desk when I rap on the heavy oak door. "Come in, Libby. I'm trying to get some ideas for decorating my new office. What do you think of burned-caramel?"

"As a color, or a dessert?"

She chuckles and continues. "Should I choose cloud-white, porch-white or antique-white?"

"White comes in shades?"

Sighing, she sets down the samples. "I called you here to thank you for your support. Everyone came through in the crisis, but without you, I doubt we'd be celebrating today."

"That's nice of you to say, Minister. I'm happy it all worked out."

"It's just a shame Julian and I have lost a friend in Richard."

"Yes, that is a shame." I suspect she'll find it in her heart to forgive Richard, eventually—especially if he becomes a British MP.

"He succumbed to the glamour of politics, you see. Perhaps it was inevitable, being around me." She sighs as if the weight of the nation rests on her petite shoulders. "Power is seductive, Libby, and corruption is all around us. Few can maintain their principles as I have."

"You're an inspiration to us all, Mrs. Cleary."

She nods graciously and smiles: I'm just confirming what she already knows. Picking up a file folder from a corner of her desk, she says, "Do you know what this is? Your new contract."

"Oh? But mine doesn't expire for a couple of months yet. I assumed you'd leave that to the new Minister."

"Of course not, Libby, you're coming with me to education."

My heart sinks. Although I'm pleased at this proof she likes my work, the last place I want to go right now is back to my old Ministry.

"Minister, I really appreciate the offer, but I'm afraid I'll have to decline."

"Decline?" Her smile vanishes. "But your home position is in Education. And Margo's even found a way to swing a ten-percent pay increase."

I'm amused to see that Margo believes righteous Libby would accept a ten-percent payoff for her silence. Although I could use some extra cash to pay down my postcrush Visa bill, I'm not tempted. "It's not about money, Minister. I left Education because the issues had grown stale for me. Culture is still relatively new and exciting."

More important, it's one media crisis after another at Education. With the book taking shape, I can't afford to get beaten down during my day job. I haven't forgotten what Elliot said about staying in the eye of the storm.

"But I've put so much work into training you, Libby, and you've finally captured my style. You must come."

I might have wavered there if she hadn't taken full credit for my hard work. "Your confidence means a lot to me, Minister, it really does, but I want to stay here. You see, I've started a creative project on the side and I just can't take on other challenges right now. However, I do have some talented colleagues at Education who'd jump at the chance to write your speeches. I could share what I've learned with them."

She rearranges the paint chips rather violently for a few moments. Finally, without looking up, she says, "On your way out, tell Margo to set up interviews with those writers."

I turn back at the door. "Thank you again, Mrs. Cleary."

"You're welcome... *Lily.*"

I smile as I close the door behind me, sensing that the name "Lily" has just been etched in granite.

To: Roxnrhead@interlog.ca
From: Mclib@hotmail.ca
Subject: Life

Hi Rox,

I know I haven't kept up my end on the e-mail front lately, so I hope this catches you before you leave for Ireland. Things are definitely on the upswing here. For starters, the Minister gave me a gift before she left for Education, which suggests she's relenting. It's a huge hardcover volume of quotations, which I love, and an equally hefty palette of makeup. Truly, Rox, it's the largest all-in-one kit I've ever seen. I spent the morning in the staff washroom trying various looks, the envy of every woman in the can.

But on to more important things... I made dinner for Tim Kennedy on Saturday night. Well, you know me better than that: I actually bought a lasagna at Senses and passed it off as my own. The evening went well—although Cornelius would disagree. Tim brought Stella, his fat, disobedient Jack Russell with him. Corny took her down with one well-aimed whack and she spent the next two hours wedged under my dresser. Interesting, since Tim claimed on the night we met that Jacks are the "toughest breed on the planet." He finally lured her out with lasagna and shut her in the den. I shut Cornelius in the living room and Tim and I retired to the bedroom to consummate our reunion—to the romantic soundtrack of hisses and howls. Three days later, it's subsided to occasional grumbling and I trust Corny will soon stop asking to move in with his favorite aunt Rox.

Can't wait to see you!

Libby

Available in March from
the author of *Carrie Pilby*…

# Starting from
# Square Two

by Caren Lissner

Twenty-nine-year-old Gert Healy thought she
would never have to return to the craziness of the
dating world. Would never have to worry about
what to wear and what to say and whether she
was pretty enough. But the death of her husband
two years earlier has forced her to clad up in
miniskirts and leather jackets and brave it…again.
But does Gert have it in her to fight through the
singles crowds in search of a second miracle?

It's back to square one on everything. Well, actually, she's done it all before. Square two, then.

"Debut author Caren Lissner deftly delivers
a novel that is funny, sarcastic and
thought-provoking. (4 stars)"
—*Romantic Times* on *Carrie Pilby*

RED
DRESS
I N K
™

RDI03043-TR